VALE OF DREAMS

FEY SPY ACADEMY BOOK TWO

ALEX RIVERS

C.N. CRAWFORD

SUMMARY OF AVALON TOWER

A brief refresher:

At the start of *Avalon Tower,* the Fey have taken over northern France. Fifteen years earlier, after experiencing a famine, the Fey invaded France from their own kingdom, Brocéliande, a magical realm. After the invasion, modern technology started to fail, disrupted by Fey magic. The Fey also created a magical boundary, a veil that separates Fey France from the rest of the world. Anyone who touches this misty veil will die unless they possess an enchanted orb to pass through. Since the invasion, the Fey king, Auberon, has been hunting demi-Fey, scapegoating them for the famine in his kingdom.

Avalon Tower is a secret spy organization located in the hidden realm of Camelot, where anti-Fey spies have been training for centuries, starting during the reign of Arthur. At Avalon Tower, human—and now demi-Fey spies--learn about Fey culture and language. Their goal is to infiltrate Fey France and gather crucial information. Romance is strictly forbidden at Avalon Tower, as it is believed to create distractions and lead to poor decision-making that prioritizes romantic partners over the group's mission. We are introduced to two spies, Alix and Rein, who are killed by Fey soldiers while Alix is distracted, deeply in love with Rein.

Nia is a human raised in Los Angeles. She saves up money working in a bookstore for a vacation in the south of France. While she's there, something unexpected happens—she discovers that she can enter and exit the veil without dying. She also encounters a group of demi-Fey on the run from Auberon's soldiers and helps them to safety by hiding them in the veil. Turns out, she's a demi-Fey with magic, which was news to her. When she leads them to their contact, she discovers it's her ex-boyfriend, Raphael, a gorgeous demi-Fey who broke her heart years ago. Raphael identifies her as a Sentinel—someone with the magical power to control the veil. This is an incredibly important role in Avalon Tower, and Raphael demands that she begin training as a spy. She's essentially forced onto a boat and taken to Camelot against her will.

At Camelot, she has no option but to join the spies. During training, she practices the Fey language and culture. She is also subjected to antagonistic bullying from the Pendragon clique, particularly from Tarquin Pendragon, a descendant of Arthur's sister. He's also the nephew of Wrythe Pendragon, one of the Tower's leaders. However, Nia's new friends—Tana, Serana, and Darius—help her get by. Tana, who possesses the power of prophecy and augury, reveals that Nia is, in fact, the new Lady of the Lake—a role that has not existed in centuries.

Magical history permeates every stone in Avalon Tower. Merlin was one of the first knights of Avalon Tower, and his portrait hangs throughout the institution. Another, more sinister portrait also adorns the walls—that of Mordred Kingslayer, the son of the evil queen Morgan. Mordred once invaded Avalon Tower, and his forces killed scores of people, including King Arthur. Now, everyone at Avalon Tower believes Mordred is dead, having perished in a battle against Merlin, and that his evil son, Auberon, rules in Brocéliande. A prophecy declares that his family, the House of Morgan, will one day destroy Avalon Tower. For this reason, Raphael has pledged to annihilate the entire House of Morgan, starting with Auberon.

Raphael and Nia end up in close quarters on several missions, and their relationship develops as they grow closer and can't fight their attraction. Nia also discovers that she possesses a second power – telepathy, she can read the minds of those she touches. Only Raphael and her close friends know of that power, because everyone in Avalon Tower believes that those with more than one power are unstable and dangerous—like Mordred was.

At one point, Raphael and Nia travel to the *Château des Rêves,* where a terrifying Fey prince known as the

Dream Stalker holds his hedonistic parties. While there, they steal a map from him, which Raphael hopes to use to find his sister in the Fey realm. The Dream Stalker realizes they have stolen his map and traps them in a horrifying waking nightmare. At the last moment, they manage to escape. But Nia is horrified to realize the Dream Stalker (prince Talan) has been in her thoughts for years. His voice is eerily familiar, and she has been hearing his sometimes violent, sometimes seductive thoughts. Still, she escapes his palace without him ever looking directly at her, so he cannot identify her.

Back at Avalon Tower, Nia passes a series of trials to become a Knight of Avalon. In the final trial, Raphael makes her so angry she can hardly think straight. But emotions drive her magic, and during the trial, she discovers a new power—a primal power thought to be lost to time. It turns out Nia can combine both her telepathy and Sentinel powers to control people's minds. She demonstrates this by controlling the mind of Wrythe Pendragon. At this point, she is granted an Avalon Steel torc, signifying a status for a knight that has not existed since Merlin.

She and Raphael are sent on one final mission together, where they must pretend to be newlyweds in Fey France to spy on the enemy. There, they finally admit their feelings for each other, and they bang.

But Auberon is not done with his invasion plans, and they discover that his army will be attacking England next. They rush to Dover, where they fight a brutal battle against the Fey alongside the British army. As the Fey forces close in, Raphael is captured, sacrificing himself to save Nia. By the end of the book, Nia despairs, knowing Raphael must be enduring horrific conditions in the Fey realm.

One night, something calls Nia out onto the Lake of Avalon, past Nimuë's tower, where the former Lady of the Lake once lived. She takes a boat out onto the lake through the mists, and finds a veil. Using her Sentinel powers, she lowers the veil. What she finds there shocks her: the lost island of Avalon, a snow-covered, ruined kingdom with an ancient, towering castle. The entire kingdom is abandoned—except for one person. It turns out Mordred Kingslayer is still alive. He has been trapped alone on the island for fifteen centuries, allowed out only one day every hundred years. And what he tells her is shocking: **Auberon is not Mordred's son**.

In fact, he loathes Auberon. Auberon was the son of his archenemy, Merlin, but used magic to convince people he was the true heir to the Fey throne. In reality, **Nia is Mordred's heir in the House of Morgan**, condemned to destroy Avalon Tower. This means her lover Raphael has her on his kill list, but he just doesn't know it yet.

She is not, in fact, Prince Talan's sister.

Mordred offers to help her find Raphael in Auberon's torture dungeons—if only she will help him destroy Avalon Tower once and for all—just as the prophecy has predicted.

BONUS CHAPTER - TALAN

Talan's perspective.

I wake up in a languid tangle of limbs, the scent of perfume hanging in the air, sickly sweet. Shadows claim most of the room, the heavy curtains drawn tight against the morning light. Or, for all I know, the afternoon light. Only a sharp glint of the sun pierces through a crack, casting a sliver of gold across the stone floor.

My head rests between someone's breasts. I can't remember her name, but I do remember the way she screamed mine.

Right now, my bed cradles the sultry forms of two naked women—one with long black hair that cascades over her shoulders, the other with white-blond curls that frame her sleeping face like a halo. It's her full, round breast that I'm lying on.

So, no, it's not as terrible here as I imagined it would

be when my father, the king, ordered me back to the bleak landscape of Brocéliande. He thinks he'll force me to marry a countess—but that is something I have no intention of doing, and it didn't take me long to find other women here to keep me company while I work on a plan to forge my own fate.

The women's breaths rise and fall in a rhythm that lulls me back toward the edge of dreams. Last night, I drifted into their dreams. For hours, I wandered through their fantasies of coronation, of scepters and crowns, of ruthless rule.

They're not getting near the throne, but they can, perhaps, ease my boredom while I'm stuck here.

I turn my head to kiss the blonde woman's nipple, my tongue flicking over it. As I do, the dark-haired woman grabs my bicep. She's awake now, pouting at me, pulling me away from the blonde. Her large, green eyes blink. "You hardly paid any attention to me last night, Prince Talan. It's not fair."

She licks her lips, and her hand slides up to my face. She's gorgeous, voluptuous, but right now the cloying scent of her perfume is overpowering. She leans in, kissing me, and her soft, sweet lips make me forget the perfume. My tongue flicks against hers, and she moans into my mouth.

My hand slides down her spine, and I press her naked body against mine. I can feel her arousal as her thighs wrap around mine.

From behind, the other woman is awake now, eager

to get my attention. She's kissing my neck, thrusting her hips against me, her breath quickening. Her soft lips brush over my skin, and her hand slides down my abs. She does not want to be left out.

This is, by any measure, a delightful way to wake up, in the arms and legs of two gorgeous women. And yet... why do I feel vaguely empty? Perhaps it was the two bottles of mead I drank last night, clouding my pleasure. Or maybe it was the bitter knowledge that I didn't know them at all, and my bed would be cold and utterly empty if I'd been born penniless.

When a loud knock sounds on the door, I disentangle my limbs from theirs, resisting the pull of their hands, their whining protests.

"Give me a minute," I shout at the door, but it's for the women, too.

I'm not entirely convinced I'll be going back to bed, and I have literally no idea what time it is.

I pull on a pair of trousers and brush back my dark hair.

The knock comes again, harsh and abrupt. Whoever is knocking is already on my last nerve. Is that any way to approach a prince?

My jaw tightens as I fling open the door to find the Duke of Wace, his gaunt, pale features like a specter always haunting the halls of power.

He is draped in the tacky, ostentatious finery of a man who desires more than he's worth. His mouth is a thin line, and his skin has a smooth, waxy sheen.

"Your Highness. I must speak with you."

I glance at the two women, who stare at me expectantly.

I nod at the hall. "Outside."

I close the door behind me, scanning the corridor for any signs of movement. I've been doing my best to keep this part of the castle empty because the last thing I want is prying eyes reporting on me. So far, I've scared away every guard my father has sent to stand outside my door.

I'm relieved to find that we are completely alone because anyone overhearing us is likely to report immediately to my father.

I fold my arms. "Now, what the fuck do you think you're doing waking me at this hour?"

"It's nearly dinner, Your Highness."

Light slants in from a towering window, and I can see now that it has the purplish hue of dusk. "Right. Anyway, why are you here?"

The duke's eyes narrow, and they shift from side to side. He looks nervous, and I suspect he should be. "I have always wanted Arbreth Castle, you know."

"That belongs to me. Why the fuck would I give you a castle, Wace?"

"All I'm saying is that I will help you, if you help me."

My jaw tightens. "And what makes you think I need your help?"

"I can, of course, be very discreet," he says quietly, the tenor of his voice as grating as a saw on stone. "About what you plan to do. My wife can see things, you know. She can see into people's thoughts, their desires."

I step closer, and cold fury slides through my veins. "And what does she say about me?"

All the color drains from his face. "Only that you have plans… that you're ambitious, and believe you can do better than your father…" He clears his throat. "Of course, you would make an excellent king."

"Are you blackmailing me, Wace?" I hiss. "A castle for your silence?"

The silence between us thickens like gathering clouds before a storm. His mouth opens and closes.

I'm not waiting for another response. Didn't he know that only a fool would threaten me? I grin widely as tendrils of my magic surround his mind, trapping it. Fragments of his latest dreams flicker in front of me. He dreamed of sitting on a golden throne that slowly sank in a putrid bog. He wore a crown made of thorns, piercing his flesh, drawing blood. Somewhere, in the distance, he could hear his wife's flirting laughter. Who was she talking to? Someone richer, more powerful than he. He calls out to her and no one answers. The throne sinks deeper. He's already up to his waist in mud.

Wace's dreams are hardly complex to figure out. He's desperate for more power, more wealth. Always terrified it will go away, that it will never be enough. That his beautiful wife will leave him for someone richer. His true terror is isolation, abandonment.

Inside his mind, I begin to weave a living nightmare,

like my mother would have done—stitching, binding delicate filaments. But my threads are those of terror, and I knit for him a vision of utter and complete isolation. He's alone now, trapped in a dungeon, forgotten by time. Until even the stone falls away, and he floats in a void, his consciousness severed from his body. He's been here forever, and he will remain here forever—a disembodied soul whose life meant nothing.

A scream rips from his throat, and he runs toward the window, throwing himself through it. Glass shatters, and his shriek echoes through the air as he falls to his death.

Cold air whips in through the shattered window, and I sigh. I'll need to get that fixed soon. Then, I need to pay that man's wife a visit.

I turn back to my room, and pull open the door. I glance at the two women, who wait eagerly for me, bodies splayed out to entice me. But death hangs in the air, and I will need more than two bottles of mead tonight to forget that grim episode.

CHAPTER 1

No matter how many times I hear the roar of a dragon, it always fills me with bone-deep terror.

A dragon cry rips across the night sky. The sound rumbles down to my spine, and fear coils around my ribs, robbing me of breath. I shut my eyes, then exhale slowly and press my body to the cold concrete rooftop. On this mission deep in enemy territory, it's hard to avoid the sound of dragon calls. Their ear-shattering bellows are the relentless requiem for the Second Fey War.

I glance at the dark sky over Bristol, my breath misting. A few snowflakes dance in the air, but it's a moonless night, and I can't see the dragon.

Through the magical conch in my ear, Serana sighs. "That was a loud one."

"They're all loud," I mutter.

She's somewhere on the streets below me, keeping to the shadows, avoiding the warm glow of the gas lamps. Fey soldiers are roaming around occupied Bristol, and we're doing our best to avoid them. Even fully glamoured, we would draw suspicious stares, skulking in the shadows as we are.

Somewhere nearby, our soothsayer, Tana, is drinking in a pub. She has the best assignment of the night. She's probably sitting by a fireplace, eating savory steak and ale pie.

The cold air nips at my fingers and cheeks. "Tana?" I whisper. "Anything in the tea leaves? It's freezing out here."

A second goes by before I hear a breezy murmur through the conch: "You can't rush tea. It takes time to drink it. If I rush it, I'll get a rushed reading," she says. "One second."

I fiddle with the conch in my ear, irritated by the ragged edges scraping my skin.

Inwardly, I curse the Fey—for ruining human technology, for invading France and England. For capturing Raphael and doing gods-know-what to him.

My Raphael, who once waited for days in the woods for a family that he never saw again. Raphael, who'd told me he was desperate for me the way a starving man craves fruit...

The thought of his sorrowful silver eyes makes my throat tighten. I miss him with a gnawing emptiness that makes it hard to think straight. I replay the final moment before the Fey captured him, mentally reviewing every detail. My thoughts spiral into obsession. I can't stop trying to figure out what I did wrong, how I could have stopped it. The tiny moments and decisions that could have led to a better outcome.

What would the brutal Fey do to a high-ranking knight of Avalon Tower? I don't want to think about it, and yet, the thought rings in my skull in an endless loop.

We have to get him back. If they manage to break him with torture, Avalon Tower's agents will start disappearing one by one, like pawns captured in a gruesome game of chess.

"Nia? Hello? Are you listening?"

Serana's sharp hiss in my ear jerks me from my dark thoughts, and I clench my teeth and try to focus on the street again. "I'm sorry. What?"

"I said that I see him now in the tea leaves," Tana says. "The commander is wearing a black cloak. His silver hair is streaked with black. And as the cards foretold, he's coming your way soon."

"How long?" Serana asks.

"In three days."

"*What*?" Serana sputters.

"No, sorry. I got a bit of pie crust in the tea leaves. It's in about fifteen minutes."

My muscles tighten and my pulse races as I glimpse armored Fey rounding the corner. "Serana, there are two guards a block away. Armed with spears. Watch out as they get closer."

"What *is* a block?" she whispers. "That's an American thing."

I scramble to come up with an estimate. "Looks like maybe three hundred feet?"

"What's that in meters?" she presses.

These were things we never covered in Avalon Tower, as I was the only American. "I don't know. A hundred meters?"

I watch the armored Fey as they march closer beneath the golden light of the gas lamps. Despite their gleaming armor, they move with ease, their metallic eyes alert, searching for interlopers like me. Once, seeing Fey soldiers prowling England's streets was unthinkable. Now they're everywhere—marching between London's glassy skyscrapers, soaring on the backs of dragons above the coast.

When they invaded the south, they'd quickly pushed the British army to the north. They now wage a bloody war in Scotland against the humans. Camelot is one of the few places in England still free from the Fey—but that's only because it's hidden with magic from the rest of the world.

Tonight, we're here to find a way to attack them in their own territory, to surprise them in the heart of the Fey kingdom—in Brocéliande itself.

And while I'm at it, I plan to rescue Raphael, too. I need him back so badly, I can taste it, like blood on my tongue. The problem is that Auberon has sealed most of the portals in and out of the Fey realm, and the ones that still exist shift location. Even when found, they require a special key to unlock them—a key possessed only by the highest-ranking Fey. And that's exactly how we ended up here tonight, waiting in the shadows for a captain with a key.

There's no sign of him yet, but two armored Fey guards are marching closer to Serana's hiding spot. My fingers tighten, breath shallowing with tension, but as they pass, they don't seem to notice anything out of place. I exhale in relief and push myself onto my elbows, teeth chattering from the winter chill that slips under my wool coat to bite at my skin. We still have a few minutes before our real target arrives.

Serana sighs. "You know where I'd like to be? Under a blanket, drinking a hot toddy."

"Or jasmine tea," Tana suggests.

"No. A hot toddy with plenty of whisky," Serana says firmly.

"It's like you're reading my mind," I whisper.

"In a warm room, overlooking Lake Avalon," she continues.

"I don't want to go back to Avalon Tower so soon," Tana says darkly. "Wrythe, Tarquin, and all the Pendragon arseholes are out of control. And this human-only Iron Legion club they just started is so gross."

I grimace, knowing what she means. Wrythe is power hungry and hates all demi-fey, me in particular. Tarquin, his nephew, is just as bad.

"I can't stand their 'pure human lineage' shite," Serana mutters. "Did I tell you that Tarquin described me as tainted and corrupted? I asked by what, and he said monstrous blood. The chinless twat. His family is inbred, and *I'm* the monstrous one because of too much genetic diversity?"

"Shh." Someone appears at the edge of the street, and I squint, trying to see him better in the murky light.

Not our target. This man has red hair, and he lacks the brash arrogance of a military commander.

"Are you sure he's supposed to show up now?" I whisper.

"The future is always shifting," Tana says. "But I'm as sure as I can be."

Time is running out for Raphael. This absolutely *has* to work. Because if this fails, I'll be forced to get help from someone dangerous, violent, and deeply unhinged: my father, Mordred, who once broke into Camelot to go on a murder spree, then spent the next fifteen hundred years plotting more vengeance in isolation. He's a revenge-obsessed Fey Heathcliff, a Poe story come to life, and I don't trust him. Paintings all over Avalon Tower depict him sawing off women's heads. Call me crazy, but I think working with him might be off the table.

I try not to dwell on the fact that his blood runs through my veins.

My heartbeat picks up as the captain finally staggers into view two blocks away, his silver hair gleaming under the lamp light. He totters along the sidewalk.

"Serana, I see him," I whisper. "He's turned onto this street. Two blocks away. Uh, two hundred meters, I guess? Get ready."

He stumbles forward, and I hold my breath. He's big, but I've seen Serana take down men twice her size.

The operation will be fast, and—

A shout rings out behind him. He lurches and turns, then lets out a laugh. A large group of Fey soldiers turns the corner behind him, calling his name. Their voices carry on the wind.

My heart skips a beat. "Wait."

"What's going on? What are those voices?" Serana can't look out without revealing her position.

I quickly scan the group. "He's not alone. There are five Fey with him. All military. All armed."

"How drunk are they? I can probably take them."

Frustration sparks through me. For a moment, I consider telling her to risk it, but I quickly quash the thought. I'd never forgive myself if something happened to her. "Not drunk enough. They'll cut you down fast. There are too many of them."

One block away now. The Fey clap the captain on his back, and one of them slings an arm around his shoulder.

"We won't get another chance," Serana says. "You said it yourself, Nia. We *have* to do it tonight. I'm going for it."

"*No,*" Tana and I say at once.

"We need that key!" Serana insists.

And she's right. We need it more than anything. Without a surprise attack on the Fey realm, they will destroy the British army and the allied forces. And no one believes they'll stop with that. Auberon will take over the rest of Europe. Maybe the entire world.

My heart twists. If we don't fix this, Raphael will die in their dungeons.

"Don't move," I say. "I have an idea."

I crawl to the edge of the roof. A rusty drainpipe lines the wall and runs three stories down to the pavement.

I pull off my wool coat, then hoist myself over the edge of the roof, gripping the top of the pipe. It groans under my weight as I start to shimmy down, and something snaps. Dread blooms in my chest. A fall from this height would crush my skull. Frantically, I slide down faster, palms scraping along the rusty metal. With another crack and a lurch, the pipe disconnects from the wall. Fear slams into me. Creaking, the entire thing pulls away from the stone, and I plummet, arms flailing. I grab at a window's ledge, sudden pain shooting through my fingers as I cling to it, but I manage to hang on, my heart thundering. I scramble and find a foothold on the top of a lower window.

I'm still about fifteen feet above the street, but there's no way to climb down. No time, either. Bracing myself, I make a jump for it and land *hard* on my feet, the shock sending waves of pain through my body. Ignoring the impact of the fall, I limp into the light of the gas lamps.

I'm glamoured to look like a full-blooded Fey, with dark steel eyes and sharply pointed ears. I wear the white dress of one of their healers.

I walk toward the soldiers, glancing shyly at them and looking away whenever one of them catches my eye. One leers at me and whispers something to his friend, and they erupt in laughter.

I walk past them, making sure I'm in the path of the captain. A few feet away from him, I pretend to trip and stumble to my knees, crying out. The captain rushes over to me without a thought, reaching out. I take his hand, thanking him in Fey.

And then I summon my powers.

Two magical forces live inside me. One of them, Sentinel powers, lets me break through magical energies. The other lets me read minds. But when they entwine—strands of crimson and violet coiling together—they create something else: the power of mind control.

As our fingers touch, I slip into his mind, and his thoughts wash over me. The captain's name is Adoran, and he's drunk, celebrating good news he got from home. His wife gave birth to a healthy daughter. As soon as the Fey beat the human army, he will go back to Brocéliande to see her. They live in a cozy home in the capital city of Corbinelle. I feel his unbridled joy at the idea. Him, Adoran, a father! Does she have his gold eyes?

I force myself to block those thoughts as I push further into his mind. Sometimes, mind control is difficult. But in this case, it's ridiculously simple. Adoran drank copious amounts of mead tonight, and his bladder is about to burst. I tug at that thought, whispering of streams and waterfalls and trickling water. His need to pee increases tenfold at my suggestions. He'll never make it back to his room in time. What he needs is a dark alley.

I pull away from his mind and stand, curtsying, and thank him again. After I break into someone's mind, I'm always haunted by their thoughts—the ghosts of someone else's memories flitting around inside my brain. For a moment, I fantasize, anticipating the day I'll get to see my golden-eyed daughter before I recall that I don't *have* a daughter. I sweep his thoughts from my brain and hurry away from the group.

Already, the captain is telling his compatriots that he'll join them later. The poor man is bursting for a piss. Glancing back, I see him turning back toward the closest alley, the one where Serana waits for him.

I walk away, and as soon as the sounds of the group fade around the next corner, I double back, hurrying toward the alley. Adoran is stumbling to the wall, already fumbling with his belt as a figure unfolds from the darkness. Quick as a whip, Serana's arm twists around his neck, squeezing. Adoran kicks and buckles, then crumbles into her arms, unconscious.

"Nicely done."

She lays him on the ground, smiling at me as she goes through his pockets. "There's some money here. And a letter."

"It's from his wife." I can still feel the elated joy he felt as he read it over and over.

"That's nice." She purses her lips. "No key."

"It's circular," Tana whispers through the conch. "Maybe one of the coins in his purse?"

I pick up his limp arm to examine a silver bracelet on his wrist. "No. I'm betting this is it."

Serana tries to turn it, looking for a clasp. But it doesn't look like it will budge. "It's stuck *on* his wrist. I'm betting they welded it onto him to make sure it's not stolen. Ah, well."

She unsheathes her long knife.

"Wait!" I grab her arm. "What are you doing?"

She frowns at me. "Cutting his hand off."

"You can't do that! My daughter was just born. My wife is waiting for me back in Corbinelle!"

Serana stares at me. "Are you for real? Get a grip, Nia. You're not him. He's your enemy. He's here to *kill us all.*"

His memories still whirl in my thoughts. I give her a beseeching look.

She raises her hands in despair. "Fine! I'll try to take it off without cutting his hand, okay? But I might have to break one of his fingers. Does that offend your sensibilities, or would that be okay?"

The memory of Raphael's beautiful face pushed

Adoran's thoughts from my mind, clearing away the cobwebs.

"Do it now." I quickly step away, the thread between Adoran and me still too fresh for me to watch.

I hear Serana grunt, and after a few seconds, she joins me.

She rolls her eyes when I look at her. "He'll be okay, but he'll need a healer for that thumb. Happy, Nia?"

"Delighted."

She opens her palm, holding the bracelet, and blood streaks her fingers. "This is it. We have it."

"Check it for writing," Tana says. "The location and time for the portal should be inscribed on the key."

Serana points to some runes etched inside the bracelet. "There. Um. It says…uh…this is definitely *Neh*, and that letter is *Moh…*"

I sigh and hold out my hand, and she drops it in my palm.

"It says *Glynn Nathan*," I say, reading the Fey runes. "That's Saint Nectan's Glen in northern Cornwall. And here are the dates…"

I read and reread them, my heart plunging. *No, that can't be right.*

"Fuck." Disappointment crushes my chest, and I start to wheeze, then cough. I pull out my inhaler, taking two puffs, and wait for my lungs to open again.

"What's wrong?" Serana asks.

My eyes sting, and I close them for a moment. "The portal closed three days ago."

"Fuck!" Serana shouts. "The key is worthless."

She's right. The portal is long gone. Our hope of finding our way to Brocéliande lies crushed, and I know what that means. I'll have to do the unthinkable, an act of pure and utter desperation—madness, perhaps.

Another secret I'll need to swallow, even from my closest friends.

I need to talk to my father.

CHAPTER 2

The salty wind toys with my hair as our boat sails up the river. Up ahead, mist twines around golden towers, and dawn tinges the fog on the lake with rosy gold. The ancient snow-frosted city of Camelot spreads out on the shore, crowned by the castle. No matter how grim the future seems, the sight sends warmth spreading thorough my chest. *Avalon Tower*. This feels like home.

I am still clinging to a desperate hope that someone in MI-13 will be able to use this little bracelet. The alternative, seeking help from my father, is one of the most dangerous ideas I've ever entertained. According to a prophecy, those of his bloodline are fated to destroy Camelot, and Mordred has already tried. Centuries ago, he left Avalon Tower full of corpses—Arthur's and Guinevere's included.

To protect Camelot from the prophecy, Raphael has

pledged to slaughter all of Queen Morgan's descendants. Long ago, the Fey king Auberon convinced the world that he was the true heir to Queen Morgan's throne. And since then, that's what everyone has believed. Raphael is sure he must kill Auberon.

But what, exactly, would my beautiful lover do if he learned that it was all a mistake? That I was the one on his kill list? Would he murder me, too, or would he sheathe his blade?

Right now, no one knows the truth about me except my father. It doesn't matter how much I distrust the man—our secret is a thorny vine that twines us together in a poisoned garden for two. No one else can come within these walls. It's an alliance I never wanted.

While I'm mulling this over, Serana and Tana join me at the prow to stare at the gilded docks as we approach.

"The city looks even more crowded than when we left," Tana says.

I nod. "More fugitives coming in all the time."

"Even if we take in only the families of the Avalon agents, we'll be running out of space soon," Serana says.

"We don't have any other option. We can't let people's loved ones get captured. They could be used as hostages to turn agents." Tana glances at me. "You haven't been eating enough, have you?"

My appetite has all but disappeared. I'm not sure if it's the loss of Raphael or the secrets that stuff me so full, there's room for little else. "When Raphael gets back, I'm going to eat a seven-course meal."

"Don't be daft, you can't wait for that," Serana says. "You'll wither away."

I tighten my grip on the ship's rail. "I will get him back soon, and I'm not in danger of starvation."

"Stress does the opposite to me," she says. "That whole time I was waiting in the alleyway, all I could think about was apple fritters."

As we glide into the narrow canal, the mist thins. The dawn-kissed stone of Avalon Tower rises above us. Apple trees line the canal, covered in a light dusting of snow. The rising sun washes the crooked timber-frame buildings in gold. Shouts ring out around the wharf as longshoremen and sailors bustle around the docks. I'm desperate to get moving, to jump into my next plan.

I may be home, but I won't rest until Raphael is home, too.

The moment the ship is properly moored, I hurry down the gangplank, my breath puffing in the air. I stride rapidly through the cobbled streets, Tana and Serana falling behind me. I march as quickly as I can beneath stone archways and through crowded streets, heading for the castle. As the street opens up into a square, Avalon Tower's walls loom over shops selling tarot cards and old books. Water streams from stony gargoyle heads in a fountain, and steam rises from the basin in the cold air.

"Slow down, Nia," Tana calls out from behind me.

"Nia!" Another voice—one I haven't heard in days.

I turn, surprised to see Viviane, dressed in a green

cloak, poking her head out of a shop door. The sign above her reads *Enchanted Brew Coffee* in gold letters. Her blue eyes sparkle, and she beckons for us to follow her.

She hated me once. Threatened my life as soon as we met, and a few more times after that. Then she started to teach me everything she knows, and now, I'm deeply relieved to see her again.

The three of us follow her down a narrow road next to the café.

She turns to look back at us, and I'm surprised to see that there are dark circles under her eyes and her platinum hair is tangled beneath the cowl. She usually looks like perfection.

"I forgot you wake up stupidly early," I say.

"That's not the only reason I'm here. I knew you were coming this way, and I wanted to catch you as soon as you came in from the docks." She cuts a furtive glance over my shoulder. "Do you have it?"

I raise my hand to show her the bracelet. "Yes, but it's of no help. The portal closed days ago."

Her pale eyes open wide, jaw clenching. Her nostrils flare, and for a moment, I fear she's about to throw her hot coffee at me, but instead, she says coolly, "That's not good."

"Is there any chance we could use it to open a new portal?" I ask.

She shakes her head. "Merlin would have known, but that knowledge was lost to time long ago."

My eyes sting. "Fine. We need a new plan. Should we get back to the Tower to work on it?"

"No. That's why I was waiting for you here. We can't talk about anything at the Tower right now. Let's go to Knight Fall. They've opened it early for us. There are people waiting for us already."

"The tavern? Why?" Realization hits me. "We can't talk around Wrythe and the other Pendragons."

"Exactly. They're getting worse. Wrythe now wants all missions to go through him. I have almost no authority at this point, and neither would Raphael if he were here. Wrythe has been disbanding demi-Fey task forces. He says we need at least one Pendragon agent in each team. Otherwise, he says we're vulnerable to betrayal."

Serana edges forward into the conversation. "He can't do that. Can he?"

Viviane closes her eyes, sighing. "Until Sir Kay returns, the Seneschal is the top-ranked commander in Avalon Tower. I'm afraid it's within his authority."

I turn to my friends. "They'll be serving breakfast soon at Avalon Tower. You two go back. I'll work on a new plan at the tavern."

Tana blinks sleepily. "Are you sure—"

"Sounds good to me." Serana grabs Tana's arm. "It's Tuesday. They'll be doing scones, and Nia doesn't have an appetite, anyway. Thanks, Nia, you're my favorite person ever. Come on, Tana, let's go. I could eat my way through the stone walls of the Tower at this point."

Viviane stares after her. "She didn't put up much of a fight. Come along."

She briskly leads me back into the town square and past the burbling fountain.

We pass shops and pubs with painted signs and magical symbols. We sweep past a bakery, the mullioned windows stuffed with fresh bread, pies, and sugary marzipan confections. For the first time in ages, I actually feel hungry.

Viviane's long legs carry her past the crowded shops at a fast clip. I wheeze, trying to keep up. My asthma worsens in the winter. I pull out my inhaler for two more puffs, and my breathing opens up a bit.

As we reach another small town square, the Knight Fall Tavern looms over it. Made of aged stone with a steeply pitched roof, the tavern almost looks like an gothic manor house. Warm light beams from lead-framed windows, and esoteric symbols glimmer on the door frame. When we get closer, I feel a familiar thrum of magic from within, a tug between my ribs.

Nivene, the other Sentinel, is in the tavern, waiting for me.

As if hearing my thoughts, Viviane turns to me before she pulls open the door. "Nivene is trying to convince me to lead a coup and throw all the Pendragons out. Which, frankly, sounds tempting at this point."

"Of course she is."

Avalon's other Sentinel has no patience for diplomacy, but a war with Wrythe would be dangerous beyond belief. The Pendragon leader would probably rather help the Fey kill us all than give up his seat of power.

I step inside behind Viviane. The tavern has crooked stone walls, rough-hewn wood columns, and cozy alcoves lit by candles. At this hour, the tavern is mostly empty, apart from a man in a cloak nursing a steaming cup of coffee by the fireplace.

Across the room, I spot Nivene sitting at a round table in one of the corners, her red hair fiery in the candlelight. She beckons us closer, already impatient, and I slide into an empty seat beside her.

Viviane pulls out a chair. "Tell her the bad news, Nia."

I shake my head. "We have the key, but the portal closed days ago."

Nivene's shoulders sag. "Well, fuck."

I swallow hard. "Do either of you have another idea? *Anything?*"

The disappointment on their faces is answer enough.

Viviane drops her head into her hands. She's desperate to free Raphael, too. She's known him even longer than I have, and she depends on him. Now, she seems lost. In Avalon Tower, it can be hard to find someone you can truly trust, so when you do find that person, you want to protect them with your life.

"This just makes it all the more urgent," Nivene hisses. "We can't have Wrythe running the show. He'll destroy us all. Without Raphael or Sir Kay to hold him back, he'll take apart Avalon Tower stone by stone—"

"I am *not* about to start a mutiny right now!" Viviane snarls. "It would be a gift to Auberon."

"Don't be an idiot," Nivene says. "Wrythe has already pitted us against each other. Pendragons and humans on one side, demi-Fey on the other. And anyway, who said mutiny? I'm simply suggesting a slight shift in the command structure."

Viviane's fingers tighten into fists. "You said we should arrest Wrythe and kill anyone who gets in our way."

"I was brainstorming. If you have an issue with slaughtering the Pendragons, we can put a pin in that and circle back later. I'm open to alternatives. I mean, we have both Sentinels on our side—"

"I don't want to join a mutiny," I say.

"All I'm saying is that if you both *do* come around to my plan, the other agents will join in," Nivene adds, folding her arms. "If we get rid of the Pendragons, we can invest every available resource into finding another way into Brocéliande. It wouldn't hurt to kill the people stopping us from making progress. Think about it: we kill a few in a brutal fashion, and the rest will fall in line out of fear."

Viviane sighs and looks at me. "Okay, let's ignore the mob boss here for a second. We need Raphael back, and your psychic friend thinks we can free him. She's seen it in her cards. And she said specifically that it's supposed to be you. So, if anyone has an idea, it would be you."

My breath catches, and a storm rages in my thoughts. Mordred claims he can get me to Brocéliande. Viviane said that the knowledge of opening new portals to Brocéliande is lost to time—but Mordred is literally from the time of Merlin. He fought and survived a battle against the great wizard.

But what will my allies do if I tell them the truth? I don't imagine they'd be into the idea of forming an alliance with Avalon Tower's worst enemy.

Before I have a chance to form a sentence, I see Viviane's eyes flick up over my head, and her jaw clenches.

A cold and familiar voice echoes behind me. "Well, what do we have here?"

My skin chills, and I swivel in my chair to see Wrythe Pendragon standing in the doorway, arms folded.

"Hi, Wrythe, grab a seat," Viviane says, not missing a beat. "We were just about to order breakfast."

"No thanks, I'll stand." As he walks closer, his gaze slides to me. "I see that our illustrious Sentinel has returned from her mission. But for some reason, she decided to stop in a tavern instead of reporting to me in Merlin's Tower."

I drum my fingertips on the table, trying to act casual. "I ran into Viviane by sheer luck. And she's the one who sent me on the mission."

His blond mustache twitches, and he adjusts his scarf, probably to remind us who he is. The scarf is embroidered with the Pendragon insignia, a shield with a crown and a severed head in the center. He lifts his chin. "I'm the Seneschal, lest you forget. Everyone should report to me."

"Is that right?" Nivene mutters. "Because I'd rather report to a drainage pipe." For once, she doesn't shout.

"What was that?" Wrythe takes another step closer, narrowing his eyes.

"She said she likes to report to the manager types," I blurt. "Like you."

Wrythe arches an eyebrow. "Right. Good. I wouldn't want to have to court-martial anyone for insubordination."

Viviane claps her hands together. "Fantastic. Well, if that's all, I actually do need to finish hearing Nia's report."

Wrythe nods. "As do I. So, Dame Nia, did you manage to find a key into Brocéliande?"

Reflexively, I let my sleeve drop a bit, hiding the bracelet. "Unfortunately, no. The portal is already closed."

He nods. "Perhaps your next mission requires the experienced hand of a Pendragon officer, like my niece Genivieve or my nephew Tarquin."

Tarquin, who tried to beat me to death. That Tarquin?

Viviane's lips tighten into a thin line. "Her team

included three knights, one of them with Avalon Steel, which is more than any of us have."

"And yet, they failed." Wrythe shrugs. "I think we need to disband that particular team. It's not working out.'

I stare at him in shock. "The portal would be closed no matter who went on that mission."

Wrythe yawns, but I think he's faking boredom. "We have a new policy enacted as of today. Every team we send into the field will contain a human agent, preferably a Pendragon. We deem this safer for everyone."

"Are you suggesting we will be safer with humans, who move sluggishly and have zero magical skills to help us?" Nivene says acidly.

Wrythe ignores her, keeping his eyes on mine. "Furthermore, all newly appointed demi-Fey agents need to go through a mandatory three-month training course in which they'll learn more about what it means to assimilate into human society. What our traditional human values are. You are, after all, living in our world. And we have welcomed you here, but you must learn our ways."

I stand, stunned. Wrythe glances at me, and for a moment, I think I see a flicker of fear cross his face.

"I'm from L.A. I don't need to learn about the human world."

He winces. "Be that as it may, the moment we start making exceptions for one person, it's going to be chaos. I'm afraid we will be taking a hard line on this."

I stare at him, and I notice his hand slide almost imperceptibly toward the pommel of his sword.

During the final trials, I mind-controlled him. Since then, he's made sure to stay as far away from my touch as possible. His obvious fear is a little satisfying, but it's probably not helping my situation. "Well, I'd better get to work learning about humans, I guess," I mutter. "Though I suspect I know a great deal more about normal human behavior than you do, Sir Wrythe."

Furious, I stride out of the tavern. The morning sun has risen higher in the sky, and I blink in the light. My heart thuds, and my face is hot with anger. I now understand what Nivene was talking about. Wrythe is trying to kneecap the demi-Fey until we're no longer a functioning part of Avalon Tower.

Maybe Nivene is right. Not about the slaughter, but…

I catch sight of a person with blond, gleaming hair marching toward me between ramshackle stone shops, and my heart sinks. Great, the only person who could make this day worse.

His pinched nostrils flare as he grins at me. "Hello, hello," Tarquin croons. "None other than the illustrious Dame Nia. The Avalon Steel, or so they say."

"Fuck off, Tarquin, I'm not in the mood."

He puts his palm on his chest, his expression hurt. "First of all, it's *Sir* Tarquin now. And is that any way to talk to someone who looks after the safety of your loved ones?"

"My loved ones?" My stomach flips as I try to figure out what he means. Is he talking about Raphael?

Behind him, a woman runs toward me, waving and smiling like a maniac. My pounding heart registers her identity before my brain does. For a second, I stare at the familiar face so out of place here: large lips overdrawn with red liner, bleached blond hair growing in dark at the roots, thin frame and gaunt cheeks.

"Nia?" Her voice is too loud, and it echoes off the stone buildings.

My jaw drops for a few seconds before I manage to find my voice.

"Mom?"

CHAPTER 3

Guilt. Once I get past the shock, guilt washes over me.

What do others feel when they see their parents after a long time apart? Love, probably. Connection. Familiarity. Excitement.

For me, it's just a black hole of guilt. All the letters I should have written her but didn't. All the times I didn't miss her. The relief that she was finally far away and I no longer had to look after her.

She walks toward me, her bony arms outstretched, and I can't avoid noticing the slight stumble in her step, that unfocused stare. It's six in the morning, and she's either drunk or high. Maybe both.

She pulls me into a hug, all jagged angles. The familiar odor of cigarettes and alcohol envelopes her. She's wearing an expensive suit that I haven't seen her wear in years, with a silky cream shirt beneath it. But now, the clothes hang off her skeletal frame.

"Oh, Nia," she shouts. "I've missed you so much, my dear girl."

It sounds so caring, so motherly. But I instantly notice the way she glances backward to make sure Tarquin hears her. With Mom, every place is a theater, and there's always an audience to impress. She's probably already clocked by Tarquin's accent and clothes that he comes from money. She knows the role to play for him—the loving mother.

And again, I feel a stab of guilt as those thoughts flit through my mind. Why can't I just believe that she truly meant what she said? Sure, she has her own warped survival skills, but she really does love me. She *must*.

"I missed you too, Mom," I say automatically.

"Did you? Last time you wrote me was over a month ago." She laughs as she says it, as if she's just teasing. But I know she felt abandoned.

I stare at her, unable to make sense of her appearance in this place. "What...what are you doing here?"

Her eyes widen, and she touches my arm. "Well, this lovely gentleman, Sir Tarquin, said I was in danger because of the European war with the Fey. He said that because you work here, the Fey might want to abduct me. For leverage. He paid for me to come all the way to Camelot. I had my own suite on the ship. Honey, I didn't know you had anything to do with this Fey war."

I glance at Tarquin. "Because my role here is supposed to be secret."

He's looking down at his nails. "Ah, well, yes, the thing is…most of us were raised here in Camelot, so *our* family is safe. For outsiders such as yourself, who knows what could happen? I was, of course, only trying to help."

I hold my mom by the elbows. "You were never in danger. There was no way they could have found you all the way in California."

"In the war, Nia." She shakes her head. "I really never could have imagined. You were always so scared of taking risks. So timid. Everything was always such a big worry for you. Always fretting."

"No, Mom, I had a normal number of worries." I just didn't want her lighting the sofa on fire again, or driving high as a kite and crashing her car into an abandoned Pizza Hut, or—

She pulls out a cigarette. "Tarquin told me you're the transportation. I realize that being a driver isn't the most glamorous role, but surely you could have told me about it in a letter."

"That's not my title." I can feel my face flushing. I'm torn between wanting to brag about my Avalon Steel and hating myself for even caring what she says in front of Tarquin.

She smiles a little too broadly, glancing back at Tarquin. "Young Sir Tarquin told me your job was to get people where they needed to go."

"Mom…can you give me one second? I want to thank Tarquin for bringing you here, and then I'm all yours."

"Of course. He's a perfect gentleman. You should be very grateful." She says this pointedly, lowering her chin and raising her eyebrows.

It's a long, meaningful look, and I know she thinks he's a catch.

I walk over to Tarquin, fantasizing about smashing my fist into his thin nose. "What the hell do you think you're doing?" I hiss at him.

His nostrils flare. "Honestly, I thought you'd be happy." He waves at Mom and smiles. "All the outsiders have been bringing their families into Camelot for safety, but you somehow neglected to bring your own mother."

"She was halfway across the world. She's not in any danger, or at least she wasn't until you brought her here. You *know* that."

"Oh, Dame Nia," he says. Still smiling, he leans forward and whispers, "I'm going to enjoy introducing your train wreck of a mother to everyone in Camelot. I want everyone to see exactly why someone of your rotten pedigree does not belong here at all. That's the thing we always seem to ignore, isn't it, when we pretend we're so accepting of the demi-Fey? Because the fact is, your mother *shagged* one of those monsters, didn't she? You're not just half corrupt. You're entirely corrupted. The child of a beast and a slag, that's the breeding of your kind. And we're all fine with it now, aren't we, here in these accepting new times?"

After days of sleeplessness and lack of food, and then the conversation with Wrythe, I'm about to lose my temper. I want to bash his pasty face in. But of course, that's what he wants—some way to prove that I can't control my beastly Fey impulses.

He flutters his fingers at my mother with a fake smile. "Nice to meet you, Mrs. Melisende."

"Oh, call me Brandy," my mom laughs lightly. "Mrs. Melisende is my mother."

Trembling with rage, I watch him walk away, then let out a long breath and turn to face Mom. "Where are you staying?" I manage to say with a tight smile.

"Mr. Pendragon found me a cute place a few minutes from here." She blinks. "It's a bit small, to be honest, but he assured me it's only temporary."

"Okay. Um...did you have any breakfast?"

"I don't eat breakfast, Nia. Have you already forgotten? I know it's been a long time, but I didn't think you'd forget everything about me so soon."

"I didn't forget you, Mom." Of course she doesn't eat breakfasts. Why waste the calories on food when you can simply use them to drink?

I return to her and put my arm around her shoulder. "Let me walk you back to your place, then. It's a bit cold for you to be outside right now."

"I was hoping you'd show me around."

I clear my throat. "Maybe later. I have a job to do."

"You need to drive someone?"

I grit my teeth. Naturally, Mom can't know what I really do. "Not exactly. Something else."

As we walk, she loops her arm through mine. "Nia, if you want to land a nice man like Tarquin, you really need to dress nicer. There's dirt all over that cloak. When did you start wearing cloaks? It's a bit strange, I think. And it covers up your figure. You want a clean, sleek line without pockets."

"Land a nice man..." I'm so annoyed, I can hardly form clear thoughts at this point. "Mom, Tarquin's not... there's no way in hell—"

"Oh, honey." She pats my hand. "I know you think you're not good enough. But he obviously cares about you. Do you really think he'd go through all the trouble of getting me here if he weren't interested in you romantically? Now you just have to lure him in. He introduced me to his cousin Ginevra, and she's beautiful, you know. She looks like I did when I was your age. She might be able to tell you where to shop."

"Oh, gods," I mutter. Ginevra hates me as much as Tarquin does. Possibly even more.

Everything about this is a nightmare. Being with my mother suddenly peels away the layers of confidence and worth I've found here. Underneath, I'm still the girl who would never be good enough. "Let's not talk about clothes right now. What about you? How was your trip?"

"Long. But it was nice to have the suite." She smooths her shirt. "You know, I was in this area about twenty-five years ago. Not Camelot, but Cornwall. Tintagel, I think. Lovely place. Great fried scallops."

A shiver dances up my nape. "Was it twenty-seven years ago, perhaps?"

She frowns at me. "How did you know that?"

I let out a long sigh. "Just a lucky guess." I'm twenty-six. I was conceived when my mom was in Cornwall.

"You could have sent for me, you know. You live in a castle now? You left me in that roach-infested apartment so you can live in a castle? They were trying to evict me when Sir Tarquin sent for me."

"Sorry, Mom."

"You're my only child." She sighs deeply. "I've always said that the best thing I ever did, my proudest achievement, was raising you. But I guess parenting doesn't guarantee a child's loyalty. Well…fine. This is where I'm staying."

She waves at a two-story white stucco building with dark wood beams that crisscross the front. A sign hangs from a steep, gabled roof: *Branwen's Inn.*

It looks nice enough. Leaded-glass windows overlook flowerpots, and the smell of coffee and baked bread wafts through the air. I was afraid that Tarquin would place her in the worst location in town. But that's not what he's planning. He wants her nearby and accessible so that he can introduce her to all his friends and acquaintances. To prove that all demi-Fey come from a twisted, dysfunctional background, and that none of us should be here.

But I'm not worried about anything Tarquin's shitty friends might say. I'm worried for my mother's safety—and my sanity.

"You know." Her voice trembles, and she tucks my hair behind my ear. "You don't even look happy to see me."

I smile at her. "Oh, Mom, of course I'm happy to see you."

At least my training as a spy has improved my ability to lie.

CHAPTER 4

I sit on the bed in our room, sipping chamomile tea. In the dark night outside, rain drums against our windowpanes. Warm lamps light up our space. Serana stands beside me, tossing throwing knives against the wall with a steady *thunk, thunk, thunk*.

"Do you know what?" she says. "This is way more fun than practicing my glamouring magic."

In the adjacent bed, Tana is muttering to herself. Tarot cards are spread on the bedsheets, and five empty cups of tea are piled on her nightstand. There are flowers in her dark braids, and she wears a bright yellow dress. She looks a million times better than I do, or so I imagine. I feel faded and worn.

When I was a teenager, I had a Joy Division shirt that I wore all the time and washed every week. By the end, it was tattered and almost translucent, more like a memory of a shirt than an actual shirt. That's how I feel right now. A threadbare version of myself, hardly recognizable.

The sense of warmth I had at coming home to Avalon Tower has already turned to ice. Here, in the tower's gothic halls, a cold cloud of suspicion hangs over every conversation, frosting the atmosphere. My trio was gone less than a week, but that was all it took for mistrust to fester. In that week, tensions between the "Iron Legion" and demi-Fey have escalated, becoming unbearable. Wherever I walk, humans whisper and stare at me. Some give me dirty looks. Most of them have probably already signed the Iron Legion pledge to inform on us.

With most of the elite knights fighting in Scotland, there are few demi-Fey left here to band together. We're outnumbered.

I try to imagine how Raphael would handle it, but I can't exactly picture it.

Over lunch today, my mom told me a story about attacking an accountant with a high heel after he insulted her at a party. As I listened to her ramble, my mind raced about Mordred. As insane as it seemed, I was leaning toward allying with him.

"Damn it!" Tana shouts.

If calm, dreamy Tana shouts, it means something terrible is probably going to happen. My pulse kicks up a notch. "What is it?"

She sighs. "The streams of time are entangled. They

crisscross every which way, stars misaligned, omens misread." Her hands are shaking.

Serana stops tossing her throwing knives and turns to face her. "Sorry, what?"

Tana looks up from her reading. "The future is fucked. Never mind. Go back to what you were doing. It's fucked, but I need to find out more."

Serana tosses another knife. *Thunk.*

"Serana, can we have some quiet? I have a headache," I mumble.

"Because you haven't slept normally in months," Serana says. "And you haven't eaten normally. Do you know what you need to do? You need to channel your aggression like I do."

She holds a knife out to me by the hilt.

Reluctantly, I grab it from her. She points to a spot on the floor by my bed. "Stand here." Too tired to argue, I obey. "Now, imagine that target is the face of someone you really hate," she instructs. "Can you see it?"

"Tarquin," I say immediately.

"Good. Go for it."

I can almost see his thin face before me, the long nose and flared nostrils. The thin lips. Gritting my teeth, I toss the knives, one after another in rapid succession. They hit two feet below the target, clattering off the stone.

"Good on the aggression," Serana says, nodding, "except you're supposed to *aim*."

"I did. I imagined his face." I point at the notches in

the stone where the knives hit, right at crotch height. "And I hit the target."

Serana stares at me, her mouth open. "Right. Okay. Not sure if I'm impressed or concerned."

"All right, hang on," Tana says from her bed. "Am I losing my mind? The cards don't make *any* sense. I've checked the stars, but the sky is too cloudy for a proper reading."

"What about the crystal ball?" Serana asks.

"Absolutely not. It's *tacky*. You know what I need? Goat entrails. One can really see the future clearly in proper entrails."

My eyebrows shoot up. "Tana, I swear, if you start spreading goat entrails on your bed, I'm transferring rooms."

A knock sounds at the door, and I'm relieved by the interruption. Goat entrails?

"Yeah?" I call out.

"It's me." A deep voice pierces the door.

Darius. I hurry to the door and yank it open.

He smiles from the doorway, holding a dinner tray with a silver dome. He saunters in, sets the tray on a desk, and gives me a hug. "I missed you ladies."

"I thought you were in Scotland!" I say, stepping back.

Serana walks over and grabs him in an aggressive bear hug.

"Serana, you're crushing me," he squawks, disentangling himself. Going to the bed, he leans over and kisses

Tana on the cheek. "I *was* in Scotland. They sent me here to report to command and get some supplies. But I have to return in two days."

"How is it there?" Serana asks.

He frowns. "Bad. We're being pushed back. I don't know how much longer we can hang on. There's been talk about retreating to Ireland. They're even worried Auberon could breach Camelot's magical defenses and destroy Avalon Tower. The prophecy of Queen Morgan could happen in our lifetimes."

A sharp silence fills the room, and a chill ripples over my skin. "I'm sure that's not the case."

"Why?" says Darius.

It's *very* hard to keep this secret from them.

I clear my throat, eying the tray. "Just hopeful. Did you bring dinner?"

"Oh. I didn't want to eat in the dining hall," he says. "It's full of the fucking Iron Legion."

"It's really hostile, isn't it?" says Tana.

He pulls the dome off the tray. "Well, I brought extra."

Underneath, there's a basket of fresh bread rolls with steam pouring off them and a plate full of sliced blue cheese.

"Is that Stilton?" Serana asks, already reaching for it.

"Stop!" Tana leaps from her bed. "Stilton is almost as good as goat entrails."

"You're wasted here," I say. "You should be in marketing. 'Stilton: almost as good as goat entrails.'"

Tana grabs the plate, staring at it. "I don't eat it, but I can see the future in cheese. Especially if it's ripe like this."

"I'm just going to have a little nibble." Serana grabs a piece and pops it in her mouth.

"Serana!" Tana yanks the cheese plate away. "You just ate the fate of the Italian military."

Serana's eyes widen guiltily. "Sorry."

Darius hands Serana a roll. "Have some bread."

Tana stares at the cheese as she carries it to her bed. "It's the same as the cards. The war cannot be won here. It must be won in Brocéliande. But when I try to find the way there, it just shows the same figure, and I can't make any sense of it."

Dread chases down my spine. I think I already know who the figure is, a man who has lived alone for centuries, twisted with fantasies of revenge.

"What figure is that?" Darius asks.

"In the cards, he appears as the Emperor." Her gaze flicks to me. "That showed up in your reading, too, remember?"

"Must be Auberon," Serana says.

Tana shakes her head. "No, I always see Auberon as the reversed King of Swords. Tyranny."

I swallow hard. "Weird."

Her dark eyes shift to me. "Any idea who the Emperor might be?"

My skin grows cold. Do I tell them?

"Maybe Sir Kay?" Darius suggests.

"Wrythe?" Serana asks. "He certainly thinks of himself as an emperor."

My pulse is racing, electrified. I can't keep this information to myself forever. Even if I wanted to, Tana will piece it together, one reading at a time.

Slowly, I say, "I know who he is."

They turn to stare at me.

Sweat chills my skin. "When you gave me the reading, you told me he represents one of my parents."

Tana's eyes widen. "Oh, right. Your father, I thought. Do you know who he is?"

My blood roars, and I try to keep my tone light. "It turns out my father lives on the lost island of Avalon."

"Hang on, your what lives on the lost what of the *what*?" Darius stares at me.

"That island sank," says Serana. "Like Shalott. The war between Merlin and Mordred drowned all the islands in the lake."

My fingers dig into my palms. "No, Avalon is still there. I found it two months ago. After Raphael was captured, I felt something calling to me from the mist. I thought it was a Lady of the Lake thing. I ended up in a boat, sailing through the fog. It was hidden by a veil, but I could get through that with my Sentinel powers, and I found the lost island of Avalon. It didn't sink. It's just hidden by a veil. And my father lives there. He's been there for fifteen hundred years." My throat goes dry. "He said he could help me save Raphael."

They stare at me, mouths agape.

"You never said anything," Serana said. "Why did you never—"

"It's Mordred," I blurt.

Serana's jaw drops. "Mordred. As in…Mordred Kingslayer? The man who slaughtered hundreds of people in this very tower?"

My stomach twists. "That's the one."

"That's impossible," Darius says.

Tana stares at me, unmoving. "No, that makes perfect sense. It explains everything I see. He is the way to Brocéliande. He can get you there."

Serana looks horrified. "Hang on. Are you telling us that you're Auberon's sister?"

I shake my head. "We're not related. In fact, Mordred *hates* Auberon. Mordred is Queen Morgan's son. Auberon is Merlin's son. They were on opposite sides of the war for Camelot. The Court of Merlin versus the Court of Morgan. Merlin's court won out, and he trapped Mordred on the island and hid it behind a veil. Nimue then trapped Merlin, and their son, Auberon, claimed the throne for himself, using his magic to convince the world it was always his."

Serana frowns. "So, Mordred could be an ally?"

My nose wrinkles. "Not really. He still wants to destroy Avalon Tower. In return, he said he would help me free Raphael. And I know it sounds completely fucking insane, because he wants to kill us all, but I want to take him up on his offer." Maybe I'd risk destroying this place for Raphael.

A thorny silence settles over the room. Serana distractedly picks up another piece of cheese and takes a bite from it.

At last, Darius inhales sharply. “So, he can never leave the island?”

“Once a century, he can get free for one day. Which means my mom knew him less than a day…never mind. That’s not important.”

Serana steps closer to me. “Maybe you can accept his offer. If he can’t get out again for another, what, seventy-three years, then how much harm can he do? Maybe you could just play along with his bargain.”

“Play along,” I repeat.

“You’re a bloody spy, an Avalon Steel spy,” says Darius. “Mordred is an asset. Tell him you will help him destroy Avalon Tower and then don’t. Manipulate him. Use him. Get him to open the way to Brocéliande so you can save your gorgeous boyfriend, and then, when he wants you to fulfill your part of the bargain, you just fuck off. Or kill your dad. Whatever.”

My chest unclenches. “You’re not worried about the prophecy?”

Tana sighs heavily. “What I see right now is that Mordred is the only way forward into Brocéliande. He’s not lying about being able to help you. We’ll have to worry about the prophecy later. Burn that bridge when we come to it. One thing at a time, yes?”

Serana nods. “It sounds unhinged in a way, but we are absolutely running out of options. We’re running out of time here to save Raphael. And with the way Wrythe is acting, I'm sure he doesn't want Raphael back. In fact, I bet he actively stands in the way of Raphael's return. I think if things keep going the way they are, he'll be imprisoning all of us demi-Fey as corrupted traitors."

My breath quickens. Suddenly, I'm filled with energy. I'm going to get Raphael back, and for the first time in a while, I feel electrified with optimism. "I'll go there tonight. See what Mordred has to say."

"Yeah, I didn't want to mention it before, but there's a small problem," Darius says. "There's an Iron Legion cadet downstairs in the Astolat Atrium. He has one of those coat-of-arms badges they wear to make themselves important. This one looks like he's on guard to see if anyone specifically from *this room* is going anywhere. He's keeping watch on the demi-Fey."

"They've been following me around ever since I got here," I say.

"Same here," Serana says.

I turn, staring out at the rainy night. "Looks like I'll be sneaking out the back way, then."

The window swings open. It's not designed for climbing in and out, so I can barely squeeze my ass through the opening.

Inside the room, Darius watches me scoot out, his forehead creased with worry. The cloak I'm wearing is bunching up, and I've packed too much into the pockets

—dagger at my side, my inhaler. A sleeker ensemble would make this easier.

I barely manage to get my hips through the gap, twisting and shimmying. Gripping the window frame, I dangle above the abyss, hail pounding against my legs. I flash Darius one last smile, then scale down the wall, slotting my toes into tiny gaps in the stones. I glance at the sheer drop below me. The earth looks impossibly far away, but there's a stone gargoyle a few feet below our room. I make him my goal.

I lower myself and grab onto the statue. Lightning flashes, illuminating the gargoyle's horned, leering face. The statue is slippery, and I nearly lose my footing, but soon enough, I'm hugging the gargoyle tightly, arms and legs wrapped around him. I haven't been this close to another creature since Raphael was here.

"What are *you* smiling about?" I mutter at the statue.

Beneath the statue, another ledge juts out above a window, its surface covered with slippery hailstones. Slowly, carefully, I claw my way down the sheer wall, scrabbling from ledge to ledge. Darius and Serana watch my descent from above. The hail softens to rain that chills my scalp and my fingers and soaks into my wool cloak.

I climb lower and lower, avoiding the windows, clinging to the next ledge, the next gargoyle.

By the time I'm two floors below our room, I'm beyond the Astolat Atrium, safe from the lookout.

I try to open a window, prying at it with my fingernails, but it's locked. I peer into the room through the glass. It looks like an empty office.

I glance down, my head spinning at the height. Still too far to go. If I keep going this way, I'm sure to fall. Shivering in the cold, I wrap my sodden cloak around one of my hands and wait. Lightning flashes in the sky, and my pulse races as I count. One…two…

Thunder booms, and I smash the glass with my covered knuckles. Reaching through the shattered window, I unlatch it and squeeze inside. Glass crunches as I land on the solid stone floor. *Safe*. I exhale in relief.

The office door opens into an empty hall, and I creep toward the closest stairwell.

I race down the steps, my feet slamming against the uneven stones of Lothian Tower.

Once, centuries ago, my father ran up these stairs, hungry for blood and hellbent on murder.

Even if Mordred is trapped on an island, the danger he exudes is unmistakable.

If I let him get in my head—if I let him manipulate *me*—it's all over.

CHAPTER 5

On the misty shore of Avalon, I step out of the boat onto the wet rocks. Cold fog twines around me. Avalon's pale stone castle looms over an icy, craggy hill. Now, in the midst of winter, the trees are barren, and a furious wind howls between their branches. At least the rain has stopped.

What would it do to a person to live in this kind of bleak isolation for fifteen centuries?

Manipulate him, Darius said. *Use him.*

Back in our cozy room, that sounded like a great idea. But with a steeply peaked, half-ruined castle towering over me, and the haunting moan of the wind wrapping around me, I'm having second thoughts.

As I start to climb the winding path toward the castle, I remind myself that I'm doing this for Raphael. It may be freezing here, but he's in worse conditions. I can almost see his silver eyes burning like flames before me and hear him murmuring, *I've got you, love. Don't worry, I've got you.*

Whatever happens next, I can't let an ancient, usurped Fey king mess with my head.

Maybe his isolation can work to my advantage.

As I ascend the crumbling stairs, the clouds slide away from the moon. It's full tonight, and silver light pours over the half-ruined castle covered in rain-slick vines. My gaze drifts up to the carvings in the pale stone, the exquisite faces formed from twisting leaves.

And just as before, my father appears. Mordred steps from the shadows of a dark archway. His golden eyes make my breath catch, and the moon gleams off his dark, spiked crown.

Isolation hasn't diminished him, I think, nor does he seem desperate. He radiates power, so strong it sets my teeth on edge.

Focus, Nia.

Everything is a negotiation. Mordred wants something from me, and I need to make him think he can get it. I can't seem too eager, or he'll have the upper hand.

He crosses his arms, leaning against the stone archway. "I feel I've waited centuries for you."

"I had to think about your offer."

"Come inside. I'm afraid my castle isn't as grand as it once was."

He turns, leading me into a vast hall lit with torches.

The ceiling is over a hundred feet high and crumbling in places. Trees line the side of the hall, their branches heavy with apples, even though it's winter. Little silver lights twinkle from the trees like glowing ice. Columns soar high above, their surfaces intricately carved to look like curling leaves, sometimes forming faces.

Grass and wildflowers grow rampantly over the stone floor. It's disorienting—a place that can't decide if it's inside or outside, if it's summer or winter. But most strange of all, a grand table spans the hall, set with crystal glasses, white plates, and flickering candelabras.

"Expecting a party?" I ask.

"Ah, well, we set this up to celebrate the end of the battle."

I cross to the table, running my finger over the rim of one of the delicate glasses. "*We* set it up? You're not here alone?"

A line forms between his eyebrows, and he looks almost confused for a moment. "Well, I wasn't alone. Mother had this arranged to celebrate winning the war against Camelot, only it didn't work out that way. And instead of celebrating, I found myself here alone, while Auberon stole my crown. Do you know what? I hope Merlin is still conscious in that fucking tree, being crushed to death for all eternity."

"The war against Camelot." I pull my finger away from the glass rim and stare at him. "This banquet table has been here for fifteen centuries."

His expression darkens. "I'd rather not count the years since our golden age. I'd prefer to ignore that passage of time." His voice echoes off the high ceiling, the sound reverberating all around me.

"What exactly happened between Morgan and Merlin?" I ask.

"He was jealous, wasn't he? As our court swelled in grandeur, Arthur and Merlin grew more envious. We could trade with anyone back then because of our portals. We didn't even need to sail. And Arthur's covetousness started the war. He wanted our portals for himself, and he had a perfect way to justify it. Apparently, we were *sinful*. We taught the humans how to enjoy their lives, and that is forbidden. Did you know that? Enjoying things is very naughty. So, that's why Arthur made plans to take over *our* kingdom."

He turns back to look at me, and his misty breath clouds around his handsome face.

Maybe I shouldn't have asked. He's already controlling the conversation when I should be. "You know what? Maybe we shouldn't dwell on the past," I say. "I need to get one of our knights back. When we last met, you said you could help me save Raphael."

"Raphael," Mordred echoes. Moonlight and shadow highlight his sharp cheekbones, his strong jawline. His voice vibrates in the vast space, almost as if the entire castle is part of his body. I have the strange feeling that the castle takes a breath when he does. "Is that his name? The silver-eyed man that Auberon took from you? The one I met in my dreams. His mother was human, yes? Kidnapped by the Court of Merlin before they sealed up their portals?"

I nod. "I didn't know she was kidnapped, but yes, Raphael is a silver-eyed demi-Fey."

"He is imprisoned in Brocéliande."

"I know. I need to get there, and I don't know how."

He leans against a carved column. "Most of the portals in and out of Brocéliande are closed now. But mine isn't. I don't think they know about it. And that is why you're here. I am the last refuge for a desperate, shipwrecked soul washed up on my shore. But when you get into Brocéliande, then what? You'll ask for directions to the king's dungeons? Or do you think if you ask the black-hearted prince nicely, he'll release his prisoner?"

"I'm trained in espionage."

"I'm trained in espionage," he says in a mimicry of my voice. Then his dark eyebrows knit together as he studies me. He's looking for something in my expression. What is it? Is he trying to decide if he can trust me?

And then I know. I'm his daughter, and he wants to see the resemblance. And more than anything, he wants *company.*

The Fey thrive on merriment and pleasure, on parties and banquets. The man has been starved of other people for eons, waiting centuries alone for a celebration that never happened, with only memories and ghosts for companions.

I'd worried about my own desperation shining through, but he's as desperate as I am. I'm the first family he's had since his world ended, and the more he thinks we have in common, the more he'll want to help me.

I take a step closer to him, examining his features. It's easy to see the similarities between us. The thick, dark eyebrows and large eyes, the black eyelashes, the straight nose. His eyes gleam an eerie gold, while mine are dark—but their almond shape is the same.

I certainly don't have his height, but I can mimic his stance, head high and chin raised. I adapt his posture subtly, sliding my hands into my pockets like he does.

"When I get there, I can handle myself. Once I get through, I'll find him." I adjust my tone slightly, making it sound more imperious, like his.

He wants me to ask for his help, but if I seem too weak, he might change his mind. Mordred doesn't want a connection to someone useless. He respects power and strength.

With a sliver of satisfaction, I see in his expression that I hit the mark.

"You can't find him," he says. "Auberon keeps his prisoners well-hidden. But I can help you, daughter. If you help me."

I raise an eyebrow. "Help you destroy Avalon Tower?"

He shrugs slowly, flashing me a half-smile. "It is foretold."

“What does it mean to destroy Avalon Tower?” I ask. "Like, do you want it demolished, or what?”

“Every stone in every building may remain where it is. But Avalon Tower is and always has been run by the Pendragons. Arthur’s descendants. I merely want all the Pendragons to die, one by one. That’s all.”

CHAPTER 6

A chill ripples over my skin. It seems that my father has something in common with a few of my friends.

Still, as much as I hate Wrythe, Tarquin, and Ginevra, I'm not sure I can justify killing an entire group of people just because of their family name.

But I'm not really working with him, am I? I'm manipulating him.

I hunch my shoulders in the cold air. "Avalon Tower is no longer *just* Pendragons. It's not like it was in your golden age. What about the rest of us? The demi-Fey? The humans who are not Pendragons?"

"I want the Pendragons dead." He gestures at the table. "I want Arthur's line extinguished. Then we celebrate."

He really is doing all of this for a party, isn't he? It's the Feyest thing ever.

"Fine. Now, will you tell me how to save Raphael?"

He stretches out a long arm and plucks an apple from a tree. "Of course. To save him, we must learn exactly where they're keeping him."

"So, you *don't* know where he is?"

"In my dreams, I see mere glimpses. He is in Auberon's fortress, but it's a vast place, with countless dungeons, cells, and torture chambers. I need to think." He takes a bite of the apple, closes his eyes, and leans his head back against the column.

I grit my teeth in frustration as I turn back to look at the banquet table. He's actually still got ancient wine in the decanters. Dust and snow cover the plates and the faded gold tablecloth. There are food trays with silver domes on them. I hate to think of what's underneath them.

I have no idea what Mordred is doing right now. Eyes closed, he seems deep in thought. He begins to hum, an eerie, haunting tune that raises the hair on my nape and pulls my attention from the banquet table. The song is uncanny, strangely familiar, and his body glows with silver. And for some reason, I feel as if the tune is beckoning me closer.

After a while, movement catches my eye from above, and I glance up to see a cloud of silver moths fluttering down from the ruined ceiling. As Mordred hums, they twirl and dance in the air, their wings ignited by the slate-silver moonlight. Mordred holds out his hand, and a moth lands on his palm.

He opens his eyes and clamps his hand into a fist, crushing it. The rest of the moths scatter, flitting away from him. He opens his hand again, and my breath hitches. On his palm is a jeweled silver moth, its wings decorated with tiny, sparkling stones.

"Take it," he says.

I take it from his palm, a lifeless moth made of metal.

"This moth will be my ears and my eyes. Carry it into Auberon's castle. Once it's inside, I will be able to see and hear everything that goes on in the fortress. I will be able to find your Raphael. And the moment I find him, the moth will lead you to him."

"You make it sound almost easy."

"It will not be easy. Steer clear of Auberon—that goes without saying. And his dark-eyed son, too. The Dream Stalker is dangerous, one of the few remaining with primal powers."

"What *are* his powers, besides invading people's dreams?" I can't take my eyes off the little creature in my hand.

"Just stay away from him and focus on the moth."

"How do I get into the fortress? Castle Perillos is surrounded by towering walls."

"The portal will take you straight into the castle's garden. You won't need to get past the walls—you'll already be inside them. Once you're in, it's not heavily guarded. There are hundreds of entrances into the castle itself. I don't know whether any of the doors to the towers will be open, so you may have to get creative."

"How do we open the portal?"

Mordred narrows his pale blue eyes. "You don't need to worry about that. Follow me, do what I say; that's all you need to know."

Spoken like a true parent. And incredibly, this revenge-obsessed weirdo might actually be the *better* parent of the two.

"Come with me." He turns, stalking across the hall.

I follow him through a heavy set of oak doors. As I step outside again, the cold wind stings my cheeks. He leads me into a vast garden. Large stone dolmens rise from the earth like an overgrown Stonehenge in the moonlight. They are carved with spirals that seem to circle endlessly, like obsessive thoughts spinning back in time. They remind me of Mordred.

He stops before the stones and nods at them. "Walk through the ley portal. Surely you can see it."

The hair on the back of my neck stands on end. A faint buzzing sound thickens in the air like the hum that emanated from the Fey veil. I concentrate on my powers, summoning my Sentinel magic, and darkness spreads between the stones, a black tear in the landscape, as if some unknown hand had ripped a fragment of reality, leaving this hole in its wake.

I stare at it, my jaw dropping.

"These ring stones are a bridge between worlds," Mordred says. "There are numerous gateways to Brocéliande and other magical realms in Avalon through our carved stones. But since Brocéliande closed its borders, only a Sentinel or someone with a key can pass through this portal."

"Just Sentinels?" My heart sinks. My mind was already spinning with the possibility of unleashing dozens of Avalon agents directly into Auberon's castle. We'd end the war within a day.

"A Sentinel can forge the path between worlds and walk through it."

I grip the little metallic moth, then slide it into my damp coat pocket. "Auberon has his soldiers walk through portals that he opens from Brocéliande, but they've got keys."

His golden eyes flick up to the full moon. "And I have no idea how to make them, so you'll need to steal one of theirs if you want to get your lover out of Brocéliande. Now, are we going to talk all night, or are you going?"

I pull my cloak tightly around me. "Do I look like I could blend in there? I wasn't expecting to go right in tonight."

He narrows his eyes. "You look a mess. You can't be seen wearing that."

He touches the collar of my coat, and his magic thrums over me again. I look down to see my damp wool coat transform into a black gown with a lacy décolletage and a low-slung silver belt. It even has discreet pockets, and when I slide my hand inside one of them, I find the bejeweled moth tucked inside, along with my inhaler. My dagger is still wrapped around my waist, sheathed in dark leather that matches the dress.

I look up into his haunted golden eyes. "How many powers do you have, exactly? Is it true that your diametric powers are what drove you to massacre those in Lothian Tower?"

"Is that the story they're telling? *Diametric powers*? Absolute nonsense. The Pendragons are fucking idiots." He casts a critical eye over me. "Right. The dress looks good. Unfortunately, I can't do anything about your stunted height. I can fix the deformed ears, though."

"Deformed?"

"Human." Frowning, he brushes a fingertip over the top of my ears, and I feel the tingle of glamour magic whispering over my ears.

"How does it look?" I ask.

"Perfect. And your eyes. They need to shine like ours do—dark steel for you, I think—and you need our sharpened canines."

Magic buzzes uncomfortably over my eyes, and I blink. "How long will this last?"

"Years, unless I remove it. You still mostly look like yourself, with a few tweaks. Tell me, could anyone there recognize your face? The Dream Stalker or the king, perhaps?"

My mind searches through all our encounters. I was in the same place with Prince Talan once, but he never looked at me. I was watching him carefully in the cabaret hall. The entire time he was tormenting me through dreams, I was on a different floor than him. He was in my head, but he never saw my face.

"I don't think the prince has ever seen me, and I doubt that anyone else would recognize me."

"Good. A complex glamour that would change your features significantly would fade quickly. But this can last much longer."

I hesitate. "There might be another problem. He hasn't seen me, but he's sensed me. I hear his thoughts sometimes. They've gone dark in the past few months, and that made me think he might be back in Brocéliande. And if I end up in his thoughts again, he might sense me. He called me 'the little telepath.'"

Mordred leans closer. "You hear *what*?"

"His thoughts. I hear other people's, too. I'm telepathic, but usually, I have to touch someone to hear their thoughts. But with Talan, I don't need to be anywhere near him."

"Do you hear anything useful in his thoughts? Battle plans, for example?"

I shake my head. "I wish. No, it's mostly dark, poetic, lonely." *And sex. Lots of sex.* "I didn't even know who I was hearing until a few months ago." All these years, I'd had a private radio broadcast straight from the mind of the crown prince of Brocéliande—a man feared and desired in equal measure.

"Now, *that* is interesting. So, he might sense you the moment you come through the portal?"

I shrug. "I got close to him once before, in the Château des Rêves, and he found me through my thoughts. He taunted me, then pulled me into a waking nightmare."

The wind rushes over us, and Mordred's black hair sweeps over his sharp cheekbones. "Well, that complicates things, but it's not insurmountable. Before you go in, you must shield your mind from him. As a Sentinel, you should be able to do it. Imagine a cloud of mist or fog in your skull. No, imagine *the veil* itself. Conjure up its hum in your mind and the shimmering cloud of mist. Block him from entering with a magical barrier. Do it now."

I close my eyes. My heart flutters, and I summon the image of the veil in my mind until I can hear its hum, feel the electrifying buzz over my skin, and see the pearlescent mist roiling in my thoughts. My skin prickles as though I'm approaching the actual barrier. "Okay. I think I've got it."

He shakes his head. "No, you don't. It's not powerful enough. Do it again. Really focus. You need it to last effortlessly while you're there."

"I *am* focusing." I tighten my fists as the imaginary veil hums in my mind.

"Focus *more*. You can't let down your guard when you're there. If you and the Dream Stalker have this connection, you must get it right."

I try again. And again.

Mordred berates me and snarls at me, losing his patience several times. He's far from the patient teacher that Raphael was. But finally, he claps his hands in what I think is satisfaction.

"That's good enough." He turns to the dolmens, and his black cape catches in the wind. "Go on. And remember exactly where the portal leaves you off, because you will need to return the same way."

"Okay. And how do I find the portal key I need to get Raphael back?"

"It will take a while, but my moth will help us. Eventually. Tonight, you should try to free him from his dungeon. Find a place for him to hide in Brocéliande. You and I will work on the key later."

My heart speeds up at the thought. I might see Raphael again, *tonight*. I should have come here sooner.

And telling him whose help I used to get him out? That's a problem for future Nia.

I step closer to the dolmens until I'm standing inches from the rain-soaked stone.

This portal isn't like the veil, a crisscrossing wall of magic that I could unravel. It's a continuous vortex of energy that pulls at my Sentinel magic, a black hole drawing me in.

The moment I touch the stone, I fall into the portal. Hard.

CHAPTER 7

The portal slings me onto the cold, rocky earth. Snow whirls around me, and cold air stings my skin.

My thoughts swim with dizziness and an overwhelming sensation of wrongness, something that should never have happened. The winter wind shrieks in my ears, whipping snow into my face, as I pick myself off the frozen earth. The dress Mordred gave me is stunning, but I can't say it's keeping me warm.

Hugging myself, I survey the wintry landscape. The scene echoes the one in Mordred's dolmen garden, almost as if one is a darker reflection of the other. I'm shivering in a barren, thorny garden where twisted briars grow over jagged rocks that jut from the earth. The towering walls to the fortress rise above me, and night bramble crawls over the icy stones, but I can hardly see the castle with the snow in my face.

A weeping willow stands nearby, and I scramble beneath the gnarled branches to get out of the lashing snow. I glance up though the boughs, and my breath hitches. The storm clouds are sliding away from the moons--*two* moons that shimmer in the sky, one round and silver, the other half-waxed and dark red. I knew that Brocéliande had two moons, but actually *seeing* them is different. Our briefings don't do these celestial bodies justice. The silver and red moonlight cast a ghostly aura on my surroundings and on the looming tower walls that surround me.

I've read Fey poems of Brocéliande, and there are two kinds. In one set of poems, Brocéliande is described as lush meadows of wildflowers and honeyed sunlight. In the second, the realm is a harsh place, an inhospitable landscape lashed by wild tempests.

Judging by the current conditions, the second version is more accurate.

As the howling wind lets up a little, I peer around the willow trunk.

Just like Mordred promised, the portal took me within the walls. I'm in Corbinelle, the capital city of Brocéliande, a few hundred feet from Castle Perillos. It's even bigger than Avalon Tower—practically an entire city of pale stone frosted with snow and ice. The fortress comprises seven towers altogether, looming over the landscape like a mountain.

The central tower stands at the forefront of the vanguard, its wooden doors barred to the world. Above the enormous doors, a moon and a raven, the symbols of Queen Morgan, my grandmother, are carved into stone that gleams with ice. Auberon has worked his fiction into the castle's very stones.

High above the frozen earth, stone bridges connect the seven towers, and stairwells crisscross between buildings in complex patterns. My gaze flicks all the way up. The spires stretch to the red-tinged clouds. In some windows, golden lights twinkle, beckoning me closer with their warmth. Torches are affixed to the walls outside, washing the stone with warm light.

Shivering, I shove my hand into my pocket and brush my fingers over the metallic moth. Its ice-cold surface stings my fingers.

Now, to get *inside* the castle. As the snow dies down, I fold my arms over my chest and march toward the entrance. There's not a ton of security here inside the fortress walls, but there is some. As I near the castle, I realize that guards flank either side of main doors.

The King's Watch, probably. If they see me out here, I could be reported to Auberon's spies and goons, the police force that he uses to maintain his rule in Brocéliande.

I dash across the courtyard toward one of the smaller towers instead, one with a stone bridge that spans two towers, doing my best to stay in the darkness. If I can find a way up to that bridge, I might be able to get in through a door.

The cold air nips at my fingers and cheeks as I hurry

closer to a cluster of vines clinging to the wall. I glance over my shoulder, looking for signs of life. In the distance, shadows are moving by the surrounding walls —patrolling guards.

Shit. They're marching my way, and I slink back behind a column to hide. As I wait for them to walk past me, I feel a familiar tug, then a faint voice, a low, velvety murmuring in my mind.

It takes me a few seconds to pinpoint what it is.

It's the Dream Stalker's haunting presence, dangerous as a blade at the throat, seductive as silk caressing the skin. Prince Talan's thoughts brush against my mind, just as they've done so many times before. For the past several years, I fell asleep to the sound of them, the promise of exquisite ecstasy or pain, depending on his mood. And now that I'm close to him, his voice is back.

How strange that I've been hearing his innermost thoughts for years, like a dark lullaby in my thoughts, and he *still* has no idea who I am.

Already, I can feel our connection forming—the silky strands between us, delicate as a spider's web.

In the frozen night, cold wrath climbs over my skin like hoarfrost, a rime that glazes my soul. Tonight, I find no solace in the dark. I wander silently among a garden of thorns. Let vengeance's flame guide me through this desolate path...

My fingers curl into fists. I have to sever this connection right now. I close my eyes, imagining the hum of the veil, the crackling buzz of its intensity. I think of a misty magic, twisting and churning inside my skull. Shivers dance over my skin.

Instantly, the prince's thoughts go silent, blanketed by the fog in my mind. I exhale with relief.

The patrolling guards have passed by, oblivious to my hiding spot. I watch them walk away. When they're at a safe distance, I grab at the vine, tugging it a few times to make sure that it's sturdy. I'd read about dragon-claw vines, but never seen them in person. They're unique to Brocéliande and stronger than any plants in our world. It has giant thorns, but they're sparse enough and large enough that I can use them almost like rungs. Admittedly, it's much harder climbing in a damn dress than it would be in pants.

I hoist myself up the vine toward the bridge. Reaching it, I pull myself over the edge and land with a thud on the icy stone. My heart pounds as I hurry across the bridge to an oak door. When I pull it open, exhilaration fizzes in my chest. Narrow, candlelit stairs wind upward. I start up them, huffing from exertion.

I climb several flights of stairs and reach an archway, crossing into a vast gothic hall with a rib-vaulted ceiling and long, mullioned windows. Moss and delicate wildflowers grow over the floor and on some of the walls. From this vantage point, I can see the city of Corbinelle over the exterior walls. Lights twinkle in distant windows, and a river snakes through the landscape. It reminds me of Camelot, except the stone buildings are a pale white instead of gold, and towering oaks grow throughout the city, and along the river. Dark mountains rise in the distance, illuminated in shades of rose and silver by the double moons.

My heart tightens at the strangeness of this world. Somewhere nearby, Raphael is waiting for me. Time to find out where.

I take the silver moth from my pocket and place it on a wooden table—Mordred's eyes and ears in the castle. "Go find Raphael," I whisper to the moth. "Then take me to him."

I wait for a long moment, then another. At last, one wing trembles and then goes still again. I inhale deeply, watching as both wings flap and the moth silently rises. It floats a few feet above me, then flutters down the hall.

Alone, I take in the eerie grandeur around me.

Red-tinged moonlight streams into the corridor, and shadows gather above me in the ribbed arches. Portraits of Fey royalty hang on the walls, and in the ghostly torchlight, they almost seem alive, making my heart stutter. Candlelight from chandeliers dances over a painting of King Auberon in a golden crown, wielding a sword at twilight. But there are more paintings of a man I don't recognize. He almost looks like Talan, but with blond hair and a platinum crown. He stands at the prow of a ship. In another image, he's leading men into battle on a horse. A third image depicts him on a throne, his silver-eyed gaze leveled sternly at the viewer, almost smirking.

Beneath one of the portraits are the words PRINCE LOTHYR.

Vaguely, I remember learning about him, the golden prince who drowned two centuries ago, fighting for the king in a civil war.

There's only one painting of Talan here. He's sitting by a table, holding a goblet of wine, his lips curled in a wry smile. Nothing heroic, but as I glance at the dark look in his eyes, a hot shiver skims over my skin.

Distant music floats through the hall, and I move deeper inside, investigating my surroundings and making sure no one is nearby. As I pass a mirror, I check my reflection, and I'm startled to see the dark sheen of my steely eyes. My cheeks have gone bright pink in the cold, and I turn my head, examining the glamour. My pointed Fey ears protrude a little from my dark hair, just the way they should. I curl my lips to see sharpened canines. Perfect.

If anyone sees me here, I'll pretend to be a guest at the fortress. From what I learned at Avalon Tower, dozens of noble families are invited to Auberon's castle every week.

Already, I'm growing impatient for the moth's return.

I only have Mordred's word that it will guide me, but of course, he could be lying. What if the moth serves some other purpose? For a moment, I wonder if I should make my own way in the fortress to look for Raphael myself before I lose my chance .

But just as that thought enters my head, the moth zooms back. It circles around my head three times, and I hurry after it.

Its pace is erratic, moving twenty feet in a flash, then slowing to a crawl. It never moves too far from me, giving me time to catch up. Occasionally, it hovers in midair for a long while, seemingly waiting for something. Every time it pauses, I slip into the shadows to wait. Whenever the silver moth moves again, I do, too. I pass windows overlooking courtyards and push through doors into the biting air, taking vine-covered bridges between towers under the starlit sky. From one of them, I look out over the kingdom of Brocéliande to see the vast expanse of distant, flickering lights beyond the castle walls.

As I move through the castle halls, up and down stairs, beneath flickering candles in chandeliers, I never meet any living soul. I suspect Mordred must be orchestrating my journey through the emptiest parts of the castle, making sure that no one sees me. Maybe he never actually found Raphael, and he's still searching for him.

The castle is byzantine, with stairwells that zig and zag between buildings, and it feels like I've been walking for hours in a labyrinthine path. If I didn't have the moth with me, I'd be utterly fucked when it comes time to get back.

The moth leads me outside to a narrow set of stairs between buildings. The icy wind whips over me, and I hug myself, teeth chattering in the cold. As I walk down the stairs, the shadows seem to grow thicker, the stone rougher. At last, the moth flutters up to a heavy oak door.

I pull the door open into a dark corridor, but this one looks different than the rest. Gone are the portraits, the banners and sigils, the coats of arms, the chandeliers. Instead, my way is lit by flickering torches fixed to the walls, and the ceiling is lower, only a few feet above my head. Cobwebs and moss cling to it, and it smells musty and dank.

I cough, my asthma irritated by the damp moldiness, but I follow the moth down a flight of twisting, turning stairs. Excitement ripples through my chest. Clearly, I'm going to the dungeons.

Near the bottom of the stairs, something shifts in the shadows, and I freeze at the unmistakable sound of a throat clearing just ahead of me.

The moth dances to and fro around me in frantic warning, but I can't make out who's standing there. My hand moves to the hilt of the dagger at my hip. The moth flutters back into the shadows of the stairwell, disappearing from sight. Quietly, I sneak farther down the stairs, peering out from behind the doorframe at a long corridor of cells. In the distance, chains rattle. Roughly thirty feet ahead, I see a guard with a spear in front of a metal-studded door.

His armor looks rusted in places, his helmet askew. I wonder what he did to get stationed down here in the worst part of the castle, where the air smells like the bottom of a rock.

He doesn't see me yet, hiding in the darkness of the stairwell. Even from here, I can tell he won't be easy to take down with my little knife. He's large, armored, and has the strength of a full Fey. A sword hangs at his waist, and his weapons have a much longer reach than my blade.

I'll have to use another approach. I shift the belt with my sheathed knife, hiding the weapon behind me, then stumble into the corridor, one hand leaning against a stone wall as if for support.

"Who goes there?" he barks, gripping his spear.

"It's me. I'm here," I say in Fey, slurring my words like a drunk. "I was looking for my room but…this isn't it."

He eyes me suspiciously. He's not a fool. To get lost *and* get all the way down here would take a ridiculous lapse of judgment. "Who are you?"

"I'm me!" I laugh stupidly, then let my smile fall. "I'm a musician, obviously. Did you not hear the concert? It was amashing…" Slurring my words, I take another step toward him, pointing my finger at him. "You should have come to hear it. Next time, you *must* come. I insist."

I'm desperate to get a look inside the cells, to search for Raphael, but I have to take care of this soldier first.

His tense posture relaxes. As alert as he is, the sight of a small woman in an evening gown is a welcome distraction. Still, he shifts his spear. "That's far enough. This isn't your room. Go back up the stairs."

I notice the silver moth fluttering behind him now and keep my eyes on it. "They really loved the music we played. There's this one song that they asked for again and again. 'Fly into His Face.' You know it?"

He frowns. "That's a weird name for a—"

The moth zips down, straight into his face, and he swats at it, stumbling back. I leap forward, dodging the tip of his spear, and touch his bare cheek. My powers unfurl, and I slide into his mind.

Cadoc, that's his name, and he can't wait for his shift to end. They've been sticking him here ever since the morning he was late to His Majesty's procession. But he won't complain. He needs this job desperately. He'll be here, watching this one special prisoner, until he's done his penance. His life is miserable, anyway, so he might as well be down here.

His lover, Odelia, left him last month for a lord. He's spent every night writing her poetry about his heartbreak, emptying bottles of mead down his throat, but he can't let himself fall apart. His father has lost his job, and Cadoc needs to keep the money coming in for his family. Just this morning, he called the chatelaine a cunt under his breath, and he still doesn't know if his superior heard him. The chatelain said, "I'll speak to you later." What does that mean?

I flip through his thoughts, searching deeper. *The*

prisoner. Does he know anything about a beautiful, silver-eyed demi-Fey?

The prisoner has been here for some time. Captured in the war with the humans, but they didn't put him with the rest of the rabble. He's too valuable, for some reason. Doesn't seem particularly valuable to Cadoc. Just another half-breed mongrel…

My heart skips a beat. Raphael.

I invade Cadoc's every thought, sifting through ideas, memories, everything he knows. I'm ravaging the inside of his skull, grasping the threads, then pulling the strings to bend him to my will.

Now, Cadoc wonders if the prisoner is *literally* valuable.

Maybe he's rich. In fact, he's probably rich, or they'd leave him with the rest, right? If Cadoc will just do this tiny thing, just unlock the door, the prisoner might reward him handsomely. Yes. That's what he should do. Odelia will fall back in love with him, and his father will get his job back in the stables. Cadoc absolutely shouldn't question this drunk lady more because she's a distraction from what's really important. She's just a tiny woman, a drunken musician, not worthy of his notice.

When I withdraw from his mind, he stares at me, dazed. Then, without a word, he pulls a skeleton key from his belt and opens a door into yet another torchlit stairwell.

I follow him down a flight of stairs, the air growing staler, like wet earth and mushrooms.

My heart is pounding as he leads me to another wooden door. He slides a second key into a rusty lock, turns it twice, and pushes the door open.

I can hardly breathe.

"You," he says into the darkness. "Get up."

I step inside, trying to see in the dark.

In the corner of a grimy stone cell sits a shirtless man. For a second, I almost don't recognize him. Dirt smears his body, and his hair has been shorn. But when he raises his head, his silver eyes gleam in the dark cell, and my breath leaves my lungs.

Raphael.

CHAPTER 8

Raphael's eyes widen as he sees me. I'm starting to adjust to the dark, and I can get a better look at him.

His jaw drops, but he stays silent. He has just enough of his wits about him not to call out my real name.

Scars mark his skin, barely healed over—and it looks as if his collarbone was broken and not healed properly. Under his skin, a bone juts out about half an inch.

I grit my teeth, and the magic within me roars.

My hand shoots out, and I grab Cadoc by the face. I push my powers into him, whispering that all his dreams are just within his grasp. Money, fame, a promotion, his old love back in his arms. No subtlety anymore, I simply burn through his mind with fantasies and desires, scorching his true self until his mind turns to ash. He becomes a puppet fully under my control.

Leave us, I order. *Wait for us above.*

He swivels like a doll on a string and stumbles up the stairs.

"Raphael." I crouch down, clasping his face between my hands.

"Nia," he rasps. "You came for me."

"Of course I did. I'm getting you out of this godforsaken place now."

He pulls back a little, and his pale eyes flick to the stairwell. "The guard. He'll call for backup."

"No. He'll stay where he is. Trust me on that."

He leans forward and rests his forehead against mine, closing his eyes, and I know he's weak as hell. Otherwise, he'd be springing out of here.

"How did you find me?" he asks, his voice hoarse. "How did you get here?"

An answer he *really* doesn't want to know. "I'm here alone. I met a source who helped me. We'll talk about all of that later. Right now, we have to get moving. Can you stand?"

I sit next to him and slide my arm around his waist, helping him up. He slumps against me.

"You're here alone? I don't understand why Avalon Tower would send you alone. It's incredibly risky. The King's Watch lurks unseen all over the kingdom. What if you were captured?"

I swallow hard. "They didn't exactly send me."

He pulls away and leans against the wall. "So, you came into the enemy's kingdom against orders, recklessly and on your own, because you wanted to get me out?"

"Did you expect me to leave you here forever? They were moving far too slowly, and I had to figure it out myself."

"Why couldn't you work with Avalon Tower on this plan?"

"Do we really need to talk about this now?" I hiss.

"You recklessly came to break me out, just like I couldn't let you get captured. Because the only thing on my mind was you. And now the only thing on your mind is me." His haunted voice echoes off the stones.

"Of course I've been thinking about you. What did you expect?"

There's something unnervingly despondent about the way he's speaking, but I can't expect anything different after what he's been through.

I touch him, urging him toward the stairs, and he drags himself up the steps. I follow close behind in case he stumbles, staring in fury at what they've done to him. His back is a network of scars, and my heart clenches at the sight of it. Right now, I want to hunt down Auberon and his fucked-up son and cut them into ribbons.

I look for the moth, but I don't see it. It doesn't matter, anyway. Cadoc can be our new guide.

Near the top of the stairs, Raphael glances at me, his cheeks gaunt. But I wonder if he's finding a bit of his old strength. Something shines in his eyes, perhaps the realization that freedom is just around the corner.

We reach Cadoc, and Raphael tenses, but I raise my

hand to assure him it's fine. Cadoc is staring vacantly at the wall, his mind consumed with the fantasies in which I drowned him.

Give the prisoner your coat. Lead us out. We need a way out of the Castle Perillos.

I slam him with my powers.

No one may see us.

His jaw sags, and his eyes are dazed. He drops the spear, and it clatters to the floor. He pulls off his blue soldier's coat and hands it to Raphael, who pulls it on. Bending over, he sucks in a breath before picking up his spear again and shambles up the stairs. We follow Cadoc up the outdoor stairwell and through the hallways of the castle, taking care to avoid any area that might be occupied.

Unlike Mordred's little moth, Cadoc can't magically see and avoid other people walking around. But he knows which ways are less used, which corridors are mostly forgotten, and where the guard patrols are.

Twice, he tells us to hide in empty rooms behind closed doors while he scouts forward, checking for anyone who might see us. He does it all as if he's half awake, his consciousness rambling over the scorched earth I left behind. I've never unleashed my mind control like that, and I wonder if he'll *ever* snap out of it, or just stumble through the rest of his life.

He leads us up one stairwell after another, then down a narrow corridor. He opens a door.

"You'll have to wait here…leading you out through

the kitchen, but part of the staff is still there. Cleaning up. Should be fine soon. In here…yes. Good? No one will look."

"Fine." I glance inside the small room, a library where a fire is burning. At least it'll give Raphael and me time to talk a bit, figure out our next move. I give a whisper of a command to Cadoc.

"I'll wait outside," he stutters, prompted by my order. "Keep a lookout."

"That's a good idea." I take Raphael by the hand and lead him into the room.

Raphael follows me and closes the door behind us, then drops down onto a red velvet sofa. He runs his hand over his shorn hair. The cut is uneven, his features gaunt—but he somehow looks gorgeous as ever. "Tell me how you got here, Nia."

I sit next to him and brush a smudge of dirt off one of his high cheekbones. "I got here through a ley portal. But I won't be able to get you back that way. It's only for Sentinels. So, I need to hide you until I can find a portal key here in the kingdom. Then we can both get out."

He covers my hand with his, but then he pulls it away again and stares into my eyes. "That's the problem, love."

I have a sinking feeling in the pit of my stomach. "What problem?"

"Avalon Tower doesn't know you're here. And now you want to stay and search for a portal key, putting your life at risk? One of Avalon Tower's only Sentinels?"

Frustration simmers. "Well, I don't have to do it now, but you need to hide until I can get it. I can work it out with Vivianne, if that makes you feel better, but I can't exactly go to Wrythe or any of the other Pendragons. They don't trust any of us demi-Fey right now. Do you have any idea where you can hide in the kingdom until I can return?"

I touch his back over the soldier's coat.

His silver eyes gleam. "There are a few old assets here that I think I can connect with. As long as I'm out of the dungeon, I'll be fine on my own." He takes a deep breath. "But I'm not going back with you. I'm going to find Ysolde first, and it might take a while."

My breath catches. "Did you hear something about your sister?"

"I was in a cell with a few criminals before they separated me. They said they believe there's a dungeon here just for demi-Fey. A fortress of some kind. Not for spies like me, but the civilian demi-Fey they captured long ago. The guy just didn't have any idea where it is. But if she's alive here, that's where she'd be."

There are dark circles beneath his eyes. I so badly want to bring him home with me and give him a warm bath and feed him.

"Okay. Maybe we can bring her back with us," I say. "I'll work with Nivene and Viviane on that, too. We'll figure something out. The assets you mentioned, maybe. Just stay safe for now, and I'll get you out later." I stare into his beautiful silver eyes. "I can't stomach what they did to you in the dungeons. I want to find the royal family and batter their faces in right now."

"Nia, when you go back to Avalon Tower, I need you to work *with* them," he says. "You can't go rogue. This is the whole problem."

"You keep talking about a problem..." The feeling in the pit of my stomach is like watching a storm roll in on the horizon, the sky darkening, clouds roiling—a tempest that's going to drown me. "What *is* the problem?"

"You shouldn't have come here alone for me. You shouldn't be letting emotions drive your decisions," he says quietly, a sigh in his voice. He rests his forehead against mine again.

"It worked, though, didn't it? I got you out." With a feather-light touch, I brush my fingertips over his jaw, where a bruise darkens his skin. I wish I had his healing powers.

He closes his eyes. "Yes. And I would have done the same for you. And then I'd probably hunt down Auberon for revenge. I'd make the worst, rashest decisions that could get a lot of people killed. I would do that for you, and my emotions would get the better of me."

I feel the world going cold. "What are you saying?"

He pulls away from me again. With a wistful look, he brushes the back of his knuckles over my cheekbones. "This isn't easy for me, Nia. You were all I thought about in there. You, and the last moments before I was captured."

My stomach drops as I feel the storm approaching. "Why don't you just say what you need to say?"

His expression is agonized, and he tears his gaze away from mine. "I can see another world where we're together, and there's no war and no Auberon. Where our lives spread out before us like sunlight over a vineyard, where we don't have to risk our lives and look over our shoulders. Where no one will break our bones to wrench every last secret from us. But that's another world, Nia. Not this one."

My chest splinters open. "Just say it."

His eyes shine with sorrow, his brow furrowed. "We can't be together. We never should have been. Back in Dover, when I thought you might be captured, I would have sacrificed all of Avalon Tower for you. And here you are, on a mission by yourself, talking about hunting down the king or searching for portal keys. You could have been captured. And then what? One of our only two Sentinels, an Avalon Steel agent, would be in their dungeons. And Nia, you don't know what it's like...I'm lucky I didn't break. We have to be thinking as clearly as possible in this war. We can't have our decisions clouded by love. I don't want you risking your life for me, Sentinel or not."

"But I made the *right* decision to get you out of there."

A line etches between his eyebrows. "You came here

alone." A ragged edge tinges his voice. "And believe me, I would have done the same if I thought it was the best way to get you out. Love drives us to make the most reckless decisions, but that's not what the world needs from us. The world needs us to be thinking clearly, rationally. I appreciate that you came here for me, but I hate it, too, because you never should have risked your life. I need you to go back now, and I need us to think like trained spies again, not like lovers. We never should have broken the rules in the first place. Because…I kept replaying that day in my mind over and over, the day I was captured. Every time they were beating me or torturing me, it looped in my mind. Every stupid misstep I made. The ways I could have made a better decision. I don't for a second regret giving myself up to save you. I regret that I wasn't thinking rationally and clearly that day, because half my mind was on you the entire time, and the fear of losing you was like nothing I'd known before. I kept making bad decisions. And that's what will happen to you if we let this go on. This ends with you dead, and it will be my fault. I can't do this. I can't…"

He stares into my eyes like he's searching for absolution.

I swallow hard. "You don't know that it ends with one of us dead."

His eyes mist, and he looks lost for words for a few moments.

My heart breaks for him, for me.

"Nia..." He struggles to compose his thoughts, and right now, I have few coherent thoughts of my own.

"I get it."

"I think Alix died because she was in love, because her mind was off the mission, because all she could think about was Rein. It ended with them both dead. Everyone knew how she felt about him. I'm not letting that happen to us. I'm not letting that happen to *you*."

Pain twists in my chest. My eyes sting, and I shake my head. "I still need to get you out of here, Raphael. One way or another."

"With Avalon Tower. I'll find the assets, look for my sister. I'll get myself out of here with *their* help. If you come back here, it should only be because Avalon Tower sent you. Don't come on your own, and don't come without them knowing you're here. Promise?"

I nod. "They'll know who the assets are, so I can find you?"

"Yes. And once I get back, I'll only do what *Avalon Tower* needs. Not what I decide on my own, because..." His voice breaks. "It's not how it's supposed to work. *You* are the Lady of the Lake. You have to be focused. The world needs you. We need you. But we need you focused on Avalon Tower, not on me."

I blink the tears from my eyes. "You really think you know what's best for me?"

Raphael brushes a tear from my cheek. "I think your mission here was nearly suicidal, and it's my fault."

"Well, Raphael, I always knew you would break my heart. It's not the first time."

He touches my arm, his eyes burning brighter. "Nia, I just want you to be safe. Because if you end up in that dungeon, I will lose my fucking mind." An agonized edge laces his voice. "I want you to get out of here as quickly as possible. Right now. Where's the portal you came through?"

"It's in the fortress courtyard, near the weeping willow."

"Then go back through the portal. Don't return unless Viviane orders you. I'll be here."

My chest aches. "Fine."

He grabs both my hands in his. "I think I will always love you. But this is the way it has to be."

Another tear runs down my face, and I can hardly speak. "Please look out for the King's Watch," I manage, my throat tight. "I don't want to have to rescue you again."

He turns from me, a pained expression in his eyes as he stares at the fire. "As long as I'm not dragged here in chains, I can look after myself. I can manage. I promise. I'll find a way to make contact if I can."

I feel my chest hollowing out. "That's it, then?"

Cadoc opens the door. "It's safe. Come on out."

Raphael stands and walks from the room without another glance. I let out a shuddering breath, feeling as if my heart has been shredded.

We cross into a kitchen. It's dark and empty, just like I feel. Cadoc unlatches a door at the back.

"This stairwell goes all the way down," he says. "The kitchen staff use it. If there are guards at the bottom of the stairs, they won't be paying attention to anyone leaving. As long as you move quickly, you should be fine. But you should go separately. Yes?"

Raphael nods and looks at me. He reaches for me, then lets his hand drop, giving me a cursory nod instead. "Thank you, Nia. This is goodbye for now."

The finality of those words is a door slamming in my face.

I can't say anything. I feel as if my voice has been robbed from me.

He turns away and steps out of the door.

This was always how it was going to end with Raphael, wasn't it? With heartbreak. I knew that from the start.

CHAPTER 9

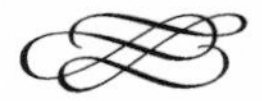

Right now, my magic is erratic, and Raphael would tell me not to use it. But if he can take care of himself, then I can make my own decisions.

I need to make sure he reports *none* of this.

I turn to Cadoc and pour myself into his mind. I find his recent memories from the moment I showed up. I picture a white snowstorm, and I unleash it on these memories, burying them, making them disappear. Cadoc's legs buckle under the onslaught, but I keep going until nothing of the past hour remains in his mind. Even if questioned by the King's Watch, he won't be able to explain how the prisoner escaped. I doubt he'll be able to recall the prisoner at all.

Follow me, I command.

I lead him back the way we came, through the corridors and back to a wider hall. I plan to send him to the guards' quarters, then leave through the kitchen and make my way to the portal, but I don't want to risk letting Cadoc out of my sight too close to the kitchen. I'm about to erase his most recent memories when the sound of footsteps interrupts my thoughts.

I turn, and my heart skips a beat.

From one of the arches, the silhouette of a tall, broad man crosses into the shadowy hallway, towering over us. When he takes a step forward, a shaft of moonlight illuminates his face.

Ice crystallizes around my heart as I stare at his coldly beautiful features.

The Dream Stalker stands before me, and the world tilts beneath my feet. Time seems to slow.

Here is one of the most powerful Fey in existence, and right now, his attention is locked on me. His broad shoulders block my way, and his dark eyes pierce me, the pupils nearly black, framed by thick eyelashes and straight eyebrows. The moonlight sculpts his high, sharp cheekbones and casts a silver sheen over his tan skin. Thorny tattoos climb his neck. Maybe it's because I've heard his thoughts for so long, or maybe it's his other-worldly beauty, but the man is hard to look away from.

He's a million times more dangerous than the King's Watch. If he figures out who I am and what I'm doing here, I'll live out the rest of my days being tortured to death. And if the stories about him are true, the prince will be drinking champagne while it happens.

His expression is unreadable, but his dark eyes slide from me to Cadoc.

Fuck. Have I lost control of the veil protecting my mind? Has that spiderweb of connection drawn Prince Talan to me like a moth to flame? Or in this case, perhaps it's the deadly flame that's been drawn to the helpless moth.

Quickly, I summon the veil in my mind again, shielding my thoughts. I can't let him recognize me.

Cadoc seems to awaken at the sight of the prince. "Your Majesty." He bows deeply.

But Talan's eyes are back on me, staring down from his considerable height. A strand of his dark hair falls, sweeping over his cheekbone. "Who are you?" he asks quietly. "And what's going on here?"

"Your Majesty." Cadoc bows again, his movement erratic, stunted. He's still in the throes of my mind control, struggling to make his own decisions.

I follow with my own deep curtsy, eyes fixed on the floor. *I'm nobody, I'm nobody, I'm nobody.*

"Tell me your name," the prince says, "and what, exactly, you are doing in the countess's hall. Only she and her people are staying here, and I do not recognize you two."

"Your Majesty, I was merely showing this guest the way to, uh…" Cadoc frowns in confusion. He has no idea what he was doing or why.

"There's a cloud over your head." A bored smirk tugs at his lips as he idly flicks his fingers toward Cadoc.

A surge of magic hits the delicate tendrils I'd woven around Cadoc's mind, severing them instantly. Blinding agony shoots through my skull. It feels like I've been stabbed in the brain, and I clench my teeth against the pain and try not to scream.

For a moment, I think, *Raphael was right.*

The pain fades a little, and Cadoc stumbles back. His mouth opens and closes, but no sound comes out. He stares at the prince, then at me, his eyes widening. "What happened to me?"

But Talan isn't paying him any attention. His gaze is fixed on me, and I feel the full force of his dark magic thrumming over my skin. Goosebumps prickle my flesh, and a shiver dances along my spine.

"Well. That's interesting," he murmurs.

"Your Majesty," Cadoc shouts. "This woman...I don't know who she is. She did something to me. She's an intruder. She got into my mind."

My head still throbs, and I can hardly think straight. I tense, glancing at the open archway to the stairwell on the other side of Talan. It's twenty feet away, but even if I ran, Talan would be right behind me.

My heart is a tempest. Maybe I should throw myself down the stairwell to my death while I still can. I don't think I'd withstand torture as well as Raphael did, and I really don't want to find out.

"We must report this!" Cadoc says. "The chatelaine must know. The king must know!"

"There's nothing to report." Talan's voice is glacial, disinterested. "This is none of your concern. Leave now."

"Your...Your Majesty?" Cadoc is struggling. Talan severed my control over him too sharply, and he can't string a coherent thought together. "She...she did something. I...there's something wrong with me. She's dangerous...dangerous...she is..."

Talan arches a black eyebrow at me. "Well, maybe I like dangerous women."

"You're insane, just like everyone says," Cadoc blurts. Then, realizing what he said, he shakes his head. "No, I didn't mean that. I don't think that."

"What did you say?" Talan asks, and a quiet, controlled rage laces each word. "Please repeat that."

Outside, the wind rises, rattling the windowpanes, shrieking through cracks, as if the world outside mirrors his anger.

Cadoc goes pale as the snow, and he points at me. "I didn't say it. I didn't...the intruder...she should be interrogated. Executed. Treated no better than a demi-Fey."

The air goes cold around me, the torchlight flickering, nearly snuffing out.

Talan gestures to Cadoc, and the white-haired guard falls to his knees, his eyes open wide. He trembles, screaming. Outside, lightning flashes, and thunder rumbles soon after. Snow whips at the windows.

My thoughts are spinning out of control, frantic as the frozen storm outside. I am going to die here in Brocéliande.

Talan lifts his dark eyes to me, and the expression I

see there is positively lethal. "That is what will happen to you if you try to escape, intruder. Understood?"

I swallow, glancing at Cadoc as he twists in pain. "What are you doing to him?" I ask.

"Oh, nothing. He's merely dreaming. He's dreaming of pain." Talan lazily twists his fingers in the air, and Cadoc lets out a shriek.

"Stop it!" I hiss.

"You're worried about the fate of the man who wanted you executed?" Talan cocks his head at me, then makes a twisting motion with his wrist. Cadoc slumps forward on his hands and knees, moaning quietly.

"Leave now," Talan says to Cadoc, his voice as smooth as silk. "Tell no one of this, or I'll pay you another visit while you sleep."

Shaking, Cadoc rises to his feet and skulks out of the hallway, into a stairwell.

Talan prowls closer, a hunter stalking its prey.

My blood roars.

I'm alone with the Dream Stalker, a fate worse than death.

CHAPTER 10

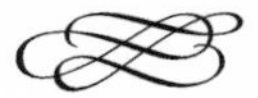

The wind shrieks like a banshee, snow whipping against the towering windows. If I were worthy of my Avalon Steel torc, I'd jump through that window, shattering the glass and plummeting to my death. Better for a spy to die than be captured.

And yet, what is his plan?

If he wanted me arrested, he would have let the guard stay. He wouldn't tell him to leave and not say a word to anyone. The prince has something else up his sleeve.

He's looking at me like a cat watching a glass at the edge of a table. Maybe he'll smash me, maybe not. But either way, I have his interest. Beyond that, I can't read his expression, but this arrogant prince on a power trip ignites a molten rage inside my veins. I loathe this man like I've never hated anyone before.

The torchlight dances in his dark eyes as he stares down at me. "Let's start with your name."

"I'm Severine."

"No. Your *real* name."

"That *is* my real name."

He cocks his head, and a lock of ebony hair falls before one of his eyes. "If I desire, I can wrap you in a dream, girl. And in that dream, you will feel compelled to say your real name a thousand times. You will say it for days, for weeks, until you starve half to death, until the word no longer has meaning. So, let's try this again. What's your name?"

Thunder rumbles outside, rattling the diamond-shaped glass panes.

I feel it then, a touch of his velvety power, brushing at the edges of my mind. Threatening to wrap around me, to envelop my reality. He really will do it unless I act fast. The shield in my mind isn't strong enough. There wasn't enough time to practice.

Lying works best when it is laced with truth. I can give this evil fucker a crumb.

I narrow my eyes at him, jaw tightening.

I should be acting like a meek girl, intimidated by the crown prince. But Raphael's words still echo in my mind, and the state of his ravaged, tortured body burns my thoughts like a brand.

"Fine, it's Nia." I spit out the words. "Vaillancourt." My words come out sharper than they should, while my mind is whirring, making up a story that would work, that would convince him I'm not worth his time.

"So, *Nia*. What are you doing here?" His voice is so uncannily familiar, and the sound of his deep, velvety voice as he speaks my name sends a strange rush of heat through my blood.

My pulse is racing out of control. Some Fey can hear a heartbeat while standing nearby. I wonder if he's one of them.

I lift my chin. "My family and I are tenants on farmland we don't own. And we're short on money. I met a lord one day who was slumming it in one of the country taverns, and he promised to lend us money, but he wanted me to get it from him in person. He told me to sneak in here at night when it was less guarded."

A look of irritation crosses Talan's handsome features. "Ah. And this so-called lord? Who is he?"

When I last saw Talan, he was with a retinue of followers, and I'd invaded their minds—nearly losing my own identity in their thoughts. For weeks, I'd occasionally get confused, thinking that I was actually one of them, and I still remembered each of their interior worlds. One of them is his cousin Lumos, a womanizer, desperate to be like Talan, though he's also driven by relentless jealousy of his cousin. And since Lumos has little charm of his own, he often tries to lure women with promises of money. But he hardly keeps track of their names.

"Lord Lumos, he's called. He was so generous with

his offer. He told me he would cover our debt and give me a little extra to carry us through the winter."

The Dream Stalker's eyes dance with dark amusement. "Is that what he said? And what did he want in return for this surprisingly generous loan?"

My fingers tighten into fists. "I think he was just being nice. He told me he can afford to be nice because he's very important, that he's close to the royal family. He said that he once saved you from a wild wolf."

I remember Lumos's thoughts about the wolf incident. Talan always downplayed it, said that it was more a badger than a wolf, and that he'd never been in danger in the first place. Lumos told the story about the wolf whenever Talan wasn't around.

"It was a badger," Talan says with a sigh. "So, you're here for money."

"Without the loan, we'll be destitute. You can ask him about our conversation a few weeks ago."

Even if my story were true, he'd never remember a common woman he met in a tavern. He spends half his life drunk.

Talan's dark eyebrows draw together. "And how did you enter the fortress, Nia?"

"I bribed a guard with the last of our money."

Talan's body goes still. Behind him, the torches flicker. "You're lying again."

My heart skips a beat. "I bribed him. I don't want to get anyone in trouble, but I can tell you what he looks like."

"You bribed no one. You used your powers."

"My powers?" I frown at him and concentrate on my telepathy magic. I might need those tendrils of red really soon. Already, I can glimpse Talan's own magic, brushes of energy that threaten to tighten around my skull, to send me into a waking nightmare. His magic is like a silken caress that turns sharp as a serpent's tooth, prodding at my mind. I try to block him out with my mental veil, but I feel like it's about to shatter.

He closes the distance between us, staring down at me from beneath his long eyelashes. "I'm getting impatient, Nia. I saw the threads of your powers in that guard's mind. You were controlling him."

"Mind control? Impossible. Primal powers are long gone from this world, and even if they existed, they would belong to someone powerful. Important. Not to someone like me."

Lightning flashes outside, and it glints off his dark eyes. "Except I can see that you are more than you pretend to be."

Fuck.

"I tire of this game," he says with an indifferent sigh. "Fortunately, no one lies to me in the dream realm."

Talan's silky powers tighten around me, enveloping me in a shroud. I have a sliver of a second to react before he enters my mind. I lash at the tendrils of his power with my Sentinel energy, and his eyes widen with surprise, a line forming between his brows. Gritting my teeth, I dive in with both my powers, intent on breaking his mind, but searing pain rips through my skull.

His magic wraps around him, a protective barrier. Then it slides around me again, and it starts to probe. I stumble back, breathing hard, heart hammering. Panic drags its claws through my chest. Out of ideas, I turn and run for the stairwell. One step, two steps—

But Talan moves in a blur, fast as lightning, and is already between me and the stairs. He grabs me by the throat and the waist, whirls me around, and flattens me against the wall. He has me pinned now, helpless, and my pulse races.

His thumb gently brushes over my throat, and his magic slips around my body, snaking up toward my mind. His dark eyes gleam. He's intent on wrapping me in a waking nightmare, but my own power cracks and lashes like a whip, refusing to let him get a grip on my mind.

Then, all of a sudden, he lets his magic fall away, though he doesn't release his grip on my waist and throat.

"There it is." A deep whisper that reverberates over me. "That's the power I was talking about."

My fingers tighten into fists. I've managed to hold him off from entering my mind, and he's not putting any pressure on my throat. In fact, though he swiftly pressed me against the wall, he did it without hurting me. Still, I have no doubt he can snap my neck like a twig. I'm completely in his control right now.

"Let's try this again," Talan says. "How did you enter the fortress?"

"I..." My throat is dry. "I used my powers on the guards at the front gate. I made them think I had an invitation."

He leans closer, and my gaze dips down to his full, sensual lips for just a moment.

"Good," he whispers. "Let the real Nia out. You are more powerful than a typical telepath. You have mind control powers. A primal power. You don't look like a threat, but someone would be stupid to underestimate you. Tell me, am I right about that?"

There's a haunting quality to his voice that shivers over my skin.

"My magic is weak. I can hardly make anyone do anything. I have to touch people to use it. And it fades quickly—otherwise, I would've used mind control to make Lumos bring me a bag of gold."

"Where are you from, Nia?"

"From a farm on Lauron."

Lauron is a small Brocéliande village, about forty miles from Auberon's fortress. It's tiny enough that I feel confident that Talan doesn't know the people there. More importantly, Cadoc's brother lives there, and Cadoc's memories of his recent visit are still fresh in my mind.

Talan still has me pinned against the wall. "Really?" he says. "I hunted in the area once. There was a feast in the evening in the town square. I remember they served a roasted wild boar. But I don't recall seeing you. I daresay I would have remembered your face."

During Cadoc's visit, his brother recounted the dinner with the prince endlessly. "I was there, of course. But you might be misremembering that day. The feast was in the afternoon. And we didn't serve boar—we cooked the stag that you hunted down. I picked the herbs to season it from my family's garden. I just don't like being the center of attention, that's all. Are you happy now? Can I go?"

He stares at me for a long while. I'm acutely aware of his touch, the heat from his hands radiating through the fabric of my dress and warming my throat. Then he nods and releases his grip on me.

That was a test, and I passed. He believes me.

"How come no one has heard about this until now?" he says. "A Fey with a primal power? Surely the king would have taken interest."

"Attention from powerful people isn't necessarily a good thing for a commoner like me."

"Interesting. And you think the king might do something to you if he found out about your powers?" His deep, rich voice vibrates through my ribs.

"Perhaps. And who knows about his advisors?"

"Quite true. Or his bloodthirsty son." He steps back. "Well, Nia, I have good news and bad news."

I exhale slowly. "Yes?"

"The bad news? I'm afraid you won't see Lumos tonight. He has another woman over that he promised money to. Or rather, he's bent over another woman that he promised money to."

My jaw drops in feigned horror. "Is that what he wanted from me?"

"But the good news is, I can pay your rent." He flashes me a smile, and his face transforms in a way I hadn't quite anticipated—so shockingly beautiful and disarming, I nearly forget what a monster he is. "As a prince, I would be more than happy to pay the rent of my chief mistress. My maîtresse-en-titre, my official courtesan. You."

I stare at him. "What are you talking about?"

His eyes flash. "It's quite simple. I'm in need of a mistress. And here you are."

As I stare up at his looming form, the realization sinks in. Cadoc was right. Talan is completely unhinged.

"I'm not going to be your mistress. You've got to be joking."

"It seems like fate, Nia. You've broken into our castle at a perfect time because I was really enjoying myself in the human realm, in my Château des Rêves, and then I was ordered back here. My father demands that I marry Countess Arwenna de Bosclair of Val Sans Retour. Her family is rich, and the coffers in our treasury are empty since he invaded France. We are flat broke. Apparently, the countess is the answer to all his problems, but I don't want to marry her."

"Why not?"

He narrows his eyes. "Tell me, do I seem like the

marrying type to you? I don't want to live in this bleak castle. I belong in the Château des Rêves, enjoying myself with whomever I want. But if I publicly introduce a new mistress, it will humiliate the countess enough to delay the wedding plans. Really, it's an old tradition here in Corbinelle, and my father himself has gone through many mâitresses-en-titre. Most of them ended up dead." He shrugs. "A new mistress will be enough scandal to throw the wedding into question. Her family will not want their daughter to marry while I'm so publicly entangled with a glorified whore, especially one from such meager provenance. And here you show up, the answer to all my problems."

I stare at him, breathing hard. Gods, he's truly an asshole. But this isn't the whole story. "You're leaving something out. There are any number of people who could be your glorified whore. Why me?"

His dark eyes grow half-lidded, bored. He looks down, toying with one of the rings on his fingers. "What a wonderful gift. A farm girl no one here really knows, possessing a power that no one would suspect. A power that I could very much use to my advantage." He looks up again, and his gaze sharpens on me. "I suspect you know little of court life, but a favored mâitresse-en-titre can wield a considerable amount of influence. Not that you would *actually* wield influence, but you will wield *my* influence over others, and that is very appealing to me, indeed. It's also surely a better life than scrambling for half-rotten potatoes in the dirt, yes?"

Except that I fucking hate him, and I'm not sure I can mask it after seeing Raphael.

Then again, I haven't managed to mask it so far, and my instinct tells me that has him intrigued. He's used to people leaping at his offers, and refusing him might raise me in his estimation.

"I'm not going to be your mistress, and you should find someone else. You have a ruthless reputation, and these few minutes with you have done nothing to dispel it. Frankly, I'd rather light myself on fire in the courtyard than be the whore of a hedonist prince."

A dark smile curls his lips. "What a coincidence. That is actually an option if you defy me. What would you prefer, really, Nia—living as my mistress, or burning to death outside?"

He goes very still, studying me closely, and his attention sharpens on me like a knifepoint. I don't think he expected to be turned down, but my refusal has piqued both his curiosity and his rage.

"Being a mistress would ruin my reputation," I say.

He lets out a sharp breath. "*What* reputation? For someone like you, a little rustic of pitiable peasant stock, getting fucked by the prince is the greatest honor you could hope for. But I'm not even ordering you to be a real mistress. I'm ordering you to fake it. And in return, you are elevated far above the station that the gods chose for you. The mistress of a handsome prince. You'll have proximity to the throne, to real power—and all you have to do is everything I say."

His voice is a low rumble that blends into the sound of thunder.

My breath goes shallow. The shocking arrogance of this guy. "Proximity to power, without actually having any. What a gift."

"No, you won't have power. But you will have the appearance of it, which is more than you have now. And I get what I need—power over my father. Politically speaking, and likely otherwise, you're worthless. *But* you can manipulate minds in a more straightforward manner than my own magic. I can bend people's dreams, but you can bend their will while they are awake. With you under my command, I can force the council of nobles to ally with me against my father."

My blood pounds hard. He wants to rebel against his father? "And would people believe that you'd choose a mistress from pitiable peasant stock, since you are so obviously contemptuous of people like me?"

He shakes his head slowly. "I've been known to shock the court with outrageous decisions."

"Why would you want to rebel against your father?"

"That's not any of your concern. You are my subject and will do what I say. Even if I tell you to light yourself on fire in the courtyard, which is increasingly tempting. But if you must know, my father has small dreams and wastes time. He squabbles in a war with the humans, emptying our treasury." He shrugs slowly. "Why not get rid of the human problem once and for all? Why not take everything they have?"

My blood turns to ice at the thought of his solution for the "human problem." I'd heard about everything he'd done when he invaded Brittany—a massacre. The streets running with blood, cities echoing with screams. The man didn't just manipulate nightmares. The man *was* a nightmare.

"You want to kill all the humans?" I ask.

"Why not?" he says casually. "And the half-breeds, too. Why spend every last piece of gold on the human problem when I could just end it?"

I restrain myself from lunging at him and trying to bash his head against the wall. "Oh. So, you are as bad as they say."

"And what else do they say about me?" he asks, his voice icy.

I hold his gaze. "That you torture people for fun while drinking champagne. That even your father thinks you're too murderous and unhinged to trust with any real power after what you did in Brittany."

His eyebrows rise, and he leans against the wall. "Is that right? Champagne and a torture show. I must say, it sounds like quite an evening."

In his thoughts that I'd overheard, he seemed mostly a pleasure-seeker. But at other times, I'd heard his thoughts as he fought ferociously, carving through the bodies of his enemies.

I narrow my eyes. "You have everything you want. A palace. Servants. Any woman or man you could possibly desire. Why spend your days slaughtering people instead of enjoying life?"

"You're quite imperious for a runt-sized pig farmer, do you know that?"

"I didn't say it was pigs."

"But it is, though, isn't it?"

I swallow. "There are pigs, yes."

"How many did you manage to keep through the famine? Two? Three?"

"A few."

"In any case, you just said it yourself, little intruder. Why spend my days slaughtering people when I could do anything I want? Maybe that *is* what I want."

He lifts a finger to his lips, his face suddenly alert. Now, it's much quieter around us. The storm outside has finally calmed, and the music has gone silent.

"The banquet is over," he says. "I should make an appearance. And you can't be seen here. If any other guards find you in the palace right now, there are bound to be questions. We need to make you look as harmless as possible. Return home. I'll go on another hunting trip to Lauron within a few days. There, we will meet by accident and fall madly in love by your pig farm."

Return home.

I exhale with relief. I can't believe my luck. He's letting me *go*? I nod. "Fine."

He arches a dark eyebrow. "I can see your mind running. Wondering how you should handle this. So, let me clarify. There's only one way. *My* way. If you think you can disappear, I'll remind you who I am. I'm Prince Talan de Morgan, the Dream Stalker, the man who tortures people for fun. I can find any soul in Brocéliande when they close their eyes. And unless you intend to remain eternally awake, I will always find you. Don't make me chase you, Nia. You won't enjoy what I'll do when I find you."

Lucky for me, I don't live in Brocéliande. As soon as I'm out of his sight, I'm leaving through the portal, back to Avalon.

Shadows slide through his eyes. "Remember that I know your secret. You're right about one thing. A villager with mind control powers? King Auberon would view it as a threat. We all would," he says, his voice darkly melodic.

"I understand. I'll be waiting for you in Lauron."

He gestures at the stairwell. "That's where you were going, wasn't it?"

"Yes."

"Good. I assume you won't have any problem leaving the same way. You seem capable enough. I will see you soon."

Like fuck you will. "I'll be waiting."

I step into the cold stairwell, my heart still thrumming in my chest. I cannot believe how perfectly that worked out. I break into a run down the stairs, fleeing toward freedom.

CHAPTER 11

I run across the fortress's courtyard, my feet flying over the snowy grass and my heart in my throat. I can't believe that I'm alive, that I'm out of his sight. I can still see Cadoc's tormented face in my mind as Talan's magic overpowered him and hear Talan's cold, distant voice murmuring, *He's dreaming of pain*.

I don't slow as I near the portal, the misshapen rocks jutting from the earth. As I sprint closer, I summon my magic. Energy crackles down my arms and fingers, and I send tendrils of my Sentinel power ahead of me. Just as I reach the rocks, they shimmer, and a dark portal yawns open between them. I fling myself into it, falling through the air.

Pain jolts through my limbs as I land hard on my hands and knees. I glance up to see Avalon's dolmens all around me. I'm back in Mordred's home again. Here, the air smells rich and musky, like rain-soaked moss. The moon bathes the standing stones in haunting light. *Silver* light. I never thought I'd love simple, pale moonlight so much.

I cough, gasping for breath. I'm wheezing hard, my asthma returning with a vengeance. I pull out my inhaler, puffing twice, drawing the albuterol into my lungs. Coughs rack my body as I breathe out.

"Well," Mordred's low voice says behind me, "that was exciting. Sorry about your sweetling breaking your heart after all you went through to save him."

I'm still coughing. My skull is throbbing, a dizzying headache building.

Mordred circles around me and kneels, staring intently at my face. "I told you to avoid the Dream Stalker, and what do you do? You agree to be his lover instead. Just a few minutes after Raphael ended things, you've already seduced a prince. Impressive, in a way."

"Is that what you think seduction looks like? You really have been alone a long time." Apparently, the silver moth worked. Mordred was able to see and hear everything that happened to me.

"Well, by choice or not, you've fallen into a unique opportunity."

The cold earth nips at my hands, freezing my fingers. Once I've caught my breath, I push myself up. "A unique opportunity to pretend to be a glorified whore of a murderous tyrant? I'll pass."

"No, I don't think you will." He straightens. "What

are you pouting about, wench? I thought you wanted to take down their wretched empire. What better way to do it than getting close to the prince? You share his bed, and you learn every one of their secrets. It's a golden opportunity."

Slowly, I stand. "The man just threatened to torture me, and you think I should run back into his arms? You're failing at parenting so far." Though frankly, he's not necessarily my worst parent.

"You're a spy, aren't you?" he hisses. "I thought spies were good at spotting assets. You're in a position to use Auberon's own *son* against him. And anyway, I didn't see him *actually* hurt you."

Not with his hands, I suppose. "His magic hurt when he severed my control over that guard. Now I can't use my telepathy. It causes too much pain."

He shrugs. "Those who play with fire often get hurt. You might find that extremely painful from now on, but it *will* still work. And anyway, any granddaughter of Queen Morgan doesn't shrink from a little pain."

"Look, Auberon's son wants to destroy humanity. He wants to kill the demi-Fey, too. You know, demi-Fey like me?"

"So, don't go along with his plan. Use him, manipulate him, and when the time comes, kill him. You're in a position to stop him."

Mordred's suggestion is so unnervingly similar to Darius's words from earlier that a shiver runs along my spine. "Use him, manipulate him, and kill him. Are you speaking from experience?"

"As a matter of fact, yes. It's what I did with my first wife, Cwyllog, a human from Camelot."

Terrific. I'm surrounded by psychopaths. I rub my temples. "I barely kept him out of my mind. The first time I fall asleep near him, he'll tromp through my dreams and learn everything about me."

The moonlight illuminates half of Mordred's face, sparking in his eyes. "You can protect yourself from that. Summon a veil in your mind, like I already taught you. Do it before you go to sleep, when you wake, and whenever you feel the Dream Stalker near. In time, you'll gain more control over it. You just need to practice. And of course, your magic will only grow stronger in the Fey realm."

I frown. "What do you mean?"

He looks at me in surprise. "Well, I thought it was obvious. According to the prophecies, you're the Lady of the Lake."

"So?"

"Magic begets magic. If you spend a long time in a magical domain surrounded by Fey, your magic will grow. Your powers as a Sentinel, as a telepath, and as the Lady of the Lake will increase."

I shake my head. "I'm not doing that. We have an agreement: you help me get Raphael out. And I need you to find out where Raphael's sister is, because he's refusing to leave without her. That part of the bargain isn't completed. He needs to get out of Brocéliande. I'm assuming the silver moth works?"

He tilts his head slightly into the shadows, and for a few seconds says nothing. A golden speck flickers in his eye, looking almost like a moth taking flight. "Auberon is in his library, talking to one of his generals about an upcoming assault. In the kitchen, the staff is cleaning up after tonight's banquet, and a maid just hid an unfinished loaf of bread in her bag, probably taking it home. The guards are patrolling the walls of the fortress, though the one in the eastern tower is nodding off. The moth works. I have eyes and ears throughout Auberon's fortress. We will get your sweetling out."

"Can you also find out what Auberon's plans are?"

"Eventually, but it'll take time. It would be much faster if you'd just seduce the prince."

"No."

The branches cast sharp, claw-like shadows that rake a ghostly dance over the planes of his face. "Have it your way."

Exhaustion washes over me. What time is it, anyway? I desperately want to be back in bed. "I have to get back. I need you to remove the glamor before I go."

He shrugs and brushes his fingertip over my ears, and I feel his magic buzz and tingle over my skin, my eyes stinging. "There. Now you look *human* again." There's more than a faint note of disdain in the word.

I nod. "I'll return tomorrow."

He smiles at me. "Will you? How considerate. But haven't you forgotten something?"

I fold my arms. "What?"

"Your part of the deal."

I shake my head. "I'll help you take down Avalon Tower once Raphael's sister is located and we get them both back here."

He narrows his eyes. "I'm aware that humans become frail and stupid as they age. I assure you, it's not the same with Fey. I may be over two thousand years old, but I'm not an idiot, Nia."

"Our deal was—"

"Our deal was that we work together. I get your man out; you help me take down Avalon Tower. And I have your first errand." He retrieves something from his robe. Another silver moth. "You planted one in Auberon's fortress. Now do the same in Avalon Tower. I need eyes and ears there, too."

My stomach clenches. "I'll do that after Raphael is here."

"You'll do it today, or you'll never find your way back to this island. I'll make it disappear. Brocéliande will be out of your grasp, and the man you claim to love will linger there forever. He'll likely be captured again, returned to their dungeons. Executed. I know he just broke your heart, but you're not going to let him *die,* are you?"

My heart slams. I can do it. Plant the moth, then tell Viviane about it so that she can take measures of precaution against it. It's a dangerous game, but the alternative isn't great, either.

This isn't *just* about Raphael. Maybe he can even free his sister and find a way to survive there in hiding. But the prize I can't give up is the portal. I can't relinquish access to Brocéliande.

But there's one little problem—I have only Mordred's word about what the moth does. How do I know it's not a weapon as well as a magical wiretap?

"I don't even really know what this moth is." I narrow my eyes. "It could be a bomb that kills us all."

His smile deepens. "Ah, good. You *are* intelligent. I was beginning to wonder if you were my daughter after all. Of course, you're right. All you know is what I told you, and I could be lying through my teeth. I've been known to lie once or twice."

"So, you understand why I won't do it, then? I mean, you literally just told me you married your first wife to learn her secrets and then murdered her, so I guess I'm not getting a trustworthy vibe."

"It was for the greater good of the Fey. Anyway, you'll do it. You just need some assurances." As he unsheathes a long dagger, the wind whips over us, toying with his black cloak. His blade glints in the moonlight.

My breath stills in my lungs.

"Do you know what a Hemlock Oath is?" he asks.

Vaguely, I remember that term from my studies as a cadet in Avalon Tower. "It's a dark magic ceremony, practiced by Fey. The oath-takers bind their lives to a promise, and if the promise is broken, they die a horrible death, as if poisoned by hemlock."

"You're right, essentially, but I don't know why you call it *dark* magic. I'd call it useful magic. Humans made up something much worse, didn't they?"

"What are you talking about?"

"They have binding covenants written on parchment, the language complex and tedious. An elaborate, arcane process navigated by advocates and proctors in the inns of court."

I stare at him. "Are you talking about lawyers? Contracts?"

"And when the covenant is broken," he goes on, "the proctors battle each other, sometimes for years, while their pockets and purses fill with gold, until finally, the winner is chosen by a be-wigged magistrate in a robe. Now, *that's* a strange and dark practice."

"Point taken."

He rolls up his sleeve. "We Fey are more pragmatic. We make an oath bound by blood. We write nothing down because the terms are simple and incontrovertible. If anyone breaks the oath, he dies. No need for the inns of court. Now, you and I will perform the oath, whereby I swear that the moth only serves as my ears and eyes and cannot kill anyone directly. And then *you* promise to place it in Avalon Tower. If one of us fails, we die, writhing in pain. Simple. Yes?"

I don't truly have many options. I need Mordred's

portal, but I need to make sure we protect ourselves against his spying.

"Fine," I finally say. "How does this work?"

"Usually, there would be a ceremony, sometimes a sacrifice, but it's late, and I can't be bothered. We mix our blood and recite the words of the Hemlock Oath. Then we each make our vows."

He holds out a palm and traces the blade along it. As blood starts to drip from the gash, he hands me the blade, and I place the tip on my palm. Grimacing, I slice quickly, not letting the lacerating pain show on my face. I clench my fist.

Mordred seems satisfied with my stoicism, like this is another test that I just passed. He holds out his bleeding hand, and I grip it with mine. Our blood mingles, dripping on the cold earth.

"Repeat after me," he says. "In hemlock's kiss, our fates entwine. In blood-signed bonds, oaths enshrined. Break the seal, and death is thine."

As the wind howls over us, whipping at my hair, I repeat the words. With the words spoken, heat burns through my palm. I grit my teeth as magical energies buzz through my open wound, crackling along my veins.

"I, Mordred, Scion of Morgan, King of Avalon, swear that the silver moth that I gave you will be used only to listen and watch. It will be my eyes and ears in Avalon Tower and will do nothing else." He raises his eyebrows at me. "Now you."

"I, Nia Melisandre, swear to place the silver moth in Avalon Tower."

He squeezes my hand, his expression darkening. "You will place it there *tonight,* where it can't be found. And you will leave it there for as long as I need."

"Fine," I grit out. "I will place it today where it can't be found and won't remove it for as long as you need."

"And you will remain silent about it, tell no one about the moth or of my existence."

Fuck. My heart thunders. "That's not what I agreed to."

"Of *course* it's part of the agreement."

"And will you also swear as part of your oath not to hurt anyone at Avalon Tower who isn't a Pendragon?" He has me cornered, and he knows it, but I'm going to get as much out of this bargain as I can.

"It's not as though I can *leave* here, Nia. I couldn't kill them even if I wanted to."

"Swear that you don't want to anyway."

"Fine. I can swear an oath that I, Mordred, Scion of Morgan, King of Avalon, have no targets for vengeance other than the Pendragons. Happy?"

I swallow hard. "And I will not tell anyone about you or about the moth's existence."

He releases my hand. Blood drips to the ground, and smoke rises from the spatters. When I look at my palm, the cut has already closed. All that remains is an angry red line across my palm.

"So." He hands me a new silver moth. "Now that we *trust* each other."

I take the moth from him and shove it into my pocket.

I wouldn't *trust* this man to do my laundry, and I suspect the feeling is mutual.

But no matter how we feel, our fates are threaded together.

CHAPTER 12

By the time I finally get back to Avalon Tower, the rising sun is spreading a rosy blush across the Camelot sky. I've been gone for less than eight hours, but it feels like days, maybe weeks. My legs burn with weariness, and it hurts to keep my eyes open.

Somehow, the fatigue dulls the pain of the heartbreak. A breakup doesn't sting quite so badly when you feel as if you're under water.

I stumble into the door of Lothian Tower and push through it into a stairwell, my legs shaking. It smells comforting. Like home.

It almost feels impossible to walk the rest of the way to my room. So. Many. Stairs.

I lean on the stairwell as I climb, trying not to imagine my father rampaging through here with a blood-stained sword in his hand, just like he did centuries ago.

But when I get into my hallway at last, it's hard *not* to think about it. Hanging on a wall is a large painting that I've seen a thousand times and noticed the day I arrived in Camelot. It's a painting of Mordred thrusting his sword through a naked woman, corpses littered the ground around him, and it captures his cold beauty incredibly well, even his smile as he slays the woman—cruel and mocking. It's the same smile I saw on his face just a few hours ago.

This is the Fey to whom I've bound myself in a Hemlock Oath, this heartless creature.

The silver moth is ice-cold and heavy in my pocket, and when I slide my fingers in, the wings feel sharp as blades.

Mordred is trapped for another seventy-four years, at least, but doubt nags at me. Who is using whom? Mordred has millennia of experience over me. What made me think I could outsmart the ancient heir to the Fey throne, who has had centuries to plot his revenge?

I force myself to keep walking until I reach the circular stairwell that leads to my room, then drag myself up. At the top of the stairs, I push open the door, blearily staring at a dark-haired cadet guarding the stairwell. He wears a coat of arms on his blue uniform jacket, one with a stag and an iron helmet and swords. He's one of the brand-new Iron Legion sentries, part of the Pendragon cult, set up to spy on the demi-Fey. He goes pale as he stares at me, his jaw dropping open.

Right now, he's wondering if he fucked up.

"Aren't you..." He sputters. "How did you—"

"Dame Nia of the Avalon Steel? I was in the library all night. Did you not notice me leave? Not a very attentive guard, are you? Close your mouth, darling, you'll catch flies like that." I brush past him and climb the stairs.

Reaching my door at last, I open it softly, my bed calling to me, and creep inside. Serana is gently snoring, and Tana is asleep as well. I stumble across the room to my desk and the wooden case that Amon gave me when I returned from Dover. The case houses my Avalon Steel torc. I unlatch it and pry open the lid, running my finger along the torc lying on the smooth red interior, admiring its rosy sheen. Only King Arthur, Merlin, and a few powerful Fey from Arthur's court wore Avalon Steel torcs. Now, I have one. What does it say about me, that I'm willing to work with the man who murdered Arthur?

I let out a long sigh. Espionage is a delicate act of playing people against each other—a tightrope routine between one total disaster and another. We have to keep secrets, even from our allies.

Gently, I lift the velvet off the bottom of the box, revealing a hollow underneath where I keep a hidden key. It's the key to the French cottage where Raphael and I spent a glorious week together, pretending to be newlyweds. It's the only thing I have to remember Raphael by. Holding it in my palm is helping me steel my resolve for what I'm about to do next. I close the box, and I slip the silver moth from my pocket. With a tightening throat, I drop it just behind the box—a spy device for an enemy of the Tower.

I let out a long, slow breath. There. Mordred's demand is done.

"Nia?" Tana's sleepy voice rises behind me. "You're back!"

I snap the case shut and whirl around, blood rushing to my face. I want to tell her about it, to warn her. *Anything* she says, Mordred will hear. But I can't. Mordred forced me into this impossible position, lying to my closest friends with a fatal oath.

"Morning," I say, trying to act natural. "I have good news."

"What happened?" she asks.

"Why were you gone so long?" Serana asks, now awake, too. She rubs her eyes.

"I found a portal that leads to Auberon's fortress in Brocéliande. And I got Raphael out of his dungeon. Then he broke up with me and is refusing to leave Brocéliande until we can find the dungeon where his sister is held." My heart tightens at the thought of him.

"What?" Serana flicks her red hair out of her eyes. "Wait a minute. I have so many questions. You rescued Raphael, and he dumped you?"

"He suddenly cares a lot about the rules of Avalon Tower."

My eyelids are already drooping, and dizziness clouds my thoughts. All the energy has leached out of my body.

"Nia, are you alright?" Tana asks.

"I need sleep," I mumble.

"Right. You haven't slept for two days," Tana interjects. "Rest for a bit. We'll go get you something to eat. We can talk about everything once you feel a bit better."

"But if there's a portal, we have to tell Viviane," Serana says. "This is a game-changer."

"*We* will talk to her," Tana says. "With Nia once she gets some sleep. She looks like she's going to collapse."

"Thanks." I crumple into my bed and pull the blankets up over myself.

As I start to fall into a deep sleep, I see Talan's hauntingly beautiful dark eyes in my mind.

Soon, the Dream Stalker will be trying to find me, to claim me as his mistress.

* * *

TANA AND SERANA wake me way before I'm ready. I've slept for two hours, but somehow, it seems no more than four minutes. I feel like I've been ripped from the darkest depths of sleep, dredged from the lake of dreams. My thoughts are still sludgy, under water.

Walking between them, I drag myself through the

hallway. They're leading me to a debriefing meeting that can't wait in the Lady of Shallott Tower.

Blinking, I clutch a blue teacup, its porcelain surface covered in stars and moons. I take a sip. Slowly, the two shots of espresso are starting to work their magic in my veins, clearing my thoughts just a little.

I glance behind me, bleary-eyed, to find two Iron Legion cadets trailing us. I curl my lip at them, snarling. They blanch. Of course they're scared of someone who can control their minds. What they don't know is that I don't have any desire to feel that skull-shattering pain again anytime soon.

Tana pulls me into a narrow hall. "Detour," she mutters.

Sipping my coffee, I survey this new hall. I've never seen this one before—so cramped we have to walk single-file, with Tana in front of me and Serana behind. There's hardly any light, and a few cobwebs hang from the ceiling.

"This used to be a servant passageway," Serana explains. "Back in the days when Avalon agents didn't want to see the help. It isn't used much today, but it's a handy place for a smoke break, apparently."

"Nice." My voice echoes, and so do the extra footfalls behind us.

We're still being followed.

"Whoops, my shoelace is untied," Serana says. "You two go ahead. I'll catch up."

I glance over my shoulder at her. She's kneeling,

fumbling with her shoelace in the cramped stone passage. Her red hair hangs down, and her body blocks the hallway. One of the Iron Legion cadets glares at her as he catches up.

His lips press into a thin line. "You can't just block the hall."

Serana is working on the slowest shoe-tying job in the history of shoes. "Sorry. I forget how it goes sometimes, you know? Do you make the bunny ears first, or…you know what? I'm going to tie a knot if I'm not careful."

Tana hurries ahead, and I rush to keep up with her, leaving Serana and the fuming Iron Legionnaires behind.

At the end of the long passage, we turn into a wide corridor once more and slip into a stairwell. My legs burn, shaking a little from fatigue.

"Who, exactly, was the Lady of Shallott?" I ask.

She turns to me with a small smile. "You know, Shalott, the beautiful island in the lake with the weeping willows?" She frowns. "Oh, it's not there anymore, is it? I think it drowned in the war between Merlin and Mordred. Anyway, Elaine was a countess. She was madly, passionately in love with your father, but he cursed her, trapping her on the balcony of that tower with a mirror and a loom. So now, it's named after her."

I swallow hard. The stories about Mordred weren't getting any better. "Why did he curse her?"

"She didn't support his attack on Camelot. She was worried for him, I think. She tried to talk him out of it. I think she saw that it would go badly for him…Shalott had a small army, and she refused to send her forces to aid him. Mordred took it personally, so he cursed her to stay trapped out there on the balcony, weaving her tapestries in isolation. Her only contact with the rest of the world was through watching people in that mirror. They say Auberon broke the curse, rescued her from this tower after the battle, and dragged her into Brocéliande to be his bride. But she never got over her love for Mordred, and she died of a broken heart. Now, her ghost haunts this place, and in the dead of night, she rattles the doors and windows, demanding to come inside from the cold. I talk to her sometimes, but it's hard to understand what she's saying. She's always crying."

A shiver ripples over me. I'd really made a pact with one of the worst people I'd ever met. "Sounds like a nice place for a meeting."

"It's private. Somewhere you can talk without the Pendragons or their cult members eavesdropping. It's going to be just three of you: you, Nivene, and Viviane. Serana and I will wait for you outside the door to get you back without harassment."

I'm wheezing as we reach the top floor, and Tana gestures for me to open the door to the pale stone balcony.

I find Nivene and Viviane sitting by a blazing fire pit, both of them clutching teacups. The air is crisp and cool, just above freezing. The sun dazzles with that crisp light that often follows a rainstorm.

"We were followed," says Tana. "The Iron Legion. Serana stalled them, though."

"Good," says Viviane.

I survey the terrace, where ivy climbs the walls. On one side, a large weaving loom stands before a mirror. Within the loom, the threads form the shape of a web. As I peer at the glass of the mirror, its surface shimmers and ripples like lake water. Then it transforms into a vision of the bustling streets of Camelot—the cobbled twists of Malevile Lane, then the ramshackle shops of Dark House Walk... The vision is gone again in the next moment.

"Is that her mirror?" I half suspect that the sleep deprivation has me hallucinating. "The Lady of Shalott's?"

"That's the one," says Viviane.

For a moment, I think I can feel her heartbroken presence whispering cold over my skin, and I shudder. I glance at the mirror again and feel as if I've been bathed in ice water.

"Helloooo?" Nivene snaps her fingers at me. "Are you awake? We need the debriefing to begin."

"Hang on." Viviane hands me a small brown paper bag. "Tana told me you haven't had breakfast."

I open it to find a sandwich of fresh bread, Cheshire

cheese, and a fig spread. My stomach rumbles. "I love you."

"That's too much emotional expression for me, thank you," says Viviane shortly. Her smooth blond hair gleams in the dazzling light.

I glance up at her. "I was talking to the sandwich." I take a bite. Delicious.

"You look like shit," Nivene says.

"It's been a long night," I reply, my mouth full. "A long several nights. Sleep has been elusive."

"So we've heard," Viviane says. "So? Tana and Serana told us something rather extraordinary. They said you found the lost Isle of Avalon, where Queen Morgan used to rule. It's been missing since the Fey War. We all thought it drowned, like Shalott."

My mouth is full, and I nod.

Viviane narrows her eyes. "That alone already sounds improbable. It's been lost fifteen hundred years, but I suppose you are a Sentinel. Then they told me that apparently, you found a portal on the Isle of Avalon, one formed from ring stones. And although Auberon closed his borders, you could get through as a Sentinel. They said it leads directly to Auberon's fortress, where you found Raphael. Honestly, it almost seems too good to be true. Why didn't you come right to us?"

Ah. Well, it *is* too good to be true because I left out the part where I had to make a deal with the Butcher of Lothian Tower. Mordred, the slayer of innocent women.

Curser of Countesses. I glance at the magical mirror again, my blood running cold.

"It's true," I say. "I found Avalon."

"When did you find it?" snaps Nivene.

Fuck. Of course she's the type who'd immediately be able to suss out when I'm leaving out something important.

I sigh. "Months ago. But I thought it was just abandoned. I didn't realize it was useful until I found the portal. It's mostly just a ruined castle and barren apple trees. Nothing of value except the dolmens."

"We need to get to Avalon," Viviane says. "Scope it out. And then, if it's really all you said, we can launch the attack."

Viviane's eyes flash. "A portal into Auberon's fortress? It's Sir Kay's wet dream. We gather a few hundred soldiers and agents and storm through the portal. We Kill Auberon and Talan, and every other royal member of Auberon's house. We cripple the Fey's command. End the war. The Court of Morgan will lay in ashes."

A pit opens in my stomach. I haven't told them yet that Mordred is what's left of the court of Morgan—and so am I. "We can't send an army through. Only Sentinels can walk through the ley portal. That's only Nivene and me."

Nivene nods. "Just like it was before the first invasion. There were ley portals that only Sentinels could walk through. There were many on Avalon and across

England. The biggest one was in Stonehenge, of course, but there were more. A bunch in Ireland. One or two in America. Any Fey with Sentinel powers could go back and forth through them using ley lines. But around the time that Auberon invaded France, they stopped working. We assumed Auberon shut them down, but maybe he didn't know Avalon was still there."

Viviane's pale blue eyes sparkle. "And these ley portals...are you sure we can't use them to get other agents through? We did it with the veil."

"The veil is different," Nivene says impatiently. "Sentinels can control that. But with the ley portals, it's the opposite. They control us."

I nod. "When I went through, it felt like the portal's magic was pulling me, like intense gravity. I fell into it, hard. It drew on my Sentinel powers to pull me through. I wasn't summoning anything."

"Ah." Viviane nods. "I knew it was too good to be true. Okay, so we have a portal that only you two can get through. Fantastic."

"And that's why I can't get Raphael out," I say. "Also, he's refusing to leave until he finds his sister."

Viviane sighs. "Well, it's still better than nothing. Maybe we can still use it to assassinate Auberon or Talan. And we can finally get in touch with our assets in Brocéliande. We haven't contacted them for fifteen years. Okay, keep going. How did you break Raphael out?"

I clear my throat, calculating how much I need to

omit. "The portal led to a courtyard within the fortress wall. So, I got into the fortress easily and found him in the dungeons, mind controlled a guard, and then I came back and collapsed from exhaustion."

"That was dumb and risky," Nivene says. But she looks at me with something that almost feels like respect. "So, hang on, when you mind controlled the guard, did you read anything important in his mind?"

"Not really." I stare out at the mist coiling off the cold lake. "Oh, and the Dream Stalker found me—"

"He *what*?" Nivene sputters.

"Nia!" Viviane shouts. "I think it's high time you tell us the entire thing from start to finish."

I do, skipping over the parts that include Mordred and his silver moths. They ask a lot of questions, and I find myself lying again and again to avoid mentioning the Kingslayer. As I weave together a web of lies, my gaze flicks to the mirror. My chest aches. The Lady of Shallott wasn't the only woman he'd cursed to live in isolation.

I finally finish and have a much-needed bite of bread and cheese.

Viviane and Nivene stare at me, stunned.

"So, we have a few days," Viviane finally says.

"We don't know how long, exactly," Nivene says. "To get this ready, we'll have to move quickly. Get her cover story ready. He could arrive at the village sooner."

Viviane nods. "Yeah, I'd honestly prefer that you leave tonight, before Wrythe gets a whiff of this."

"Hang on..." I say. "What are you on about?"

"We need to go through our contacts," Nivene says. "We'll have to use the sleeper agents. The assets we mentioned."

"That goes without saying," Viviane agrees.

"*What are you talking about?*" I press.

"It's a good thing that her cover story places her in Lauron. You can get there quickly," Viviane says.

They're ignoring me now. Am I a ghost haunting this place, too?

"Hello!" I shout. "What's going on?"

They look at me. "Well, we're discussing how best to proceed with the Talan thing."

"What. Talan. Thing?"

"His courtesan thing, obviously," Nivene looks at me, frowning. "Come on. I know you're tired, but we need you to be much sharper than that."

"There's no courtesan thing," I say in disbelief. "There can't be. I fully intend to return to Brocéliande on missions, but not as his mistress. Talan will figure me out immediately. He's the Dream Stalker."

"Nia," Viviane says softly, "as spies, we spend years cultivating connections with Fey nobles. If we can get an agent undercover as a kitchen maid in a baron's house, it's a huge win for Avalon Tower. There's never been anything *remotely* close to this. No one ever got close to the royal family. To be in a romantic relationship with the prince himself...it's an opportunity we can't pass on."

My heart hammers. "I was with him for twenty minutes, and he came very close to invading my thoughts, to discovering every secret about me. He's the Dream Stalker. Viviane, you know what he can do. The first time I fall asleep around him, he'll step into my mind and find out everything I know. Then I'll be stuck in Brocéliande as well as Raphael."

"As a Sentinel, you can shield yourself from his power," Nivene says. "It's hard at first, but you'll get the hang of it. You create a veil in your mind. I can teach you how to do it."

That's what Mordred said, too.

Viviane's eyes blaze. "You told us yourself. He wants to murder all the humans. *All* the demi-Fey. He's worse than his father. All the more reason to stay close to him, to stop him if you can. You cannot pass up this opportunity. We can create a cover story for you. By the time he gets to Lauron, you will be a Fey farm girl. Then, you learn all the prince's secrets, yes? Get him to let his guard down around you, at least for a few days. Figure out his weaknesses. Find a way to get Raphael out. Then we take down the Dream Stalker and his father, and the war is over."

"You really think Talan the Impaler will let down his guard around me?"

"He must like something about you," says Nivene. "I couldn't say what. But if he hated you, you'd be dead by now."

"I wouldn't say he liked me. He called me imperious."

Viviane frowns. "I've never thought of you that way."

I shrug. "I was really angry when I ran into him, and I didn't care what he thought. I think it's safe to say I gave him an attitude."

"Well, maybe your instincts were right. He probably doesn't encounter someone who gives him attitude very often. Maybe it intrigued him. Maybe that's what got you this role."

I stare wordless at them. "You really want me to do this?"

This is insanely dangerous, but we're desperate. Losing the war. On the brink of Avalon Tower tearing itself apart. And maybe it isn't the worst idea to have a backup plan that doesn't involve Mordred.

"It's a lot to ask, I realize that," Viviane says. "And if you refuse, I'll understand—"

"*I* won't understand," Nivene interrupts. "We all put our lives in danger to fight Auberon. You have the best shot out of any of us."

"Not the best way to put it, but I see her point," Viviane says, glaring at Nivene. "Our forces are losing miserably. Raphael is still stuck in enemy territory. The Iron Legion are tearing Avalon Tower apart, and I feel like we'll be thrown out of here soon. Nia, I can't see any other way. Can you?"

I swallow. She's right. But to form an alliance—even fake—with the Dream Stalker? I shiver. He's like the devil himself. "I'm going to need to bring an inhaler with me, and it will be a risk getting caught with it.

Unless you have some magical solution to asthma. Serana will need to glamour me incredibly well."

Viviane nods. "Well, she's already done that."

I clear my throat. "Right."

"I'll go with you," Nivene says. "You won't be alone."

Dread skims up my spine. "Let's do it, then. I'll become the mistress to the worst person in the world."

CHAPTER 13

Our boat floats through Avalon's lake, cool mist wrapping around us. We're disguised as messengers tonight and armed to the teeth with bows, swords, and leather satchels of supplies.

I've been practicing nonstop with the veil in my mind, strengthening it.

What I'm not prepared for is what might happen if Mordred pops out of his palace. *Surprise! I'm Nia's evil partner.*

As Nivene and I pull our small boat onto the island's shore, I'm terrified he'll jump out to criticize the job Serana did on my glamour, although to my eye, it looks nearly identical to his work.

We step onto the shore, and I adjust my quiver of arrows.

As we climb the winding path toward the castle, the island looks deserted. A few snowflakes drift through the air, twinkling in the moonlight. Right now, the only sound around us is the gentle lapping of the lake's waves on the rocks and the rush of the wind through ruined castle walls.

I hope that Mordred knows enough to hide tonight.

"This is incredible." Nivene looks up at the castle towering above us. "Imagine the magic forces that hid this island for so long. We *all* thought it sank into the lake with Shalott."

"Still very much here." I glance at the dark arch where Mordred appeared last time. Nothing yet.

I suppose, with his little spy devices, he knew that I was about to show up with Nivene. But Mordred is still a mystery to me, and I have no idea what he'll decide to do.

Nivene follows behind me, and I glance back at her before I cross into the castle. Her hair glows with a purplish sheen under the moonlight. "Did you explore the castle?" Nivene asks.

"Not too much," I say cautiously. "It's not in a great shape."

"Still, it's worth checking out—"

"Yes, but not tonight. We don't have time."

"Right." Nivene sighs. "My sister Alix would have loved seeing this."

I lead her through the castle doors, into the hall with the banquet table set for a party centuries ago that never took place. Nivene is marveling at it, wondering what it's doing there.

My muscles tense at every sound, and my breath catches with every movement out of the corner of my eye. Fortunately, Mordred is still nowhere to be seen. When we reach the double doors at the end of the hall, I push them open, and we cross into the courtyard, where the ley stones wait for us.

"I can feel their magic," Nivene whispers by my side.

I've known Nivene for a while, but we've never gone on a mission together. It's truly a sign of Viviane's desperation that she's sending MI-13's only two Sentinels together.

As we get closer, I feel Nivene's power mingling with my own and reverberating around the towering rocks.

"Do you feel that?" I ask. "Not just the ley portal, but our powers combining?"

She smiles, and I realize I've hardly ever seen her smile before. "Yes. My magic used to twine together with Alix's in the same way."

When I glance at the dolmens, they glow faintly with our red Sentinel magic, like the light of Brocéliande's moon. In the grassy space between them, a dark portal opens, a shadow yawning between the stones. Larger this time.

I stare at the gaping hole.

When we go through that portal, I'll be better prepared. I've read everything in Cadoc's thoughts—the layout of the fortress's grounds, the placement of security details.

"Once we get through, let me take the lead. We take

the horses to the eastern wall, and we avoid the soldiers at the main gate. At that gate, they mostly stop people coming in, not going out. That's where Raphael left from."

She nods, smoothing her coat. We're dressed in the sleek black outfits of Fey messengers, tight trousers and a fitted jacket with buttons down the front. "If they try to stop us, can you handle them with your mind control?" she asks.

"Hang on." I close my eyes, tugging at the violet threads of my telepathy. Immediately, pain shoots through my skull, so fierce that I want to vomit. Staggering back, I let my magic sputter and die. Since the Dream Stalker severed my connection to Cadoc, this has happened every time I try to use that power. My primal magic for which I earned the Avalon Steel torc? It's basically hot garbage right now.

I wince. "Maybe if it's life or death, but it feels like my sinuses are going to explode."

"Okay. Well, if anyone gives us trouble, we can slit their throats and then bury the bodies in the cold earth. I do enjoy that sometimes."

Silence stretches between us. "Great. Good times. Are you ready?"

She nods. "Let's get on with it."

I reach out and touch one of the dolmens. Its cold, ancient magic slips into my chest, winding around my ribs, pulling me closer. I stumble forward into the portal. For one heartbeat, I'm in both places at once—

two sets of ring stones, mirroring each other. Then I fall hard onto the frozen ground between the jagged stones of Brocéliande, snow stinging my hands. I hear Nivene swearing under her breath from the force of the fall.

Snow whips through the air, and I glance up at the castle in the distance. But as I do, I see a shadow moving toward us and the glint of steel under the night sky. Shit.

"Halt!" his voice booms, echoing off the towering outer walls.

He's running now with his sword drawn. We've just materialized out of nowhere, right in front of a guard.

I scan him as he runs closer. He's tall, even for a Fey, and heavily armored. His coppery hair streams behind him. We can probably still take him, but we can't afford to let him shout for reinforcements.

But as he gets even closer, I realize that I know his name. In fact, I recognize him through Cadoc's memories.

"Riwanon!" I call out, grinning wide. "Imagine meeting you here."

He slows his running, then stops when he's only a few feet away. His forehead crinkles. "Do I know you?"

I wrinkle my nose. "We were together for military training. Don't you remember?" I ask, sounding hurt.

Cadoc hates Riwanon, who often uses his position to harass the women working in the kitchen. And Riwanon loves nothing more than to wax about all the women he shags during training.

"Oh..." He blinks. "Right. You're...uh..."

"Adelaide." I take two steps toward him, tilting my head shyly. Riwanon once told Cadoc that he slept with so many women in the training camps that all their names blended. "Don't you remember our night together? I thought it was memorable."

Slowly, his expression grows more hostile, his eyes narrowing with suspicion. And with a sinking feeling, I realize my mistake. Of course. A man like Riwanon who brags nonstop about his prowess with women is obviously full of shit. He didn't seduce a single woman during training—possibly ever.

And I just blew my cover.

On the other hand, the distraction worked. While I was talking to him, Nivene slipped behind him. I give a nearly imperceptible nod, and she leaps forward to jam her dagger into his neck, her lips curled back with ferocity.

He tries to scream, but with the blade in his throat, it comes out as a gurgle. Somehow, he's still on his feet. Blood spilling from his lips, he swings his sword violently in a wide arc.

I pull the knife from the hidden sheath in my sleeve and dart forward, kicking him hard in his chest, my boot connecting with his ribs. He loses his balance, falling backward over one of the jagged stones that jut from the earth. Incredibly, despite the knife in his neck, he's still alive. Adrenalin crackles through my veins, electrifying me.

Nivene and I are both upon him. I stab him twice in

his side as Nivene wrestles his sword away. Everything unfolds in nearly complete silence—just grunts and hisses whispering in the night air. At last, Riwanon's large body slumps motionless on the grass, blood trickling from his lips.

This is a disturbing reminder of how difficult the Fey are to kill.

"Wow." Nivene is breathing hard. "This fucker was tough."

My heart slams hard against my ribs. "There's blood on your face."

She leans down and wipes it off with Riwanon's cloak.

We do our best to clean ourselves of the blood, then hide the body in the dark tangles of the night brambles that climb the walls. They'll find him by tomorrow, but by then, we'll be well out of Corbinelle.

"Come on," I whisper. "This way." A winding stone path leads us along the perimeter of the grounds, and it will take us to the stables. To my right, the pale, sharp-spired towers rise into the air like stone gods.

"This place is fucking huge," she breathes.

When I was here the other night, I didn't go anywhere near the stables. But Cadoc has, and that means I know where they are. It's always bizarre, following someone else's memories as if they're my own. Even long after the connection is severed, my mind is shot through with flashes of feelings that I can't quite place. An apple tree makes me wistful for someone

Cadoc misses, and an empty guardhouse near the castle makes me flush with embarrassment.

But I also feel fear, and that comes from me. What if the stables are heavily guarded? What if Talan senses I'm here again and hunts me down, finding me inexplicably dressed as an armed messenger? I focus, strengthening the veil in my mind.

I lead Nivene east, hugging the castle's outermost walls in the shadows. We pass a stone fountain, one where raven-shaped spigots spew water into the wintry air and water burbles in the basin. We walk past a rookery, where a few birds stir, ruffling their feathers.

"The tavern we're heading for should be a safe spot," says Nivene. "The owner of the Shadowed Thicket is anti-monarchy. Or at least he was fifteen years ago. But anything could have changed since then, so we still need to be cautious, yeah? I don't even know if our contact will be there. If he is, let me do the talking. He's going to be cagey."

"Tell me about him again."

She leans in close to me. "His name is Meriadec. He's one of Avalon's sleeper agents in Brocéliande. What do you know about the Scorched Earth Revolution?"

I try to recall what Amon taught us during training. "Two centuries ago, the commoners revolted because of wealth inequality and dwindling food. And it failed."

"Right." Nivene nods. "Interestingly, it happened just a short time after the French Revolution ended. Some scholars believe there's a connection. People were dying in the streets, hardly more than skeletons, eating leaves and moss. And the nobles had six servants each *just* to serve them their breakfasts. One to pour coffee, one to butter the bread, and so on."

"That's very specific. You almost sound like you were there."

"My mother was."

I should be used to the fact that Fey live for centuries, but it still catches me off guard. "Wow."

"So, the commoners revolted, just as you say. But there was one tiny difference between the French Revolution and the Fey revolution. Unlike Louis XVI, Auberon had dragons."

My stomach flutters. I can't quite imagine the horror of a dragon-scorched landscape.

"Humans weren't the first thing Auberon unleashed his dragons on," she continues. "He started with his own people. Half of Brocéliande burned to death. Auberon blamed the revolutionaries for killing his son, the crown prince Lothyr. He lost his mind. The revolutionaries were left as nothing but ashes, and all the leaders were executed in front of the castle. Ripped limb from limb, their entrails dragged—"

"I don't need the details."

"Anyway, Meriadec was part of that Scorched Earth Revolution. And probably one of the few who survived. Years ago, we established contact with him, and he worked with us for a time. Whether he still will—well, I suppose we're about to find out."

I point ahead at the large wooden stables. "We're here."

I slip inside, Nivene following close behind. The timber and stone structure is unguarded, dimly lit by oil lamps that cast warm light over the horses in their stalls.

I beeline to Holly, a dark mare that Cadoc loves. She's fast and reliable but isn't one of the royal horses that'll get noticed when we get to the gate. Nivene crosses to another stall, eying a large white horse. "Not that one," I whisper. "It belongs to the prince's cousin. Take the brown one over there. His name is Madog."

She quickly turns and grabs Madog. We saddle both horses, then lead them outside. Once we clear the stable, we leap onto our horses. Holly snorts, maybe realizing that I'm not her usual rider. I pat her neck, then trot her back toward the gate in the eastern wall.

There's an art to going past enemy sentries. You can't avoid their eyes completely, because that looks suspicious, but you can't stare at them like some sort of weirdo, either. Raphael once taught me how to do it. You picture someone you know, but not too well. Like a neighbor you see a few times a week. You imagine that it's him, and that you've just seen him the day before. If you manage to convince yourself, then you give him just the right kind of casual smile. That sort of short recognition of connection between acquaintances who avoid small talk with each other.

I exchange that look with the guard. He nods at me, then opens the gate.

Relief sweeps through me.

We ride out of Corbinelle, into the night, and the wind rushes over us. I take in the landscape, silver-red in the moonlight. It's not long before we pass charred stone walls, abandoned villages of crushed roofs and blackened stones, and a collapsed bridge with jagged stones that tumble into a river. Clearly, when Auberon fears a threat to his crown, his response is swift, brutal, and bloody.

THE SHADOWED THICKET reeks of yesterday's booze, sweat, and dirt. This tavern is the sort of place people visit in search of one specific aim: getting obliterated.

When we step in, hours after midnight, there's only a handful of patrons left. Most sit alone. A trio of men are trying to sing together, though it sounds like each one is singing a different tune.

"Any idea how to find him?" I ask Nivene.

"Give me a second." She sidles up to the bar, then waves over the bartender. "We'll have two...whatever."

"Two whatever coming right up." He picks up two smudged glasses, then pours a pale golden drink in them.

Nivene takes a long sip from her mug and licks her lips. "This is good. Almost as good as the mead I drank at my coming-of-age dance, back in Saxa." She speaks loudly, clearly.

The barman seems to freeze. He stares at her for a long while, then leaves through a door in the back.

"He seems to recognize the pass phrase," Nivene whispers. She takes another sip, looking around her.

I bring the glass to my lips. I'm not an expert in Fey meads, but even to my untrained palette, this stuff is nearly undrinkable. It tastes like fermented cough medicine. No wonder the pass phrase starts with "this is good." These words were probably never uttered here by mere chance.

Within another minute, a man sits down on the bar stool next to Nivene. His long brown hair is pulled back in a ponytail, and he wears a maroon cloak. His cheeks look gaunt, his skin pale.

"Hello, Meriadec," Nivene says.

"Nivene." He takes a sip of mead from Nivene's glass and stares at me over the rim. "Are you going to use my real name in front of strangers as a matter of course, or just around the pretty ones?"

"You can trust her," says Nivene. "She's a demi-Fey from Avalon Tower."

"I trust no one." He shoves her glass back into her hand. "That's why I'm still alive. Where's Alix?"

"Dead." She says this with almost no emotion.

His hazel eyes widen. "I'm sorry to hear that. Your sister was a decent person. Honorable. And she never pissed me off, which is more than I can say for you."

Nivene smirks. "Well, she would have appreciated your touching eulogy. We need your help."

"No."

"No? This is your moment, Meriadec. The moment you've been waiting for. This is your chance for revenge for everything they've done. For the Scorched Earth Revolution—for everything."

"They don't serve revenge here. Only that absolute swill in your glass."

"What happened to the Meriadec I met twenty years ago? The one who was ready to die for the cause? To, quoting your own words, 'introduce the human guillotine to Brocéliande'?"

He narrows his eyes. "*That* Meriadec was abandoned by your lot. That Meriadec was left to fend for himself in another famine-ravaged kingdom. Just as the famine was spreading, your lot lost interest in us. And when Auberon imagined he might be faced with another revolt, he started killing anyone he thought of as disloyal. Burning villages. Mass executions. Half the people I know died in Auberon's torture dungeons. I spent four years in the forest, hiding from the King's Watch and living on acorns and pigeons. And now you want me to die for my cause? That's the thing, Nivene. For all intents and purposes, I *did* die for the cause."

I wince at his words. No wonder Raphael was so desperate to get his sister out.

"We didn't lose interest," Nivene whispers. "Auberon closed the borders. The only undercover contacts we could maintain in the Fey Realm were in France. Brocéliande became impossible. We could only get back in here when Nia found an ancient ley portal."

Meriadec narrows his eyes. "Is that right?"

"Fill me in. What did we miss after the borders closed?"

"You must know about the start of the famine?"

"Yes. We have demi-Fey knights who escaped Brocéliande after it started."

"Right, so all the crops failed, and the commoners were starving. No one knows why, but Auberon scape-goated the demi-Fey and their allies. He called them enemies of the kingdom. Of course, the famine had nothing to do with the demi-Fey. Sometimes, nature just turns rotten, doesn't it? But Auberon was clever. People were ready to turn on him. They knew that those in Perillos castle ate lavishly while they starved, so he directed their rage elsewhere--at the demi-Fey. *They* caused the famine, he said, with their mixed blood, polluting our land, an offense to the gods. They conspired against us. They conspired with human allies to destroy us all. And when most of the kingdom was half-dead with starvation, he promised to invade the human world. They're the real enemies, aren't they? And France is now Auberon's breadbasket." He shrugs. "At least we're not eating grass anymore. We have France's wheat."

I touch his arm. "Speaking of those demi-Fey agents from Brocéliande, one of them is looking for his sister here. Have you heard anything about a fortress just for demi-Fey prisoners somewhere in the kingdom?"

Meriadec shakes his head. "I don't think they keep many demi-Fey prisoners alive."

My heart sinks.

Nivene leans in closer to Meriadec. "Listen, Meriadec, we have a real chance to get close to Auberon and his son now. *Really* close."

He snorts. "I've heard *that* before."

Nivene grabs my shoulder a little too hard. "Talan wants this woman to be his mistress. His maîtresse-en-titre. He's going to look for her in a few days, if we get her cover story straight."

Meriadec stares at me in disbelief, his jaw dropping. "You can't be serious."

"It's true," I say. "And trust me, I want that monster dead."

He snatches Nivene's drink again and takes a long sip. "Tell me everything."

"Sure," Nivene says. "I'll just get us another round of those terrible drinks."

CHAPTER 14

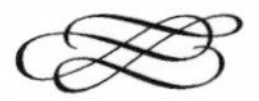

For three days on my new farm, I've been waking at sunrise, feeding the chickens and the two pigs, mending the fence, and cooking meals.

Meriadec found us a small, abandoned place in the most isolated part of Lauron. There's no one around for miles—just our tiny timber-frame cottage nestled on snowy rolling hills, with a thatched roof and smoke coiling from a brick chimney.

Meriadec believes that we have to really get into our characters, to play the role for real.

I grip a few weeds, tugging them out of the earth, and breathe in the clean air. The wind nips at my cheeks and fingers.

The moment we arrived here, we prepared the cottage thoroughly, setting it up to be my childhood home. We went through our cover stories, talking them over, polishing every detail.

Meriadec says a cover story should be as close to the truth as possible. On our way here, he spent a day interrogating me about every painful detail of my real life before coming up with our fake family dynamics. Naturally, my fake family involves having one parent who's a complete train wreck and another I never met.

We set up the house, taking care to leave empty bottles of mead lying around, and then we started playing our respective parts. By the time Talan arrives, the dynamics will be perfect. If anyone in his retinue scouts ahead, they'll see exactly what they expect to see: a small, dysfunctional farming family harvesting mostly rotten vegetables from the wintry soil.

Now, as I sit in the dirt in our fields, a subtle thaw spreads through the air. The snow has been melting the past few days. As I gently pry an onion from the wet earth, the cold soil stings my fingers. I inhale the rich scent of the earth and hold up my find. There aren't many edible onions. Most of them are covered in a dark mold, rotten from the inside out. But this one is actually good, and I feel immense satisfaction when I drop it into the near-empty basket.

"Nia! Nia?" I hear a voice calling.

I stand up, stretching my back. "Yes, Father?" I call back.

Meriadec steps around the low fence that surrounds the onion field, holding a bottle. "My dinner!" he slurs.

"I still have half the field to pick, and I need to finish mending the fence."

"You're starving me, girl." He scowls at me, but for a second, his eyes flash, a recognition of the imaginary game both of us are playing. But that look disappears instantly, and he's back to being my drunk dad. He waves a hand at me. "Your worthless sister is in a rotten mood again."

He stumbles off. I wonder if he's *actually* drunk. He's the type to really commit to a role. I turn back to the field and let out a breath.

I'm feeling oddly better about things. Maybe this is what everyone needs after a breakup: onion farming. Every morning, I've felt a sense of peace as I watch the sun rise over the rolling hills. I could stay in a place like this for good.

While I've been here, the volume has been turned down on my most pressing worries: Mordred and his magic moths, Prince Talan, Raphael wandering around the forest. For now, I let myself believe that this is who I am: Nia Vaillancourt, Meriadec's daughter.

I finally finish pulling the onions from the cold earth and trudge back to our little cottage. As I walk, weariness seeps into my bones.

Nivene is in the kitchen, arms folded, staring sullenly. "There's nothing to cook."

At this point, we're authentically starving. We've hardly eaten a thing in the past few days—fried onions, a few carrots, and dried herbs. France might be Auberon's breadbasket, but the bread isn't making it out to rural peasants like us.

"Look at this." I remove the single healthy onion from the basket. "Isn't it amazing?"

She looks at it, then at me. "It's a fucking onion."

Nivene, unfortunately, doesn't do so well on an empty stomach. Last night, as we lay in our beds, she whispered that if Talan didn't show up soon, she'd eat all the pigs and be done with it.

"It's a *good* onion," I point out.

"Whatever. And yesterday, you found a weird-looking carrot—"

"It looked like a penis, and it was delicious."

"And that one potato. You're driving me insane."

"Father said you were in a rotten mood."

"Well, Father can bite my—"

"Girls," Meriadec shouts from the doorframe, clinging to it for balance. "We have visitors. They're coming on horseback." His eyes are wide, face pale. He heads out the door again.

Wordlessly, Nivene and I exchange a quick look. I turn back to the counter and start to chop the onion.

It's another few minutes before Meriadec stumbles back into the kitchen. Talan follows right behind him, bowing his head to fit into the small space. Two armored soldiers lurk close behind the prince.

My heart races. Talan looks completely out of place here—the rich, velvety fabric of his dark cloak is obviously worth more than the farm. His cold, unearthly beauty stands out here like a marble statue in a field of rough scarecrows. He casts his dark gaze around the rushes strewn over the floor, the simple furniture of rough-hewn wood, and the rustic beams. I can't say it smells amazing in here, and it's obvious how much a prince does not belong in a place like this.

Meriadec's face is pale, his voice quivering, playing the act of the terrified but drunk villager quite well. I'm not sure how much he's acting. More than likely, he really *is* terrified. He nods vigorously. "This is His Highness, Royal, High…Prince Talan de Morgan."

"Your Highness." I give a cursory curtsy, then lift my chin.

Talan had called me "imperious," so I can't change it up too quickly. He saunters over the rushes like he owns the place, casually taking it in—the counters of rough-hewn wood, the fiery hearth, and the ceramic pots hanging from the ceiling, nearly hitting his head. "We were passing by on a hunt, and I realized how hungry I was. There's not a tavern for miles, and sadly, one of my idiot guards scared our stag away."

Meriadec waves a hand at him. "We'll get you fed, Your Highness. My Nivene is an amazing cook."

"It is a nice farm," I say, "which is why I hope we can stay here, but since our taxes are so high, it won't be easy."

"Nia," Meriadec barks.

Talan's lip quirks. "And what's your name?"

"I am Nia Vaillancourt," I say. "And this is my sister, Nivene."

"It's a true honor," Nivene says, her voice sounding high and nervous. But I know her body language well enough to see the charade. She's cool and calculating, ready for anything.

This is the crucial moment of our plan.

"And you're the cook?" Talan asks.

"I…I didn't know we were about to entertain guests," Nivene stammers. "But I can kill one of the chickens. My cooking isn't fit for such esteemed—"

"I'm sure it will be fine," Talan interrupts, looking bored with all of this already. "And while you're making dinner, perhaps your sister might show me around." His dark eyes flick to me, and the corner of his lips curls in a sardonic smile.

"Of course, Your Highness. I will show you the apple grove." I bow slightly, making the lines sound just *slightly* rehearsed.

I'm performing a complex juggling act of multiple fronts, and the wrong move might end with all of us dead, burned to a crisp by dragon fire. Talan assumes that I'm playacting for my family and for his guards' sake, but I'm playing two characters, one on top of the other. My roles are as layered as the onions I dug up.

I can't think about it all too intently. Instead, I force my mind deeper into my surface cover. I'm Nia, the farm girl with an attitude forced into league with the prince.

"Perhaps I could see your house first," said Talan.

He wants to see if anything seems out of place. He doesn't trust me at all, of course.

"It's just a small cottage," I reply. "Surely Your Highness has seen—"

"Indulge me."

"Nia," Meriadec half-shouts. "The prince asked you to show him the house. I'll pour us some mead."

"Fine." I gesture at the small room. "This is the kitchen. We have two bedrooms."

"Let me see."

"It's just my father's room, and the one where my sister and I sleep." I beckon him up to our bedrooms, taking a narrow, crooked flight of stairs. Meriadec's room is a mess, with empty bottles of mead scattered over the floor and a few discarded clothes. It truly smells like piss.

Our room is messy, too—carefully cultivated, a staged disarray with some underwear on one of the beds.

"How will you ever live, deprived of all this?" he says.

"You can cut the attitude," I whisper. "I'm doing what you told me to do. And my sister will miss me, you know. That's why I don't want to leave. She'll be left all alone with my father."

Sunlight slants in the windows, sculpting his cheekbones with shadow. He has to stoop just to stand beneath the rough wooden beams.

He casts a critical eye around the tiny room. "Which bed is yours?"

"That one." I say, pointing at the more organized bed, the one with a knitted doll on the pillow.

Talan goes over, picks the doll up, and raises an eyebrow.

"My mother made it for me before I was born. It's a keepsake from her."

He turns and picks up a small painting from a wooden trunk. "Who painted this?"

"Nivene. She has a talent for likenesses, don't you think? I love being with her when she draws."

It's a sketch of Meriadec, Nivene, me, and another woman, all sitting outside the house. Nivene and I appear younger in the sketch, still girls. In truth, Meriadec was the artist. Nivene couldn't draw a stick figure to save her life.

"Is this your mother in the portrait?" He points at her.

"Yes. She died giving birth to me, but Nivene wanted her in the portrait anyway."

His dark eyes find mine. "Was it after her death that your father developed a fondness for so much ale?"

"Not ale, just mead. He was always that way, but it got worse when she died, then worse again with the famine."

"How does he afford it?"

I shrug. "Oh, he doesn't buy it. We never leave the farm. So, he makes his own mead. We keep honeybees and produce our own honey."

He slides the painting back on the nightstand. "Show me the apple grove."

This must be how it is with royalty, I suppose. They don't ask questions or suggest things. They just issue orders and declarations, and everyone falls in line.

Particularly when you had the reputation of being an absolute monster.

CHAPTER 15

I lead him downstairs again, through the kitchen, where Nivene stares wide-eyed. She takes a step closer. "I can show you the farm."

Talan's expression is ice-cold. "Nice of you to offer, but I'm sure you have dinner to prepare."

"We could show you the farm together," Nivene says, her eyes desperate. The jealous sister, upset at being left behind.

"Nivene!" Meriadec snaps, staggering. He grabs her by the arm. "You heard His Highness. Nia will show him the farm. Make us some food."

She scowls at her father, and I pluck a coat off the hook on the wall.

As we step out, I hear Nivene arguing with Meriadec, hysterically yelling at him that it's not fair. He's howling arguments in return, calling her worthless. I want to roll my eyes. I almost feel like they're enjoying this.

I glance over my shoulder to see that the two armored soldiers are following closely behind us. In the cold air, I pull my cloak tighter around my shoulders.

Just to the right, on the farm's rolling hills, is the apple orchard, its trees gnarled and dark. "Strangely pretty here," Talan murmurs.

"It's my favorite part of the farm. Come spring, it'll be a sea of white blooms. But the apples don't grow anymore, just the flowers." I'm making pleasant conversation for the benefit of the soldiers.

"Let's walk there for a bit," he says, then turns to look at his bodyguards. "Boys, you can keep back. The young lady and I would like to be alone."

One of them smirks at the other, not even bothering to hide his amusement. I wonder how often the prince does this.

When we're far enough from them, he leans in and whispers, "I chose the guards carefully. Most of the palace's guards are terrible gossips, and these two are probably the worst. By tomorrow, everyone will have heard about how the prince fell for a farm girl."

"Will they be shocked?"

He walks with a casual grace. "Some will, but no one expects me to make good decisions."

My lips quirk. "Because you rarely do?"

"Precisely."

I whisper, "And is our fake relationship one of those bad decisions?"

He flashes me a disarming smile. "Oh, I'm sure it will

be a complete disaster, but I don't know *how* yet, and that's always interesting."

We reach the apple grove and walk deeper between the bare trees, as far as we can from the soldiers. Finally, I stop by one of the trunks and lean back against it. "What now?" I whisper.

Talan turns to me, cocking his head. "Pretend you find me captivating. Imagine I'm Lumos."

Talan is about a million times better looking than Lumos, but I think I hate him more. "What makes you think I find Lumos captivating?"

"He was able to persuade you to sneak into my castle to see him in the middle of the night."

I smile at him. "For the rent money. Truly, I can't decide which of you is more terrible. It's like trying to decide if I'd rather get boiled to death in oil or slowly eviscerated by starving ravens."

It's what Viviane told me to do—give him attitude. I'm just not entirely sure where the line is.

I'm relieved when a playful glint sparks in his eyes. Maybe if you insult people with a smile, you can get away with anything.

"Given all the things you've heard about me, I'm astounded that you'd be willing to insult me to my face. But I suppose someone with a primal power isn't as afraid of me as everyone else is."

I shrug. "I think you kill people on a whim, whether they're nice or not. Usefulness matters to you more than pretty manners."

He brushes my hair off my face, and the stroke of his fingertip against my cheek sends a tingle over my skin. It takes me a moment to remember we're acting.

"Do you object to a monarch killing subjects to maintain order? You slaughter a pig when you need to."

"We kill them to eat, but I wouldn't go on a pig-murder spree just for the hell of it, as you and your father famously do."

"Well, perhaps the pigs aren't invading your kingdom as spies and threatening to destroy everything that you hold dear."

My heart flutters. He *really* wouldn't love the real me.

His gaze flicks up for a brief second, and he licks one of his elongated canines. "Well, this is all very charming, but we're not done yet. We need enough time to make it seem like you've captivated me with your charm."

"Are you telling me I haven't captivated you with my pig slaughter analogy? I'm borderline insulted. Most of my seductive banter involves various livestock butchering scenarios. It's not a turn-on?"

His dark eyes sparkle. With a sly smile, he toys with a loose strand of my hair. "Why don't you tell me something real about yourself, Nia?"

"Like what?" I ask in a whisper.

"Do you fall asleep easily, or does sleep elude you?"

For a moment, it strikes me as such a strange question. But I suppose to the dream stalker, sleep is his domain.

Taking Meriadec's advice, I answer honestly. "Lately, I'm awake all the time. I drink herbal teas to help me sleep, but they hardly work. Most of the time, I fall asleep after the sun rises, but it's a light, dreamless sleep."

"Well, that won't do at all. I think you have too many responsibilities here. At least when you're pretending to be my mistress, you'll be free of them. And free of all your work."

"And you? How do you sleep?" I ask.

I actually know a lot of these random details about Talan. I've been hearing his thoughts for years. The battles, the sex, the women moaning his name with their fingers threaded into his hair...and the intense loneliness when it's time to sleep.

"I seek company to sleep because I cannot stand to be alone," he says in a honeyed murmur.

I stare at him. He surprises me by telling me the truth. Even when he surrounds himself with lovers, it never seems to ease his isolation. But they all treat him with utter deference. There are no surprises for him. No authenticity. Just tedium.

He gently hooks a finger under my chin and lifts my face to look up at him. "When was the last time you were truly happy?"

He actually seems to want to know the answer.

My heart races with the intensity of his expression in his deep, dark eyes. "Months ago. But I was almost content today when I was working in the field. When I found a good onion. That probably sounds dumb to you, but it was satisfying."

"Living with your father doesn't seem like it would be peaceful to me."

"He's mostly harmless. He just needs looking after. It's like having a large child." Meriadec is right. It *is* easy enough to transpose my own experiences to Fake-Nia's.

"And who looks after you?" he asks. "Your sister doesn't seem remarkably well composed."

"I don't need looking after."

My back is against one of the trees, and Talan presses a hand against the trunk behind me. He's studying me so carefully, I'm almost afraid he's going to read my secrets.

His gaze flicks back up to the guards. "All right, Nia. If they're going to believe you became my head mistress, and that I'm bringing you with me into Castle Perillos, they need to think we had amazing, mind-blowing sex in this grove."

"I'm not going to have sex with you."

He sighs. "Your loss, but I don't actually need to fuck you right now. I just need you to convincingly fake it. Can you do that?"

"Wouldn't be the first time."

"And what was the first?"

I shrug, sticking to the truth again. "I always had to fake it with a lover I had when I was twenty. But he wasn't a sadistic torture enthusiast, so this feels a bit different. I think the worst offense he ever committed was wearing a green suit of cheap velvet with a pink shirt."

This is, in fact, true. Darren was in a bad glam-rock band and had terrible taste in clothes. He was also shit in bed. So, yes, I know how to fake it.

Talan narrows his eyes. "The outfit you describe is a worse crime than torture. And if I fucked you for real, Nia, I can assure you that you would not need to fake it." His voice is a deep, velvety whisper that sends shivers over my skin. "But for now, all we need is an illusion for our gossiping soldiers. The trees are bare, so we might need to make it look real."

My eyebrows rise. "And how are we supposed to do that?"

He crouches for a moment, then he lifts the hem of my skirt, exposing my legs to the winter air. I start to protest, but the next thing I know, he's lifting me up against the tree, spreading my legs so they wrap around his waist, under his cloak. Now my dress is hitched all the way up to the top of my thighs. His hands are firm beneath my ass, and my thighs cling tightly around his waist. As his intoxicating scent wraps about me, his mouth hovers over mine.

I grip him over his enormous shoulders, holding on.

"Is this really necessary?" I hiss.

"If I'm not mistaken, you could use actual, genuine pleasure in your life, but for now, faking it will have to do," he whispers.

I'm doing this for Avalon Tower.

My heart pounds in its cage as he stares at me from beneath his black eyelashes and the warmth of his body radiates over me. He leans down, his mouth hovering over my throat now. His breath warms my skin. "Go on. So I don't have to actually seduce you."

I hate the way his deep, purring voice makes my thighs clench around him. It's an instinct, an animal part of my brain that doesn't understand the bigger picture. The animal part of my brain wants this to be real. It wants us in the dirt, tasting each other.

My feet are hooked together behind him, under his cloak. He's wearing the softest cashmere sweater, and I can feel his body's heat through it, and the hard steel of his muscles.

My fingers wrap into his thick black hair, and the memories of some of his thoughts float through my mind. Like the time I heard him spread a woman's legs open, then lick and kiss her while she gripped his hair, screamed his name. I remember him running his tongue over a woman's nipples, and his thoughts when he'd hiked up a thirsty woman's skirt in the castle's hall, taking her hard from behind where they could have been seen.

I inhale deeply. Talan has a smoky, earthy scent, tinged with something sweet like moonflowers. Jasmine.

Okay. Fine. Why not admit to myself that I've always *liked* hearing his dirtiest thoughts? The way he practically tortures some of the women he fucks, not letting them come, driving them insane?

My breath is already quickening. For the briefest of moments, I imagine what would happen if I were one of his women. If he hiked up my skirt here in the apple orchard and did exactly whatever he wanted to me. Desire coils tightly inside me.

"I'm very curious what you're thinking about," he murmurs.

The vibrations of his voice over my throat make my thighs clench again. *After* this is over, I will remind myself of what a ruthless, terrible person he is. But now, I have a job to do. And that job involves making this seem real.

His lips, ever so lightly, brush against my neck, and the warmth radiates over me. My eyes close, and at the feel of his lips on my skin, the moan I let out isn't *entirely* fake. But I make it louder, letting it rise out of my throat. His fingers flex under my ass, and he moves his hips into me just a little. I arch my neck like an invitation. I moan louder, letting it echo through the orchard, and his canines graze over my throat. Warmth plunges through me at the feel of his teeth on me, at the knowledge that I'm completely vulnerable to this beautiful man. My pulse races. He raises his mouth closer to mine.

For just an instant, our lips brush, and he's breathing as hard as I am.

He lifts his gaze, and he stares into my eyes for a moment before pulling away a little.

He licks his full lips. "That almost sounded real, and

my soldiers will certainly not be able to tell the difference."

Gently, he lowers me to the ground, and my skirt falls to my ankles again. I feel disoriented, like I just lost myself for a moment. Like I'm snapping out of a dream. I suppose it makes sense for him.

He holds me by the hand, leading me back toward the house.

I glance at him. I'm supposed to learn as much about him as I can, but even though I've been hearing his thoughts for years, he's still a mystery to me.

"You asked me when I was last happy. What's the answer for you?" I ask.

His dark hair looks rakishly tousled now. His eyes slide to me, molten bronze in the sun. "I don't actually know. Maybe settling down with a nice, loving mistress will be the answer to that."

He flashes me a mischievous smile, and I know that the time for honesty is over.

"I'll have extra food sent to your father to make up for the loss of your labor and the chicken they're killing for me."

Oddly considerate for a monster. "Thank you. When will I join you in the palace?"

"We'll ride all the way back to Corbinelle tonight. You will join me at court, and we will have you dressed in clothes fit for a queen."

My breath catches. We're leaving already?

My mind is a battleground...a young woman gasping

beneath cold, barren branches, the fruit not yet ripe for the tasting...sacred vengeance against my enemies awaits me, blood sweeter than apples...

As I'm holding his hand, fragments of Talan's thoughts ring in my mind, cryptic as ever, and goosebumps rise on my skin. I strengthen the veil in my thoughts, blotting it out.

I suspect that while we're together, Talan and I will be playing a deadly game of hide and seek with each other.

CHAPTER 16

Getting whisked away by a prince to a castle should be every girl's fantasy. And in a way, this feels like a dream.

I lie back on the lush pillows of my bed, sipping tea, enjoying the views in my new place.

Last night, we rode on horseback to Castle Perillos, where servants immediately bustled around me, getting me anything I wanted. When we arrived, Talan left me with a small entourage of guards and servants who brought me to my room—a vast tower chamber with window views of the wild, moonlit forest beyond the castle walls.

White flowering plants climb the tall columns and stone walls, and the air smells faintly of jasmine. Outside, sunlight breaks through the iron gray clouds and streams over a rug threaded with turquoise and gold and the shelves crammed with Fey books.

A burnished mahogany table stands beneath the tall windows. After I arrived, I ate an amazing dinner there with a book of Fey history. A couple of obsequious servants brought me a lavish meal of salmon and wildflower salad, and it was possibly the best thing I'd ever eaten. And after days of eating nothing but onions and carrots, I was genuinely starving.

Breakfast this morning was fresh bread with chocolate, more mead, and a bowl of strawberries with cream. In my new chambers, I had the luxury of a hot bath in a room with a giant skylight. They even left out a bottle of champagne to drink in the steaming water.

Even my lungs feel better here. The air is free of the things that usually irritate them, like bleach or pollution —which is good, because taking out my plastic inhaler would give me away in a heartbeat.

As I sip my tea, a knock sounds on the door.

"Come in!" I swing my legs over the side of the bed.

The door opens, and a servant with braided black hair carries in a domed tray for me. She sets it on the table by the window, smiling. When she pulls off the dome, the scent of the food has my mouth watering. "Lunch is served, my lady."

Before me lies a plate of roasted pheasant, a dandelion and violet salad, and a plate of bread and cheese. More mead, of course. Always mead.

"Enjoy, my lady!" the servant calls out behind her as she leaves me in the room.

So, like I said, this is every girl's dream—apart from

the fact that I'm supposed to be the mistress of a nightmare. My beautiful Prince Charming is pathologically unable to form any kind of emotional connection with another person. He'd murder me if he knew what I really was.

I bite into the pheasant, and the tender meat, flavored delicately with rosemary and a hint of juniper berries, melts in my mouth. As I eat, I glance outside at the forest beyond the castle walls. I wonder how Raphael is doing out there, and thinking about him makes my heart ache.

I take a sip of the mead. He *did* tell me that he could look after himself. He doesn't need me thinking of him.

I will also try not think about what I heard the servants whispering this morning: that when he met me in Lauron, Talan ordered me to hike up my skirt and get on my hands and knees, and then he fucked me on the forest floor in front of his soldiers— "like a common whore" who was now "rising above her station."

As I swallow another bite of pheasant, a knock sounds at the door.

I cross the vast room and pull open the door. A man is standing in the hall in a crisp white shirt, partially unbuttoned in the front. He reminds me of a knock-off version of Talan, the way his hair looks tousled and long in the front and so many rings gleam on his fingers. It's also the way he stands casually, one hand in his pocket, the other with a black box resting jauntily against his hip.

"Well." He bends his arm and leans against the door-frame, his gaze sweeping all the way down to my hips, then my legs. He licks his lips.

I can't tell if he's evaluating my body or the simple blue dress I'm wearing. "Yes? Can I help you?

He meets my gaze, biting his lip. "Well, I can say that the prince has impeccable taste in women, but of course he has impeccable taste in everything, doesn't he? That's what makes him the prince." He barks a laugh.

"Okay." It's not what makes him the prince, but I'm not going to argue.

He runs a hand through his black hair. His skin is pale, and his hair is so unnaturally black that I wonder if he glamours it.

He nods. "Yeah, you'd be my type, you know, Nia? If the prince hadn't already claimed you for himself, you'd be my type, definitely. Interesting. Not that I'm going to tread on his territory when he so clearly values you, his royal mistress."

Two women bustle behind him carrying swaths of fabric, one with long white hair, the other with a blond pixie cut. He shoves the box into the hands of the white-haired lady, then claps his hands together, smiling at me. "What did you say your name was?"

"Nia," I remind him, though he literally just said it.

"Right, right." He points at me.

This man has a distinctly practiced indifference.

"And you are?" I ask.

"The name's Jasper. I'm in creative control of the

royal wardrobe. I'm an artist, and I've been sent here to create art."

Without waiting for an invitation, Jasper saunters into the room, looking around. "My dear friend Talan really gives his mistresses nice rooms, doesn't he? Nice. Nice. You really did bewitch him, didn't you, you little minx? Must have *quite* the snatch, but we don't judge how one gets power, do we? The power is what matters."

"Thank you?"

He turns to me, cocking his head. He narrows his eyes, and I think he's pretending to think. "Right, what are we doing, then?"

"The banquet," snaps the woman with the blond pixie cut. She cuts me a sharp look as she crosses inside.

Jasper claps again, then points at her. "Yes, Riona. Yes. The banquet. Talan has invited his new friend, and we need to get her dressed in the finest attire."

"Banquet?" I ask.

Instead of answering, Jasper drops into an upholstered armchair and picks up my half-empty glass of mead. He fills it to the brim, then takes a long sip, draining half of it. "You mind if I have a little of this? It helps me think creatively. I do my best work with mead. Do you know what I mean?"

"Not really."

He stares at me again, swirling the glass. "Do you make art?"

I flick my hair over my shoulders, staying in character as the imperious farm girl. "I'm a farmer, actually.

Onions, carrots, and pigs. Of course, there is a certain artistry to onion farming during these times of famine."

He freezes and stares at me over his glass as if he's trying to figure out whether I'm joking. "Are you being serious?"

I fold my arms. "Why wouldn't I be? The kingdom needs farmers, you know. We don't have as much to work with these days as we used to, but we still manage to pull your food from the blighted soil. And yes, there's an art to that."

"Wow. Yeah, no, I can imagine. Onions. Interesting. Interesting. And of course, I'm sure you're as layered as an onion." He laughs again.

He's highly skilled at saying absolutely nothing of substance.

He snaps his fingers again. "Riona. Riona. Bring out the—"

"It's Ranae," the blonde says acidly. "You know my name. I've worked with you every day for eight years."

He slouches in his chair, smiling. "Right. Ranae. Great to meet you. Nice one. Bring out the sheer midnight blue, please." He drains the rest of the mead in his glass, then stares at me again. "Could you get undressed now, please? Sorry, what did you say your name was, again?"

I'm positive he knows everyone's name. "*Nia*."

Undressing in front of others was a well-practiced part of our training. The Fey are not self-conscious about their bodies, and I can't ask Jasper to go into another room, even if I want him to. So, while he sips his mead, I pull off my blue dress and stand there in my brand-new white lace underwear.

He scrubs his hand over his jaw, and I can hear him mumbling, "A tiny pig farmer. Runty. Interesting, interesting. What *will* he think of next?"

I toss my hair over my shoulder again. "The prince and I met last night, and we just hit it off. I showed him our apple grove, or what's left of it. And it seems he found me intriguing."

"Obviously, that's not all you showed him," snaps the white-haired woman.

Ranae shushes her.

Until now, all the servants have been the picture of politeness, but I'm clearly on the bad side of these two women.

Jasper nods, his eyes half-lidded, like he's on the verge of falling asleep. "So, my new friend, do you like blackberry mead?"

"Never had it on the farm," I say.

"Well, we need to get you some." Jasper snaps his fingers again. "You, there, the blonde. Would you mind draping her in the midnight blue, the lake-mist silk? Shape the dress as we go, yeah? I want you to use the sheerest silk."

He slides his mead onto the table and rests his elbows on his knees. He steeples his ringed fingers, then presses them against his mouth, staring at me. "I want the plunging neckline. I want her to look like a goddess.

I want the silk to skim over her waist. Do you know what? Let's do an empire waist. And make it backless."

"That doesn't make sense," the white-haired woman says sharply.

Jasper closes his eyes and breathes in deeply. "I don't give a fuck. Make it happen, Tilly."

She shoots me a look of death, as though I'm responsible for Jasper being annoying.

His eyes snap open again. "The bra has to go. We'll do a leg slit, yeah? Show off the strong farmer legs. They're short but quite shapely. Like I always say, the prince has impeccable taste. *Unusual* taste. Use the star-woven silks, too, yes?"

"Do you know how much that costs?" seethes Tilly.

Jasper grimaces and inhales. "We don't worry about cost at Perillos, not for a chief mistress. Not when you see the gift he bought for her."

Gift?

He slouches back in the chair again and pours himself another glass of mead, chuckling to himself. "A pig farmer. That's mad, isn't it? He's always full of surprises." He waggles his finger at me, grinning. "You just never know with him. That's what makes him interesting, yeah? You think he's going to marry Countess Arwenna Blythe. She's the obvious choice for her beauty and vast fortune, but then *boom*. He brings home a pig farmer from Lauron who's never had blackberry mead. Throws the whole marriage process into disarray. Madness, you know what I mean? But that's Prince

Talan, isn't it? The man's a genius. An absolute genius. Granted, you're very pretty. I can see the logic in it. Anyone can find a pretty lady at court. But finding a lady squatting in the dirt of Lauron, pulling carrots with her bare hands? That takes a certain skill. You really never know what he's up to, do you?"

No, but I intend to find out.

As he's talking, Tilly is working her magic around me, whispering a spell that makes the dress stitch together on my body. The fabric feels gorgeous against my skin, a whisper of soft silk that falls gracefully over my hips, the sheer blue shimmering in the light. It almost feels like a warm liquid.

Tilly manages to fold the fabric over itself in just the right places so my underwear isn't showing through the dress and my nipples are covered with layers of silk.

Jasper stares out the window, looking lost in thought. "No one ever knows what he's going to do, which makes it hard to..." He trails off, but I already know what he was thinking.

It makes it hard to imitate him.

I have a feeling Jasper will be running out to find himself a girlfriend from a farm in Lauron.

As she works, Tilly glares at me like I murdered her firstborn. "He hasn't just been with farmers. Seamstresses, too."

I wonder what gifts he gave to Tilly.

"Could you twirl, darling?" Jasper narrows his eyes at me. "Yes. Yes. That's the one, isn't it? For the banquet. I tell you what, my farmer girl, all the other women are going to be outrageously jealous of you with this dress on. And we haven't even got to the real showpiece yet."

He picks up the black box from the table and opens it.

My jaw drops as I stare at the jewels gleaming before me—a necklace made of dozens of teardrop-shaped diamonds, which hang from delicate chains. The gems have a faint silver-blue sheen to them.

When I turn to see Tilly and Ranae, the vicious expressions on their faces tell me everything I need to know about what this means.

Ranae licks one of her sharp canines. The corrosive envy in the air is palpable, toxic.

Tonight, the courtiers and servants alike will be out to get me.

CHAPTER 17

Haunting music floats through a heavy set of oak doors. Two guards dressed in blue coats flank the doors to the banquet hall. One of them raps his staff, and the doors groan open, wood scraping over stone. In my beautiful new dress, I take a step into the gothic-arched doorway.

As I stand in the entrance, a guard slams his staff against the stone floor. "Miss Nia Vaillancourt, guest of His Royal Highness, Prince Talan, has arrived."

In the castle's vast banquet hall, every bright, glittering Fey eye turns my way. The haunting hum of the music fades to silence. Dozens of crystal goblets pause mid-sip as the drinkers stare at me. Moonlight flows in from towering stained-glass windows with images of winged creatures and forest scenes, and the kaleidoscope of light glints off the guests' heavy jewels.

This hall is the size of a basketball court, with

soaring carved stone columns that stretch to a high ceiling. A small orchestra sits in a corner, their bows stilled. Two long banquet tables line the longest walls, with a third connecting them, far at the other side of the hall. Light from candelabras sends gold flickering over a sea of elegant Fey faces, flower crowns, gossamer dresses, and rich brocade jackets.

I take a deep breath. I'm deep in enemy territory. A place I absolutely do not belong.

My heels clack over the flagstones as I cross inside, and my heart pounds while I scan their faces. Spies thrive in the shadows, and here I am, drawing attention like a firefly in the night.

Clearly, the rumors have spread about me.

All eyes are on me—including Talan's. At the center of the tables, on the far side of the hall, he's lounging in a chair. His rings and lopsided crown gleam in the candlelight. He wears a black jacket with silver buttons that sleekly fits his muscular body.

For the benefit of the crowd, he's giving me a smoldering look. His dark gaze sweeps down my body to take in the sheer material, jaw set tightly in contrast to his indolent pose. I know his expression is just a performance, but I suddenly feel acutely aware of my body.

A cool draft whispers over my skin through the translucent fabric of star-woven silk. I take a step closer, and the fabric against my thighs feels like a soft caress. Some in the crowd shift their attention to him, watching him as he stares at me. His gaze brushes up my body again, then locks on my face.

I have no idea where I'm supposed to sit. There's one empty chair next to Talan, but I assume that's for the king. This is a level of royal protocol that I didn't learn at Avalon Tower.

I raise my chin, smiling, and I cross behind one of the tables, heading for Talan.

A murmur ripples over the room.

I keep my eyes on the prince. He's still striking a louche pose, slightly slouched in his chair. There's something truly luxuriant about how comfortable he is in his own body. And when he turns and arches an eyebrow at me, his expression is searing. The torchlight dances in his dark eyes like matches burning in the night.

I flutter my fingers in a little wave at him, and I can feel whispers ripping over the crowd of Fey.

As Talan beckons me with a sultry smile, I exhale with relief.

At least I know where to walk now. The music starts to swell again, but I can still feel everyone's eyes on me with every step.

When I reach Talan, he pulls me into his lap. He sits in a chair large enough to be a throne, and he drapes one of his arms around my waist. I find myself acutely aware of the steely muscles beneath his velvety suit and of the heat radiating from his hand through my thin dress, onto my skin.

From his lap, I cast a look around the banquet hall. As far as the Fey nobility are concerned, I'm a paradox. Thanks to Jasper, I'm wearing the finest clothes, a style and fabric reserved for the upper echelon of the Fey world. The most expensive jewels in the hall. And yet, impossibly, they don't know who I am. I am a commoner. A nobody. They're not used to envying people like me.

I suppose that's why the gossip keeps spreading—the story about how Talan ordered me onto all fours to fuck me in the dirt. It takes the sting off their jealousy.

I glance at him for just a second, and he gives me a wicked smile. "Where *did* I find you?"

If I didn't know what he was really like, I might even be charmed by him.

I give him my best flirty look, biting my lip, playing along. I pick up his goblet of mead and take a sip, simpering at him over the rim.

One half of me feels the tangible chill of being unwelcome—the commoner so sexually bewitching that a prince has invited her into the sacred court of Perillos. No one likes an interloper. The other half of me can only focus on the feel of his hand on my waist through the sheer fabric. And when his thumb brushes over my skin, my blood heats. Sometimes, the mind doesn't know the things the body does.

Talan's fingers stroke slowly up and down. "Nia, you look delicious tonight. I can almost taste you."

His voice is low but still loud enough that the people around us can hear him. All part of the performance.

I lift my chin and smile at him. "Thank you. You, too."

My pulse races, breath quickening. My body only knows that his scent is intoxicating, and he looks like a fucking Adonis.

I turn from the intensity of his expression to scan the room again, and he lets his hand rest casually by my hipbone, his forearm just below my belly.

To my relief, I actually see a friendly face at the far end of the table: Nivene, my alleged sister, was apparently invited to the palace, too.

I turn my head toward Talan, whispering, "You invited my sister here."

"I thought she belonged at court with you."

This is *brilliant.* We were planning to find a way for me to invite her over, but I was hoping I planted enough hints for the prince to do it himself. And it worked.

I catch her eye and wave.

She sits with the lowliest of the guests: the rich merchants and bankers who occasionally get invited to the palace, those without a drop of aristocratic blood. She's chatting with her neighbor, a thin man with spectacles. She waves back at me.

A guard standing by the large golden double doors slams his staff three times on the floor. The sound echoes around the room. The low murmuring in the hall fades to silence, and everyone turns to look at the doors.

The only one who seems completely relaxed at this point is Talan, who lifts his goblet, signaling for a servant to bring us more mead.

The doors open, and King Auberon steps into the hall.

He does look a bit like Talan, though not half as beautiful. He has the same strong jawline and dark eyes, the same tan skin and high cheekbones, but his face is fuller, his hair lighter. Long and braided in some places, his brown hair flows over his black cloak. A platinum crown gleams on his head, and unlike Talan's, it's perfectly balanced.

The sight of him makes my blood run cold.

Everyone in the hall stands, as do I. While the servant refills his goblet, Talan stands last, languidly rising with a heavy sigh, as if he can't be bothered. He slides his hand around my waist again—and given how much taller he is than me, his arm brushes just below my breasts. I glance up to see him taking a sip of his newly filled mead.

As the king marches closer, his coppery gaze cuts to me. His lip curls just slightly.

Talan's already done with the formality of standing, and he pulls me into his lap again, arm draped below my belly. His thumb brushes over my hipbone.

"This is your new friend, Talan? I trust you examined her thoroughly before you brought her into our presence." The king's voice booms over the hall, and he somehow makes it sound like the filthiest double entendre.

Laughter ripples through the room, ringing out like delicate chimes, and Talan's fingers tighten around me, as if he were actually protective of me.

The king crosses to his throne, the chair next to Talan and me. Goosebumps rise on my skin. This is probably the closest an Avalon agent has ever been to the king of the Fey.

Before sitting, Auberon grabs the back of the throne, and he cuts a sharp look at Talan. "If only Prince Lothyr could be with us tonight."

Talan's muscles tense as silence fills the hall, but he doesn't show much of a reaction. He merely takes another sip from his wineglass.

Auberon rakes his gaze around the hall. "We have been at war for decades. First, we defeated the forest dwellers who tried to overthrow my rule. Now, we fight against humans and half-breeds. Our enemies are all around us. So, I demand that if you see *any* signs of treason, of espionage, conspiracy, or sedition, you must inform my King's Watch immediately. Anyone caught shielding traitors or concealing secrets from the Watch...well, I don't need to tell you about the gruesome consequences, do I?"

He pauses, allowing that to sink in, then resumes. "We are here to enjoy our feast. And I trust you know that everything I do is to protect the peace and safety of the realm. I alone can keep you safe from the human scourge that cursed our land after they tried to starve us with their manmade famine. I alone can keep your families fed. But you must trust in your king and tell my Watch what you learn. If you see the dull, deformed appearance of a demi-Fey hiding in our kingdom, turn him in. Help me protect you. Here in Brocéliande, we have no sanctuary for enemies of the Fey."

The guests break into a round of applause, and a few people call out, "Here, here!"

I focus on breathing normally.

I can practically feel the power crackling from the king. As he sits on the throne, the rest of the guests sit as well.

The prince lifts his goblet. "His Majesty, my father, and esteemed guests. You may have noticed this jewel I have discovered."

I steal a glance at Auberon's expression. He is staring directly ahead, his face frozen like a statue, mouth flattened into a thin line.

He knows that Talan is about to fuck with him, doesn't he?

Talan raises his glass higher. "I would like to raise a toast to the enchanting Nia Vaillancourt of Lauron, whom I had the fortune to meet while on a hunting trip. I have invited her to Perillos as a companion and dear friend. Truly, her wit and beauty are unmatched in Corbinelle and I daresay in all of Brocéliande. Miss Vaillancourt graces us with her beauty, and we are all the richer for it. Let us celebrate our stunning new guest at court, to whom I pledge my eternal devotion."

Low muttering rumbles around the room, and people whisper behind their hands.

A beautiful silver-haired woman is glaring at me, her cheeks pink, lips pressed tightly together with fury. Jewels gleam from her throat and dangle from her ears. An angry flush has spread over her chest. When I see people looking her way, it doesn't take the skill of a trained spy to know that she must be Countess Arwenna Blythe.

It was bad enough that I was a farm girl sitting in his lap, but now he just called me an unmatched beauty.

A half-smile graces Talan's lips. "Now, we are here to be merry, are we not?"

My throat goes dry. Those closest to me—the nobles whose seats are close to the king's—all stare at me with naked hostility. I'm sure that the billion-dollar necklace at my throat isn't helping. These are the highest-ranking aristocrats, the dukes and earls. Here I am, out of nowhere, a threat to their influence on the prince. Minutes ago, they could comfort themselves with the image of him fucking me in the dirt in front of his soldiers. I was a whore with expensive baubles. But the public compliments? The pledge of eternal devotion? That changed the game. I may be a mistress, but he's now elevated me above Arwenna.

Down at the far edge of the table, the expressions are more calculating. The lesser nobles and merchants are wondering if they can somehow leverage this surprising development in their favor. Some of them are eying Nivene with renewed interest, suddenly realizing that she and I must be somehow related.

The only one who shows no reaction to my introduction is the king himself. He stares stonily ahead, not sparing either his son or me a single glance.

Talan raises his goblet higher. "I am sure you all wish my *dear friend* and I the best."

I smile at the banquet hall.

The guests clap and raise their glasses, but no one cheers or even smiles. Talan is the only one here willing to risk his father's wrath.

Dread crawls over my skin as I think of the danger I'm in now. Surely the king wants me dead.

Talan's arm slides around my waist, and his lips brush over my cheek. Heat radiates from the place where his mouth makes contact with my skin. With a hitch of my breath, I realize how much he *relishes* the chaos he just created.

I turn to him, nestling in closer. "How much trouble am I in?"

I feel the muscles of his forearms flex against my belly. His lips brush the shell of my ear, and the warmth of his breath kisses my skin. "Careful, darling."

His thumb rubs my hip again like he's trying to soothe me.

I feel as if his magic is radiating from that point of contact, tingling over my skin.

"It might seem like no one is listening," he whispers, "but some of our guests are very talented at reading lips, and others' hearing is enhanced magically. So, if you want to talk about how I fucked you hard up against the wall on the way here, now is not the time."

I get his meaning clearly enough.

The serving staff place endless dishes in front of us. There's a plate of enormous oysters, each one served with the pearl, and roasted carrots, buttery bread, cheese and berries, and roasted boar. I eat, perched on Talan's lap, taking just enough sips of mead that I don't look suspicious. But I'm not here to get drunk.

The tension in the hall washes over us like a cold fog, chilling me. Even with delicious food like this, it's a grim atmosphere for a banquet.

My gaze sweeps between bites to look at the guests, memorizing their faces, remembering who they talk to. I file away every detail in the recesses of my mind. I try to figure everyone out based on what they're wearing and where they sit. I can guess their role, their place in this hierarchy. Those closest to the king are the most important, and Arwenna isn't far away. There are nineteen noble families, each with representatives in the king's advisory council. I believe that I've spotted four of them sitting around me, all glaring at me with obvious loathing. I think Talan's little ruse has fucked up the plans of many powerful people in Brocéliande.

Talan loosens his grip on me, then lifts me by the waist off his lap. He stands and raises his glass. "How could I forget? I have yet *another* announcement to make." A dark smile curls his lips.

My heart sinks. What now? This isn't an undercover relationship like one from Avalon Tower, because I have no idea what he's actually up to.

A sharp silence pierces the hall, broken only by the echo of Talan's shoes as he walks behind one of the wings of banquet tables. He prowls with lupine grace down to the end and stops just a few paces away from Nivene.

I hold my breath. There's a dangerous chill in the air.

All eyes are on Talan, and the air in the hall grows icy, darker. In all the candelabras in the room, the candlelight sputters. Talan drops the pretense of enjoying himself with me, and the look in his eyes is frigid as the air. Lethal. A shiver dances over my skin.

The hall is so silent, he doesn't need to speak loudly. "There is a traitor among us."

CHAPTER 18

The world seems to tilt beneath me, and I grab the chair's armrests. I have to employ my entire self-control *not* to look straight at Nivene, though I'm watching her from the corner of my eye.

She maintains her composure, looking at the Dream Stalker with nothing but the curiosity of a calm onlooker.

I allow myself a closer glance—quickly—and I notice the way her knuckles tighten around her goblet.

Fuck.

Talan leans forward and puts an arm on the shoulder of a Fey man with wavy black hair, thick eyebrows, and a white cravat. "Lord Ael here has been spying for the humans. In fact, a guard he knows released one of our prisoners. A demi-Fey spy named Raphael."

Nivene glances my way just for a second, her eyes widening slightly. I'm still holding my breath.

Lord Ael's face pales, now white as his cravat. "What?" Lord Ael stammers. "I never…is this because of the blue dragon—"

Talan's movement is so fast, so smooth, I nearly miss it. The man's chair topples over, and the next thing I know, he's lifting Ael by his throat, as if the Fey noble weighs nothing. The man's eyes bulge, his face reddening and feet kicking as he tries to take a breath. He's clawing at Talan's hands.

"In His Majesty's court, there is only *one* punishment for traitors." Talan's voice is ice-cold. With his free hand, he reaches inside his jacket and pulls out a dagger. The blade glints in the candlelight. For just a moment, the prince releases Ael's throat. But as he does, he slashes with his dagger, carving right through the man's neck. A simple, elegant swing that sends blood arcing over the flagstones. The Fey falls to the floor, legs kicking as he grabs at his throat, emitting horrible gargling sounds. I stare, willing it to be over. Time seems to slow to a painful crawl as the crimson rivulets stream over the floor, the stains spreading on the delicate embroidered rug.

The woman next to him—his wife, I presume—is sobbing. She covers her mouth with her hand, trying to stifle the sound of her cries. At last, Ael's body goes still. His green eyes stare lifelessly up at the ceiling, where candleflames gutter in hanging chandeliers. Blood glistens around him, and a deadly silence settles over the room, broken by the sound of that woman's sobs.

Only King Auberon keeps his composure, taking a bite of the roast boar as if nothing happened at all. I'm pretty sure he's been eating this whole time.

Talan stabs his dagger into the table and turns back to the hall. His venomous smile makes all the heat leach from my body. "Well? That was exciting, wasn't it? It's awfully quiet in here. How about some music? Play something fun, for the love of the gods." He nods at the musicians, then picks up Ael's glass of mead and drinks the rest of it.

Lady Ael cries into her hands, trying to be quiet.

Two violinists and a piper begin playing a cheerful musical piece, their faces pale with fright. A few servants hurry to carry the dead lord's body away.

I stare at Talan as he saunters back to me. He gives me a dazzling smile as he holds out his hand. "Dance with me."

All eyes are upon me. Faintly, I can see the sheen of blood on his dark jacket.

"It would be my pleasure." I stand and take his hand.

We're trained on Fey dances in Avalon Tower, and yet I still somehow don't feel prepared. It's one thing to dance with Serana or Darius under the bright lights of the training room. It's quite another thing to dance with the Dream Stalker seconds after he slit a man's throat, then drank his mead.

He pulls me in, leading me in a close dance. Awkwardly, my head comes up to his chest. Still, he dances gracefully, every step in the right place, commanding my body with ease to move with his. He's the kind of dancer who makes his partners seem skilled, even if they aren't. I just let him lead.

Quickly, other couples join, twirling around us. Maybe it's the mead, or maybe it's the coppery scent of blood hanging in the air, but I'm starting to feel dizzy.

I glance up, my gaze catching on the large, brightly colored butterflies fluttering above us as we dance, their wings shimmering.

"We can talk now." He leans down, whispering. "The music covers our voice even from the keenest of listeners, and no one can read our lips as we move."

I stretch higher onto my tiptoes so I can whisper. "That was brutal. What the fuck was that?"

"Just keeping everyone safe from traitors and spies, my love. Your heart has been racing out of control all evening, and I have to wonder why. Something surprising, farm girl? I thought you'd heard all about my reputation."

"Maybe I'm a little surprised. I didn't realize I'd ever meet anyone worse than the merchant who tried to shag one of our pigs, but here we are." I smile up at him as I say it, taking the sting out of it.

"I'm below the pig shagger in your hierarchy of people?" he murmurs softly. "Truly, I am cut to the quick by the poor opinion of a diminutive, half-starved, woefully uptight onion farmer. How *will* I recover from this mortal wound to my soul?"

"Why worry what anyone thinks when you're the best at everything? Killing, manipulating, fucking…"

"So you've heard."

"You're quite the full package, aren't you?"

An arched eyebrow. "A full package. I've heard it described that way. I don't usually brag about it in polite society, though clearly, there's none to be found before me. Or below me, in this case."

"You truly don't care what others think, do you?"

"I would be a masochist to dwell on what other people thought of me. I've been despised since I took my first breath. So, I don't really give a fuck what they think. You are not unique or original in your assessment. But I can say you are the only one who says it out loud, so at least you make it interesting. Perhaps it almost makes up for the fact that you're the size of half a person and you loathe having fun."

As we dance, I'm a little distracted by the feel of his powerful muscles shifting slightly beneath his clothes.

Obviously, there are some things I will not be saying out loud. "I say what I think because we're not taught courtly manners in Lauron."

"That is apparent. And that is why they can't stand to have you here."

"Your father certainly doesn't seem happy," I whisper.

"Yes." His lips curl in a wicked smile.

"This might be fun for you, but you've put me in danger."

"You truly make an art form out of being overwrought, don't you? I've given you a life fit for a princess, and you're still upset about it. Don't worry, I won't let anyone harm a hair on my faithful mistress's head. But now I really do need your skills."

"Now?"

"Yes. One of our targets is right here. Duke Ker-Ys. My sources claim that he has been plotting some kind of treason."

"And you're not just going to slit his throat or enter his dreams?"

"No, I need him alive. And dreams are complicated. Some peoples' dreams are intricate and detailed, full of their lives. Others are fantasies and fears, and some barely dream at all. Duke Ker-Ys dreams almost every night that he is counting green beads. Hundreds of green beads. I cannot manipulate his dreams, nor see anything in them. His own tedium is a powerful shield. That's what I need *you* for."

"You want me to read his thoughts and see what he's planning?"

"No. I don't care what he's planning. If I wanted to know, I'd have him arrested and interrogated. I want you to take control of his mind and make him confess to me privately."

My breath quickens. I've become entangled in Talan's murderous web. "What's the point? You can slit people's throats with impunity. Why do you need me to make him confess?"

"Don't worry about why. Just do as I ask. Do you understand what I need? I need him to talk to me privately and confess all the details of his treason. To me only. Not to anyone else."

"I understand," I say. And I do. Slowly, the pieces are sliding together in my mind. If he arrests the duke and gets a confession, he will only take down the duke. The duke's son will simply take his place, and Talan will gain nothing. But if the duke confesses to the prince in private about his betrayal, Talan will gain leverage over him. Ker-Ys will be in Talan's pocket. A duke on the council of nobles, voting and acting every way Talan needs. Not to mention, Ker-Ys might expose or fabricate additional conspirators whom Talan could blackmail.

"Pay attention." He twirls me, and I lean into his arm, my head thrown back. I get an upside-down glimpse of the dancers spinning on the floor. Then he pulls me upright. "Did you see the man with the deep green jacket trimmed with gold?" he asks.

"Yes. Dancing with a woman in a silver dress with a flower crown."

He lets out a short laugh, one that almost sounds like surprise. "Very good. The woman is Lady Breval, a tedious old witch. Ignore her. The man is Ker-Ys. He's your target."

I nestle my face against his chest, but my eyes are on Duke Ker-Ys. He's easy to pick out in a crowd, with a shock of long white hair, bronze skin, and eyes that glitter like emeralds. I whisper to Talan, "My powers only work with touch."

"Don't worry. Ker-Ys will ask you to dance. He is nothing if not predictable. And when you dance together, you'll get your chance."

I almost feel guilty at the part I'm playing in this macabre and twisted play. The stage is set, the curtain is rising, and I will play a starring role in the ruthless pageant of Talan's making.

But I don't dwell too long on guilt. After all, everyone here is an enemy who'd kill me in moments if they knew who I was.

When the dance ends, Talan bows deeply and brushes a kiss across the back of my hand. His dark eyelashes flick up, and he gives me a faint smile before dropping my hand and sauntering away once more.

I'm about to return to my seat when Nivene stumbles toward me, giggling. "Sister!" She grabs my arm drunkenly. "Can you believe this? Us, dancing here, with all these important people?" Her face is flushed pink, and her dress is a bit askew. She leans against me, struggling to keep her balance.

"Yes, it's all our dreams come true," I say.

She has her hand up as though she's whispering, but her voice comes out in a loud imitation of a drunk girl. "I danced with the owner of the biggest wine cellar in Brocéliande. He has so. Much. Wine."

She tugs on my arm as she falters.

At least, I *hope* this is an imitation of drunkenness.

"Are you all right?" I ask.

"I'm fine," she murmurs. "It was just a lot of really good mead. And wine. And sparkling wine…oh, wow, the room is spinning really fast."

"Maybe you should go lie down," I suggest, playing along.

"That is such a good idea." She giggles. "Just…lie down. In my huge bed."

"Right."

"Where is my bed?"

I sigh. "I'll ask someone to show you to your room."

"Nooooo…I don't want to admit that to strangers. They'll think I'm a farm girl idiot who can't handle her mead. Just show me the way yourself."

"Fine. Here. Lean on me. We'll look for it together." I have no idea where her room is, but that's not the point of this charade.

I lead her through the doors, relieved to be out of the noisy hall, even for just a second. We cross into the hallway, where a swooping stairwell curves to the upper floor. Out here, the masonry is exquisite but haunting, winged creatures slaying each other with swords and their bare hands. Moonlight pours in through the windows—silver in some places, red in others.

I glance behind me to make sure we're alone. "Please tell me you're not really drunk."

"Of course not, but we can't talk in there. Half the room would be listening. My room's up the stairs."

Arm in arm, we climb the stairwell, and she leans on

the curving stone banister, still feigning drunkenness in case anyone is watching.

"Holy shit, that was unnerving," I whisper. "The prince, just cutting that man's throat at dinner. Do you think Lord Ael is really a traitor?"

"It's possible." She leans in close. "I'm not privy to every secret agent passing on information to Avalon Tower. But we know for a fact that he's not the one who let Raphael go."

"Right. And what do you know about Duke Ker-Ys? Talan wants me to mind control him, to force him to confess treason. In private."

Nivene frowns. "If he wanted to get rid of Ker-Ys, he would have made the confession public. So, I assume he wants you to do it for blackmail purposes?"

We reach the upper floor, where chandeliers hang from pointed vault arches high above us. Stone statues of knights line the corridor.

"Yes, I think blackmail," I whisper back. "What do you know about him?"

Nivene sighs. "Okay. This is where it gets more complicated. Ker-Ys *is* likely plotting against Auberon, but not with the help of any humans or our agents. Just out of his own self-interest. The problem is, one of our assets has been involved in this. His name is Goulven, and he works with Meriadec. Ker-Ys has no idea that he's aligned with us. If you force a confession out of Ker-Ys, that might land our asset in the torture chamber, giving up every secret he knows."

I swallow. "How do you know all that?"

She shoots me a sharp look. "I'm a trained spy, Nia. It's literally my job to uncover things like that with my sharp deduction skills. Also, Meriadec told me."

I exhale. "Okay, so I can try to remove Goulven's name from his confession, if I can."

"If you can't, Goulven is fucked, and hopefully, he doesn't break under torture," Nivene says darkly. "But if there's no way around it, get the confession with his name in it. He knows the risks, like we all do. And fortunately, he doesn't know about you and me."

I swallow hard as dread dances up my nape. "Right."

"I nipped back to Avalon Tower earlier today," Nivene says. "Briefed Viviane and Wrythe."

My jaw drops. "Wrythe, too?"

"There was no way around it," Nivene says grimly. "He realized you were gone and demanded to be included. Anyway, we have our instructions. First of all, the Fey are advancing quickly through Scotland, getting closer to Edinburgh and Glasgow every day. If they get there, the casualties will be astronomical, and the war on Scotland will be lost. The Americans have sent troops, buying us some time, but it's not looking good."

I swallow. "How long?"

"A month at the most. Our sources report on special strategy plans that the Fey have. You and I need to get our hands on them. If we do, we might be able to reverse the tide of the war."

"Any idea where to start?"

"None. Keep your eyes open."

We pass thick, gothic-arched doors inset into the walls. I think her room actually is around here. "Okay, what else?" I whisper.

"We need to prepare for a possible assassination attempt, like Viviane suggested. It will be aimed at Auberon and Talan, at the very least. We need you to map their living quarters. You're the only one who can get close to them. Figure out the guards' schedule, and preferably figure out any routine that the king or prince have. Note anything we can use. With your information, we'll be able to plan our attack."

"Got it," I say. "I'll get the intel. And what's the plan for Raphael and his sister?"

"That's not in the mission scope."

"I know that's not in the mission scope," I hiss. "But he's a knight of Avalon. We need to make sure he's okay and get him out of here."

"No," Nivene says firmly. "That's not our mission. We're doing this to stop the war. And like I said, Nia, we all know the risks."

Frustration coils in my chest.

Nivene stops before a grandiose wooden door flanked by torches. A flicker of movement turns my head, and I glance at a maid on the other end of the hall, dressed in black and carrying a basket of clothes.

"Can I help you, my ladies?" she asks, hurrying closer to us.

I clear my throat. "My sister had a bit too much to drink. She needs help getting to her bed."

The maid bows. "Of course."

"Don't need help, I fucking..." Nivene slurs, pulling away from my grip. She nearly falls down, and the maid quickly grabs her arm to stabilize her.

"Just get her to bed," I whisper to the maid. "Before she embarrasses me anymore. She's only just arrived at court, and she's making a spectacle of herself."

The maid sets down her basket and nods at me.

I hurry off through the corridor, back to the banquet hall.

Nivene's words still echo in my skull like a dirge. *We all know the risks.*

But I'm not okay with leaving Raphael here.

If Avalon Tower won't help get Raphael back to safety, then perhaps Mordred Kingslayer will.

CHAPTER 19

By the time I return to the banquet hall, King Auberon is no longer gracing us with his presence, but everyone else is still dancing and drinking. The thick perfume of wildflowers floats through the air, and the ghostly sounds of the Fey music echo off the high ceilings.

With glass after glass of mead, the guests are spinning and twirling around the floor between the banquet tables.

In the far corner of the room stands Talan. Leaning against a stone column, holding a crystal goblet of mead. He's talking to one of the nobles, who wears a jewel-encrusted brocade jacket, and while Talan's body looks relaxed, his expression is predatory. The noble is literally trembling with fear, his face pale as moonlight. This is the effect my sweet, dark-eyed prince has on everyone around him.

I scan the room, searching for the shocking white hair of Duke Ker-Ys. Prince Talan doesn't strike me as the kind who would look fondly on me if I borrowed Nivene's "I got too drunk and had to go to sleep" excuse.

"Jasper, right?" A woman's melodious voice interrupts my thoughts. I turn to see her moving smooth as a panther, her silver hair tumbling in waves over a jade gown. Candlelight warms her milky skin, and her eyes sparkle in the exact shade of her dress. Arwenna is standing right before me now, peering down at me, and a shiver dances over my skin.

I look down at my dress. "Jasper, yes. He designed this today, with help."

She sips from her goblet. "Interesting. I am Countess Arwenna de Bosclair of Val Sans Retour, though I'm sure you already knew that. Jasper did my dress, too, of course, as I am to be engaged to the prince."

"Right. Well, he's very talented." I look away from Arwenna, desperately searching for Ker-Ys.

Arwenna leans in, not letting me go. "You know, Prince Talan and I have had an understanding for years. But he gets distracted sometimes. He has already had girls like you. So many, many girls like you from the dirt-encrusted laboring classes."

The look she's giving me sends a whisper of icy dread cascading down my spine.

"Girls like me?" I ask.

"Girls like you." Her voice rises, echoing off the tall ceilings. The rest of the banquet hall falls to a hush as people listen in. "Dull, inconsequential, easily forgotten. Girls who hike up their skirts, bend over in the dirt, and let the prince do what he wants. Sure, you can hold his attention for a few moments through sheer debasement. Of course, the humiliation of the peasant classes has a certain appeal to a man like him, but he will never respect you, and neither will any of us. You. Do. Not. Belong. Here."

My fingers tighten around the stem of my glass. I can feel all the eyes on me and the sharp tension piercing the room.

I lean in closer to her. Nia Melisende might be a people-pleaser, but Nia Vaillancourt is an absolute bitch in the right circumstances. I can't exactly change personalities now.

"I'm the dull and inconsequential one, am I?" I say loudly enough for everyone to hear. "And yet here you are, throwing a public temper tantrum to get my attention, demanding that I look at you. Desperate for me to acknowledge you. Because it hurts, doesn't it, to sit so far, far away from the prince? To not earn his pledges of devotion?"

Her features pale, and then pink splotches appear across her neck. "When I am queen, you will regret your words. People who cross me always live to regret it."

"Weird. You don't seem as if you are about to become queen, at least not anytime soon."

"I remember one of his girls from six months ago. He met her during some holiday trip. She was his favorite toy for a few weeks. Later, they fished her corpse from the nearby lily pond. That's what happens when the prince tires of his playthings. You get a beautiful moment basking in the warm, dazzling sun of his attention. You get little trinkets and baubles like the necklace you're wearing, and you think he loves you. Then he casts you into the shadows. Soon, they'll dig up another bloated corpse of a whore. Or they'll find you trampled by a horse. The world won't mourn the loss of another desperate harlot. But I will still be around."

"All those bodies you referenced—are you accusing His Highness of *murder*?"

Her smile falters, and panic flashes in her eyes. "Of course not. I'm suggesting they ended their own lives after they found he no longer wanted them. The nobodies like you who come from nowhere, who bask briefly in the light of wealth and power, of seduction by a prince. You'll get a taste for the intoxicating nectar of what belongs to people like me. You'll grow addicted to the prestige, the money. And when you're sent back to the dark obscurity of the filthy pig farm that spawned you, you will want to die, too. Then he will return to me. If I were you, Nia, I would get lost now before you learn how it feels to plunge from the lofty heights of Perillos back into the squalid Lauron dirt. Don't forget, Talan and I have known each other for *years*. Much longer than your two-day romp."

This monstrous harridan seems perfect for Talan,

really. But with someone like her, I can't afford to back down. Fear fuels her strength.

I sigh loudly. "Well, that's just the thing, isn't it? We all tire of the boring old things we grew up with. Those comfortable but worn-out belongings that no longer seem quite so exciting, like an old pair of slippers. He's had so long to marry you. Quite frankly, it doesn't seem like he wants to. All of this is starting to seem a bit sad, I think."

I turn sharply away from her to find Talan draped over his chair, watching us with amusement. I think he likes having women fight over him.

I walk over to a bowl of fruit laid out on the tables and pluck a raspberry, popping it in my mouth. The crowd starts murmuring again, no doubt gossiping over the scene we just caused. I pick up my glass of mead and take a sip as I watch Arwenna discreetly. Mentally, I make a note of every person she speaks to, memorizing their descriptions. Later, I'll run them by Nivene to see what she can tell me.

At last, I spot the bright white hair of Duke Ker-Ys. When I turn to look at him, I realize he's watching me, leaning against one of the hall's pillars. I school my expression to look lost—a remnant of the girl I used to be before Avalon Tower. Staring into my glass, I pretend that I don't know what to do with myself. It works like a charm. Instantly, the duke is heading toward me.

He stops a few feet away and bows deeply. "May I have this next dance, miss?"

"It would be my honor, my lord," I say shyly. I slide my glass onto the table and try to prepare myself for what will come next, the disorienting rush of mind-control powers, followed by a skull-shattering headache. I have little desire to repeat that experience, but a job is a job.

The duke leads me to the dance floor, then grabs my hand stiffly. Duke Ker-Ys isn't nearly as good a dancer as Talan. He manages to step on my toes twice within the first minute, then chuckles. "A bit clumsy, aren't you, dear? Don't worry. Enough time with us at court, and you'll learn."

I'm now desperate enough to end this dance that I start to summon my telepathy powers—the strings of crimson magic like red ribbons I unfurl. As I draw on my powers, pain lances my skull, nearly making me gasp, and my fingers tighten. I command a ribbon of red energy to slide into Ker-Ys's mind.

It's hard to concentrate on Ker-Ys's thoughts through the constant pain, but I just about manage. He's old, his mind byzantine, a labyrinth of desires and fantasies. Foremost in his mind is the way he imagines how dominant he is, dancing with the royal prince's mistress. Everyone around him can see that he doesn't fear the prince, that *he* is a real man who can lead.

But diving deeper into his mind, I find the source of those thoughts—the ever-present, gnawing terror of the crown prince and his father. What will they do if he loses their favor? Will he end up bleeding on the banquet floor, dragged out by servants because of the wild whims of a mad prince?

What will he do if that twisted prince suddenly covets his lands—or, horror of horrors, if they find out what he has planned? It's treason, of course. There's no way around it. And the way they kill traitors in Brocéliande is enough to make anyone's blood curdle. Considering what might have happened to Ael, the slow, excruciating public evisceration, he was given a merciful death. What would they do to Ker-Ys, though? Something far worse. He knows it would be worse, and that he would not be brave in the face of that punishment, that he would shriek like a girl as the horses pull him limb from limb, as they peel off his skin.

I can make his fear work against him. I could do it right now and stop this torment. My head throbs as if my brain is being skewered repeatedly with a blunt sword.

But I force myself to keep digging. I have to make sure he'll keep his mouth shut about Goulven.

I run deeper into the maze of his mind, searching for the plot to take down Auberon. I glimpse it there—the meetings with several lower nobles—and then a shady individual called Goulven. A commoner who could help with some of the more unsavory, bloody tasks.

I clench my teeth and ram my powers into that memory, crushing it. I wipe the name Goulven from Ker-Ys's mind. He doesn't remember what he's called or what he looks like. In fact, he's not even sure if he was there.

Done.

Now my body is shaking with pain, skin sweating, my jaw clenched. I feel like I'm about to throw up. Just a bit more…

I focus on Ker-Ys's fear of discovery.

Talan already knows, I whisper into his thoughts. *He must've unearthed the secrets in your dreams. That grotesque display with Lord Ael was a warning for you, a prelude to the fate that awaits you. Talan probably intends to arrest you after the banquet. But there is hope. Just a tiny, flickering glimmer of hope. The only chance of leniency is if you confess first. If you give away the other conspirators' names, Talan and his father might show mercy. In fact, maybe Talan hasn't told King Auberon yet. You must confess to Prince Talan alone, away from prying ears, and throw yourself on his mercy...*

I pull away, the agony still ringing in my skull like a cursed bell.

Ker-Ys is pale, looking as sick as I feel, but I mask my pain as best I can.

"Are you all right, my lord?" I ask.

"I need to speak to the prince," he croaks.

I blink innocently. "Of course. I have his ear. I could talk to him, set up a meeting for you in a few days."

He's shaking, sweating. "Now. Please. As soon as possible."

Clenching my jaw, I spin, catching the eye of Talan.

He waits in the shadows, his gaze on me. He lifts his chin, and light from the stained-glass windows streams red and blue over his sharp jawline.

I walk with Ker-Ys toward Talan, my fingers still delicately touching his wrist. I keep the thread of magic between us alive, though it feels like a white-hot needle in my skull. Talan leans back against the column, raising his goblet to me. A lock of his dark hair falls before his eyes. With a rakish smile, he says, "There you are, my love."

"My prince," I say. "The duke wants a word in private."

Talan sips from his glass, and his rings glitter in the light. "The night is early. Perhaps a bit later."

I can feel the duke's hesitation and give him a prod, stoking his fear into complete terror.

"Please, Your Highness," he stammers. "It's…quite urgent."

Talan's twinkling eyes meet mine, and I see a flicker of…something there. Admiration? No, it must be amusement.

"Fine. Follow me." The prince sighs. He practically tosses his goblet onto the table, and without another word, he turns to saunter from the hall, all eyes on him.

"Of course, my prince." Ker-Ys hurries after him, and I follow.

The large doors groan open, and we cross out into the corridor. I stare at Talan's broad form as he walks before us. His crown is still askew, and he pulls it off to drop it on the head of a knight's statue that we pass.

From the hall, he pushes through a wooden door to a small library. A fire burns in the fireplace, and I drop into a wooden chair upholstered with deep red velvet, the magical connection with Ker-Ys stretching painfully. Talan opens a liquor cabinet, uncorks a bottle of wine, and pours us three glasses of claret.

With his wine, he perches on the edge of his desk. "What's all this about, then, that you had to pull me from a party?"

"Your Royal Highness," the duke blurts, "I must confess. I've recently learned of a terrible conspiracy against you and King Auberon. A few of the lower nobles are conspiring, I'm afraid. Riling up the commoners. They complain that the king spends too much on war, too little on them. They complain that the men from their baronies are dying in the war. These conspirators are turning the common people against the royal house. There's talk of getting the army on their side. I can tell you their names."

"Interesting." Talan arches an eyebrow. "But I'm ever so curious. How, exactly, did you learn about this conspiracy, Ker-Ys?"

"I...I have my sources. I..."

I send another surge of magic into our connection. *He knows* I whisper in his mind. *Come clean. It's the only way to escape a traitor's death.*

"I was part of the conspiracy, Your Highness." The

duke starts sobbing, his body trembling. "But I realize now how foolish it was. That's why I've come clean, you see. To demonstrate my loyalty. To show you that I atone. I will do anything now to prove myself. I am not a traitor."

"Your loyalty. Of course, I demand nothing less." Ice slides through his tone. "And your coconspirators? You'll give me the names of those you've been working with?"

"I can give you the names of the nobles, of course, my prince. As for the commoners…I've never really met any of them. I think I saw…I don't remember…a shady man…"

Talan's expression looks almost bored now. "I don't give a fuck about the peasants. Nia, will you give us some moments alone?"

"Of course."

At last, I can release the threads of magic between Ker-Ys and me. It takes all of my self-control not to stumble on my way out of the room. As soon as I shut the door behind me, I grunt with pain, grabbing my head in both hands. Spots dance in front of my eyes, and nausea turns my stomach. I lean against the wall, trembling with the effort not to puke in one of these stone alcoves. My legs are shaking, and I want to drop into a bed and never move again.

I hunch against the wall and sip the wine. I'm not sure how much time passes before Talan opens the door again. With the hammering, jaw-clenching headache, it seems like hours, but maybe it's only a few minutes.

Talan closes the door behind him, and he peers down at me, eyes twinkling with curiosity. "What's wrong with you?"

"Using my powers is painful now, ever since you brutally severed my connection to Cadoc. Now, when I use them, I feel like someone is trying to hack their way out of my head."

"Ever since we first met?" He hooks his finger under my chin, lifting my face to his. He's examining my face.

"Yes."

"Why didn't you mention it?" He lowers his hand.

"Does it matter? You need me to do this, and none of the healers can know about it."

He frowns, staring at me, then pulls out a silk handkerchief and hands it to me. "Right. Of course. I suppose it doesn't. Your nose is bleeding."

I dab at my nose. Red streaks across the blue silk.

"I'll walk you to your room," Talan says. "You look half dead."

"There's no need," I say sharply. "I can get there on my own."

He glances at me. "Has it ever occurred to you that when a prince of the Royal House of Morgan says he is going to do something, he isn't asking for your approval or permission? I said I was going to walk you to your room, and I will. And I will send my healers for you. I do whatever the fuck I want, love, and when I die someday, I will have no regrets. It's the privilege of being me."

Despite the harshness of his words, his voice has a smooth, lyrical cadence that I find strangely soothing.

He offers his arm to me, and I lean against him.

He dips his head to my level. "Come on, then, I can't have you causing a scene in the hall. I already know how tetchy you get. Even without a headache, you're wound tighter than a drum, with no release in sight."

I close my eyes as I let him lead me through the hall, reminding myself that I can't get comfortable with him —not even for a moment. Because I saw in Ker-Ys mind what Talan would do if he knew the truth about me, and it would make this headache seem like a day at the beach.

CHAPTER 20

Light streams through the windowpanes in my room, painting my silky bed sheets with diamonds of coral. I allow myself to luxuriate in that single moment of contentment.

For two weeks in this castle, I've alternated between bad sleep and a constant state of wakeful hypervigilance. No wonder Talan described me as *wound tighter than a drum, with no release in sight.*

The moment I walk out of my room, my senses kick into overdrive. I'm constantly scanning for information and threats, wary of danger, perpetually fearful of someone discovering the truth.

Throughout it all, I feel what Mordred spoke of. My powers are growing, a nervous energy within me itching at my mind, threatening to burst.

At night, I've been drifting into a restless half-sleep. Just as Mordred taught me, I summon the veil in my mind before I fall asleep. And that *is* managing to keep the Dream Stalker out of my thoughts, but it's also keeping me from having proper dreams.

Dawn is the time when I can feel like myself again. Right now, as the peach morning light streams into the room, everything seems temporarily perfect. In the quiet of morning, with the birdsong outside, I'm at peace. A few moments of just being Nia, curled in a soft bed, before I throw myself into the lion's den again.

As I stretch out, a gentle, nervous tap sounds at the door. I close my eyes, inhale, and become Nia Vaillancourt, Prince Talan's chief mistress.

"Come in," I say.

The door opens, and my handmaid, Aisling, tiptoes inside. "Good morning, my lady. Should I give you a few more minutes of sleep?"

I've asked Aisling to wake me every morning as soon as the sun rises. Even if I'd love to stay in bed longer, I want to get some work done before the rest of the castle starts to stir. A dawn wakeup is an almost unheard-of request for the aristocracy of Brocéliande, but not quite so strange for a simple farmer.

"Thanks, Aisling. I'm getting up. The gods smile on those who rise with the sun."

She pushes through the door with a tea tray and slides it onto the table by my bed. Steam coils from the teapot. She tucks a strand of her auburn hair behind her ear. "They didn't tell me that you'd be rising this early, but I'm fine with that, of course." She sniffles, and I see that the tip of her freckled nose is red.

"Are you all right, Aisling?"

She nods and opens my wardrobe, then starts to rifle through the clothes for dresses. "Oh, well. Not really. My husband left me long ago. And I thought I'd found love again at last. Not that I even really wanted love again, but I wanted someone to talk to. And also I thought if we got married, I might be able to do something else with my life, you know? I guess I wanted something more…I always dreamed of living out in the countryside, learning how to paint. Not that I mind being here."

I understand how she feels. I used to feel trapped in a life of empty bank accounts and looking after my mom. "Maybe you don't need a partner for that. You never know when your life might take an unexpected turn."

Aisling's expression brightens, and she nods. "I suppose. Never mind. It's a nice day today, positively sunny. I've heard about the Dream Stalker…" She freezes, and her freckled cheeks flush bright red. "Apologies, my lady. He hates to be called that."

I shrug. "I won't tell him."

She relaxes, smiling at me. "I've heard it's connected to him. My daughter says His Highness controls the weather with his moods. Can you imagine that? All grown up now, she is, but she still doesn't know her arse from her elbow." She tuts, shaking her head.

"I haven't heard that one."

"Well, I told her nah, that's nonsense. First of all, the prince is never in a good mood, between you and me. Second, that's not how his magic works, is it? It's the Dream Stalk...you know. Dreams. And his tongue does magic things. Runs in the royal family, that one. The Royal House of Morgan. Magic tongues."

"His tongue—what?"

She nods vigorously. "He can cast enchantments with his tongue. Or is it his saliva? Haven't seen it, of course. It's not like I often get to see the prince's tongue. And he rarely does it, I suppose. He's more into killing. No offense."

"None taken."

She sets out my clothes as she talks. "Anyway, my daughter has all sorts of silly ideas. Listens to whatever the cook says because she saw the cook's bare chest once, and she can't stop thinking about his muscles. I said to her, Aela, I said, half the men in in Brocéliande have perfect chests. We're Fey. It's not like we're human. We have cheekbones too, you know? Not like humans. Do you know what they look like? I've seen one in a picture book. They're like a bloated toe with a face drawn on. Like a bowl of quince sauce with eyes. That's not us Fey. And do you know what else? I once caught the cook fondling the uncooked bread dough in a way that I would call...well, I would call it unsavory. I really would, with the look he had on his face. The way he violated that dough with his hands...and do you know what that lump of uncooked dough reminded me of? A human face, really. So, that's what he fancies, I imagine. Humans. Imagine that." She tuts and shakes her head, and a corkscrew curl dangles before her eyes.

I let her words wash over me as I sip from the tea. At first, Aisling's frequent word barrages made me dizzy. But slowly, I'd grown accustomed to them, until they became a crucial part of my morning wake-up process. Now, along with the strong tea, her stream of consciousness jump-starts my brain.

She sets out hot water next to my bed for me to wash my face and fluffs a fresh towel. "...and she told me, that's not a sea dragon, that's a whale. Can you imagine that, Nia? A grown woman talking about whales and other such myths? I'll go get your breakfast, my lady. Where will you be eating today?"

"I think I'll take breakfast down the hall at the balcony of the Barenton Tower in twenty minutes."

"Very well, my lady. I'll set it out there. There will be an execution today, so that's exciting."

My heart speeds up. "Of whom?"

She smiles brightly. "Traitors. Spies. People secretly working with the humans, even after everything they did to us. I won't be sorry to see them dealt with. We're lucky we have the King's Watch looking out for us. The humans and the demi-Fey caused the famine, you know."

I swallow hard, mastering control over my expression. "Oh. Did they find actual demi-Fey? How horrifying."

She shakes her head. "Gods, I hope not. I think Fey traitors. Who knows what the humans are paying them for their treachery? Get dressed, then. I'll bring your breakfast to the balcony."

She bustles out of the room.

I force myself out of bed at last and spend a few minutes washing in the sun-drenched bathroom. I pull on the dress Aisling left for me—a luxurious material, periwinkle with a pale silver bodice and bell sleeves. Then I sit down by the desk and pull a blank piece of paper from a drawer. I pour myself another cup of tea. Carefully, I write a coded message, summarizing everything I observed yesterday. I detail the new guard that joined the roster, the section in the eastern wall overgrown with vines, Count Cian's affair with his butler, and the change in the patrol route. Any detail I can think of to help plan the assassination.

Sipping my tea, I write in tiny letters, using a code that should be unbreakable, so I'm not doing this as quickly as I'd like. My encryption skills are still quite basic since I missed most of those classes during training. When I'm done writing, I finish the tea, then roll the paper to slide it up my dress sleeve. I pull on a blue cloak over my dress.

The moment I open the door, my shoulders tense a little. I never know when someone might be watching me here. As I stride through the empty halls, I keep scanning for movement, but I don't see anyone. Just the morning light washing over the stone floor, the cracks greened with moss, and the flowers that grow around the leaded windows—primrose and foxglove. I turn a corner, and a servant passes me carrying a fresh bouquet of flowers. He bows slightly as I pass.

When I peer out the window, my heart skips a beat. I take a step closer to the window, my breath clouding the glass. There, far below me, is a stone courtyard, where a large wooden platform has been set up. Ten metal blocks have been arranged on top of it, with curved indentations where necks will lie. My blood goes cold. Are these for real spies working with Avalon Tower?

Goosebumps spread over my skin.

I walk on, and reaching the balcony, I step out into the wintry air, hundreds of feet above the snow-dusted earth. My gaze flicks over the walls. Most of the city of Corbinelle spreads out to the west of here, so the view to the east is one of a landscape of frozen trees. The Paimpont River carves through the forest, and it widens to a lake with a metallic gleam, with mist coiling from its surface. It's serene today—the air chilly and crisp, the sunlight glinting off the snow like diamonds. I drop into a chair, with a heated brazier just by my side, warming the air. When my gaze flicks to the lake, I feel a sharp pang of homesickness for Avalon Tower.

The door creaks open behind me, and Aisling steps onto the balcony. She slides a tray onto the table in front of me—one with hot bread, tea, mead, and strawberries. "Here you are, my lady. I had the cook make more of those rosemary-seasoned rolls that you like. I kept an eye on him this time, made sure he wasn't doing anything untoward with the dough. You know, when I was a little girl, I used to dream about a giant bread roll the size of a house that I could live in."

"Oh?"

She stares out at the landscape. "I can see why you like this spot. It really is the most beautiful place in the castle."

"And it faces east," I say with a smile. "So sometimes, I think I can almost see my village from here."

"You poor thing. You must miss it so much."

"Oh, but I'm so lucky to be here, Aisling." Smiling, I start to butter one of the rolls.

Of course, the real reason for this spot isn't the gorgeous view or my supposed yearning for my home in Lauron. It's that from the Barenton balcony, I can see the main gate and one of the patrol routes. From this vantage point, I can make notes of everyone coming and going, and the different guards and their habits. On top of that, one of Auberon's tower bedroom windows is visible from here. So far, I've glimpsed him twice. All these things go into my daily reports for Avalon Tower.

By now, I've mapped every nook and cranny in the fortress—except for the prince's and the king's chambers. Mistress or not, I'm not allowed into either of their bedrooms, and I desperately need to find a way in.

Even more worrying, I've found no information about the war in Scotland. No mention of the Fey plans I'm supposed to uncover. Every day, thousands are dying in that war, and I can't learn a thing. We're running out of time.

"Well, enjoy your breakfast," Aisling chirps, and she leaves me alone on the balcony.

As I eat, I watch the guard shift change before the open gatehouse doors. I watch closely as a merchant passes through. While the guards are changing, they don't inspect him as they usually do.

Then I tense as a familiar figure strides along one of the lower bridges between the towers. He's so far away, I nearly miss him, but Talan has a strange way of catching the eye, as if he sucks in all the light around him. I stare as he descends a stairwell, heading for the courtyard, black cloak trailing behind him.

What's he doing up at this hour?

He crosses the courtyard, walking purposefully to a spot by the wall that I've already noted, one hidden by brambles and hedges. With the morning sun coming from the east, that area is cast in shadow. No one in the courtyard would see him as he stands there, waiting.

And it doesn't take long for me to see who he's waiting for.

A rider comes through the gate, dressed in the black jacket of a messenger—one of dozens that go through the fortress every day. He seems to be riding toward the closest stables, but he's not taking the most direct route. And as he passes Talan, he discreetly tosses a package to him. No, not a package—a crimson envelope. Talan slides it into his black cloak and stalks back toward the castle.

Why would a prince need to receive secret messages? Part of his plot against the king, I suppose.

I frown. Whatever he is up to, it is definitely worth reporting back to Avalon Tower.

I rise and brush the crumbs from my clothes.

With my new information stored away, I take the spiral stairs all the way down to the lowest level of the castle. A guard waits at the door, he follows me as I step into the courtyard.

My skin prickles. Whenever I leave the palace, someone follows me. Is it because Talan suspects me of lying, or is he trying to protect his secret weapon against the king?

I step outside, my boots crunching in the crisp snow. As I cross a hedge, I pretend to stumble. I let the parchment in my sleeve drop into my palm and quickly shove it under the thorny hedge. Then I rise, laughing awkwardly and brushing the snow from my cloak. I keep walking. One of Nivene's people will pick up the message and get it to her, and she'll take it to Avalon tonight.

As I turn back toward the castle, something shiny draws my eye, glinting in the sun.

Mordred's silver moth flutters over the snow in plain sight as I watch it, then flies away.

I pull my cloak more tightly around my shoulders.

My father wants to see me.

CHAPTER 21

I wait until the middle of the night to use the portal, slipping through the shadows of the courtyard. I've already figured out that when the gatehouse guards are changing shifts, they are the most distracted.

Under the starlight, I hurry over the cold earth, the icy wind nipping at my cheeks. I glance back at the castle, where almost all the lights are dark. Shadows pool in the empty courtyard. I hurry past the large willow tree to the portal's jagged stones. Glancing around me, I don't see a single person—just the vast expanse of wall and the vines climbing the stones, rustling in the wind.

Taking a deep breath, I step closer to the portal, its magic already vibrating over my body. A dark tear opens before me, and I plunge into it. I fall to the ground, the cold earth biting into my palms and my knees.

Looking up, I see Mordred standing before me, surrounded by the towering, carved dolmens of Avalon. Moonlight shines off his spiky crown. "There she is, the heir to the House of Morgan. Can you feel the heft of your ancient crown yet, weighing down your skull?"

I stand, brushing myself off. "I hope this is important. Nothing will give my cover away like popping in and out of a portal to chat to Auberon's mortal enemy."

"How sharper than a serpent's tooth it is to have a thankless child..."

"You've read Shakespeare?"

"Mmm. The first thing I do when a hundred years rolls around and I get my single day of freedom is to get my hands on as many books as possible."

"And the next thing you do is find the comfort of an American woman visiting England?"

"Something like that. And speaking of comfort, are you enjoying life in Castle Perillos? It looks luxurious to me. Those fine clothes. The banquet with dancing. Breakfast on the balcony. You'll want to stay longer, I wager."

When he said the words *banquet with dancing,* a slight edge slid through his soft tone.

My fingers tighten. "Absolutely not. As soon as Auberon and Talan are dead, I'm out of there. I really hope this is important. Can you get to the point?"

"I seem to remember that you wanted to bring your lover home to Avalon Tower."

Hope sparks in my chest. "Yes. He's not my lover anymore, but yes. Do you have any ideas about how to get him across the border?"

The wind whips at his dark cloak. "I have a way."

My heart skips a beat. "How?"

"Apparently, your *new* lover, the Dream Stalker, has a key to one of those gateways that Auberon's soldiers keep using. It can be used to transfer a few people from Brocéliande to Prydyn. Scotland, I suppose, as you know it these days. Auberon gave the key to him because he wanted the Dream Stalker to join his war against the humans. But Talan, being the conniving cunt that he is, avoided that."

I think it over. "So, how do I get the key from Talan?"

"It's in his room, in the top drawer of his desk."

"How do I know the key still works? I spent days on a mission in Bristol for one that was useless by the time we got our hands on it."

"It still works. Trust me."

Fatigue is making it hard for me to concentrate, but I try to sharpen my thoughts. "I can probably get into his room, but not without him knowing. And once he finds that the portal key is gone, he's going to know it was me."

"That's why I made this for you." Mordred pulls a silver bracelet from his pocket—one that looks very similar to the key we took from the officer in Bristol.

"This is an exact replica. It won't work, of course, but unless Prince Talan decides to go to Scotland after all, he'll never find out." He hands it to me.

I shove it into the pocket of my cloak. "What do you gain from this?"

"What I get from it is fulfilling the agreement I made. I help you get Raphael out, and you help me destroy Avalon Tower. Have you forgotten how bargains work? You're going to need to trust me."

I'd rather trust a scorpion. "Fine. I'll let you know if I manage to get the real key."

He smiles. "No need. I'll be watching."

"Okay. Is that everything?"

"No. I have a warning for you also. You met a viperous woman called Arwenna."

"I'm aware."

"She's going to try to kill you. She recently procured a deadly poison intended for your gullet."

My throat goes dry. "Ah. Maybe I went a bit too far with insulting her."

"See? I have done nothing but in care of thee." A smile flits over his lips. "And no, I don't think it has anything to do with your insults. She wants you dead because she wants to be Talan's wife. It's as simple as that."

"Any suggestions on how to avoid the poison?"

"So far, she is hesitant. She's worried that the poison will be traced back to her and she will lose her chance at marrying him. She needs to find someone in the kitchen she can bribe. I'll let you know when that happens."

Damn it. This is going to make it very hard to enjoy any food. "Thanks."

He glances up at the moon, and it gleams in his pale blue eyes. "Don't you ever wonder how this all came to be, Nia?"

"Why don't you just tell me things straight out?"

He meets my gaze. "Because manipulation is what being Fey is all about. If you'd been raised by me, you'd know that by now."

I narrow my eyes. "But it's more than that, isn't it? You want me to stay here as long as you can because you've been trapped here alone for fifteen centuries, planning a banquet that never happened, and you're desperate for company. All the Fey are gone from your court, and now you can only see the world pass by through your little spy moths. Now you must know how the Lady of Shalott felt, I suppose."

Starlight glints in his pale eyes as he stares down at me. "No, I do not, because she betrayed the Fey like Merlin did, and it's my job to avenge the dead. We are nothing alike. And that is why you need to know how this all came to be."

"What do you mean, she betrayed the Fey?"

"She never wanted me to go to war with Arthur. She refused to raise her Shalott army to help me, even though together, we could have changed the tide of the war. We could have won. So, Mother went with only the Avalon warriors. And what was she supposed to do? We had no other choice. Arthur wanted to take over Avalon. Merlin wanted Morgan's throne for himself. I managed to kill Arthur, Guinevere, some of the others in Lothian Tower, but it wasn't enough while Merlin still lived. He hunted Mother and me down, and the real battle began. He destroyed everyone in the House of Morgan except me. I was too strong for him."

"Are they all dead?" I ask quietly.

"I assume so. And during these centuries, I've been planning to slaughter the House of Merlin, to wash Avalon in their blood. I refused to let a scion of Merlin sit on my throne, pretending to be the true king. But Merlin, that covetous prick, trapped me here and created Brocéliande. He hid his cowardly son from my wrath, hid all their court. They tricked the Fey into believing Auberon was their true king, and now Auberon rules as a usurper in his own false kingdom. A pretender on the throne. Nimuë, Lady of the Lake, couldn't forgive Merlin. So, we all ended up trapped in the end, didn't we?"

I rub my eyes. "Okay, that's enough history for tonight. Is there anything else urgent you've seen in the spy moths?"

"From the moth in Avalon Tower, I've learned that the Pendragons' machinations involve devising some sort of new weapon they plan to deploy against Auberon's armies."

My eyebrows flick up. "Well, I have no issues with that. Anything else?"

He sighs. "Yes. Perhaps this is something you will care about. Your friends in Avalon Tower will taste the bitter draught of betrayal soon. Do you have issues with *that*?"

A chill runs up my spine. "What do you mean?"

"Those demi-Fey in your room? Tana and...Serana? And that Darius fellow. Too bad about what's going to happen."

My heart pounds harder, and I take a step closer. "What's going to happen?"

He clicks his tongue. "The Pendragons are planning a night of terror. Tonight. Assassins in the dark. Anyone they see as an enemy, and that's anyone with Fey blood. Your friends assume they're safe in their tower room. They're wrong."

My breath shallows. "Why didn't you tell me this as soon as I got here? I have to warn them." Without another thought, I'm turning to rush back to the lake's shore.

Mordred grabs my arm, his fingers tightening on my bicep. "If you don't go back to your room in Brocéliande, your cover will be unmasked. And then what will happen? You'll end up on one of those little execution blocks."

I look up at the moon. "I have a few hours. I can get there and back in time."

"That little freckled maid will find you missing from your bedchamber at dawn."

"Mordred. I *need* to warn them." I tug my arm free. "You knew I would as soon as you told me."

Mordred glances over my shoulder, and a distant look crosses his blue eyes. "Perhaps I was hoping to see if you were made of stronger stuff. Sometimes sacrifices have to be made. But no, so easily you cast everything away into the cold winds."

"Yeah, well, I'm happy to say I'm not you." I look around the empty, barren space. "Perhaps if *you* were less like yourself, you wouldn't end your life so alone." At that, I turn and start running. I have just about six hours to row the boat to Avalon, warn my friends, and get back.

CHAPTER 22

As I run up the stairs of Lothian Tower, my lungs are screaming. My asthma is always much worse in the winter during physical exertion. I've grown complacent because it doesn't seem to bother me in Brocéliande.

But tonight, after I rowed across the lake, then ran upward through the streets of Camelot and up several flights of steps, I'm wheezing, gasping. The anxiety isn't helping, either. *Please don't let me be late. Please don't let me be late.*

There's no Iron Legion cadet standing guard against the nefarious demi-Fey in the Astolat Atrium, and I take that as a bad sign. Someone called them off. Is that because there's no more need to spy on these demi-Fey?

Please don't let me be late.

I reach the door to our room and slam into it, tumbling inside. I half-expect to find my friends with their throats slit, but to my relief, the first sound that welcomes me to the room is Serana's snores.

Tana sits up in her bed, her hair frazzled, eyes blinking in confusion. "Nia?" she mutters sleepily.

"Quick," I blurt, breathing hard. My lungs are shrieking with every breath, sounding like a broken whistle. "The…key…we…must…lock…" I can't keep talking, my head is spinning. I stumble to my nightstand and fling the drawer open, hoping to find my extra inhaler still in it. Instead, I find three combs, a book titled *Vampires Stay Hard,* and glitter eyeliner. I blink, gasping for breath.

Someone sits up in my bed. I draw my knife, ready to fight.

"Nia!" Darius says.

"Darius." I exhale. "What are you doing here?"

"Sorry," he says. "I didn't want to stay in my own room. The atmosphere is getting *very* hostile, so I figured since you're gone, I could bunk here a few days."

"Where…my…stuff…"

He opens the second drawer in the nightstand, and I rummage in it, finding the inhaler. I put it to my mouth, taking two deep puffs and drawing them into my lungs.

"Lock the door," I blurt, still half out of breath. "Assassins coming."

"What's going on?" Serana mumbles, rubbing her eyes. "What are you doing here, Nia?"

Darius, to his credit, functions much better when awakened. He leaps out of bed and scrambles to find the room key underneath a bunch of Serana's things. Within seconds, he's at the door, turning it in the lock.

I clutch my inhaler to my chest. "I've come to warn you. The Iron Legion is attacking tonight. Targeting all demi-Fey in the tower. What other demi-Fey do we need to warn?"

"No one," Tana says. "Apart from us, they're all in Scotland. Viviane is in Ireland, preparing a backup base of operations."

"Oh," I say, feeling ill.

That's why the Iron Legion chose to strike today. Just three demi-Fey to take down—easy to overcome, but a terrifying message to the rest.

"How did you get this information, Nia?" Serana asks. "I thought you were in Brocéliande."

"I was."

Darius frowns. "So how did you get a warning about the Iron Legion?"

Mordred's Hemlock Oath has me limited in how much I can tell them. "It doesn't matter. The point is, they're coming."

Serana stares at me. "Was it Mordred?"

Darius shakes his head. "But how would *he* know what's happening at Avalon Tower? He can't leave Avalon."

I'm not about to drop dead from the oath just to fill them in. "It was a source I trust for information. That's all I can say."

"It doesn't matter," Tana says. And for just a second, I

see her glancing at my palm, where a trace of the scar from the Hemlock Oath is still visible.

Serana turns to her weapons chest and flings it open. She pulls out a curved blade and swings it twice.

"Here." Tana walks over to me and hands me a water bottle. "Drink. You look like you ran all the way from Brocéliande."

"I sort of did." I take a long swig to find that it's cold jasmine tea, Tana's drink of choice. Right now, it feels like heaven.

"Darius, axe or sword?" Serana asks, sticking a knife in her belt.

"Do you have that nice blade that I gave you for your birthday?" Darius asks.

"No, it's at the blacksmith's. I wanted the pommel adjusted."

"What's wrong with the pommel?"

Serana's red hair gleams in the moonlight. "Nothing, I just like them bigger."

"It's not the pommel's size that matters, it's—"

"Hello!" I say. "Assassins, remember?"

"Give me an axe," Darius says sulkily.

Serana throws him an axe, and he deftly catches it in one hand and twirls it.

"Nia? Are you armed?" Serana asks.

"I just have a dagger."

"Here." She hands me the curved blade.

"You don't need it?" I ask.

She pulls out two nasty-looking maces and grins at me. "I feel like breaking some bones."

"I think I'm going to hang back for this one," says Tana. "But I'll cheer you on."

"You do that, hon." Serana eyes the door.

"That's much appreciated." I smile at her.

All of us stand, prepared.

"When, exactly, are they coming, Nia?" Serana says.

"I don't know. Sometime during the night."

"And you're sure it's tonight they're coming?"

I hesitate. "Pretty sure."

"Because if we wait here awake all night like twats and nothing happens, I'm going to feel a bit miffed."

"I can't be—"

The door handle starts turning slowly, and all of us fall silent, tensing. I hold my breath. The door shudders.

"It's locked," someone says outside.

"Never mind," another voice answers. "Those old locks won't withstand a few kicks."

Darius glances at me, the grip on his axe tightening.

"Ready?" the voice from outside says.

A second later, the door thumps and shudders. Then it booms again. Before it happens a third time, Serana smoothly turns the key in the lock and yanks the door open.

A masked man stumbles forward into the room, the open door catching him by surprise. Serana's mace whooshes, slamming into his arm with a sickening crunch. He screams, and a second man follows him through the door. I hurl one of my knives at him. It sinks into his side, and he staggers, falling back.

By then, three more men barge inside, one of them hurling himself at Darius. Serana is fighting another, her maces flashing as she swings them. The third guy tries to catch her from behind, and I sink my sword into his thigh. He screeches in pain, tumbling to the floor.

Darius manages to disarm the guy who's fighting him, but another man leaps at him, stabbing him with a nasty knife. Darius grunts, falling back. He's clutching his side, tumbling to his knees.

In a fury, Tana screeches, throwing a teapot at the man. She follows it with a barrage of teacups, all shattering.

And then, just as suddenly as they came, they retreat, falling over themselves to get out of the room. They drag one of their wounded away, kicking the door shut as they go. Serana is ready to run after them, but I grab her arm. "Darius," I say.

"Right." Her eyes flash, and she turns around, rushing to Darius.

He's in the fetal position now, grabbing his side. Tana kneels next to him, and she rolls up his blood-soaked shirt. I'm relieved to see it looks like a shallow gash.

"I don't think it's too bad," Darius says, wincing with pain. "Ugh. I shouldn't have let him get me like that."

"You were fighting two of them." Serana yanks open her desk drawer and pulls out a first aid kit.

"They fought hard to get all of their friends away," I say.

"Of course," Tana says grimly. "They didn't want one of them caught and interrogated."

"Well, keep an eye out for a bunch of Iron Legion assholes limping tomorrow," I say.

"Nice moves with your blades, Nia," Serana says, dabbing Darius's cut with alcohol. "Hard to believe you're the same girl who showed up here less than a year ago."

"It wasn't as good as Tana's teapot maneuver."

"She's the legendary Teapot Dame," Serana says. "Sworn to strike down villains with her kettle and cups."

"You can laugh, but if the tea in that pot was hot, his face would have melted off," Tana points out.

"Who's laughing?" Serana says. "Tomorrow, I want you to start teaching me all you know in the dark arts of tea violence."

I grin, breathing out a sigh of relief that we made it relatively unscathed. No matter what Mordred said, coming here was the right call.

I glance at Darius as Serana sews his wound closed. It'll leave a scar, but he'll recover. Running a hand through my hair, I say, "I can't stay. I have to get back to Brocéliande before my maidservant notices I'm gone."

"Ooooh," says Serana in a high-pitched, fake posh voice. "My *maidservant*."

Tana's eyes shine as she touches my shoulder. She

leans in closer, whispering, "Watch your back. The cards show me endless danger for you."

I pull back and smile at her, trying to look as if this doesn't rattle me. "Endless danger? Must be Wednesday."

* * *

As I'm taking the stairs back down to my boat, I hear wild, raucous laughter coming from one of the common rooms. There's only one person whose laughter sounds like a braying hyena.

Tarquin.

I stop dead in the middle of the hall. I should be running outside, but I'm certain Tarquin was behind that attack.

I pivot and march through the torchlit hall to the common room. I push it open and hide in the atrium, where a red velvet curtain shields me from their view.

When I peer around the corner, I see them. Tarquin, Horatio, and a bunch of their lackeys sit at an oak table, several empty wine bottles between them. Torchlight wavers over their drunken faces and the stacks of books all around them.

"I'd fuck the tall one," Tarquin says. "What's her name? Serana? Yeah, I bet she's proper filthy. You can just tell, can't you? She's into proper weird stuff."

"She looks like a biter." Horatio guffaws. "I'd go with

the creepy one. The one who acts like she knows the future. Bet she takes it up the khyber."

"I bet she'd see syphilis in her future if she took you up on that, mate," Tarquin says.

A bunch of their friends jeer and make fun of Horatio.

"Well, I suppose it doesn't matter anymore, does it?" Tarquin says. "That ship has sailed. No one will be taking any of them up anything."

My jaw tightens. With every moment, with every word from their lips, I'm feeling fonder of Mordred's goal. *Kill the Pendragons.*

It's not so mad after all, is it?

"Why has that ship sailed?" a drunken female voice calls from the other side of the room. "Did they leave?"

"Oh, yes." Tarquin laughs. "They left."

There's something familiar in the woman's voice, and I shift a bit closer so I can see her in the shadows.

My heart sinks.

It's Mom.

Dressed in a bright pink sundress that makes no sense in winter, her face flushed to match it, she leans against one of the Iron Legion goons, eyes glazed. She's smiling that smile she wears when she wants to placate a guy.

"Hey, Brandy," Tarquin says. "Do that bit again. From the movie you played in."

"Oh, you boys have heard it so many times." My mom giggles.

"It's always so cool to hear it again. You know what big fans we are of your film."

My throat is dry. When she was young, back in the eighties, mom was an actress in one film. That was back when electronics worked, of course. It was some sort of comedy. She made me watch it a bunch of times. It was terrible, but Mom always mentioned it to everyone. Her fifteen minutes of glory.

Now, my mom stands up, and to my absolute horror, mimes as if she's showering, washing her hair. Then she turns around, her eyes widening. She covers her chest. "Why, Jason," she says, her voice slurred from the drink. "I didn't know you were here."

And Tarquin, Horatio, and two other guys all shout the next line together: "Well, what would you do if you did know?"

Mom gives them a lopsided grin. "Oh, you boys. You're terrible."

They all laugh hysterically, and Mom laughs with them.

"You're so much fun, Brandy," Tarquin says. "I can see where Nia gets all of her qualities."

At that, more of them laugh.

I stumble out of the common room and find my way outside to the cold air. Once I do, I promptly throw up all over the grass.

It's clear that this is not the first time my mom has spent her time hanging out with the Iron Legion. And it's clear why they're keeping her around: Nia's mother, the great joke. I should never have left Camelot with her still here.

I force myself to walk toward the boat, out by Nimue's Tower.

As I cross the bridge, I can hear their laughter echoing in my thoughts, and I wipe a tear from my cheek.

Tarquin has no idea what's coming for him.

* * *

MY BODY SHAKES with exhaustion as I stumble through the portal back to Brocéliande. I wait, crouched by the wall, until the coast is clear. As luck would have it, it doesn't take long.

I hurry across the snowy courtyard, pulling my cloak tightly around me.

The sun is rising already, a rosy blush spreading over the kingdom. I'm late. Too late. Aisling will have knocked on my door by now. She'll have entered the room and seen the empty bed.

But I push that thought away. No point worrying about it unless she's suspicious.

My breath puffs around me as I hurry across the snow, and I reach my tower. I dash up the stairs, then stride through the hallways to my room.

When I reach my bedroom, I find the door slightly open, and my stomach sinks.

I step inside silently to find that Aisling is standing

by the bed, the tea tray in her hands. She turns to look at me, and my mind whirrs. "And where were you, my lady?"

Time slows down.

I know what Nivene would do. A quick stab to the throat, and she'd be gone. A loose end tied up. It's the best course of action. Anything else would place me in a problematic position.

I smile. "I woke up early and went for a long walk in the gardens."

She frowns, eying me, my disheveled clothes, my flushed face. "It must have been a very long walk, my lady."

And there it is—the tinge of suspicion.

I look at her and force myself to think about Tarquin and my mother. About the attack on my friends. About Mordred's warning of Arwenna's poison. Of all the people dying in Scotland because I still haven't provided any useful intel about the war. About Raphael's crushing rejection. My chin trembles, a tear trickling from my eye.

"Oh, my lady, what's wrong?"

"It's just..." I say with a choked voice. "It's been so difficult. I know it's stupid, you see me in this gorgeous bedroom, with all these clothes, and amazing food, and with you looking after my every need. And of course, I'm grateful. But...I just feel so lonely here. Without my friends. Without my father. I don't know if you realize, but the women here don't really like me very much. And

I woke up in the middle of the night, and I just couldn't sleep, and I needed to get out, and..." By now, I'm sniffling, my voice cracking, tears streaming.

"Oh, my poor girl!" Aisling wraps me in a hug. "It'll all be alright. Here, get back into bed. I'll go get you some fresh breakfast. Maybe you should stay in bed and rest for a bit today."

I pull off my cloak. "Thank you, Aisling. You're taking such good care of me."

"Think nothing of it, love. You just rest, okay?"

"Okay," I say meekly, curling under the blanket.

But rest is far from my mind. If tonight's taught me anything, it's that I haven't been working hard enough. I need to start making riskier moves, getting more information faster.

And it begins with getting closer to Talan.

CHAPTER 23

I stalk the halls of Perillos, dusky light radiating through the windows in shades of molten gold kissed with rose. If I'm going to get into Talan's room, this is the time of day to do it. I sift through my memories for all the thoughts I've overheard from him.

In the somber, dusky veil of twilight, light withers to mortal hues. Silence enshrouds me, and I'm buried in ashen grey. The burning sun, snuffed out like a life cut short...

His thoughts can be strange, nearly impenetrable, but they give me a sense of him. Twilight can be beautiful, but it always feels like a lonely time to me, when the daylight starts to die. I remember it being worst on Sunday nights, for some reason, when the sun started to set. It was always such a sorrowful feeling of having missed out on fun, a certainty that I'd spent too much time alone, that I'd be headed into another day of corrosive loneliness at school, where I always seemed to say the wrong thing or wear the wrong thing...

So, even if his thoughts were wrapped in strange phrases, I understood him.

Outside Talan's room, an armored soldier stands in the hall, gripping a pike—a member of the King's Watch. I take a deep breath and try to look serene. As I near the sentry, I summon the image of the veil in my mind, feeling its power hum over my skin. My protection from Talan's invasive magic.

The guard glares and shifts his position to block me. "Is the prince expecting you?"

I put my hand to my chest. "I'm his chief mistress. Of course he is."

Everything about the guard is silver—his armor, his eyes, his long hair. He peers down at me. "Are you the one from Lauron?"

"What do you mean, 'the one from Lauron'? How many mistresses does he have?"

"It's just that I'm from Lauron," he says softly, "and I've never seen you."

My blood runs cold. "Well, we were at the outskirts of town."

He narrows his pale eyes. "And your accent." He speaks slowly. "It's not quite right for a Lauron farm girl, is it?"

My heart slams. "Is it really your place to question the prince's chosen?"

His gaze sweeps down my body. "It is my job to protect the king and his family, so yes. What do you have on you?"

I look down at my dress—the sheer, pale blue cloth, the gold embroidery, the lace in just the right places to hide everything. "What could I possibly have on me?"

The truth is, I *do* have something on me—the replica key wrapped around my wrist. And I don't want this guard going anywhere near it.

His jaw clenches. "I'll search you before you go in."

"Do you really think the prince wants you touching his mistress?"

"As I said, my job is to protect him. And something isn't right about you."

I swallow hard. "Oh, forget it. I'm not letting *you* touch me. The prince will hear of this." I turn to walk away from him, and he grabs my arm. "Get your hand off me," I snap.

But his grip is iron. He's hostile, suspicious, and I need to change his perception. So, when he yanks me, I let go and topple backward onto the floor. Agony shoots through my wrist, and I grunt with the pain, which is quite real. "Why are you hurting me?"

"I didn't mean to." His face blanches. Good. His fear and guilt are already clouding his mind.

The door swings open, and Talan leans against the doorway, his hair looking tousled. "And what, pray tell, is going on here? Did you hurt my mistress?"

My mind races. I have to take control of this situation. I need to control the narrative, to make sure that Talan finds out only the information I want him to hear.

"Your Highness—" the guard begins.

"He says he suspects me," I cut in, rubbing my throbbing wrist. "He suspects me of not really being in love with you. He thinks I'm a fraud, apparently, and that our relationship is a sham."

From the floor, I shoot Talan an expression that says, *He's found us out.* As if we're together in the guard's suspicion.

Talan turns to the guard and raises his black eyebrows. "And you hurt her?"

"I didn't mean to. I just don't think she's who she says she is," the guard stammers.

Slowly, I stand, still cradling my injured wrist. "He's threatening to report me to the king for being a fake."

I know the reaction this will get.

Talan acts swiftly. In a blur of movement, his dagger arcs through the air. The guard grabs his neck, his blood spilling onto the flagstones. I step back, my heart racing, and stare down at the guard as he bleeds out. My legs feel weak, and my head is clouded. Guilt carves through me. The man was only doing his job, like I was doing mine. And unfortunately for me, he was fucking good at his job. But it was either him or me, and if I'd let this conversation take its natural course, I'd be the one bleeding on the floor.

I look up at Talan, my mouth going dry. For the

briefest of moments, I see something unexpected on his face. Is it regret? Guilt? But before I can make sense of it, his expression settles into a mask of cool composure. Sheathing his dagger, he brushes his dark hair away from his face. "He belonged to the King's Watch. He was good at his job. But that's the problem, isn't it? I can't have someone good at his job watching me, informing on me. I need an idiot as my sergeant-at-arms. Now he's a problem I no longer have."

The expression he shoots me is ice-cold.

I swallow. "Right."

"Guards!" he calls.

At the far end of the hall, two guards hurry around the corner. They stop to stare open-mouthed at the body at the end of the hall, watching the man's blood run in rivulets between the flagstones.

"Get someone to clean this up," Talan says. "And I'll need a new sergeant-at-arms, one who will not treat my mistress as if she's some sort of criminal." He leans against the doorframe and folds his arm, a ghost of a smile playing over his lips. "What brings my mistress here, exactly? And did my chivalrous protection elevate me above 'murderous pig-shagger' in your estimation?"

My mouth opens and closes. This is not how I'd expected this to happen. I stare down at the guard's body. "I've quite forgotten why I came."

He opens the door to his room and steps inside, pausing to look back at me. Sunlight from the windows behind him gilds his dark, tousled hair and outlines his broad shoulders. "Are you coming in, then?"

Silently, I follow him, and he closes the door behind me.

Once inside the huge room, he leans against a column and gives me a wry smile. "How may I be of service, my faithful mistress?"

I try to remember the little speech I'd prepared, the one I'd gleaned from his thoughts. "Nivene isn't around, and everything is so quiet. I've spent too much time in my room by myself." I shrug. "Maybe I don't like to be alone at dusk, is all."

"And here I thought you felt nothing but disdain for me." His voice is a quiet, silken drawl as he steps closer. "Are you after something from me, love? The sweet release of a lover's touch, a night's solace in my bed, to scream my name for real this time? That's usually why women show up at my door, but I can't say that grim spectacle was the best start to the evening."

My heart stutters.

Fuck. I've been thrown off guard already. I need to reflect his own thoughts back at him. "No, it's just that I wanted some company. It's a feeling I get when the sun is setting, when the dying light fades to a mortal pallor. It reminds me of the intense solitude a person must feel in their final breaths, when someone is alone with their pain."

A line forms between his eyebrows. "Oddly enough, I

know exactly what you mean. Have a seat. I'm pouring myself wine, if you want some."

I follow him across the vast, vaulted chamber, my heart beating faster. Light spills from arched windows onto a four-poster bed made of twisting, gnarled dark wood. The blankets on the bed are a velvety purple. A table and two chairs stand beneath the windows.

He crosses to a mahogany desk and uncorks a bottle of wine.

I glance up at a stained glass rose window. It's an ouroboros—a serpentine dragon eating its own tail, a symbol of creation and destruction. This is Talan's sigil, and it is strangely fitting for him.

A tapestry hangs on one of the walls, depicting a dark, snaking river with weeping willow trees drooping into the water.

"That's beautiful," I say as he hands me a glass of claret.

He glances up at the window. "That's the drowned Isle of Shallott."

My eyebrows flick up. I'm still trying to reorganize my thoughts, to compose myself after everything went so badly awry. I'm trying not to think about how this lovely claret looks like the blood of the man Talan just killed. I take a sip of the wine and relax a little. It's heaven, in fact—berries and oak infused with sunlight.

The light catches Talan's eyes. They are dark as ebony, but at this angle, I can see a vibrant ring of copper around the iris. How did I never notice that copper before?

"Why did you choose Shallott to hang on your wall?" I ask.

"That's where my mother was from, before the isle was drowned in the human war."

My curiosity sparks. "All the way out in Lauron, we don't really hear that much about what happens at court. I never heard about your mother."

When he looks at me again, the copper is dazzling. "She died a long time ago. They say a demi-Fey turned her in to the King's Watch, trying to curry favor with my father."

I swallow hard. "Is that why you hate humans so much?"

He's studying me closely, and my breath catches. "Tell me, Nia, why can't I see into your dreams? I can't get in your head at all."

As he speaks, I feel his magic prodding at the edges of my mind, trying to look for a weakness, a serpent's fang of power nudging at my thoughts. I clench my teeth and fight to stay in control. There's danger in the intensity of his gaze, and I stare out the windows at the mossy walls surrounding the castle. "I have no idea, Talan. I don't know how your power works."

I turn back to see him sipping his wine. He's wearing a black, short-sleeves shirt, baring the skin of his lower arms. A tattoo twists up one forearm and over his bicep, disappearing into his shirt. Thorny vines, I think, that reach all the way up to his throat, stopping just below his chin. No, not vines, I realize, leaves of a willow branch, drawn to look sharp.

He's standing so casually, so relaxed, but he's still trying to break into my mind, and I can feel my defenses about to shatter like glass.

CHAPTER 24

I swallow hard. Agony shoots up my wrist from my earlier fall. It's difficult to protect myself from his magic when I'm in pain, but I have to pretend that everything is fine. The Fey heal quickly—well, the *real* Fey.

I need to distract him.

Stepping closer to him, I trace the path of his tattoo with the tip of my finger, inhaling his masculine scent. "A willow branch. Are they in Shalott, too? Because they're in the tapestry."

His full lips part. "So I've been told. They're on my family crest. Not Auberon's, but my mother's side. When Mordred trapped her in the tower of Camelot, they say the willows in Shallott turned bone-white with sorrow."

My finger pauses. "And she died here, in Brocéliande?"

"Executed. Burned at the stake." His eyes narrow, and his thick eyelashes cast shadows on his cheeks. "For spying."

My breath goes quiet in my lungs, and I pull my hand away from him. I can't stay here long. I was hoping to find a way to sneak back in later when he isn't around, but I don't see any other doors leading into the room except the main one, and we're far too high up for me to climb in through the window.

I need to get him to leave me alone in here so I can rifle through his things.

I glance at his desk, where books lay open on a stack of papers, and lean against a windowsill. "So, do you have the night off from torturing?"

He scoffs. "I'm bored of using the rack. The screaming gets on my nerves sometimes. So high-pitched, the way they shriek."

I swallow hard. I *think* he's joking, but I can't be sure.

I raise my glass and smile coyly. "Well, congratulations. You continue to be the worst person I know."

"Do I get a prize for this honor?"

I rack my brain for something—anything that I overheard in his thoughts that might give me a second alone.

...the taut cherry skin yields as my teeth pierce it, and the tart flavor bursts over my tongue. Cherries and cream, the nectar of the gods when the rest of the day has left me wanting...

Someone special to him used to bring them to him, and now he loves them.

I lick my lips. "I think you deserve a prize, yes. When I was little, before the famine, if we did something worthy of celebrating, my big sister used to bring cherries for me."

He takes a step closer, the copper in his eyes ignited in the dying sunlight. "I adore cherries."

He takes another sip of his wine, eyeing me over the rim of his glass. I have the faintest inkling that he likes having me here.

"Give me a moment." He turns and crosses to the door.

He steps outside, and I can hear him talking faintly to the new sergeant-at-arms.

I hurry to the window and examine the latch up close so that I can describe it later in my report to Avalon Tower. If the assassin can find a way to climb up here, he'll have to figure out how to unlatch this. Unfortunately, it doesn't look possible. The windows lock from the inside.

I pivot and rush over to his desk, my heart slamming against my ribs, and open the top drawer. Just as Mordred told me, the gateway key is inside, along with some parchments, a container of ink, several quills, and a wicked-looking dagger with a few drops of dried blood on it. I slip the replica key from my pocket and switch it with the real key. My blood roars in my ears. If he catches me—

From the other side of the door, I hear the guards

obsequiously pleading with Talan to let them remain at their posts. I *think* I hear him curtly say he will find a servant, then footsteps moving away from the room.

I have a few more seconds, and something draws my eye. Underneath a pile of papers, I notice the corner of a crimson envelope—the letter Talan collected early that morning. The secret message.

I should leave it alone. I should just be happy with the key, and yet…I won't get another chance like this.

I slip the envelope out of the stack, making a mental note of its exact position. With relief, I see that the seal is already broken. I open it and take the pages out. The first page looks like an architectural plan of some sort. My pulse is racing so fast, I can hardly concentrate, as part of my brain is still wondering what sort of horrific fate awaits me if I'm caught. What I find is a series of stone towers and buildings surrounded by a stone wall. A fortress, maybe. A river runs into the fortress itself and seems to flow into a cavern labelled WATER MILL. I scrutinize the diagram for a few seconds, memorizing it as best as I can, then flip to the next page.

Is this an accounting report? There's a list of supplies and their prices. And at the top of the page, it says BLUE DRAGON PROJECT. My jaw drops.

Those are the words Lord Ael said just before Talan killed him. This must be *why* Talan killed him. Not because he was a traitor, but because he was about to tell the world about…whatever this is. Is this related to the secret strategy in the war in Scotland? And if so, why is he keeping it secret from Auberon?

I'm about to flip to the next page when I hear rapid footfalls in the hall and the sound of male voices. Quickly, I slide the papers inside the envelope and shove it back where it was, then hurry to the window. The door opens as I pick up my wine again and casually take a sip, and Talan saunters inside, a lock of his hair falling in front of his eyes. Moving at a languid pace, he drops into an armchair as a blond servant bustles into the room, carrying a tray of cherries and cream. She is sweating, and a few strands of damp hair cling to her pink cheeks.

Talan gestures for me to sit, and I ease into a chair next to him.

"Your Highness," the servant stammers, sliding the tray onto the table.

"This is my reward, Nyfa, for being the worst person in the world," he says to her. "Everyone needs one area to really stand out in, don't you think?" He plucks a cherry from the bowl. "And every kingdom needs a torturer. Is it my fault that I happen to be good at it?"

"No, Your Highness."

"Do you think I'm the worst person you've ever met, Nyfa?"

She pales and shakes her head. "No, Your Highness."

His eyes glint with amusement. "But Nyfa, your dreams say that I'm a sadist. And they say that you like it, too."

I glare at him. "Stop tormenting the poor girl. She just brought you cherries."

"You may leave us, Nyfa."

She bows, and I glance at the desk. My heart skips a beat as I realize I haven't put the envelope back in exactly the right place.

Nyfa practically runs from the room, and the door slams behind her.

And there it is again, the feel of silk wrapping around me and the sharp edge of his magic trying to penetrate my thoughts. "It's like there's a barrier inside your skull. It's intriguing."

I grab a cherry from the bowl. "Maybe there's nothing in there. Maybe my mind is empty."

"I doubt that very much." He leans over the table. "In fact, I feel like you're hiding something from me. I'm not getting the real Nia. Tell me something that is actually true about yourself."

"And what about the real Talan? Do you spend your days torturing people, or are those just rumors you play along with?"

"Nice deflection. Tell me a true thing about yourself. And just to warn you, if I'm paying close enough attention, I can tell if someone is lying."

I take a deep breath, realizing the brilliance of Meriadec's directives. *Keep it all as close to the truth as possible.* He'd already set me up for this.

So, I look into Talan's blazing copper-ringed eyes and tell him something true. "I always wanted a family like other people had. A dad who read books to me in bed, or a mom who made sure I had what I needed. Someone who'd wake up at night when I was sick instead of letting me look after myself. I wanted them to clean up after *me* when I vomited and not the other way around. I wanted someone who was always there so I didn't have to wonder how long I'd be alone..." I swallow hard, as I realize I'm straying too far into my own life. I sigh and give him a small smile. "But we get the family we get, don't we?"

He inhales sharply and twirls his wineglass. "Well, Nia, that is certainly true. And what happened to your man with the cheap velvet suit? Why didn't you make a family with him, like other people?"

"He left me for a singer." Also true.

"So, the man is a fucking idiot. Would you like me to torture him to death? I would use the rack again, if it made you happy."

I blink. "I believe his own music is torture enough."

Talan gives me a smile that steals my breath for a moment, but it fades. "You told me a true thing, and now it's my turn. No, I don't go into the dungeons. I don't need to torment people physically to get what I want. I kill them, if it suits me, but I've never seen a rack in my life, nor do I want to. Why use such a brutal instrument? I can invade people's dreams and make them feel the most exquisite pain in their minds—or pleasure, depending."

"Okay. But I told you two truths. One about my ex,

and one about my family. Tell me another thing," I venture. "Who was your mother spying for?"

His expression is inscrutable, and he gives me a casual shrug. "They say she never fell out of love with Mordred. That she was always trying to find him. She believed he never died. They say that he was truly our worst enemy, that he had made claims to the throne. That's what they say. But that was a long time ago, when I was too young..." His gaze shutters, and he seems to collect himself. "Anyway, not to worry. You might loathe me, but you are mine now, and if anyone tried to burn you at the stake, I'd make them wish they were never born."

I finish the last drop of wine in my glass and know I need to leave. If I don't, my nervous glances at his desk will give me away.

I slide the empty glass onto his table. "Well, thank you for entertaining me while the sun went down. I'll leave you on your own now."

I stand to leave, desperately hoping he never notices that little shift of the envelope.

"Nia." Talan's soft voice stops me, and he stands. "I can see from the way you are holding your arm that your wrist is hurt."

My heart slams hard, and I wonder if he'll realize I'm not healing as quickly as I should. I shrug. "I just fell on it badly. Maybe twisted something. It will be better in no time."

"I can heal it."

"How?"

He holds out his hand. "Give it to me."

My breath is still shaky as I rest my wrist in his hand. He traces his fingertips over it, a line etched between his eyebrows. Then he glances up at me. "I heal with my mouth."

"Sure. Whatever it takes."

He brings my wrist to his lips and kisses my skin.

A hot shiver runs through me as he runs his tongue over the place where it hurts. The sharp pain softens into pleasure, and as his tongue laves my skin, I'm no longer thinking about who he is. No longer able to think of anything except the way his mouth feels on me.

There's obviously more to his magic than just healing, because as his tongue moves over me, a sensual heat pulses between my thighs. My nipples peak under my dress, and molten heat slides through me. Part of me wants to yank my arm away from him, to stop this pulsing of warmth in my core. But I'm transfixed, my breath becoming shallow as I imagine him kissing my hips, stroking me. Murderous prince or not, I can't stop thinking about how it would feel for him to spread my thighs and kiss...

With a racing heart, I pull my arm away. "It's fine now." My cheeks are hot, and my breath comes in rapid little gasps.

Surprise flickers in his eyes. "Are you sure? Because your heart is beating wildly out of control, and you sound breathless."

He's fucking with me. Of course he's fucking with me. "I'm fine."

His gaze dips to my breasts, and one of his hands clenches into a fist. I look down to see my headlights on, high beams in action, and I fold my arms in front of my chest. Jasper doesn't really do bras.

A sensual smile curls the prince's lips as he looks into my eyes. "You can stay longer, if you like."

I turn to the door. The pain in my wrist is gone now. "I'll see you later, Talan."

When I glance back, I find his eyes locked on me. "How strange. I like the way it sounds when you say my name."

"When do I need to see you again? For the purposes of our fake relationship?"

"Tomorrow, actually. I want you to join me at the High Council. I don't need your particular skillset just then, but I want you to know who everyone is."

I do my best to look unimpressed. Bored, even. But inside, I cannot believe I'm about to go into the heart of their government, to find out exactly how the Fey operate. Nivene, Viviane, and even Mordred were right: coming here as Talan's fake mistress was absolutely an opportunity I couldn't pass up. None of us at Avalon Tower had any information about what went on at the High Council meetings. And after fifteen hundred years, I'm going to be the first spy to infiltrate the heart of their discussion.

I shrug and sigh. “Fine,” I say, sounding like I couldn’t give a fuck.

As I leave the room and step into the hall, my gaze lingers on the scarlet stain on the stone floor.

CHAPTER 25

A guard follows Talan and me as we walk up the sweeping stone stairs to the High Council's chamber. We're arm in arm, the perfect picture of romantic love. Through his finely tailored black suit, I can feel his muscles flex as we walk. I try to think about anything other than his body and survey the hall as we approach the chamber of the High Council.

The stone walls are engraved with vinelike patterns and sigils—the raven and moon of Morgan, my grandmother. His insignia marks the stones, too—the Fey runes for an A and an M, for *Auberon, House of Morgan.* Auberon's great lie carved into the castle's stones.

But there are other symbols on the wall that were struck off the stone at some point, dashed from history. They left one, just over the large, arched door to the High Council Chamber—an E and an S entwined. *Elaine of Shalott*. And around it, her name and her willow branch sigil.

Talan glances at me as we approach the heavy oak door and brushes his fingertips over my arm, like he's reassuring me. The door swings open, and we cross into a great hall.

A long table sits in the center of the hall, and the Fey rise from their ornate chairs as we walk in. There are about twenty of them, and all eyes locked on me.

Nervously, I gaze around the room. Banners with crests hang between towering windows, and torches affixed to the walls cast dancing light over the hall.

The council is comprised of Fey nobles I recognize—all men, except Arwenna. Her pale blond waves are draped over a silver gossamer dress, and she keeps her eyes steadily on the table before her.

King Auberon sits at the head of the table, glaring at us as we enter. With a brisk gesture, he motions to the foot of the table, where two chairs sit empty. "You're late."

I feel the metallic Fey eyes burning on me as we take our seats.

I wear a serene, slightly stupid smile, but inwardly, I'm scanning *everything*. This is a fucking incredible opportunity. The intel I'll gather here will be invaluable for Avalon Tower. *This* is where they will be discussing military strategies. My report from this meeting could tip the balance of the battle raging in Scotland.

Auberon's crown gleams in the torchlight, the points

looking sharp as daggers. "The first order on the agenda is the war," he says. "It is going much slower than we anticipated. The human armies, though inferior, are like cockroaches. We stamp out one battalion, two crop up somewhere else. Humans are not difficult to kill, but there are so *many* of them. Scuttling around like bugs."

Arwenna stands. "We need to send the dragons in. We need to *end* this with fire, once and for all. Why are we using our dragons so sparingly? Send the entire fleet. Scorch the earth. We can fight a pestilence with the heat of dragon fire."

A man in a black cap—Lord Sorchelle, I believe he's called—clears his throat. "The humans have already demonstrated that they can maim and even kill our dragons when they put their best efforts to it. We can't afford to keep losing—"

"Are you scared of losing, Lord Sorchelle? And they say women don't have the mettle to win a war," Arwenna shouts.

The council explodes with shouting, nobles screaming over each other. Chin in hand, Talan watches it with amusement twinkling in his eyes. Finally, the king slams his palm onto the table, and the council members grow quiet.

"Your Majesty," Lord Sorchelle says, giving Auberon a pointed look.

"We can send three dragons on a single assault," Auberon says. "Scorch one strategic target and see how the humans handle it. If it works, we send more."

I can't believe my luck that I'm overhearing all of this, and my heart races. The nobles start arguing about the best strategic target. In my head, I'm compiling a list of the locations suggested.

"What about Glasgow?" someone shouts. "One of the largest cities in the country. Burn it to the ground. The humans will capitulate immediately."

Arwenna's eyes gleam. "Exactly."

Talan sighs. He looks absolutely bored with this discussion. "We can always burn more cities," he says with a shrug. "The fewer humans, the better. But if we want to pick *one* strategic target, it should be a military base. We should target the largest supply base the humans have. It's stationed in southern Scotland. Demolish it, and their forces will be cut off from supplies." He gives a laid-back smile. "*Then* we can burn cities at our leisure."

"I agree with Prince Talan," Arwenna says quickly. "Strategically, that's much better."

"I disagree!" someone shouts.

I look toward the speaker, surprised to see that it's none other than Ker-Ys. I thought he was in Talan's pocket, so what's he doing arguing?

"We need to destroy the humans' morale, not their supplies," he goes on. "We need to crush their spirits."

More shouting erupts, and Auberon slams his hand down again. "Silence. I will not have you squabbling like peasants in the High Council. I have heard your ideas, and I am ordering an attack on a strategic target. The military base."

Why am I not surprised that Talan's idea wins out?

I'm desperate to get this information to Nivene. She needs to carry it back *immediately* to Camelot. They need to set extra ADGs in the supply base—the anti-dragon guns we used when the Fey attacked Dover. Back then, we managed to wound one of the dragons severely. If they can take one of the dragons out this time, the Fey might be wary of using them again. That could change the tide of the war.

I listen to every detail as they talk about the logistics and the funding of the Fey army, frantically committing as much as I can to memory. Every piece of information is crucial.

Each time Talan speaks, Arwenna hurriedly agrees with him. And in each and every case, Ker-Ys votes against Talan's suggestions. Talan seems to be amused by the entire thing. It takes me a while, but I finally figure out what's going on. For whatever reason, Talan has instructed Ker-Ys to disagree with him. Talan seems to want to cement the idea that Ker-Ys is opposed to him, though I don't yet have any idea why.

I tune out a little as the discussion moves from war strategy to domestic matters that don't concern me, arguments about estate borders, a law about dungeon security, and the planning of a large banquet that's supposed to take place soon. Mentally, I'm still reviewing the details concerning the war, making sure I got every important fact. Avalon Tower doesn't *really* need to know how many roasted ducks will be served during the banquet.

Talan has an opinion on everything, but often, he seems to choose the opinion that would infuriate as many council members as possible. He relishes spreading mayhem in the council, pitting the nobles against each other. He delights in making people nervous. I suspect this is some kind of game to him, and maybe that's what all of this is about after all. Does he really want to avenge his mother against the humans, or is this just the way a bored, clever man amuses himself?

Now they're discussing a forest that one of the nobles wants to cut for logs. Lord Sorchelle hangs a large map of Brocéliande so they can determine the exact area that's to be cut.

Talan leans forward. "The southern forest would make more sense. Logistically, the logs would be easier to move."

He has the same expression of boredom on his face. However, whether it's because I've been hearing his thoughts all my life or because I've grown to know him a bit during the past weeks, I notice a shift. This is one of the first times I've heard him sound like he actually cares about something. There's an almost invisible tension in his body, his jaw clenching just a bit too tightly. Why on earth would he care about some forest in some random baron's territory?

I squint at the map. It's just a small forest, nothing special about—

Holy shit.

A river runs through this forest, and the river has a strangely sharp bend in it—one that looks just like the sharp curve I saw on the map connected to the Blue Dragon Project.

The fortress doesn't appear on this map, though. They don't *know* about the fortress.

I would never have noticed it if it weren't for this discussion; Brocéliande has thousands of rivers. But now that I'm focused, I can't unsee it. It's almost certainly the same river.

Talan doesn't want woodcutters there because he's keeping a secret military base in that very location.

The king doesn't seem to give a fuck about the forest, and he puts it to a vote. As they vote, Talan clenches one hand into a fist.

Ker-Ys votes against Talan's suggestion, and this time, the prince doesn't look amused.

It's close, but Talan wins by just two votes. He drops back into his seat, slouching again, like he's barely paying attention.

The meeting keeps going, but my mind is still buzzing, ignited by this new information.

As soon as I get a chance, I'm going to make a foray to Talan's secret base. I'm certain that *this* is a secret at the heart of his plans.

* * *

THE COUNCIL DEBATES different items for almost six hours, and by the time Auberon calls the meeting adjourned, I'm desperate to get to a pen and paper so I can write down everything about the planned attack in Scotland while the details are still fresh in my mind. I also need to fill in Nivene on everything about the Blue Dragon Project.

But, of course, this being a Fey event, no meeting ends without a lavish, wine-and-mead-soaked banquet. The moment the meeting concludes, we move to another hall nearby where long tables are set with food and wine and lit by glowing chandeliers. A string quartet plays a hauntingly melodic tune.

Talan lounges in a chair, and the colored lights from the stained-glass windows gleam off his ringed fingers.

I stand near him, trying to look like a relaxed, simple farm girl. But mentally, I'm reviewing everything I've just learned, gleaning every detail that could be useful.

I hang back behind Talan's chair and glance at the wall. A few feet behind him, there's an alcove with a bench and cushions partially hidden by a velvet curtain, a cozy little nook that offers a view of the gardens. It's the perfect place to hide while I'm committing things to memory.

I drop onto the bench, but it's not long until a dark-haired Fey saunters over, wine sloshing out of his glass. He reminds me of Jasper with his black hair, rings, sleek, dark clothes, and studied air of indifference. Another Talan imitator, but there's something vaguely familiar about him.

He looks over me with a faint smile, dragging his eyes down my dress, then up again to my face. "Nia, is it? I've heard so much about you. I'm Lumos de Morgan, Marquis of Klarvel. I heard you were at the High Council. Is that right? I don't even have an invitation."

My heart skips a beat. Of course he's familiar. I've been inside his head, and when I first broke into Perillos, I pretended to know him. "Hello, Lumos. We have met, you know."

His eyes widen. "Have we?"

"I was told that you charm so many women that you don't remember most of them, so I guess it's true."

He gives me a devilish smile. "Did we, you know…?"

"No, nothing like that." I glance at Talan. A red-haired woman is draped over his chair, laughing hysterically at his joke, just ten feet away. I turn back to his cousin. "It was business. I have eyes for only one man."

Lumos leans against the side of the alcove. "Is that right? Because you don't seem particularly interested in the prince." The contents of his wine glass spill on the floor. "The rumors are he doesn't even visit you at night. Very strange, considering who he is. And you know, usually the women he's with throw themselves at him, but you're over here in the shadows, almost like you wish you were somewhere else."

Fuck.

CHAPTER 26

I inhale deeply. "Perhaps I like to give the prince some space. You can't miss someone who is always clinging to you."

Talan glances back with a mischievous smile, then raises his eyebrows when he sees Lumos. He rises from his chair, prowling closer. "Is my cousin boring you?"

I shrug. "We were just catching up, although he doesn't remember me."

Talan sits on the alcove bench next to me, leaning back against the pillows, a wine glass in his hand. He ignores Lumos, and the look he's giving me is positively smoldering. "Would you mind fucking off, cousin?" he says with an arrogance bordering on contempt, still holding my gaze.

"Aww," says Lumos, "was your lover ignoring you? Is the bloom off the rose already? Or did you choose her simply because she's the one woman in Corbinelle who doesn't give a fuck about the prince?"

Lumos is obviously drunk, I think, and his voice is too loud. It echoes off the vaulted ceiling, and a hush falls over the room.

Slowly, Talan's dark gaze slides to Lumos, and the air grows colder around us. "You're drunk again, Lumos. Time for your nap, I think, before you say something you'll regret. You don't want to lose your head."

Talan takes a sip of his wine and leans against the alcove wall, looking bored. But the threat was delivered like an arrow to the throat. Lumos's cheeks redden, and he turns away. With a dark smile, Talan watches his cousin skulk off.

A House de Morgan power play in action.

Talan meets my gaze again. Arching an eyebrow, he beckons me closer. Another power play, as he's not coming to me. But we haven't been playing the part well enough—we're on a stage with an audience before us, and we should be playing the roles of two lovers in lust. Rumors have already spread.

I move closer to him and drop into his lap. He smells delicious, musky and tinged with jasmine. His arm slides around my waist, and his body is pure, unyielding muscle against the thin fabric of my dress. His lips are by the side of my face, his breath warming the shell of my ear. "My little farm girl, you're going to need to fake some interest in me." His hand slides over my thigh, and

I feel the heat of it through the translucent fabric of my dress.

I whisper back. "What do you have in mind, exactly?"

"Nia, love, you're going to have to kiss me." The deep sound of his voice in my ear strokes over my skin like a sensual caress.

Warmth creeps over my cheeks, and his hand moves over my hip. Only the thin fabric of my dress separates us, and heat ripples out from his palm.

My gaze dips to his full, sensual lips, and my pulse races.

It's just a kiss. All part of the spy game, of course. Agents of Avalon Tower must do all kinds of things on our missions. Things we normally wouldn't dream of, like kissing the enemy.

I feel their eyes on us, watching. Waiting.

I lick my lips, and his gaze flicks down to my mouth. His pupils dilate, the copper blending to black. His thumb strokes languidly up and down on my hip, then circles over the hollow of my thigh, sending hot tingles in the wake of his touch.

I lean forward, my mouth hovering just over his, his breath mingling with mine.

"Nia." There's a fierce, ragged edge in the way he whispers my name, his lips so close to mine. "I hear your heart racing. You can lie to yourself, but you can't lie to me. I think you're interested in me after all."

Oh, he has my interest. I loathe him and fear him, but

I'm also painfully aware of how breathtakingly beautiful he is, this man with the dangerous smile, the seductive eyes, and the muscled body of a Fey warrior.

This close to him, his body warms mine. I lean into his chest, and it feels like pure steel. I brush my thumb over his full lower lip, my heart racing. His breath hitches, and I'm surprised that I have this effect on him. I search his eyes and find an unexpected hunger there instead of his usual detached expression. It's a strange and powerful feeling to have captured the full force of Prince Talan de Morgan's attention. He's enraptured.

My lips move closer to him, and the rest of the room fades, along with the sound of the quartet and the voices echoing in the hall.

Closing my eyes, I brush my lips against his. Tentatively. Questioningly. But already, even with that light touch, heat is blooming in my core. I feel as if sparks are dancing over my skin.

That gentle taste sends warmth plunging through my body. His hand strokes up my back, and his fingers lace into my hair. Slowly, he flicks his tongue over my lower lip. My lips part, and I press my mouth harder against his. I'm not sure whose tongue slides in first—his? Mine? All I know is we kiss—a deep, sensual kiss—and I lose track of the world around me. Kiss? He's savoring me, exploring me. I shift positions, straddling him, my dress hitching up to my thighs. I kiss him more deeply, and as his tongue brushes against mine, I forget where I am while an exquisite ache builds inside me. His hand slides to the small of my back, pulling me closer to him, my breasts brushing against his hard chest. He groans faintly as he kisses me.

I slide my hand under the hem of his shirt and trace the warm skin, the carved abs. Gods, his body is perfect. As he kisses me, my hips rock against him, and I hear another light moan from deep in his chest.

He nips at my lower lip, and I pull away, catching my breath. My lips are still close to his, my heart racing. Darkness has spread through his eyes, devouring the copper. I want to rock my hips against him again, I want to kiss him again, but I'm trying to control myself. This is all for show. That's all. He's still gripping my hair, his expression smoldering, half-lidded, lips parted. Ravenous.

And as for me? I don't want to admit to myself how much I want more. I'm literally here to *kill* this man.

"Is that enough?" I whisper through heavy breaths. I'm shocked to realize I almost want him to say no.

"You did well," he whispers. He moves his hand around and cups the side of my face, his thumb brushing over my cheekbone. "But I'm going to need to visit your room at night. There are rumors going around, apparently, that we don't spend enough time together."

"You'll stay in my room?" I whisper. This is a terrible idea. I can't be around him, that close to him. His seductive power will absolutely disrupt my ability to do this job. "Is it really necessary?"

He arches an eyebrow. "You're welcome to take the floor."

"Such a gentleman."

As I narrow my eyes at him, I remember that everyone is watching us, that my dress is hitched up. That we're not alone, though the rest of the room has gone silent. The only noise at the moment is the string quartet, and when I gaze around the hall, I find them all staring at us.

For a few heated moments, I'd nearly forgotten everyone in the room.

I shift on his lap, pulling down the hem of my dress, my cheeks going red.

I need to keep my distance from him as best I can. His allure is *dangerous,* and I will lose myself in his seductive charm instead of doing my job.

I'm here for an assassination. *That* needs to be at the forefront of my mind.

My heart is still hammering, my chest flushed as I slide off his lap and walk away from him. I smooth out my dress, painfully aware of everyone staring. Arwenna is giving me a death glare, her face white, jaw tight.

As I stand, someone offers me a strawberry tart, and I pluck it off the tray, eager for a distraction. My breath is still shallow, my heart still racing. I force myself to stop thinking about how it felt when we kissed.

I focus on the tart instead.

Strawberries don't grow in Brocéliande; they have to be imported from France. They're considered an incredibly expensive delicacy, served only on very formal events. Most of the tart is made of Brocéliande korriberries, harvested from the forests. But there's a single large strawberry on top.

I have no appetite, but my fake persona would gobble this up—the poor farm girl who lived through a famine.

As I bring the tart to my lips, something silver flutters up. It's Mordred's moth. It skitters in the air, circles around my tart once, and flies away.

A warning.

Thank you, Mordred.

I shoot a nervous glance at Talan, but he's already gone from the alcove. He's back in his chair, and one of Arwenna's dark-haired friends is perched on the armrest. She has gorgeous cheekbones, and her arms are covered in dark tattoos. She and Talan look annoyingly perfect together, like two frustratingly gorgeous goth Fey models. She's practically in his lap, her arm around his shoulders, breasts directly at his eye level.

I glance across the room at Arwenna. She sits next to another friend, a smile fixed on her face, but she's doing her best not to look my way. Clenching her spoon tightly, she stares at me from the corner of her eye, waiting for me to take a bite.

I can easily act drunk and drop my strawberry tart to the floor, temporarily saving myself. But that won't end the assassination attempts. She'll just keep at it. If she managed to poison my tart, it means she has someone working for her in the kitchen staff and a servant to make sure it goes out in front of me. And at some point, Mordred won't alert me in time.

I need to make sure this never happens again.

My first thought is to go over to her and use my mind control to force her to confess, but I don't want to expose my powers like that. She'll accuse me immediately, and my cover will be blown. Claiming that I suspect the tart is poisoned will draw attention as well, and people will want to know who told me. I can't even tell Talan how I know.

No, I need to figure out a more subtle approach.

The music shifts to a jauntier tune, and a few people start dancing. Guests are mingling between the banquet tables, chatting.

I turn to Talan and the woman who is now running her finger over his lower lip. Bizarrely, I feel a twinge of anger at her. My relationship with Talan is utterly fake, but she doesn't know that. On the other hand, this twat is giving me the perfect excuse to get out of here.

"Looks like you're occupied," I snap at Talan. "I'm going to go for a walk until you come to your senses."

He turns to me, a flicker of surprise in his eyes. The candlelight wavers over the perfect planes of his face, and he starts to shift the woman off him and stand.

"Oh, don't bother," I say sharply.

I turn and stalk away, the strawberry tart in my hand.

I keep up the angry act, if it can be called an act, as I

pass a few nobles from the high council meeting. With every step, I feel Arwenna's eyes on me, waiting to see if I will take a bite. When I turn her way, she quickly shifts her stare and lets out a loud, fake laugh. She'd make a terrible spy.

When I'm close to her, I brush against one of the waiters. As I do that, I tug at my powers. Abrupt pain shoots through my skull, but I ignore the piercing throb. I dive into the waiter's mind and sift through his thoughts, desires, and worries. I don't have much time, so I plant a single tiny thing in his mind and pull away. As I release my magic, the pain dissipates to a dull throb.

I pivot and stalk around the banquet tables until I'm standing across from Arwenna, then smile at her. "Hello."

Her eyes flick down to the tart—still uneaten. She brushes her silver hair behind her shoulders. "Hello," she says coldly.

I drop my tart on the plate next to hers, and I can see her effort not to glance at it. Her tart, unlike mine, doesn't have a strawberry on it. They're only for the elite, and apparently, Arwenna didn't make the cut.

"I feel like we started off on the wrong foot," I say. "I don't know many people in the palace. Since you and Talan are clearly close, I'd be glad to get to know you better."

She stiffens. "I don't think that's going to—"

A sudden crash behind her makes her whirl around.

The waiter I've mind controlled just dropped his tray, and dozens of crystal glasses shatter on the floor. All eyes are on him except mine.

The head waiter lunges forward. "You fool! Look what you've done."

"I'm...I'm sorry," the waiter blurts. Falling to his knees, he frantically begins to pick up the pieces, ignoring his bleeding fingers.

"Leave that!" the head waiter snaps. "Go get a broom. We can't have guests cutting their feet on those shards. Someone could get hurt."

Shaking her head, Arwenna turns to her friend. "The staff here are getting more useless every day. They have no standards anymore." She slides her gaze to me. "No standards for any of those we let in here these days, isn't that right, Nia?"

"I'm not sure what you mean." Might as well play dumb, at least for a few minutes. I pick up the tart and take a large bite.

"Don't you remember, Alenia, when we only let those of noble blood into the castle? All the mistresses were at least ladies and not desperate social climbers from filthy hovels." Arwenna stares at me as I eat the tart, her eyes twinkling viciously as I chew. "Those of noble breeding are the most exquisite beauties and shining intellects, and only *they* should get close to the throne."

"Is that right?"

She raises her chin and sniffs the air. "Why is it that every time I'm near you, I smell the rancid stench of a demi-Fey?"

My blood runs cold, but I pretend to ignore her, staring at the tart instead. "This tastes a bit off," I say, grimacing. "I think something's wrong with it."

Smiling, she takes a bite of her own tart. "Tastes fine to me. I don't think there's anything wrong with them. I'm not going to waste it, even if they forgot my strawberry."

"Maybe it's fine," I say with a frown. "Well, it's been nice talking to you."

I wave and saunter away, taking another bite from the tart.

Returning to my chair, I sit and wipe the crumbs from my lips. In all honesty, it's one of the best desserts I've ever tasted.

Leaning back, I fix my gaze on Arwenna. After a minute or two, her expression changes, the color draining from her cheeks. Her forehead wrinkles, and she grabs a glass of water, nearly knocks it over, then manages to grip it. With a shaking hand, she drains the water, then stares at the leftovers of her tart. Her eyes widen at the faint pink sheen on the top of the tart, where my sliced strawberry used to be.

Her jaw drops open, and she turns to me, eyes wide with horror. She covers her mouth, looking like she's about to vomit. I pick up my mead glass and raise it at her, smiling tightly.

She runs from the room.

Maybe she has an antidote, but I don't think she'll try to poison me again.

I may not be of noble breeding, but now the bitch knows who she's dealing with.

CHAPTER 27

I sink deeper into my bath, the water heating my skin. Moonlight spills through the towering windows, igniting the steam rising from the bath in coils of silver and red.

It's late, and I should be asleep. Instead, I take a sip of champagne as I let my muscles relax. After Arwenna ran away from the banquet, I left and went in search of Nivene to fill her in on everything I'd learned at the high council.

Unfortunately, she wasn't around. In fact, I haven't been able to find her in days. I returned to my room, wrote everything up, and dropped it in our secret location.

But I wasn't *just* looking for Nivene because of the report. After an evening of being poisoned and insulted, I desperately longed to see a friendly face. The loneliness in this place was starting to get to me.

Arwenna was right when she said I don't belong here.

My muscles tighten and my breath stills at the sound of an opening door. My heart slams against my ribs, and I rise from the bath, frantically grasping for a towel. Arwenna has shown up to murder me. With a racing pulse, I wrap the towel around myself and ease up a loose tile on the floor, grabbing the knife I've hidden within. Arwenna won't find me as harmless as she thinks.

"Nia?" a deep, velvety voice says from the other room. "Where are you?"

I let out a long exhalation and quickly return the knife to its hiding spot. "Talan? To what do I owe this visit?"

"To the fact that we are lovers and can't stay away from each other for even a moment. I know you miss gazing adoringly at my face, and I couldn't deprive you of the pleasure."

"Right." I clutch the towel tightly around myself and peer out into my room.

Talan has already draped himself in one of my chairs and pulled a book into his lap. His gaze flicks up at me. "I didn't expect to find you naked, which is an interesting surprise. You did know I was coming, didn't you?"

I clutch my towel. "Do you ever wonder what you might be like if you weren't born grotesquely wealthy, beautiful, and surrounded by people catering to your every whim?"

"Perhaps I'd be knee-deep in rotten onion dirt, thinking fondly of the halcyon days when apples grew. If only fate had dealt me such a hand."

"You might have developed an amenable personality."

"Sounds tedious."

I didn't bring any fresh clothes into the bathroom with me, so I'm forced to step into the room in my towel. As I walk to the dresser, I can feel his eyes upon me, though I assume an air of nonchalance. My wet hair drips down my back and shoulders, dampening the towel, and I yank open a drawer and grab the first pair of underwear and nightgown I can find. As I head back to the bathroom, I see Talan pour himself some wine. He's making himself at home.

Closing the bathroom door behind me, I discover that I've grabbed a sheer nightgown and a pair of skimpy underwear with black lace around the waist. The nightgown is also black and utterly transparent, revealing my nipples through the sheer fabric.

Scanty or not, when I walk out of here, I have to look totally relaxed and at ease with everything on display. I take a deep breath and imagine that I'm fully dressed in jeans and a T-shirt.

Opening the bathroom door, I find Talan sitting on my bed, shirtless.

I focus on keeping my shoulders relaxed, my expression serene. But it's not what I feel.

Here's what they don't teach you in Fey culture lessons when we practice being at ease with our bodies. They don't teach you how it will feel to walk out half-naked in front of possibly the most powerful Fey in the kingdom, a prince who strikes absolute terror into the hearts of everyone around him. Or how hard it is to think straight when he's half-naked, too, with a body that is perfection itself. Because my brain knows that he's a monster, but my pulse is still reacting to the sinuous tattoos of willow branches that stretch across his finely-cut muscles. I've never practiced how it would feel to walk out like this before a heart-stoppingly beautiful man whose eyes darken at the sight of me.

His jaw tightens, and that eerie Fey stillness overcomes his body. His deep, silken voice seems to ring in my skull—

I would drag you into the night's dark embrace with me and bring you to the edge...

Candlelight flickers over his powerful body. My pulse races as he drags his gaze from me and stands, removing his belt in one smooth movement.

I slide onto the other side of the bed and pull up the covers around me. "You're not planning on sleeping in my bed naked, are you?"

He rolls over, propping his chin on his palm. "And there's my tightly-wound mistress again. You were starting to seem almost relaxed for a moment, and I wondered where the real Nia had gone. But don't worry, I will keep my shorts on."

For a moment, my gaze dips to his lips, full and slightly curved. Disturbingly sensual. "Good."

"I suspect you're more worried about your own self-control than mine." His silken voice thrums over my skin. "You *did* just call me beautiful."

"Did I? Well, enough chitchat. I need my sleep." He really brings out the uptight peevishness in me, though oddly, I suspect he likes it.

I steal a quick look at his powerful chest and pull the covers more tightly around me.

"Do you ever enjoy things, Nia? Ever at all?"

"I'm not all misery. I was in love once."

"And what happened to him?"

I swallow hard. *Keep the lies as close to the truth as possible.* "He had a bad habit of running away from things. Including me. He broke my heart twice."

"Mmm." A deep murmur. "Shall I have him tortured and executed?"

Oh, my dear Talan. You've already started on that.

"No," I say. "He's not a bad person, but he chose his work over me."

He scoffs. "He sounds fucking boring."

"Were you ever in love?"

The candlelight dances over his carved muscles. "There's only one woman for me, and she is a figment of my imagination, a voice in my thoughts."

"So many centuries and not one love? Is it all the murdering? Does it get in the way of romance?"

"Not much time for love when I have subjects to torment."

"Seems like my ex isn't the only one obsessed with work."

He glances at me, and for a moment, I think there's a faint sadness in his smile. "If you saw what I see in people's dreams, you'd know why I don't love anyone."

"And what do you see in people's dreams that disturbs you so much?" I ask.

"All the things people want from me and all the things they fear from me."

I suppose he thinks no one knows or cares for the real him—the Talan who would have existed in another world, where he was a poor nobody.

I'm not about to start feeling sorry for him.

I turn and blow out the candles next to me, and shadows pool in the room, tinged with silver and red from the moonlight.

I slide down into the bed and roll over. Clamping my eyes shut, I try not to think about how close he is to me. I will not dwell on how he smells—of smoky cedar faintly tinged with perfumed flowers—and I absolutely will not entertain the memories of how many times I've overheard his thoughts as he pleasured a woman until she gripped his hair and screamed his name while he brought her to orgasm…

Nia, this is a man who would rip your throat out in a heartbeat if he knew the truth.

I close my eyes, summoning the veil in my mind.

"Why is your heart beating so fast?" he murmurs.

I curl my fingers around the blankets. "Don't you know everyone is scared of you?"

Silence falls in the darkened room. Outside, lightning cracks and thunder rolls over the horizon. "Yes," he says quietly, "but I didn't think you were."

My throat tightens, and I clamp my eyes shut.

I WAKE IN THE NIGHT, horrified to find that I've curled myself around his body—one arm around his chiseled abs, my thigh wrapped around his hips. In this position, I feel the full length of him, his hard cock pressed against the inside of my thigh. He's enormous and built like a god in every way, isn't he?

Here is my body forsaking me yet again—as I slept, I crawled to him and wrapped myself around him, lured by his exquisite beauty and his smell.

I'm frozen, my pulse racing. At the feel of his arousal, heat slides through my body.

This would all be much easier if he looked like a troll.

I glance up and find the Dream Stalker lying awake, staring at the ceiling.

Fuck.

"Sorry," I whisper. "I was asleep."

"My dear Nia, you have absolutely nothing to apologize for. You should wrap yourself around me whenever you want." His voice is a velvet caress over my skin.

I force myself to pull my arm away, slide my leg off him, and shift across the bed again. As soon as I'm away from him, I feel cold and tense. But I pull the covers tightly, gripping the sheets, and force my breathing to slow. I summon that mental veil again and drift off to sleep.

* * *

I STIR IN MY SLEEP, waking slowly. I've been dreaming of him—that he pinned me down, ripping through the sheer fabric of my nightgown. In my dream, when he pressed his lips against my throat, his canines brushed against my skin, and I wrapped my thighs around him and moaned his name.

Am I *spooning* him? My heart thuds.

I am, in fact, spooning him. Talan has turned away from me, and I've wrapped my arms around his abs. My leg is curled around his, and he's holding one of my wrists in his large hand.

But he's asleep this time, his chest rising and falling slowly.

Early morning light spreads a blush into the room.

...verdant fields rent crimson with blood... all-consuming slaughter, hellfire roars to life...

My muscles tense. The first thing I feel is horror at his violent thoughts, but then I realize something more important has just happened. I can hear what he's thinking now that I'm touching him, just like with any other person. Even with this shield up in my mind, I'm getting glimpses into his thoughts as our bodies make contact.

But what is he dreaming about? Warfare? Death? Something that's already happened or something he has planned?

I pull my arm away and untangle my legs from his.

Talan sighs in his sleep and rolls onto his back. He sits up in bed, his hair tousled, eyes sleepy. "Are you awake again, Nia?" he asks softly. "You were wrapped around me the entire night."

"I was not."

"You were moving your hips against me in your sleep."

A flush spreads across my cheeks. "Well, I was asleep, and I was dreaming you were a horse."

"I dread to think what you do to horses. And they say *I'm* depraved."

"Obviously, dreams don't make any sense. That's the nature of dreams."

"As a dream expert, I wouldn't say that."

A knock sounds on the door, and within moments, Aisling flings the door open. Her jaw drops at the sight of Talan, and she blurts an apology, then slams the door shut again.

CHAPTER 28

I sit by the windows in my room, sipping tea. Outside, the setting sun stains the clouds violet and peach. I pour myself another cup, trying to stay awake. Sleep in this place has never come easily, but last night was the least refreshing sleep of all, having waked repeatedly to find myself curled around my worst enemy.

This morning, after the prince left my room, I went back to the secret spot where I left the report from Nivene. The coded report was gone, and in its place, I found a short, encrypted message. To my relief, Avalon Tower was acting on the intel immediately. *Gone to Scotland to prepare for dragon attack,* the message read. *Lie low. Maintain your cover.*

I understand why they need a Sentinel with them, but without Nivene here, I'm more isolated than ever.

I'm not entirely sure how to find Meriadec, and I

have no chance of hearing anything about Raphael. I'm desperate to talk to someone about the Blue Dragon Project. Whatever Talan's secret plans are, I have a feeling they need to be investigated, and *soon*. There's only one conceivable reason for him to keep this project secret. Auberon merely wants to win the war. Talan wants to end the humans and demi-Fey once and for all.

Does the Blue Dragon Project have something to do with a weapon of mass destruction, perhaps? One that he intends to use in the war in Scotland?

Without Nivene and her contacts here, I need to check out the location myself.

A knock sounds on the door, and I put down my teacup. "It's Aisling!" the voice calls through the door.

"Come in!"

She pushes in, wringing her hands, her forehead crinkled with worry. "He's on his way. But are you sure this is a good idea? Usually, Jasper is used only during special occasions. Like a royal wedding or engagement. Or a royal birthday. He designed some wonderful clothes for His Majesty's birthday banquet last year. The nobility are so beautiful, so they're easy to dress. Of course, the night was marred by all the screaming because some of the demi-Fey were slaughtered and thrown in the Paimpont River. You could hear the commotion from here. And that's why I don't drink that river water, not unless you purify it with my grand-mother's special tincture. What you do is you mix garlic with honey…"

My stomach turns at her casual mention of a demi-Fey massacre, and I tune out the rest of her rambling. When Aisling gets nervous, she talks even *more* than usual.

I'm feeling very uneasy myself. My plan might back-fire if I can't keep this meeting with Jasper a secret. The problem is, Jasper doesn't strike me as someone who can be trusted to keep silent.

A knock on the door interrupts Aisling's monologue, and she hurries to open it. Relaxing in my chair, I adopt a nonchalant expression. Just another glorious day at the palace for Nia, the prince's mistress, who has absolutely no devious plans at all…

Jasper steps inside, rubbing his hands together. "Hello, hello, my lady."

I'm relieved to see that as I asked, he showed up without his assistants.

Aisling closes the door behind him.

"Hi, Jasper. Come in."

He folds his arms and leans against a stone column. "You've survived so far, my lady, which is very impressive. Some of my mates had a group pool going on. They're idiots, some of my mates. Don't know why I waste time with them. Do they really think that Prince Talan would choose someone as his mistress if he didn't know what he was doing? The man is a genius. And I said to them, no way were you going to end up slaughtered by the end of the week."

I nod. "You bet correctly."

His eyes are half-lidded as he nods. "Absolutely." He points at me, his rings gleaming in the light. "Remind me of your name again."

"You placed money on me surviving, but you don't even remember my name?"

He snaps his fingers. "Of course. Nia. Layered like an onion. I did quite well with your dress that night, didn't I? For your introduction to court. Quite well."

"It was a beautiful gown." I tip my head in acknowledgment. "And now I need your help again."

He clasps his hands together and pouts with feigned sympathy. "Unfortunately, my lady, I'm *so* overbooked right now. I am the lead creative director of the royal wardrobe, and it's always the most important royals at the top of my booking list. You know, the king, the viscounts, the earls, that sort of thing. Sorry, my lady."

I raise an eyebrow. "I'm the prince's mistress."

He nods. "That's right. Which, obviously, is not royalty. One day, if you become his wife, you won't need to pay me the large retainer required to bump you up on my list."

I pour myself another cup of tea. "But you know I don't have a large retainer. I'm the onion girl. So, why did you even bother coming?"

He scrubs a hand over his jaw, considering this. "Well, admittedly, the demand for secrecy sparked my curiosity. That, and there's been interesting rumors about you in the palace."

Icy fingers of dread trace up my spine. "What kind of rumors?"

He chuckles nervously and shoves his hands into his pockets. "You know Countess Arwenna de Bosclair of Val Sans Retour? Well, it sounds mad, really, but people are saying that she tried to poison you and ended up drinking her own poison. And I had to know if that was true."

"And you believe that nonsense?"

"Crazier things have happened, my lady. You deny it?"

I shrug. "If it happened, I was unaware of it."

"So, onion girl. You've survived the palace intrigues for weeks, perhaps bested one of the most cunning noble ladies in the court, and now you want to meet me in secret. I suppose I must know what you have planned."

"I want to perform a courtship dance for Prince Talan," I say.

He blinks at me in surprise. "But courtship dances are an ancient, outdated ritual. No one has done one in centuries. Frankly they seem...well, here at court, my lady, they are extremely out of fashion."

I sigh wistfully. "But I always read about them on my farm and dreamed of performing one. A special private dance, just between two lovers. I understand it's out of fashion, but that's why I need *your* help. Out of all people, you would be able to make it seem fashionable again. A revival of sorts. You could give this ancient ritual a modern, stylish twist. Imagine if this goes well. It'll be the talk of Corbinelle. A spectacle. Not just Corbinelle—the talk of all Brocéliande. The courtship dances are back, and the first one was created by none other than the creative genius Jasper Laval."

"Go on," he says slowly.

He's hooked. I can see it in his eyes.

I lean back in my chair. "I think the problem with the old courtship dances was a lack of mystery. They were just private dances with complex outfits, right? Now, picture this. It's nighttime. Full moon. Prince Talan goes to the lake outside the castle walls, where he's supposed to meet me. He sees no one there. But then, what's this? Something rising from the cold water. It's me, dressed as a siren. I dance for him, *in the water...*"

"Yes," Jasper mutters, snapping his fingers vigorously. "Yes! With siren music in the background. The mist settles on the water like a thin, translucent blanket. Droplets of water trickle down your skin. The prince is enchanted by the artistry."

"In the winter, though?" Aisling blurts.

Jasper blinks at her. "I'm sorry, who are you?"

"It's Aisling."

He nods. "Right. Shut the fuck up, Aisling."

I clear my throat. "It's warmer during the day, and the mist is coiling off the lake. But I'll freeze if I swim in the lake in the middle of the night."

"For a masterpiece, I'm willing to pay the price of you freezing."

"If my teeth are chattering," I say, "it might ruin the ambiance."

He sighs dramatically, then rubs his forehead. "Fine. Fine! We'll create an outfit that will keep you warm. And of course, you'll need some way to stay underwater until the prince arrives. We can't have you bobbing up for breath every few seconds like a cursed selkie."

"Yeah, I was thinking, maybe some kind of helmet for my head—"

"A *helmet*?" He looks horrified. "What is this? A courtship dance or a children's theater? No. I'll come up with a different solution. And the light...yes..."

"Light?" I frown.

"In the forest, the moonlight won't get through so well. You'll need a source of light so the prince can see you. Yes, I have a few ideas. I'll get my assistants working on it right away."

"Hang on. This will only work if it's kept a secret," I say. "If you bring your assistants in on this, they'll tell someone, and soon enough, everyone in the palace will know. That would completely ruin the impact. Of course, once we're done, they should tell *everyone*."

"I see what you mean. My assistants are not always discreet."

He grimaces, and I know the real issue. He's dying to tell everyone about this right now. Still, he knows I'm right. Only keeping this a surprise would have the true effect, without the time for everyone to second-guess if it's going to be tacky.

"But how will I do this without the assistants? There will be so many little tasks to get this right."

Gods forbid he does menial jobs himself. "Aisling can help you," I say. "She's very capable. Right, Aisling?"

She shrugs. "I suppose so. For you."

He frowns at her, forehead wrinkling. "This one? Okay. All right. Is she really capable of…you know what? Let's try it."

"And as for the price…" I say carefully.

He waves it off. "Don't worry about that. Once the prince sees my work, he won't hesitate. It'll be the most memorable night of his life, and I will be a part of it."

"How soon can you have everything ready?" I ask.

"A couple of days, maybe three."

"The faster, the better. I'm just so excited about this, you know? Now, I need to start practicing my courtship dance."

CHAPTER 29

Talan left the palace for a few days on a diplomatic mission in the far north of Brocéliande. It's day two of his absence, and I'm seizing my chance. I'm slipping out before dawn to find out what he has planned with the Blue Dragon Project.

I'm dressed warmly, with a leather bag slung over my shoulder and a dagger strapped to my waist. Most importantly, I have my new suit from Jasper tucked into my bag.

Slowly, I open the door to the hall and look around in either direction. As expected, no one is up at this hour, and I creep into the passageway.

I move swiftly, checking over my shoulder. For the last few days, I've been shaking off two people who are following me. I'm pretty sure that Talan has had his people assigned to watch me. Presumably, *Arwenna* has someone trailing me as well. I suspect any number of nobles are watching my comings and goings. I'm a popular girl.

Which means that where I'm going tonight, I have to make sure that I'm not being followed. At four in the morning, the people tailing me seem to be in between shifts, and I don't see a single soul around.

My plan is simple. Sneak outside in the dark, grab a horse from the stable, and use my telepathy powers on the soldiers at the messengers' gate. I'll ride through the day and arrive at the Blue Dragon Project by nightfall, deep in the Melian Forest.

But I needed a plausible cover, so I left behind a note on my desk: *Aisling, I'll be gone for a night. Heading home to see my father.*

I glance over my shoulder again. Still no one. I hurry down a winding stairwell, listening all the while for sounds of movement or voices. My fingers trace over the cold stones as I descend one spiral after another.

It's going to be a long day, and I'm almost considering risking discovery to get coffee in the kitchens before I go, but I decide against it. This is too important to fuck up.

By the time I arrive in the Melian Forest, where the river bends sharply into the hidden woods, I will likely be starving and cold. I'll be getting through the day on whatever I had left over from dinner last night. But a spy's life was never meant to be comfortable, was it?

At the bottom of the stairs, I push through a door

into the frigid night. The cold air stings my skin as I cross the court and make my way to the stables.

I pull my cloak tightly around me, keeping my head down. I've timed this so that not only is it still dark, but the guards by the gate are changing. Hopefully, they won't pay any attention to me skulking in the shadows by the castle walls.

But when I round the corner and head toward the stables, my stomach clenches. A soldier is patrolling, and he's marching toward me. He's too close for me to turn and run, so my only option is to act like everything is fine and hope he buys it.

"My lady." He's dressed in the deep blue of the Royal Army. His long, pale blond hair hangs over his broad shoulders, and his metallic green eyes narrow at me.

I give him a charming smile. Nothing amiss here. "I'm off on a quick journey. I'll be back in no time."

"At this hour? It's dangerous, my lady."

I wave a dismissive hand. "Oh, don't be such a silly goose! I'm not a prisoner here, you know. And the prince already knew about this. I'm going home for the night to visit my father."

I flutter my eyelashes and touch his arm. As I do, pain rips through my skull, but I summon my telepathy powers anyway, letting them unfurl around him.

Should be guarding the bloody messengers' gate. It's only me tonight. But nothing ever fucking happens at this hour, and I've gone all day without mead. My hands are shaking. I was trying to stop drinking the stuff, but now all I can think of is the sweet tang on my tongue and how I need it to calm my nerves...I just need a drink, and then I'll get back to it. I won't let King Auberon down. He did say something about spies, didn't he? Am I fucking everything up right now?

I exhale with relief. The gate is open. "Well, I'll be going."

"But you're traveling on your own, my lady? It really doesn't seem safe for a young lady to ride unguarded at this hour. Or any hour. I don't think the prince would allow his favorite mistress to travel without guards. Where is it, exactly, that you're going? Where does your father live?"

My heart thuds. "Lauron."

As I try to control his mind, pain screams through my head and nausea rises in my gut. I can't get a grip on his thoughts. Talan has really fucked up my abilities.

The soldier shakes his head. "No, not a good idea. Let me check with the chatelaine, at least. I'm sure we can organize a retinue to travel with you."

My stomach flips. The longer I stay here, the greater chance I have to implicate myself, to spin another lie that I can't get out of. And my magic is failing me.

I smile at him. "Such a worrier! You need a drink. You deserve a bottle of mead. If you go to the chatelaine, you'll miss your chance." I turn away from him and call over my shoulder, "It'll be fine. Don't worry."

Without waiting for another word, I march off toward the stables. But in the recesses of my mind, I know this is a problem I will have to take care of later.

And a dark part of me wonders if I should have taken care of the problem with the sharp finality of the dagger at my waist.

* * *

CROUCHING BEHIND A TREE, I breathe in the scent of pine. Night has fallen, and my teeth are chattering out here in the depths of the Melian Forest. Just ten feet away, a river roars past.

I left Castle Perillos ten hours ago, but that conversation with the soldier is still nagging at my thoughts. My early-morning journey turned out messier than I'd anticipated, and I have the disturbing feeling he'll be passing on the news of my trip to Talan when he gets back.

But I need to put that out of my mind now. I've come to exactly the right place. Before me, outside the forest's edge, is the fortress labeled on the map as the Blue Dragon Project. It's a towering stone edifice with mist roiling around its base. The river flows through an arched tunnel beneath it, and from the quick glimpse I had of the maps, it looked like the river opens up again within the center of the fortress.

Cold wind whips between the dark trunks, stinging my cheeks. Faint ruby-silver moonlight pierces the trees, glinting off the snow like jewels.

Behind me, the gentle snapping of a twig makes my heart jump, and I turn to see a stag standing between the trees, his breath misting around his face. He's pale white, almost ghostly. I go still, and the stag stares back at me, nostrils flaring. He runs off into the wintry woods again, kicking up snow behind him.

I shiver and turn back to watch the fortress from the shadows.

My stomach rumbles. I didn't pack nearly enough food, and now I keep thinking about the buttery salmon and wildflower salad meals the Fey make.

My thighs ache, and the cold wind bites at my cheeks. My stomach growls again, and I can only hope it's not loud enough for the soldiers to hear with their keen Fey ears.

I need to make a move soon.

From behind a tree, I survey the stone walls that surround the fortress. Dark, thorny vines climb up spiked parapets that are at least sixty feet high. I also have a view of the main entrance, a bridge that juts over the river. There's a stone gatehouse on the other side, heavily guarded, and a line of fierce-looking soldiers standing before the portcullis. They're not wearing the blue uniforms of most of Auberon's soldiers, but rather black clothes with silver breastplates and helmets. All of them are armed with swords at their waists, a bow, and a quiver of arrows. I suspect they're under orders to shoot anyone they see without question.

Going through that front gate is not an option, but I never intended to scale the walls or go through the portcullis.

Beneath that bridge, at the base of the castle, an arched stone passage runs underground. Just as I saw on the map, the river flows into that stone tunnel beneath the fortress. That's my way in.

Not that it will be a fun ride. The water churns, and sharp rocks protrude above its surface. When I'm between the forest and the castle, I'll have to stay beneath the surface if I don't want to get spotted.

I unshoulder my bag and open it, pulling out the suit that Jasper made for me. It's a shimmering silver-blue with gossamer that reaches my ankles, designed to look like a dress. The color should help me go unnoticed as I swim, but the darkness will help disguise me, too.

Ducking behind a tree, I strip off my clothes, teeth chattering wildly as the winter air bites my skin. Once I slip into the suit, I immediately start to warm up.

Next, I reach into my bag and pull out the tincture that Jasper bought for me. I pop the cork and take a long sip from it, grimacing. It tastes like fish oil mixed with bitter herbs. But then I feel something strange, a tingling on my neck that quickly changes into a burning sensation. I touch my neck gently and feel them, just like Jasper had said. Gills.

Finally, I retrieve the silver orb he gave me. I'm glad that he thought of this. Seeing the churning river water, dark as the night, I'm relieved to know that I have a source of light.

I stash the bag behind a tree trunk and cross to the river. I step in, and my muscles go rigid.

Fuck. It's cold. Even with the suit on, it's fucking freezing. The suit clings tightly to my body like the wetsuits humans wear. It insulates me and traps the heat to keep me warm, but the river is still just barely above the temperature of ice, so the chill gets through. The suit can only do so much with ice-cold water. My bare hands sting.

I look around one last time, wondering if I'll ever see the surface again, then dive in, submerging myself in frigid water. I kick my legs, moving as fast as I can, but the river is doing some of the work, too. It drags me along toward the castle, and I hold my breath. For a few moments, panic floods me as my lungs burn. But then I force myself to exhale, and the gills start working, and I stop feeling that terrifying drowning sensation. I can breathe underwater. And it's *weird*.

It's murky and dark beneath the surface. Without the light, I'd be lost. I run my hand over the silvery orb, and it begins to glow faintly, revealing my surroundings. The bottom of the river is a few yards below me. I swim as close to the bottom as I can so the soldiers won't see the light from the orb.

The current is pulling me into its churn. I'd started in the river's bend, where it was calmer, but as I dive deeper, I'm getting swept up by the swirling current, and soon, I don't know up from down. The inexorable force of the river slams me into a protruding rock. I let out a gasp, bubbles floating up from my mouth. I try to swim higher again, but the undercurrent is keeping me down, tumbling my body over rocks. I cover my head as best as I can. My hand hits a rock, and my frozen fingers fumble at my silver orb, losing it.

Fuck.

Aghast, I search for the light. There it is! It's slowly sinking in the water a few feet away from me. Swimming with all my strength against the current, I make a desperate grab for the orb and grasp it, though barely.

I'm pulled along again—there's no up or down in this darkness. I can't see the surface, just glimpses of rocks. Have I gone under the fortress yet? Then, at last, something slams into me, and I nearly lose the orb again.

No, it didn't slam into me. I slammed into *it*. Metal bars block my way, a grill to prevent intruders from the river. Like me.

The problem is, I can't swim back against the unrelenting force of the current. Unless I find a way through, I'll be trapped here until the tincture effects dissipate. I'll either drown or freeze to death.

My heart is hammering in my chest as I lift the orb and shine it on the bars. There are four of them jutting from the rocks below and extending to the tunnel arches above me.

They're not spread evenly, though. There's a slightly larger space between two of the bars. A large intruder could never get through the gap, but I'm smaller than a normal Fey.

I maneuver myself between the bars and get my head through first. But then my shoulders get trapped between the bars, and the cold water rushes over me. As the seconds go by, I start to panic. I'd scream if I could. I thrash and try to wriggle loose, my mind blank with terror.

Kicking wildly, my foot finds a hold on a rocky outcrop of one of the walls, and I use the leverage to shove myself through. My shoulders go through the bars, and with a bit of squirming and twisting, my hips do, too. I'm exhausted, and I let the current pull me along the tunnel on the other side.

A thought nags at the back of my mind—what if I'd read the map wrong? What if the river doesn't actually open up in a courtyard? I'd only had a quick glimpse at the map…

But just as I'm about to lose hope, the current starts to weaken, and I see a light below me. It takes me a few seconds to realize that I'm looking at moonlight dancing over the water above me. I'm upside down.

I spin and kick my legs, swimming to the surface, nearly crying with relief. I grip a rocky ledge, pulling myself into the air. Nearby, a massive wooden wheel churns the water, and the light of the two moons pours down from above.

I'm inside the fortress, gasping for breath. Exhausted, I hoist myself onto the ledge beside the river, propping myself up onto my elbows. I want to hoist myself out of the cold, but I still need to take in the surroundings, to check for guards.

I sit up, surveying the tunnel. A stairwell by the

water wheel leads up. A few torches glow in the darkness beyond the water wheel, where a tunnel arches over the river. As far as I can see, there's no movement anywhere, no guards patrolling in the courtyard.

Honestly, I expected more security inside. I suppose Talan might keep personnel to a minimum to make this place as secret as possible.

My feet and my hands are numb with cold, but to Jasper's credit, my body is almost warm. I hug myself and climb the stairs next to the turning water wheel. When I reach the top, I peer out into a large courtyard, scanning for soldiers. Not a single one. No movement, no patrols. Just stone towers, a water pump, and ivy-lined walls. A narrow archway leads to what seems to be a second courtyard. Torchlight dances over stone and mist. What *is* this place?

One of the towers is significantly larger than the others, and warm light illuminates the mullioned windows. Keeping to the shadows, I creep toward the tower, scanning for any movement around the courtyard or on the walls around me, but it's eerily quiet. Why are there no guards within the walls?

I reach the main tower and glance up at the windows —no bars on them.

The wooden door inset into the wall looks enormous and heavy, studded with nails. I pull the handle, and it groans open, revealing a dark stairwell. My heart pounds as I step inside. A winding set of stairs curves up. I listen for the sound of voices, of footfalls, but don't hear a thing. I start climbing, my legs aching from the frantic swim. One story up, I reach a door.

I press my ear against the wood, listening.

Silence. Slowly, I push the door open. In the moonlit room, I take in the rows of bookshelves, a tapestry, and an enormous desk with unlit candelabras. An upholstered chair stands by an empty hearth. Nothing nefarious looking, more like a giant Fey office.

I step into the hall again, climbing the stairs.

When I reach the next floor, I find a small window inset into the wooden door. I peer inside. A lantern casts warm light over a room of eight small beds—each with little Fey children sleeping in them.

My heart skips a beat. This is *not* what I was expecting.

What does the Dream Stalker want with children? I can't even begin to imagine.

My stomach churns as my breath goes shallow. I walk over to the next window and peer inside. The same decor in this room as well and four more children, asleep in beds. These kids seem a bit smaller than the previous ones, and—

My breath stills in my lungs.

While the kids in the previous bunk had the long fingers and pointed ears of the Fey, *these* kids look more human—some of their ears are curved like mine usually are, when I'm not glamoured. One of them clutches a little stuffed duck in his tiny hands, clearly a human toy.

Human children and demi-Fey children, trapped in a fortress.

What the *fuck,* Talan?

I still have no idea what he's doing here at the Blue Dragon Project. Is he using them for some sort of experiment? Harvesting their little dreams for some dark purpose?

I can't just leave them here. He's already confessed to me that he wanted to slaughter all of humankind, so it's safe to say the children he's imprisoned are not in a good place. Where to get them *to,* though? I can't bring them back to Perillos, but I could hide them until I got word to Meriadec, Raphael, or someone else.

This fortress is unguarded from within. Obviously, they think that the external defenses are enough.

That means if I take out the guards at the main gate, I can free all the kids here and spirit them somewhere safe. The guards are looking for intruders from outside the compound, but they won't expect someone coming behind their backs.

I need to wake the kids first. Just in case one of the guards raises an alarm, we have to move quickly before reinforcements show up.

I gently push open the door to the room and cross to the first bed, where a little girl with curly blond hair is sleeping peacefully. I softly touch her arm. She sighs, her eyelids fluttering open. Her eyes focus and widen in alarm, and she clutches her blanket.

"Shh," I whisper. "Don't be afraid. I'm a friend. I've come to get you all out."

She recoils in horror and scoots away from me on the bed. Then her eyes shift, and I realize that she's looking at something over my shoulder. Before I can turn, a cold metal blade touches my throat, and someone twists my arm sharply behind my back.

"Really?" a hard feminine voice says. "Get them all out? I don't think *anyone* is getting out of here."

CHAPTER 30

I freeze, my heart slamming. The blade held to my neck presses hard, nicking my skin. Any movement might be my last.

"Rosalind, go to sleep," the woman behind me says gently. "I'll talk to our visitor outside."

"Should I call for help?" the girl asks.

"No need, sweetie. I have it under control. No one is taking you anywhere." Fingers tighten around my arm, and nails dig into my flesh. "Move. Slowly."

She spins me around and starts walking me back out. With the blade against my throat, I take small, measured steps to the door, and she reaches around me to pull it open.

The moment we're outside, she slams me against the wall, her knife immediately back on my throat. Right now, with my hands and feet still numb from cold, I have no chance of fighting her off.

"Okay, then." A lock of dark hair falls in front of her face as she bares her teeth, and I realize she doesn't have the canines of a full Fey. "Start telling me who you are."

She isn't wearing armor or anything else that would make her look like a soldier. In fact, she's wearing what looks like a silk nightgown. Her silver eyes have the metallic sheen of the Fey, but her ears are round.

There's something weirdly familiar about her, but I can't quite place it.

"You're demi-Fey," I say.

Her lip curls. "Perceptive, aren't you? I suppose you don't like the demi-Fey very much. Mongrels, the trash of Brocéliande, and all that?"

I swallow hard, regretting the powerful, meticulous glamour that disguises me. She wouldn't believe me if I said I was demi-Fey, and I'm still not clear if I should blow my cover. "What I mean is, you're not Fey military. They don't accept demi-Fey."

"Obviously, I'm not Fey military," she hisses. "I belong here."

"This…this is a fortress belonging to the royal family. Or a rogue branch of them. The Blue Dragon Project. I saw it labelled on a map. Is it a weapon? Is the Blue Dragon a weapon of some kind?"

"Is it a *what*?" she asks incredulously. She blinks a few times, then lets out a snort of laughter. "Yeah, yeah, it's a weapon. It's horrific. The children scream when they use it. So, who the fuck are you?"

Slowly, I start to put together why she looks familiar.

The dark hair, the bright silver of her eyes that blends to blue. The straight, black eyebrows.

"Do you know someone named Ysolde?" I ask.

She goes still, gripping my collar with her free hand. The blade eases just a little from my throat. "Where did you get that name?"

It's her.

I suck in a deep breath. "I know your brother. Raphael."

Her eyes widen, jaw dropping open. "Where is he?"

Of course, I'd love to help with their family reunion, but I have a job to do right now. "I'll tell you what I know, once you tell me what you know. What's the Blue Dragon Project?"

She narrows her eyes. She's breathing heavily, debating whether she should kill me now or let me live. But she's not going to sever the one thread that would lead her back to her brother. "Okay, then. Let me show you. We'll take a walk down the stairs. I'm removing my knife from your throat, but make a sudden move, and I'll slit your throat so fast, you won't even have time to scream."

I give her a nod.

Slowly, she eases the blade off my neck, keeping a vise-like grip on my arm as I walk down the stairs. I can feel the blade prodding at my back.

I steady myself on the stone wall as I descend. When I push through the door into the courtyard, the cold night air hits me, and I glance up at the moons.

Ysolde's fingers dig harder into me. She snarls, "Don't even think about trying to escape. Keep walking if you want to see the Blue Dragon. Through the archway."

We're heading for the second courtyard that I saw on my way in. And as we cross through the stone entrance, I gasp. A dragon looms above us in the dark.

Except…it doesn't move. It towers over us, immobile. As she shoves me closer, details start to emerge. Like its unblinking glassy eyes. Or the handful of twigs scattered over its feet. It's painted an iridescent blue, and its surface is smooth as metal. One of its wings swoops up toward the parapet, unmoving.

A ladder stretches up its side, and a slide runs down alongside its tail. It's a fucking playground.

"I give you the Blue Dragon Project," Ysolde says, and she points the knife at my throat again. "Terrible, isn't it? The kids can climb up the rungs, dangle from its mouth, and jump into that sand pit. See? And they can walk inside its belly and look out the windows. It's a real travesty."

"Why is this place here?" I finally ask.

"It's a safe haven for the fugitive kids. The exiled demi-Fey, the displaced humans. The war in the human lands left a lot of orphans without anyone to look after them. Here, they're safe. But now I want to know who the fuck you are. How do you know Raphael?"

"Someone brought human children into Brocéliande?"

"Humans, demi-Fey. Maybe you don't think these children deserve to live, but we don't leave kids behind, no matter who their parents are."

I'm still staring up at the structure. "But *how* did they get here? Give the rest of the story, and I'll tell you what I know about Raphael."

"There was a fortress just like this back in Fey France —that's a land in the human world. But about six months ago, it was attacked. By *humans*. So, the staff evacuated the orphaned kids and moved them here. It was built remarkably quickly, with magic I assume."

"Six months ago," I repeat.

The timeline can't be an accident. Six months ago, I returned from a mission with a map of Fey secret bases. When we broke into the Château des Rêves, we stole a map from Talan. Raphael hoped to use it to find his sister. I remember how angry Talan was, how he trapped us in a nightmare again and again, nearly drowning us. He was desperate to get that very map back.

But we turned it over to Avalon Tower.

Soon after, Avalon Tower launched attacks on some of these bases, hoping to cripple the Fey military position in northern France.

I swallow hard. Maybe one of those bases was an orphanage.

"This was all a terrible mistake," I mutter.

"Really," she responds dryly.

"How did you end up here, Ysolde?"

"I was one of the first fugitives brought to the fortress in France. I grew up in it. And as we got more children, and the war went on, I chose to stay and help with the kids. I would do anything to keep them safe."

"Who paid for all this?"

"We've never known. A powerful benefactor, a member of the nobility who doesn't want to reveal their identity. Probably someone who's secretly part human. I don't really care, just as long as the funds keep coming in."

Talan knew about it. Not only did he know about it, but he seemed desperate to protect it during the council meeting. But that doesn't mean he was *the* benefactor—only that he knew it existed.

There's a possibility that he's keeping the kids alive so he can prove someone's treason at exactly the right time. Or he plans to turn the children into his own army of undercover agents.

I have to consider all the options.

But the main thing I know right now is that Ysolde will kill me if I can't convince her that I'm on her side.

CHAPTER 31

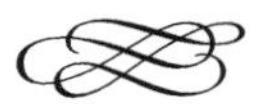

"I know your brother very well," I say at last.

"When did you last see him?"

"He's here, in Brocéliande. He was imprisoned by Auberon, but I broke him out of the dungeon. He heard that there were other demi-Fey still here. He's looking for you."

"And how do I know you're telling the truth?"

"He told me about the last day he saw you. He said your mom was human, and when Auberon started to scapegoat humans, she never thought it would go too far. She thought it was just bluster. But then one morning, when Raphael was nine and you were sixteen, soldiers banged on your door, ready to kill everyone. He said you screamed at him to run, and he did. He thought you were behind him. He waited in the forest, but you never came. A family took him in and brought him to unoccupied France."

I feel the point of the knife leave my spine, and she releases her grip on me. When I turn to look at her, I see that her silver eyes are misted with tears.

"He's really alive?" she whispers. "You have no idea how guilty I felt for losing track of him. I had no idea he was in France the whole time."

"He's fine. He lived in France, picking grapes in a vineyard. Then..." I hesitate. I don't know her well enough to trust her with the fact that Raphael is a spy. "Then he moved to England. But he's been trying to find you in any way he can since he was nine."

A single tear runs down her cheek. "I always assumed he was dead. They killed my mum. Someone brought me to the safe haven, and I was always waiting for him to show up. Where *is* Raphael now? Can you bring him to me?"

"I can get a message to him through my network, but he's a wanted man in Brocéliande," I say.

She frowns at me. "What's your name?"

"Better if you don't know." You never know when someone will be caught and interrogated. "I want to get Raphael back to England, but he won't go without you. Ysolde, he *needs* to see you. You said you volunteered to stay and look after the kids. Does that mean you're free to leave?"

She looks torn. "Yes, of course. But the kids here need me. There are four of us taking care of them."

"If you want Raphael to get to safety, I think you need to leave Brocéliande with him. He won't go without you. At the very least, you have to talk to him. Do you know a place called the Shadowed Thicket?"

"I know it."

"Go there when you can, in a few days if possible. Stay there until I can arrange a meeting. I don't know when it will be, but I'll make it happen. I'll find a way to get in touch with Raphael."

Her face has gone pale, and she glances nervously back the way we'd come. "Okay. Can you get out of here without the guards seeing you? I might trust that you know Raphael, but they won't give a fuck about what you told me."

"The way I came in is no longer an option." I shudder. "What would you suggest?"

"Are you a good climber?"

"Decent, I guess."

She looks around. "Give me a minute."

She disappears into the other courtyard, and I stand alone, hugging myself in the cold, my teeth chattering. After a few minutes, she comes back with a coil of rope. "Follow me." She crosses around the other side of the blue dragon and points at the outstretched wing. "One of the boys managed to climb up that wing, and from there, somehow, he got to the top of the wall. Scared the life out of me. You can climb up the ladder, but then crawl over the top. See how there are fake scales up there? Use them for leverage. You should be able to get onto the wing and climb up to the parapet, like you're going the wrong way up a slide. Once at the top, you can use this rope to climb down."

I eye the dragon's wing. It's doable. "That works." I take the rope from her.

"And I'll see you at the Shadowed Thicket in a little while." She smiles, and I see Raphael in that smile, her cheek dimpling a little.

I climb up the ladder, feeling ridiculous that I thought the thing was real for even one second. At the top, I grip the scales, scoot over to the swooping wing, and hoist myself up. When I reach the parapet, I grip the stone and climb, grunting as I pull myself onto the castle wall. I tie my rope to the crenellation. Before I go, I turn to look down at Ysolde.

She raises her hand in farewell. My eyes sting when I think of Raphael seeing her again at last. With a grunt, I climb down the fortress wall.

* * *

FATIGUE IS EATING AT ME, and I'm fighting to keep my eyes open. I rode for hours through the night. I'm still freezing, desperate to get under soft blankets, to feel the warmth of the fireplace heating the room.

I cross back from the stables to the castle. I've just barely made it before the sunrise. The moonlight still gleams off the courtyard snow as I trudge closer to warmth. I found only one guard by the messengers' gate, and mercifully, he didn't have many questions for me.

As I walk closer to Castle Perillos, I scan for signs of soldiers patrolling or anyone who might be following me. I see some guards by the main gate, as usual. There are none around the tower that leads up to my room.

I slip through the shadows, my legs aching with each step.

Before I pull open the door, I glance over my shoulder. Still no one around. I let out a sigh of relief.

But as I pull the tower door open, panic flares in my chest. The pale-haired guard stands at the bottom of the stairwell, arms folded. The scent of mead wafts off him, and his green eyes shine at me from the shadows.

I smile at him, but inwardly, my heart is slamming against my ribs. "See? Told you I'd be back without a problem."

He nods slowly. "And how was your trip back from Lauron? You didn't wait for me to gather the retinue."

"Well, like I said, there was no need to worry."

I start to climb the stairs, but he grabs my bicep. "So, if I checked with the soldiers who patrol the Faus-Amanz highway, they'd confirm they saw you pass about a half hour ago?"

My stomach swoops, and I'm already thinking of grabbing the dagger at my waist. "I mean, I don't think they were paying that much attention."

"There are no soldiers there. You would have known if you went through there."

I turn slowly to face his hard, metallic green glare.

"So why, my lady, would you be lying? Where did

you really go? The king keeps warning us against spies, and you're new to court. Getting invited into the High Council."

I breathe in, out.

In one swift motion, I twist my arm sharply. I merely expect to catch him unaware, but to my surprise, I manage to break his hold on me. I slam my elbow into his face, and it crunches. He cries out in pain, stumbling back.

Time slows down, the energy that has been building up in me for weeks starting to blaze through my body.

Mordred said that being here will awaken my dormant powers. The powers of the Lady of the Lake.

The guard is already drawing his sword, snarling. Gripping my dagger, I lunge for his throat, much faster than I ever used to be. He parries, awkwardly hitting me with his wrist. He knocks the dagger out of my hand, and it clatters to the stone, but he's struggling to manage his sword in the small space.

I kick him hard in the gut, knocking the wind out of him. He tries to call out, but his voice sounds choked now. I kick him again, slamming my foot into his wrist, pressing it between my boot and the wall until he drops the sword. But he punches me with his free hand, and it's not the punch of a human or a demi-Fey or anything I'm used to. It's the punch of full-blooded Fey with the strength of a fucking ox. The pain rockets through my skull, vibrating in my brain, and I stagger back. Hot blood fills my mouth.

Frantically, I grab my dagger off the floor, but by the time I'm up again, he's retrieved his sword. He lunges for me, and I try to dodge out of the way of his blade. I'm not fast enough. Pain rips through my side as his blade slices my flesh.

With that pain, more power blazes through me, and time crawls. The guard's movements suddenly seem clumsy, snail-like. I dart forward and swipe my blade across his throat in a swift, brutal arc, carving it open. He drops his sword again, gripping his neck as blood sprays around him. I watch as he slumps to the ground.

My thoughts are a raging tempest.

Footfalls, coming down the stairs. Someone obviously heard the shouting, the clattering of weapons.

But this time, I'm not going to stop for a conversation. I grit my teeth.

The moment the next soldier rounds the stairwell, I toss my dagger in a perfect arc. All the practice in the training halls of Avalon Tower intermingles with my newfound powers, sending my blade spinning directly into the man's throat. The hilt juts from his neck. Groaning, he manages to pull it out, but a gurgling noise rises from his gullet. My heart is thundering wildly, and the metallic scent of blood fills the hall.

He's dying too slowly. I grab the dagger from his hand and plunge it into his heart, severing his artery. My thoughts are roaring, my vision's swimming. What the fuck am I turning into? All I can smell is blood, and it drips from my lips. Is it mine or theirs? I feel like I've fucking bathed in it.

For a few minutes, I can't think coherently. It's just me breathing in the smell of death—until my survival instincts kick back into action.

I have to get rid of what I've done.

Right now.

I don't have another moment to waste.

I drag the bodies out into the wintry night, one at a time. It's still dark, thank the gods. But even when the bodies are gone, what am I to do with the blood soaking the stairwell?

Once the corpses are outside, I pull the jacket off the man with the pale blond hair. Guilt flutters through me as I wonder if there might've been another way, but I don't have time to dwell on it. I'm in enemy territory here. One slip up, and my severed head will end up on a pike, my limbs nailed to the gatehouse.

I carry the jacket back inside and use it to soak up some of the blood from the stairs. Then I carry handfuls of snow inside, letting them melt on the blood-streaked stairs. As fast as I can, I scrub some of that up with the second jacket. It's not perfect, but the stones are dark. I've soaked up most of the pools.

When the stairs look less like a bloodbath, I return to the bodies, dragging them by the shoulders, one in each hand. It should be an impossible feat because they're heavy as fuck, but some of that earlier magical energy is propelling me on. I hoist them across the darkened courtyard.

When I look behind me, I realize I've left trails of crimson. They're not bleeding much—their hearts have stopped. But it's still there. I'm bleeding on the snow, too.

There's not much to do but keep going.

I pull them past the willow tree, gripping them both, my knuckles white as I drag them. Frustration crackles through me at how slowly I'm moving, and I glance up at the sky. As soon as the sun comes out, I'm fucked. Anyone will be able to see me from the windows of the palace, hauling fucking corpses across the courtyard.

The first blush of dawn starts to tinge the sky, and my breath catches.

I force myself to move faster, but the pain in my side is agonizing.

At last, I get to the ley portal and feel the stones' magic shimmering over me. The hair rises on the back of my neck as I drag them toward the edge of the circle. Only Sentinels can get through the ring stones, and whatever they're carrying with them.

But is a corpse really a person? Or is it now a thing? I'm about to find out.

I glance up at the sky and see the predawn light staining the clouds pale amber. *Gods help me.* I need to do this now. I drag the bodies into the jagged stones, and the black tear opens before me. With them in my grasp, I fall through the portal.

I land hard on the cold, rocky earth of Avalon. I look around me to find the ring stones standing tall, washed in the first milky rays of morning light. The bodies made it through the portal with me.

From a distance, soft, deep laughter ripples across the garden. Gripping my slashed side, I look up to see Mordred stalking closer, his dark cloak flowing behind him. "Did you bring me something daughter? A gift. Like a cat brings a dead mouse to its owners. How sweet."

"I had to get rid of them," I say, still catching my breath.

"You're hurt," he says. "Let me help you."

"Do you have healing magic?" I ask.

He shakes his head. "That I don't, I'm afraid."

"Needle and thread?"

"Might take me a while to find them."

I glance across at the ruined castle. "Never mind. I need you to get rid of the bodies. Can you do that?"

A dark smile curls his lips. "I do remember a look in your eyes, condemning me for killing all those people in Lothian Tower. But truly, my daughter, you do take after me. I am delighted to find you just as ruthless."

My throat tightens. "Just get rid of the corpses."

And with that, I plunge back into the fortress of my enemies.

CHAPTER 32

I stagger up the stairs, gripping my side. Under my cloak, I press my hand against the slash in my waist to try to staunch the bleeding. Walking around isn't helping to stop the flow. While the fabric of my cloak is mostly soaking up the blood, I'm not sure how well I can mask the agony on my face or the panic of so much blood loss.

When finally reach my hallway, the morning light is pouring in through the windows. I don't want anyone stumbling out in the halls to find me dragging myself to my room, half-dead.

As I get closer to my door, I see Aisling carrying a tray of breakfast to my door. My jaw tightens. I'm going to have to mask this pain, to pretend everything is fine. And you know what? I learned how to do that well growing up: smile and pretend everything is great, even if the world is burning down. When the police show up, you smile and say Mom just has a fever; she'll be better soon.

Aisling turns to see me as I get closer and smiles brightly. "Oh, thank the gods you're back. I was so worried about you. Did you ask the soldiers to accompany you? It doesn't seem like you did. It's really not a good idea, Nia, traveling on your own. I'd never let *my* daughter run around the countryside alone. I was really hoping you'd be back. I brought you fruit and cheese. Did you want it here or the balcony?"

I feel nauseous, dizzy, but I smile at her, and I say, "Everything's fine. I just wanted to go home for a little bit to see my dad. He's doing great."

As I get closer, she frowns at me, clutching the breakfast tray. "Are you feeling all right?"

Fuck. "It's just a fever. I'll be better soon."

"Oh, of course. Well, I'll get you a healing brew for the fever."

My mouth is dry, and my vision is starting to go dark. "I ripped my dress."

Her eyebrows shoot up in surprise. "Not to worry. I'll fix it for you."

I hold up a hand. "No, I have nothing to do today, nothing at all. I really love mending. Especially when I'm not feeling well. Can you please just find me a needle and thread? Give me something to do while I've got a fever."

"It's really my job, my lady."

I shake my head. "You won't be out of work anytime

soon, I promise. I just need a little sewing kit to pass the time today." It comes out almost pleading.

"All right, then." With her elbow, she opens the door to my room and sets the tray of breakfast on my desk. I drop onto the bed, holding my cloak around me. For some reason, my teeth are chattering.

"You really are in rough shape, aren't you? Poor thing." She tuts. "I want you to spend the day resting. I'll bring you some tea."

"And the needle and thread."

* * *

I'M SWEATING and shaking as I drag the needle through my skin. My teeth are clenched hard, the entirety of my world narrowed to this one gash, to the needle going in and out. I'm sitting on the bathroom floor because the blood will be easier to clean up. My body feels hot and cold at the same time as I plunge the needle into my flesh again.

I grunt as I get to the end and shove the thread through. I tie the knot, and a tear slides down my face.

When I'm done, I rest my head on my shaking arms on the side of the tub and catch my breath.

* * *

HAIL DRUMS rhythmically against the window, and lightning cracks the sky outside. The tea that Aisling brought me has been helping to take away the sharp pain from my stab wound, although I still feel it as a dull throb in my side. The nightgown I'm wearing feels soft against my weary body. Jasper called this fabric veil-silk, and it does remind me of the veil—iridescent, nebulous, soft as air.

I've been in here all day. With the storm raging outside, it's almost cozy. Yes, I'm in the heart of the enemy's castle, a place where I'd be slowly tortured to death if they ever learned the truth about me. And yes, I had to kill two people and sew up my own wound earlier today.

And yet, I've had a few hours of respite. While I rested, I started to wonder if Talan could—against all odds—actually be an ally. Has his brutal, vicious, murderous personality all been a front? Or am I trying to convince myself of that because I'm insanely lonely and he has a pretty face? How easy it would be to convince myself he's a good guy and ruin the world while I'm at it.

I'm starting to see Raphael's point about not letting emotions cloud your thinking. I need data and analysis to guide me, not the allure of a gorgeous man. For now, all options are open.

I glance down at the book of Fey love poetry in my lap and flip the page. It has an almost violent quality to it, a lot of passages about raging storms, the deaths of gods, lightning igniting cities into infernos. Still, the language is starkly beautiful.

A knock sounds on my door. "Who is it?"

A deep voice pierces the wood. "It's your prince. Who else would it be?"

I swallow hard. I thought he was supposed to be gone longer.

Already, he's opening the door. Instinctively, I pull the blankets more tightly around me.

Talan saunters in, carrying a silver goblet. His rings gleam on his fingers, and the faint scent of wine and musk wafts into the room with him. His dark eyes look half-lidded as they slide to me, and his gaze brushes down, taking in the top of my nightgown.

"Usually, you wait for someone to say *come in* after you knock," I protest.

A lock of his hair falls before his eyes, and I can tell he's ever so slightly drunk. "You know, I almost missed your mutinous attitude, my favorite mistress. Everyone around me is so fucking deferential."

"Might it be your habit of slitting the throats of those who annoy you?"

He slips off his shoes. "And yet here you are, living and breathing before me, your heart still beating, cheeks pink with life, while you take such great pleasure in insulting me." He takes a sip from his wineglass, then frowns at my book. "Are you reading love poetry? A bit lonely, are you?"

I was absolutely, chest-achingly lonely here in the palace of lies I'd constructed for myself. "Just bored."

"We can get you a bucket of dirt and some onions if

it would make you happy." He plucks the book from my lap. "Is it good?"

"The writing is interesting…lots of morbid metaphors. *Love, relentless as death, tortures me at the gallows.*"

A smile ghosts over his full lips, and he traces his fingertips over the words. "Good. I like my beautiful things to have a bit of darkness in them."

"Well, that describes you perfectly."

"That makes the second time you've called me beautiful." He lets out a sigh. "We have a problem, though."

"What problem?"

"Lumos was with me on my trip, and he's still asking questions about you. He remains convinced that this is fake."

I open my eyes wide. "Wherever would he get that idea?"

He sits on my bed and slides his wineglass onto the table. "He had *all* sorts of questions for me about you. And knowing that obsessive, conniving bastard, he'll double-check everything. So, tell me about yourself so I don't get this wrong. I need to actually know you, Nia. And since I can't get in your head, you're a complete mystery to me, and I'm afraid you'll have to use words to explain yourself. It's frankly not something I'm used to."

"You already know where I'm from. You met my family. What else is there to tell?"

He leans his head back against the propped-up pillows. "Lumos, for whatever reason, thinks I'm wildly self-obsessed and there's no way I could ever possibly fancy a pig farmer unless I saw something in you that reminds me of myself. Bizarre, isn't it?"

Thunder rumbles outside, and Talan's dark gaze searches mine. Is he anything like me? That's the question. Is it possible that he's secretly saving all those human kids—that *he* is the secret benefactor?

Considering Avalon Tower is in the process of trying to assassinate him, I really need to find out.

"I've spent a lot of time pretending to be something I'm not," I say. "Not just here. At home, too. I pretend like I have everything together, that I'm in control, that everything is fine. I'm very skilled at hiding what I'm feeling."

"Because your father isn't in control, so you pretend to be."

My mother, I think, *but yes*. I nod.

Intensity sparks in his eyes, and the rings of copper seem bright in the firelight. His skin looks warm, too. Gilded. "Perhaps we do have something in common. Tell me more."

I think back to my real life—my Nia Melisende life, not Vaillancourt. There were the times my mom forgot to pick me up from school, and I'd have to make up a quick lie to the teachers so they wouldn't worry and judge her. *You know what? I forgot,* I'd say with a smile. *I'm supposed to walk to dance class today.* Then I'd make the two-mile trek home in the LA heat.

There was the time my mom fell down the stairs and

broke her jaw, and I called the ambulance. The first responders asked me if she'd been drinking, and I blamed it on a broken stair. There were the hundreds of times I claimed that she couldn't show up to school events because she had a work emergency, so I made up a career for her—she worked in PR, and she had to entertain a celebrity. When I got home, I made dinner and did the laundry.

All day long, it was a torrent, an absolute waterfall of lies to make it seem like no one needed to worry.

Clearly, I was raised to be a spy.

"When our family came to visit and people would ask after my father, I'd make up excuses for him. I'd say he was sick or working. I'd take care of everything. I learned that no one will take care of you, and you must take care of yourself. And it always made me feel like I'd never amount to anything because there was always work to do, or someone to look after, so there was no point in having dreams. So, I felt like life would pass me by. I felt like the dreams and goals that other people had weren't meant for me. I had too much to do, and it trapped me. It was like I was watching the world through a looking glass I was stuck behind."

His eyes narrow. "I think I want to hurt the person who made you think all of that."

My heart flutters. I don't want him hunting down Meriadec, and he seems like just the kind of person who might. I wouldn't want him to hurt my real mom, either. Spending time with her when she was actually paying attention to me was glorious. I remember when she'd take me to Venice Beach, and she'd buy me funnel cake, and we'd stop to watch the musicians play. Once, she bought me a kite shaped like a giant dragonfly, with bright ribbons that flowed off it. Then we'd wander through nearby art galleries and pick out pieces that would decorate our future, imaginary mansions.

"My father can be fun, too," I said quickly. "He has an artistic side. He always wants more than we have. He lives in his head and dreams of greatness but can't ever seem to get there. He's stuck in a life he didn't want. He tried to escape in any way he could, and the easiest way is by getting drunk. He wanted better for me, but he didn't know how to make it happen, and it was just his own narrow vision of what greatness was. So, maybe my own dreams got lost while I was looking after him. But things have changed, haven't they? And now I'm here. And it's not the worst thing in the world to be able to take care of yourself. It's kind of a gift to be self-sufficient."

When I look back at Talan, he has gone completely still. "I think there's more to you than Lumos could ever have realized."

"You said that we had something in common. You're hiding something, too. So, what is it?"

A line forms between his eyebrows. "Father's reign has always wrought catastrophe. He will unravel the fabric of our kingdom, like a loom weaving in reverse, until all is tangled and ruined. He turns the world into a rotten necropolis where hope withers on the vine. Where we watch our lives pass by, helpless to change our fates."

I swallow hard. When he's drunk, the words he speaks out loud sound more like his thoughts. Strange. Poetic. This is the real Talan. "But what, exactly, will you change?"

His gaze shutters, and he looks away from me. "Like I said, I will achieve our goals more efficiently."

He glances at me again, as if he's searching to see how I'll react. Then he frowns at me. He reaches to brush his thumb over my chin, just below my lips. "How did you get hurt?"

My heart speeds up. I'd just looked in the mirror twenty minutes ago, and I thought it looked much better. But of course, I didn't have the godlike Fey senses. "It's nothing."

"But how did it happen?"

My mind whirls as I try to come up with another story, but I feel crushed by all the lies, each one of them a rock weighing on my chest. Breaking my ribs. I'm desperate for something real, a connection with anyone. And I have the most insane impulse to simply tell him the truth about everything.

I'm lying to him, to Tana, to Nivene, to Mordred, to Raphael and every single person I know, and right now, I just want to scream the truth, even if it kills me.

Of course, I know that makes no sense at all, so I swallow the impulse, bitterly.

I realize I've simply been staring at him in silence for far too long.

"Nia," he says softly. "If you want to keep your secrets, you can."

"Why?"

"Because I trust you."

I blink. Strangely, my eyes are misting. "Why would you trust me?"

"I don't know. For some reason, I feel like I know you."

I swallow hard. No one knows me, though, do they?

He drains the rest of his wineglass, then stands, heading for the bathroom. "I'm going to take a bath."

"Just make yourself at home."

He turns back to me with a half-smile. "Perillos *is* my home, my mistress."

CHAPTER 33

Talan stalks out of the shower wearing only a pair of small, black underwear that doesn't leave much to the imagination. I find myself staring at the vinelike tattoos that trace over his muscles, coiling around his large bicep. For the briefest moment, I imagine running my tongue over those tattoos—and then I quickly force the image from my mind.

For the first time since I met him, he seems softer, his usual mocking expression replaced with something else that I can't quite pinpoint.

I remember to close my mouth as he crosses to the bed. The air between us feels charged. I absolutely cannot let myself fall under his seductive spell. Maybe he trusts me—maybe that was a lie. But I can't assume he's on my side until I know the truth and I have actual intel to confirm it. If I get this wrong, it's all over.

When he slides into the bed next to me, I shift away

from him, like I might be burned by his touch. As I do, I wince involuntarily at the throbbing pain in my side.

Talan, of course, notices.

His dark gaze sweeps down, and he frowns at my waist, exactly where I was stabbed. "What happened?"

"You said I could keep my secrets."

His gaze flicks up, piercing me. The copper rings in his eyes grow bright as flames. "I've changed my mind, because if someone attacked you, that's a secret you cannot keep. Did this knave stab you with a knife or a sword? What did he look like?"

I swallow hard. This is getting harder and harder to conceal. "An assassin, maybe. I didn't want you to make a big thing of it and go on a murder rampage."

"An assassin?" His voice is ice-cold, his eyes dark with anger.

"You know that since I first got here, people have wanted me out of the way. They see me as a threat."

"Was he from Arwenna's family? Sent by my father? Some other noble's mercenary?"

"We didn't get that far in the conversation."

A muscle flexes in his jaw. "Let me see. I can heal it."

Fuck. He'll see the mangled job I did with the thread.

I inhale sharply. "It might look a bit gruesome."

"Let me see." His deep voice echoes with the authority of a king's command, and his eyes are narrowed.

"Fine. But it's not pretty." Swallowing hard, I hoist up the hem of my nightgown, exposing my pale pink underwear that barely covers what it needs to. As I do, Talan's eyes flick up to me, his jaw flexing. In the cool castle air, I feel exposed before him, but the Fey aren't self-conscious.

Taking a deep breath, I pull the hem further up until the garment is just under my ribs. As I do, a chill ripples over the room, and the torches gutter, almost sputtering out. Outside, lightning cracks the sky.

"And they sewed you with thread?" His voice chills my blood. "Is this why there were reports of blood in the courtyard?"

"I sewed it. I was trying to stop the bleeding."

When he looks up at me, I can see that he has never heard of this concept before.

"It's a farm thing," I say quickly. "We didn't have access to the court healers that you have. I know it's not healing as fast as it should, so it made me wonder if there was a toxin."

"I need to know what the assassin looked like."

"He was dressed as a soldier."

"Shall I have them all killed, then? Every soldier working last night? Their entrails drawn out of them until someone confesses?"

Oh, gods. I can't tell if he's joking. It could go either way with him. I clear my throat. "That's not necessary, Talan. There were two of them, and they ran off, but I injured them severely. I think they bled to death in the woods."

"I will find whoever is behind this. Arwenna,

perhaps. There are rumors that she's been trying to kill you."

Talan stares at my wound again, and the temperature in the room cools even further. Thunder rumbles across the horizon outside, and hail slams against the window.

"Let me fix that abomination." Frowning, he turns, scanning the room. He rises from the bed and yanks open a drawer. Thank the gods for my caution: my inhaler, lock picks, and spare knives are hidden behind a loose brick in the bathroom, where they won't be found accidentally. He pulls out the little sewing kit I'd used to stitch myself, takes out a needle and a tiny pair of silver scissors, and settles next to me on the bed.

His attention narrows to the rough-looking stitching on my waist. Gently, carefully, he uses the needle to tease out the knotted thread. Then, using the small scissors, he snips the knot. The pain beneath it throbs a little as he works. As heat radiates off his skin onto mine, he pulls out the thread. I feel it tugging against my skin until he smoothly removes the final stitch. It looks slightly healed now, and there's a bad, jagged red scar, but it's no longer an open wound. Pain still blooms beneath the surface.

He glances up at me. "I can help you." He grabs my hips, shifting me down a little.

"Is this really necessary?" I whisper.

He nods, and I feel his warm breath against my skin. Already, shivers are running over my skin. His warm, strong palms root my hips in place. His lips brush against the cut, lightly at first. Testing. Then he extends his tongue, licking around the red scar. As he does, hot tingles spread from the place where his tongue meets my skin. My heart starts to race, and the heat of his mouth moves over me.

Holding me firmly in place, he kisses my skin. As his healing magic ripples through me, I hear faint glimpses of his thoughts—lust-soaked glimmers dripping with desire.

She scorches me with her stare...I will bind our bodies as a tempest of desire sweeps through us...I want to taste her. I want to hear her scream my name, our passion a comet streaking across the sky...

His tongue strokes my skin, and need sweeps through me. An aching warmth pulses in my core, and my thighs clench.

My nightgown is still hitched over my waist, and I'm acutely aware of how naked I am now. He grips the hem in his fist, holding it up, his knuckles white. My back arches, hips bucking a little.

I will brand her with a kiss...

My breath shallows, and my skin looks healed now, but his tongue brushes over the hollows of my hips. Pleasure rocks through me, and liquid heat courses down. I can hardly think straight. Under my nightgown, my breasts peak. As I breathe in and out, the delicate silk feels like an exquisite torture. I crave more of him.

I let out a moan—

Gods, I can't let this happen. I'm supposed to be spying on him, not letting him seduce me.

My fingers thread into his hair. "I think it's done now," I manage in a whisper.

He lifts his head to gaze at me, his copper-ringed eyes smoldering like embers. "But I don't think you are done with me," he whispers. "Are you?" He glances up at me, searching my eyes, as if he's seeing right into my soul, discovering my secrets, taking me apart one piece at a time. Uncovering exactly how much my body aches for him.

I'm breathing hard, and my pulse is racing. "Our relationship is supposed to be fake. That was the deal."

His biceps flex as he moves his face closer to mine, and his earthy, musky scent envelops me. One of his hands is still gripping my nightgown, and his lips hover above mine. "But you want me, don't you? Are you lying to yourself when you say you don't?"

I lick my lips, and I can't bring myself to say no. I'm sure he can read my secrets, anyway. He doesn't know who I am, but he knows what I want. Warmth radiates off his powerful body, and I feel his magic licking at my skin, stroking me.

His stare ignites me, and sensual need sweeps through me. Without even realizing what I'm doing, I wrap my thighs around his waist.

My mind is screaming at me to stop this, but I don't seem to be able to find the words as his body presses over mine, steely and unyielding.

His full, sensual lips part. I can't look away from his perfect face, from the heat in his eyes. From that intoxicating darkness in them.

I try to think clearly, but all I can hear is my own heartbeat, rhythmically pounding.

"Tell me if you want me to stop," he says.

His beauty entrances me, and I can't seem to form the words. I should be telling him to stop. That I'm already healed. But all I do is lick my lips in invitation.

His head dips, and I feel his breath on my neck. His canines graze over the throbbing pulse in my throat, feather-light, and hot tingles race over my body. Arching my neck, I invite more. He kisses my throat, tongue flicking over my skin, and my core tightens. He's tasting me, teasing me.

As my hips shift against him, I grip his hair. Slow, languid strokes of his tongue slide over the throbbing pulse in my neck. His body is steely and warm against me, his skin surprisingly soft.

Flames consume the night...simmering in a crucible of lust...

The torches seem to burn brighter around us, heating the room. I let out another quiet, desperate moan.

When he looks up at me, his eyes smolder with a hungry intensity. My blood turns molten. His heartbreaking beauty holds me captive.

He gives me a faint, knowing smile. "So, no, then? You don't want me to stop, I take it?"

"Talan."

"Yes? Why don't you tell me what you want? I already know, Nia. But I want to hear you say it."

Releasing my nightgown, he slides his fingers into my hair and tugs my head back just a little. I'm vulnerable, pinned as he brings his canines to my throat once more. His tongue swirls, and all I can think about is how it would feel to have his mouth close over one of my nipples. My breasts ache for him, and my whole body pulses with need.

As he brushes his lips over mine, my muscles melt. I'm at his mercy.

With my hands in his hair, I pull him closer, arching into him. He claims my mouth, his lips moving against mine in a kiss of incandescent heat. As his tongue slides against mine, his fingers curl in my hair possessively, and the kiss deepens, growing more demanding, wild. He's tasting me, stroking me with his tongue, and my thighs tighten around him. Quietly, I moan into his mouth, and his kiss grows hungrier. He tugs gently at the back of my hair. He has me exactly where he wants me. With a nip to my lower lip, he pulls away, catching his breath.

He raises his eyelashes, staring into my eyes. "Tell me what you want, Nia."

His body is warm, the muscles firm and unyielding against my skin, and I want to savor every inch of it. I want to run my fingers, my tongue over his muscled shoulders, his chest, his abs...

And when I look into his eyes, I feel like I'm drowning. I can hardly think straight. I'm on fire, and I can barely remember what I'm doing.

But as I catch my breath, I force myself to focus on reality.

I can't do this. Letting him fuck me for real could destroy any shred of objectivity I have.

I'm here as a spy. I'm here to figure out who is good and who is evil. To separate fact from fiction. And nothing will cloud my judgment more than giving in to him. If I do, deep down under the layers of rationality, I'll scramble to hold on to the evidence that supports what I want.

Of course, I can't give him that reason.

"I don't want this. I know the reputation you have, and I don't want to be another notch on your bedpost. If I'm going to give my body to someone, it will be for love. Not because I'm pretending."

Something flickers in his eyes, and for a moment, I think it's hurt. But then he gives me a faint smile and pulls away. Folding his hands behind his head, he lies back. "For someone who seemingly hates to experiment, you are quite adept at supplying me with new experiences."

My heart is still racing out of control, and I know he can hear it. "Being turned down for sex?"

"That's the one." He brushes his thumb over my cheek. "We are alike, you know, you and I. Left on our own to raise ourselves. We learned to play a part. We are costumed players strutting across a stage. But some day, Nia, I will learn the full truth of who is underneath that mask."

I turn over and blow out the candles.

I'm still thinking of the feel of his mouth claiming mine, his tongue tasting me.

My thighs clench, my skin still heated. I already know I won't be able to sleep tonight.

* * *

I ROLL OVER, watching him as he sleeps. He's snoring ever so quietly, his muscled chest rising and falling.

My mind is branded with that kiss, and I can't stop thinking about the feel of his tongue on my waist, on my hips, sliding and tasting me. My self-control nearly simmered away.

Now, while he's sleeping, I need to get an idea of what he's thinking. When he's out cold, he won't be able to feel me searching around in his mind.

I roll over and carefully slide my arm around his waist. He stirs a little, then folds his arm over mine. He smells amazing.

Gently, I tug at my powers. The pain sears through my mind, but I ignore it, sending a probing touch into Talan's thoughts. I can't risk digging deep. Even in his sleep, he might sense me as he has done before. And this time, it will end with my neck on the chopping block. So, I don't dig down—I caress, my powers brushing against his psyche like my lips against his. This is a seduction, not an invasion.

And in his mind, I find him dreaming of me, my arms wrapped around his shoulders in an apple grove. He kisses me hard and hikes up my skirt to my waist—

The dream is interrupted by another, one that is angry, dangerous. A suspicion. Even as he sleeps, it spins in his mind.

...a human-sympathizing spy in the High Council?

My heart skips a beat. What does he know? That someone passed on information about the attack, I suppose. A spy got the warning through to the allies. Does he have any inkling that it might be me?

Unable to restrain myself, I delve deeper after this thought, searching, probing—

His eyes snap open. I yank my powers back and summon the protective veil to cloud my mind.

His muscles have gone tense, and his dark eyes slide to me.

"What was that?" he asks with an edge in his voice.

"What?" I ask, blinking as if I'd just awakened. I slide my arm off his.

"I felt something familiar," he murmurs. "It's gone."

"Oh," I say sleepily.

"Your heartbeat is still wild."

"You startled me from a dream," I mumble. "A nightmare, actually. We were getting married." I force myself to be calm, and my heart slows down.

He frowns at me in the moonlight, then rolls over.

Gradually, his breathing slows, and I hear him mumbling something as he sleeps. *Where your fairytale comes to life...*

My breath stills, and shock courses through me. The words aren't spoken in Fey. He's speaking English. And it's a phrase that I know *very* well. *Where your fairytale comes to life* is the slogan of the bookstore where I worked back in LA.

My mind reels. All this time I was hearing his thoughts, I never imagined he was hearing mine, too.

I lie awake until dawn.

CHAPTER 34

It's been storming outside for days, and the frozen rain hammers against the leaded glass windows in my room.

Talan hasn't returned to my chambers this week. Without him or Nivene, I've been mostly on my own with only my worries for company.

I keep wondering if there's a way to misdirect Talan away from his discovery of a spy on the High Council. Maybe—if I could get out of here—I could plant evidence pointing at a different noble? It might be a good idea, but not without its risks.

The ideal candidate would be Lord Draven, rumored to have an impure bloodline, his great-grandmother a bastard demi-Fey. But I'd be condemning him to death. I'd rather choose an Auberon-loving fanatic to take out. There were enough of those.

Thunder shakes the windowpanes, and I pour myself a little wine and pace across the flagstones.

Questions swirl in my skull. Is Nivene all right? What's going on in the war in Scotland? And what about the dragon attack? I have no idea if the human forces managed to stop it.

My instructions have me feeling trapped: *Lie low. Maintain your cover.*

Do nothing.

The longer the days drag on, the more worries start to poison my thoughts.

I pivot, stalking across the room again. I find myself hoping that the dark prince will show up. At least I'd have someone to talk to.

But I did the right thing turning him down. Unless sex serves my purposes as a spy, it can't be on the menu.

There's a rustle of paper, and a note slides under my door. I pick up the envelope and see my name written in an elegant script. I open the door, peering into the hall, and spot a servant hustling away.

I turn over the envelope. Talan's wax seal is imprinted on the back, a dragon eating its tail.

Inside is a short letter in black ink written in Talan's swooping handwriting.

I have been searching for your would-be assassins. I've found nothing except that two soldiers are missing—and so is Arwenna. I believe she has been conspiring to kill you and is now in hiding. But you already knew that, didn't you?

Stay in your room until you hear from me. I'm sending soldiers to guard your door.

I crumple up the note and throw it into the fire.

When I pull my door open again, I find two soldiers marching toward me.

I'm more a prisoner here than ever.

CHAPTER 35

I restlessly stalk around my room. The moons outside my windows are huge, a ruby and diamond in the sky.

It's been almost a week since I received a message from Avalon Tower. I still have no answer to my report about the Blue Dragon Project, and I've heard nothing about Talan's *human spy* suspicions. When I leave my room now, I have to get past soldiers.

I've managed to sneak out a few times, but it wasn't easy. I haven't been able to get to the Shadowed Thicket or find Meriadoc or Raphael.

I grab my midnight blue cloak and pull it over me, raising the cowl.

Flinging my door open, I smile at the two guards. "Just going out for a walk."

"My lady," one of them says, "I thought we were supposed to guard you."

My eyebrows flick up. "I was told you were supposed to guard the room. You're the same soldiers who were here two nights ago, aren't you? We've covered this already. Remember? You're supposed to guard the room."

"Well, obviously..." he begins, stammering.

He seems like the one calling the shots. And he needs more encouragement.

Smiling coquettishly, I touch his arm. Sharp pain rips through my skull, hammering at my brain, but I push through it, sending tendrils of my magic into him. His defenses are minimal. He's young, inexperienced, and fairly lazy. *Listen to me,* I whisper in his mind. *I know what the prince wants.*

I clear my throat. "I'm sure you'll agree that the prince..." I almost can't get the words out for the pain, and I'm struggling to remember how words work at all. "Prince wants you to guard the room, not to imprison me...his favored mistress. He was very clear that I'm not a prisoner here."

My fingers tighten into fists, and I break out in a cold sweat, but to my relief, it works.

"Yes," he says with a nod, "you're right."

His friend looks unconvinced, and I brace myself. Would I need to mind control him, too? I don't think I'd be able to stand the pain.

But then he shrugs and looks at the other guard. "Okay, whatever you think."

"Guarding the room," the first one mumbles.

I hurry away before they realize that anything is amiss.

My head is throbbing by the time I reach the stairs, and nausea turns my stomach. I touch the stone wall as I stumble down the steps, wishing—not for the first time—that this place had elevators.

From the corner of my eye, I see movement, a shadowy figure. I turn to look, but it's gone, and spots dance before my eyes.

By the time I reach the bottom floor, the throbbing in my skull starts to dull. I step outside into the crisp air, heading for the garden, where the white-petaled snow-drops droop over the icy earth and blood-red witch hazel dapples the landscape.

Reaching a gnarled oak, I sit on a stone bench, as I did the night before, and breathe in the floral air, which is faintly scented with moss.

With a quick glance around to make sure no one is looking, I lift a broken flagstone with the tip of my shoe. This is one of our drop-off locations. My heart sinks. Nothing, again.

Something is wrong, I'm certain of it. Things in Scotland have gone off course for the human allies.

Worry and frustration have been coiling and twisting inside me for weeks, ready to spring. I feel trapped here.

I stand and stride back to the castle, glancing at the ley portal as I walk. Maybe I should run back to my world.

Although my heart is hammering as fast as ever, I keep my pace steady. If anyone's watching me from their windows, I want them to think I'm simply out for an evening stroll. I reach the southern tower closest to the ley portal and look around. A cold wind whips over me as I scan the wintry landscape.

My breath shallows as I stare across the courtyard at the willow tree.

I should be patient. I'll give it one or two more days before I break out of here.

I whirl to hurry back to my room, but as I turn, ice frosts my veins.

Talan stalks toward me, his black cloak trailing behind him under the claret sheen of the moonlight. His eyes are fixed on me, and the air around him is dark, his pace determined. Has he figured out who the spy is?

Instinctively, I take a step back and catch myself. I can't act scared. Visible fear will be the author of my death sentence.

Though my heart hammers, I manage a smile as he prowls closer. If I can't keep calm, he'll be suspicious.

"Nia." There's an edge to his low, silky voice. "You need to get inside."

"Why the rush?" I ask serenely. "It's a beautiful night. I just needed some air."

"I should have realized you'd mind control the guards. But I did warn you in the note that you are in danger. And it's worse now. My informants reported that someone has smuggled iron into the fortress. A large amount, in fact. We both need to get inside. Quickly."

Iron?

"I don't understand. Why would anyone smuggle iron here?"

"To kill someone," Talan says sharply. "We assume it's some sort of iron weapon. We don't know who the target is yet, but considering someone tried to kill you last week, I'd say you could be high on the list. Being my mistress has made you enemies."

I swallow hard. Is it the work of Arwenna or the assassin from Avalon Tower, sent with iron intended for Talan and his father?

"Let's go." He grips my hand firmly and turns to lead me back to my room. I follow along, my gaze trailing up at the towering palace.

And that's when I see her, a vision of white in the tower.

Arwenna.

She's standing with a crossbow in her hands. Time slows, and the wind whips at her silver hair.

I gasp as she lets loose an arrow and try to move out of the way, but I already know I'm too late.

As I brace for the fatal blow, Talan slams into me. I tumble into the snow, my teeth snapping together with a jolt. I roll to my back, looking up at the window for the next arrow, but Arwenna is already gone.

I gasp for breath, my thoughts crystallizing.

Turning, I see Talan lying on his back, gripping the

arrow shaft. It juts from his chest, just above his heart. Impossibly, it looks like he managed to grab the deadly bolt in mid-flight.

"Thank you," I whisper.

His eyes flutter, and I realize that he didn't manage to stop the bolt entirely. The tip is embedded in his chest. I scramble over to him. From the corner of my eye, I notice blue-jacketed soldiers running our way, too late to protect us.

"Is it deep?" I ask.

"No," he whispers, "but it's fucking iron."

He yanks the bolt out, and blood drips from the point.

As I stare at the crimson tip, I notice the metallic sheen underneath.

He drops the bolt and clenches his jaw. His lips are already turning a faint shade of blue.

I scream at the guards for help, a ragged note of hysteria in my voice.

I'm shocked to find that I'm screaming at them to save the life of the man I've been planning to kill all this time.

CHAPTER 36

When I reach Talan's bedroom, the guard at the door tenses. Then he nods, letting me pass. He's obviously heard what happened to the last soldier who tried to stop me from going into the prince's room.

I find Talan lying in his bed. His lips are still tinged with blue, but he's awake, clutching his chest. A soldier stands by his side.

"I want it done right now," Talan says.

He glances my way and raises a finger, indicating for me to wait.

"Sir, I'm not sure that this is the moment for such... gestures," the guard says uneasily. "Surely we need all of our manpower to search for the assassin—"

"You will do as I order," Talan says, his voice as hard as steel. "Four men guarding it at all times. No one gets near it, you got that?"

"Very well, Your Highness," the guard stutters.

He hurries out of the room.

"What was that about?" I approach his bed and sit on the edge.

"You don't need to worry about it."

"The healer says you'll be fine in a few days," I say. "As soon as your body purifies itself of the poison."

"I don't have a few days," Talan mumbles. "Too much to do."

"Well, give it a few hours, then. Even the formidable Dream Stalker needs to recuperate after being shot by an iron arrow."

"No need to be dramatic." His lips quirk. "It was just an iron tip."

I clear my throat. "You saved my life."

He glances up at me, then gives me a wry smile. "Well, I couldn't let my secret weapon die, could I?"

I sigh. "I guess not."

"I saw the arrow flying for you but not the attacker. Did you get a look at them?"

"It was Arwenna," I answer. "From a window."

"Of course."

"I thought I saw someone when I left my room. She must have had someone watching me, waiting for me to leave."

He nods, grimacing.

I pick up a little glass bottle of blue oil. "What's this?"

"It's supposed to help me sleep. It eases the pain." He winces, hand over his chest.

"Do you want some now?"

Frowning, he pushes himself up on his elbows and pulls the bottle from my hand. He takes a deep sip, then gives it to me and falls back onto his pillow. His large hand protectively covers his flesh where it was pierced, and I watch him fall asleep, his chest rising and falling. His cheekbones look sharper than usual, his dark hair tousled, black eyelashes stark against his skin.

I feel strangely protective toward him, which is insane. I'm specifically here to help plan his assassination.

But I have more questions about him than I started with, and I won't ever have another opportunity like this, with him in a drug-induced sleep. He won't wake easily or sense me at all.

I wait until I'm sure he's asleep, his breathing slow and his body relaxed, and touch his shoulder. It happens without effort when my fingers touch his skin. Unlike my encounters with others, there's no pain, and his thoughts drift closer to me like toy sailboats floating on a stream. It's effortless.

In his mind, I see a woman standing over him, her eyes dark as his, her hair streaming over a white gown. Behind her is a tapestry of a weeping willow.

His mother.

Now, a raging storm clouds the sky, lightning igniting the landscape. Thunder rumbles over the horizon.

She's led to a wooden scaffold, her hair draped over a

long, thin gown. Her arms are tied behind her back. Wind tears at the landscape, rain hammering, as she's bound to a stake with kindling at her feet. A keening sound rends the air as someone brings a torch to the wood. Talan's fear cuts me to the bone.

He wants everyone to feel like he does.

I'm shaking now, but the storm in his mind rages, sweeping the image away.

He's alone, wandering through empty gothic halls. It's like he's been in these halls in solitude for centuries.

Finally, I catch a stray thought, more of an image than a sentence. A map. I recognize it at once. I've studied this map myself for weeks, alongside other agents of Avalon.

It's a map of Scotland.

I home in on it, sliding deeper into his mind, praying that he'll stay asleep. This may be my only chance.

And as I sift through his thoughts about the war council, my heart sinks.

I see Auberon. He clenches his jaw, then motions violently with his hands, and the air in front of him shimmers, tears open, the green hills of Scotland materializing beyond. This is the king's power, I realize—the magical skill of opening portals.

Talan is poring over the map. He's the one who made the plans, not his father. He stands with the Fey army leaders, giving the orders. *He* was the one who came up with the plan to attack Dover by surprise, pouring the

Fey in through the south. He orchestrated the attack with the dragons, the veil that rolled into us.

We all assumed Auberon was the one calling the shots, deciding how and where to attack. But looking through Talan's thoughts, I see a military mastermind. He understands the field better than anyone, and he's in control. Talan whispers instructions in the ears of the generals, and he cunningly twists the High Council to act as *he* plans.

Now, he has a plan for Scotland. A ruse. A two-pronged attack to destroy the allied resistance. A trap.

It begins with three dragons attacking the logistical base, just as we already knew. But the second part is bait—exposing the flank of his army to the human forces. He plans to give the humans an opportunity they won't be able to ignore. He knows they'll take the bait and attack with everything they've got, hoping to cripple the Fey army for good.

But when they do, he'll snap the trap shut with a hidden force, routing the human military from behind. The Fey will surround them and massacre them all. Total carnage.

Even more horrifying than his plan is his satisfaction with it. Swimming through his thoughts, I can see how pleased he is with its perfection. This slaughter is the best possible outcome, and it's going to happen within two days.

Shaking, I pull away from his mind, staring at him with horror.

Deep asleep, he looks so peaceful—the beautiful monster who intends to destroy us all. The man who took an arrow for me.

But of course, he has no idea what I really am.

On weak legs, I hurry out of the room, shutting the door behind me.

I have to warn Avalon Tower before it's too late.

I have to stop them from falling into Talan's well-laid trap.

CHAPTER 37

It's late at night, but I'm thundering down the stairs, my heart slamming. My thoughts rage as I rush outside into the cold.

I lift my cloak to walk swiftly to the portal.

I have to get a message to Avalon Tower tonight. They'll have two days to prepare, to come up with a proper strategic response and coordinate it with the units on the ground. With Talan recuperating, I can easily disappear tonight without worrying that he'll show up in my room. I'll row the tiny boat to Camelot and then—

I stumble and stop in my place, aghast, staring in disbelief at the jagged ring stones beyond the willow tree.

My breath leaves my lungs. Tonight, the portal is surrounded by guards.

To them, the portal is invisible, undetectable. As far

as they know, they're standing around a few stumpy, jagged rocks with a new addition—a young sapling, freshly planted in the snowy earth between the stones.

What. The. Fuck.

I get my heartbeat under control and calmly stroll toward the guards, a tiny smile on my lips. As I get closer, I recognize one of them. It's the soldier I saw earlier in Talan's room.

Fear crawls up my nape.

"Evening, my lady," he says respectfully when I'm a few yards away. "How fares the prince?"

"He's doing remarkably well," I say. "He'll be up and about in no time. It'll take more than some iron to fell the grandson of Queen Morgan."

"That's good to hear."

I straighten, trying to gain control of the situation. "So, I see you're following your instructions." I nod at the tree.

He glances at the sapling, then turns back to me. He's clearly confused. "Oh. Um, yes. I wasn't sure if you knew about it. I assumed he might intend it as a surprise."

I let out a small, careless laugh. "Talan and I don't keep secrets from each other. Of course I know about it. I find it a bit strange, though."

The guard shuffles uncomfortably. "Well, the prince has an unusual mind. When he first told me to plant a tree to commemorate your love, I suggested that he wait until the end of winter. It is hard for things to grow at this time of year. But he liked the symbolism of it."

Sure, he does. "I see," I say, my heart sinking. "It'll be hard to get it to take root in this cold. On the farm, we never planted anything around this time."

"He was quite insistent. Perhaps if *you* suggest that we could plant later in the year, after the snow thaws..." He leaves the words hanging.

"Well, you know the prince," I say. "Once his mind is set..."

"Of course." He smiles at me.

"And I see you planted it right where he told you."

He tenses, looking back at it. "Yes. I checked several times. He was very clear that I must not get it wrong. This is the exact position he indicated."

I sigh and roll my eyes. "Royalty. You'd think he'd ask me first. After all, I know more than the prince does about gardening. The ground here is incredibly rocky, and most of the day, it's cast in shadows from that giant willow. It'll be impossible for the tree to thrive here. It'd be better to move the sapling to a sunnier location. Maybe the eastern side of the fortress."

"The prince was *very* insistent," the guard says with a tight smile. "This is the location."

"That's probably the delirium." I sigh. "Iron poisoning. I think the prince will be most grateful if you move the tree commemorating our love somewhere it can actually grow. If it dies, I imagine the prince will be furious. It will seem like a bad omen, planted by you."

The guard swallows. "With all due respect, my lady, the prince told me that if the sapling isn't right where it is when he checks on it, we will all be executed on the spot. Specifically, he mentioned ripping my lungs out through my back. So, I will keep it here, I think."

I act exasperated. "And I assume he instructed you to guard it?"

The man nods. "Four guards, fully armed, at all times. Prince Talan knows that your love is…criticized at court. He doesn't want the tree vandalized."

I consider touching him, forcing my mind into his, prodding him to leave. But if Talan threatened all four guards, I would need to mind control each of them. Impossible.

"Of course. How thoughtful of him. Well, gentlemen, I hope you have a nice evening."

They bid me farewell, and I turn away, my heart hammering.

As I stalk across the courtyard, I glance back at the portal, my thoughts roiling.

I'm now trapped here.

This is, of course, a very Talan thing to do. A random, chaotic, outrageous demand that will get everyone rolling their eyes at the capricious prince. And it hides his true intention—to keep anyone from approaching the ley portal.

Obviously, a tree planted at this very position, constantly guarded by four men, is not a coincidence. Nor does it have a single fucking thing to do with our "love."

Panic bleeds into my thoughts. He knows about the

portal, and he probably suspects that it's being used by human agents. The only bright spot is that he isn't connecting these agents to me, or I'd already be in the dungeons, my bones breaking on a rack. But why go through the charade of telling the guards that they're guarding a tree?

Because no one else knows about this ley portal. That must be the reason. Specifically, Auberon doesn't know about it, and Talan wants to control and use that knowledge for his own agenda.

Why now?

It must be because of Arwenna's attempt on my life. He's assuming that the iron was smuggled through the portal. Stupid of her to use an iron-tipped arrow right next to the prince himself. Clearly, the woman isn't in her right mind anymore. If she gets caught, I wonder if her family will have enough wealth and political capital to get her out of the consequences.

But where did she get the iron? There *is* no iron in Brocéliande. The only people who might have it are likely to be working with me.

But that's a problem for later. Right now, I have a much more urgent problem. I have two days to get a message to Avalon Tower about Talan's trap.

And I have no conceivable way of getting to them.

THE TAVERN'S lights beam warmly onto the dirt road, and as I step inside the Shadowed Thicket, the smell of stale beer hits me.

My heart thrums as I look around me. This late at night, there are a few drunks here and there. A group of men are laughing uproariously at some joke one of them made, and the jokester seems positively pleased with himself. I suddenly envy them. I wish that could be me, having a simple night with friends with no immediate worries except for tomorrow's hangover.

I cross to the barman. "Hey," I say. "Remember me?"

He wipes a glass, his expression bored. "What can I get ya?"

"I need to see Meriadec. It's urgent."

"Sorry, I don't know anyone by that name. I have a niece called Merielle, but she turned into a right twat when her girlfriend dumped her."

I grip the bar. "Oh, come on. I was here just a few weeks ago."

"And now you're here again. It's understandable. Best mead in Corbinelle."

Vaguely, it reminds me of the pass phrase that Nivene used. "Right. Okay…give me a glass of that mead."

He puts the glass he had been wiping on the counter and pours a measure of a nefarious looking liquid. I take a sip. Ghastly.

I eye him. "This is good. Almost as good as the mead I drank at my coming-of-age dance, back in, uh…" My mind is drawing a blank. “You know. Back in that place. Where I had my coming-of-age dance.”

“Uh-huh.” He picks up a new glass and steadily begins to wipe it.

“Come on! This mead is *good*. That’s the phrase, right? It tastes like piss in reality. You can’t possibly hear that often. Or really, ever.”

He stops wiping the glass and fixes his stare on me. “That mead is my ma’s recipe.”

“Oh.”

“She died in the famine.”

“I’m, uh…sorry for your loss. But I really need to see Meriadec.”

He nods. “I can see if my niece is interested. You might be her type.”

“It’s all right, Brados.”

I turn to see Meriadec shuffling over, and he takes the stool next to me. “She’s good.”

“Didn’t know the pass phrase,” Brados says pointedly, “and she insulted my dear ma’s mead.”

“Well.” Meriadec shrugs. “Can’t account for different tastes. Pour me a glass.”

Brados does so and walks off, leaving us alone.

“What’s going on, Nia?” Meriadec asks. “If any of your darling prince’s spies see us here together, they might wonder what you and your drunk father are doing so far from home.”

I eye him. “I’m going to need you to get back to the farm for a few days, at least. Talan might look for me there. You'll need to tell him that I stopped by, but I've gone into hiding. Make him think I'm still in Brocéliande, okay?"

"What do you have planned?"

I'm trying to think of how much I should share with Meriadec. I lower my voice. "First things first. Did you smuggle iron through the ley portal?"

He takes a thoughtful sip from his mug. "Nivene did, and she handed it to me for safekeeping."

"But you sold some of that iron, didn't you?" I hiss.

He shrugs. "I had a good offer for it. Some noble wanted it to off another noble. What do I care? I spent decades here starving. Every day a noble dies is a good day for us. And the revolution needs money."

"*I* was the noble!" I snarl.

He frowns at me, looking unimpressed. "Oh. Well, you seem fine. And arguably, this only helps your cover, right?"

"Except for the fact that this caused the prince to station guards around the ley portal," I say. "He knows that's where the iron came through. I'm trapped here now."

"Oh, shit."

"Yes. Very much, 'Oh, shit.'"

"I didn't know the prince even knew about the ley portal." His eyes sharpen on me. "It's *your* job to find those things out."

"Yeah, well, he's a secretive person. He probably didn't know anyone was using it. But once he found out about the smuggled iron, he realized the truth." I pause, deep in thought, then slap the counter. "Saxa!"

"What?"

"That's where I had my coming-of-age dance. Hey, Brados, my coming-of-age dance was in Saxa!"

Brados lifts his eyes from the glass and glances at me, clearly unimpressed.

"Anyway, I need to get back to Avalon Tower," I say. "I have some information I desperately need to pass on."

"From what you're describing, that's a problem."

"Worst-case scenario, I fight my way to the portal to get through. But that'll blow my cover, so I won't be coming back."

"That's not an option," he says emphatically. "Plans are in motion. You can't just blow your cover and leave us hanging."

"There's another possibility," I say slowly. I put my hand in my pocket, feeling the portal key I stole from Talan's room. "But I think I'll need help. How quickly can you get Raphael here?"

"He's in hiding on the outskirts of town," Meriadec says. "I can get him here within an hour."

"Good. Let's do that." I sip my mead. "Hey, Brados, did a young woman recently show up here? Silver eyes? Really pretty?"

Brados nods. "Ysolde. She's been here for a while. Staying in one of our rooms."

"Good. We should get her here, too. Raphael will want to meet her."

CHAPTER 38

Sitting in the back room of the tavern, I take out the stolen portal key and start moodily twirling it around my finger. I find myself counting the seconds, knowing that time is running out. I have less than two days to get from here to the gate, and then to someone from Avalon Tower's command. And instead of rushing out, I'm sitting in this dank room, waiting for my ex.

The door opens, and Ysolde steps inside. She warily scans the room before turning her silver eyes to me.

"Sorry I took so long." I stand and walk over to her. "Did you have any trouble getting here?"

"Nothing I couldn't handle," she says. Here, far from where she felt at home, she's clearly more nervous, and her tone is sharp. She's not glamoured like I am, and she looks obviously like a demi-Fey.

"Your brother will be here soon." I gesture at a

wooden table and chairs in the center of the room. "Please, sit down."

"If you don't mind, I'll remain standing," she says, leaning against the wall. She's casual, but I note how she eyes the door, her body alert. She doesn't trust me. She thinks this might be a trap. Of course she does. I couldn't expect her to fully trust me.

"Whatever you prefer." I shrug, sitting back down.

The door swings open, and Raphael steps in, dressed in a gray cloak, his dark hair wet with rain. It's grown back a little from the rough job they did on it in the dungeons.

My throat tightens when I see him, and sadness sings in my chest. There's the man who chose Avalon Tower over me.

But he's not looking at me, of course. He's looking at the sister he's missed and longed to see since he was a little boy.

Ysolde stares at him, frozen, then darts forward and grabs him in a desperate hug, her body racked with sobs.

I wait patiently. Time is short, but I have to give them at least a few minutes after all those years. How would it feel to be reunited with a sibling that you grew up with, that you spent so many years missing? I imagine for a moment having a brother or sister.

Raphael's eyes are closed as he hugs Ysolde. She's stopped sobbing and leans her head against his chest, tears running down her cheek. Finally, they break apart.

"What happened to you all these years?" Ysolde asks him.

"I will tell you everything," Raphael says, his voice cracking slightly. "Later, when we're alone. Nia probably doesn't have much time." He glances at me, his eyebrows knit together.

Ysolde sits in a chair next to me. "So, her name is Nia? She told me that you're a wanted man here. I mean, more than a regular demi-Fey."

Raphael sits, too, and scrubs a hand over his jaw. "Nia broke me out of their dungeons. The king is looking for me. If it weren't for Nia, I'd still be there. Or dead." He raises his eyebrows at me as if apologizing.

I inhale sharply. "I don't know about that, but you're right. I don't have much time."

I consider asking Ysolde to leave the room. I don't know her enough to trust her with my cover. Still, I need Raphael's help, and I need it quickly. And for what we're about to do, I might need hers as well. "I've recently learned that the Fey army is planning a crippling assault on the human military in Scotland."

Raphael frowns. "Did you alert them?"

"Alert who?" Ysolde asks.

"Avalon Tower," Raphael says. "Nia and I are agents of Avalon. Did she not mention that?"

Her eyes widen in shock. "You work with the humans? The Pendragons of Camelot?"

"Yes, of course," Raphael says. "Auberon is destroying both the demi-Fey *and* the humans. He is our enemy."

"I don't need you to lecture me about Auberon, little brother," Ysolde says sharply. "It's one thing to oppose the king, and it's quite another to work with people like the Pendragons."

"They're on our side—"

"This is a long discussion, and you can continue it later," I interject. "Right now, we don't have time for a political argument. Ysolde, like it or not, Raphael and I have to stop the Fey army from annihilating the human allies. If we don't, humanity is lost. You took care of human children, orphans of war. Imagine how many children will die if Auberon gets his way."

Ysolde rubs her forehead. "How did you find this out, anyway?"

"I'm working undercover."

"She's Prince Talan's mistress," Raphael says darkly.

I sigh. "Do you want to spill *all* of our secrets in one day? Leave something for later."

"This undercover position was a terrible idea from the start," Raphael says sharply. "I told Nivene to refuse to go along with it. Nia should be back in Avalon. It's incredibly dangerous here."

"Fine. Nobody asked you," I say, my patience at an end. "This is where we are. There's a trap prepared for the human allies in Scotland. If I can get there in time to warn them, we can prevent it, perhaps even turn it to our favor. But I can't use the ley portal anymore. The prince found out it's being used by spies, and he has soldiers guarding it."

Raphael gestures at me, frowning. "Then your cover is blown."

"It is *not* blown." At least, I fucking hope not. "But for now, I can't use the portal. Which leaves only this." I place the portal key on the table.

"What's this?" Raphael asks.

"It's a portal key that can be used to take up to four people through. Talan had it in case he was going to join the fighting weeks ago, but he didn't use it. I don't think it will take us to where the battle is now, but it will get us to Scotland." I flip it, showing Raphael the runes etched on its interior. "The portal on the Fey side will be open in Penro. Do you know where that is, Ysolde?"

"Yes. It's about two days' ride from here."

My heart sinks, and I shake my head. "Well, we need to get there within a day at most."

"That's impossible," Ysolde says.

"It's possible. We'll have to ride all night," Raphael says, "and switch horses once or twice. Meriadec can help us."

"The guy from the pub?" Ysolde asks.

"A friend." Raphael takes the portal key from my hand and inspects it. "What if it lands us in the middle of a Fey camp?"

"My source indicated that we can use it safely. He wouldn't have told me about it if it would deliver us to certain death."

Raphael's silver eyes pierce me. "Who, exactly, is your source? Can we trust him?"

Oh, sure. The Butcher of Lothian Tower is super trustworthy. You've seen pictures of him murdering innocent women all over Camelot. You plan to kill his entire family. And by the way, he's my dad. "Absolutely. We can trust him implicitly."

A sorrowful expression shines in his silver eyes. "I need to think this through. I need to plan the best course of action and—"

"We're out of time. *I've* already thought this through. *I've* planned the best course of action. I rescued you from prison. I saved your sister and found a way to get you home, and I found out about the Fey battle plans. Does Avalon Steel mean something or not? Maybe, Raphael, I know what I'm doing."

He stares at me, unmoving, until a muscle flexes in his jaw. "Fine. What's your plan?"

I drum my fingertips on the table. "The prince is recuperating from an injury he received after an assassin tried to kill me but missed. I left a note for my maidservant saying that I've gone into hiding because I'm scared for my life. I think it'll buy me a few days. You two know this kingdom much better than I do, and that's why I need you. We need to get to Penro in a day at the most, preferably even less. We go through the portal and find a way to get in touch with Avalon Tower command. I know enough about the Fey trap to use it against them, but to do that, we have to get there as quickly as possible."

"This is all moving too quickly for me," Ysolde says.

"I was still thinking of going back to the refugee fortress."

"I'm sorry," I tell her, my voice softening. "I know how you feel, but in our line of work, we always have to think and move quickly. You know this landscape better than Raphael or me. So, for now, I have to ask you to trust us. You want to help those kids? That's great. In the long run, stopping Auberon and Talan is the best thing for them, too."

And once again, I find myself desperately hoping that I'm right.

Raphael runs a hand over his close-cropped dark hair. "We're going to need weapons."

CHAPTER 39

Dressed as Auberon's black-clad messengers, we ride through the cold night, our horses kicking up sprays of snow. I wear a bow and a quiver, but even fully armed, galloping through the darkness on icy terrain is a never-ending exercise in managing fear.

Brocéliande's silver moon is a slim crescent, hardly casting any light. The red moon is half full, shading the landscape in an otherworldly, blood-hued glow. Crimson glints off icicles that hang from the trees. In this lighting, it's impossible to distinguish among hollows in the path, black ice, shrubs, and rocks. Every few minutes, my horse—a nervous brown stallion—stumbles, and my heart stutters. But we have to keep up the relentless pace if there's any chance of getting the warning to the allies in time.

Ysolde knows this land best, and she takes the lead.

In the cold air, I'm out of breath, and my lungs whistle, tightening. I pull out my inhaler and take two puffs before they start to release a little.

My mind whirls as we race across the landscape. I hope everything is in place.

We have to ride a few more hours northeast, where we'll meet a connection of Meriadec's. That's where we'll get fresh horses. Then, we'll ride on to Penro, where we can travel through the portal to Scotland.

Meriadec should be heading back to the fake farm. If the prince wakes and starts searching for me, that'll be the first place he looks.

Somewhere in the distance, a screech rends the air, maybe the death cry of fallen prey. Whatever it is, it sends my horse veering sideways in a panic. My heart races, and I lean down to soothe him with soft whispers. I manage to get him back on track, following behind Ysolde.

I'm not shrieking out my own death cries yet, but I feel nearly as hunted as that creature. At any moment, we could hear the earth-rumbling sound of a Fey legion charging after traitors.

Our disguise won't hold under close scrutiny, and Raphael and Ysolde aren't glamoured like I am.

Something snaps to my left, and I reflexively reach for my bow, but there's nothing there, just the sounds of the night. I lean closer to my horse as we ride. "Nothing to worry about," I whisper to him, trying to reassure myself. "There's no one after us. You're a good horse."

He snorts, his ears twitching. I've fallen behind, and I spur him on to catch up with the other two.

* * *

DAWN BREAKS, coral blooming in a lavender sky. Rose gleams off icicles and blushes over the snow.

Exhaustion burns through me, and our horses slow to a canter down a narrow trail.

Somehow, I've ended up in the front, and I glance back at the siblings. They look as tired as I feel, slumping over their horses. Turning around, I see a churning, icy river ahead, flecked with amber in the morning light. I pull my horse to a halt.

Raphael stops by my side. "Well, fuck."

"What?" Ysolde mumbles behind us.

"I don't think you know this area as well as you think, sis," Raphael says. "You've led us to a river."

The water is clearly too deep for the horses to cross, and we'd probably all freeze to death if we tried.

"We'll have to find a point to ford." I swallow hard. "Maybe if we ride upriver for a few kilometers..."

"We don't need that," Ysolde says, urging her horse forward. "I know exactly where we are, and it's where I wanted to be. And there's nowhere better to cross up or down the river for at least half a day of riding."

"Then how do we cross?" I ask. "Do you have a hidden raft or something?"

"No. Give me a minute." She inhales and shuts her eyes.

I exchange glances with Raphael. He frowns, and his expression doesn't reassure me. What's going on right now? It looks like she's fallen asleep on her horse.

And then, to my utter shock, I see the water in front of us grow shallower, rushing away in either direction. Impossibly, a gap appears, wide as a horse, and in that gap, the water seems to be draining.

My jaw drops. "Holy shit."

"You have water magic," Raphael says, his amazement mirroring mine.

"Yes," Ysolde says. "It developed late. I didn't know until my early twenties."

"You're like a Fey Moses," I say in wonder.

Ysolde glances back at me, frowning. "What is a Mo-zets?"

"It's an ancient story," Raphael tells her. "The humans say a man parted the sea once. And he also summoned a rain of frogs, I believe."

"Why would anyone want to rain frogs?" Ysolde asks.

"Well, it was one of ten…you know what? It's actually a long story," I say. "I'll tell you all about it one day."

She scowls at us. "I cannot control frogs, nor do I want to. And I wouldn't be able to part an entire sea. Mo-zets sounds very powerful."

"I suppose he must have been," I say. "But this is seriously amazing, too."

She pulls her horse ahead of us. "I can push the water

to a point. Follow directly after me. If you stray too far, your horses will be swept away by the current, and you'll both drown in glacial water. So, don't do that."

With that reassuring comment, she guides her horse into the parted water. Raphael follows close behind.

My horse is of the firm opinion that no, this is not a good idea. *Nope, nope, nope.*

"C'mon, horse," I whisper at him. "After the night we've gone through, you've totally got this." Soothingly, I rub his neck, whispering reassurances to him, until he follows behind Raphael's horse.

It's one of the strangest experiences I've been through. Cold river spray mists around me. As I travel through, the river closes up behind me, churning and frosting my back with water droplets. At last, to my horse's relief and mine, we reach the other side. I turn back to see the roaring river fully restored.

"That was incredible," I say, "and I hope to never repeat it."

Raphael is looking at his sister with new-found awe.

She rubs her eyes, exhausted.

"Come on," I say. "Meriadec's contact shouldn't be far off by now. We'll get some fresh horses there."

I glance up at the sky, and my stomach clenches as I see the sun rising higher above the horizon.

Our road is lined by snowy, spindly trees glazed with ice. Delirium swims in my thoughts as we exchange our horses with the contact. These animals seem thinner and older than those from the tavern. Mine constantly lags behind and stops to rest every now and then.

Ysolde, who doesn't have our training, looks to be in worse shape than Raphael and I do. At one point, she breaks into exhausted sobs.

As the sun rises higher in the slate-gray sky, Raphael gets in front of Ysole. Taking her horse by the reins, he leads the way, and Ysolde slumps in her saddle, fast asleep. I keep worrying that she'll topple off her horse, but she somehow stays on.

As the road widens, I bring my horse alongside Raphael and groan. "My ass is one giant bruise."

"That's quite the image." He arches an eyebrow. "But I know you'll get through this because I've seen you stabbed through your gut and trapped in a nightmare where you were drowned. I've seen you attacked by the veil itself. So, you'll be fine with a bruised arse, pixie princess."

I glare at him, and we ride in silence. His use of that nickname brings back many memories—our kiss in the lake after we jumped off the bridge, the nights we spent in a room watching Caradoc, and the lavender cake Raphael gave me. But they feel a lifetime away, and it's clear to me that as bittersweet as those memories are, that's all they are now.

Raphael clears his throat. "You shouldn't return to Brocéliande after this mission."

"I have to. As long as I'm in Perillos, I can help turn the tide of the war. If I weren't there, close to the prince, we wouldn't have any of this information."

"It's too dangerous, even for an agent with many years of experience. And Avalon Steel or not, you're still new to this. Before I was thrown into their dungeons, maybe I'd have gone along with it." There's a pained, ragged edge to his voice that makes my throat tighten. "But after..." He trails off.

I swallow hard. "I know it was brutal."

"They shouldn't risk your life like this. They shouldn't ask you to risk what I endured. It's worse than you can imagine, Nia. And Talan already suspects there's a spy. How much longer until he figures out it's you? That man is a monster. He's from the House of Morgan, and he'll destroy us all. Exactly like the prophecy says."

My heart skips a beat. He's certain of that point, isn't he? "Do you really believe in prophecies?"

"Yes."

I clear my throat. "I know he's a monster, and maybe I'm the only one who can stop him. Who else will?"

His jaw tightens. "If I have to, I'll talk to Sir Kay about pulling you off the mission. You cannot end up in their dungeons."

I glare at him, frustration flaring. "And how many more will we let get captured by the Fey army, brutalized by their torturers? I'll die when it's my time. Let me live my life the way I decide. And for now, let's focus on looking for the portal."

"I know there are things you aren't telling me, Nia."

My jaw tightens. *Oh, just a little niggling detail about that prophecy you hold so dear.*

"Let me focus. I should be able to sense the portal with my Sentinel powers." I close my eyes and concentrate. "I can feel it…tugging at me. There's…something here."

I look around me, my magic humming within. It's definitely here, but it doesn't feel like the ley portal. This feels more artificial, somehow, a portal that has been forced into existence with powerful magic.

"There!" I point to a fairy ring of mushrooms washed with gold in the sunlight. In the center of the circle is a faint tear between the worlds, and I can feel its power vibrating over my skin, raising the hair on the back of my neck. I imagine Auberon standing here, ripping this portal open.

"Are you sure?" says Raphael. "All I see is mushrooms."

"It's a Sentinel thing," I say. "But you see how they're in a ring and growing even through the snow? Always good to look for a Fey portal there."

I dismount, my legs aching with fatigue. Raphael follows my lead, and Ysolde slumps off her horse, half-awake. We cross into the circle of mushrooms and stand huddled together, Ysolde resting her head against Raphael's arm.

Shivering, I pull out Talan's key and turn it over in my hands. Does it need a magical phrase of some sort?

But even as I ask myself that question, the key crackles in my hand.

Power buzzes over me, and the portals blooms, swallowing us whole. The snowy landscape flickers away.

CHAPTER 40

Wind shrieks in my ears, and cold rain spatters my cheek. The portal key in my hand is suddenly blazing hot, and I drop it to the grass at my feet. It hisses, steam rising from the metal.

I look up to see Ysolde on her knees, vomiting onto the wet grass. I know how she feels. This one is even more disorienting than Avalon's ley portal.

Rainclouds churn overhead, and Raphael pulls his cloak tightly around him, staring at something over my shoulder.

I turn to see a castle of weathered stone standing at the base of a tree-lined hill. Its ancient walls tower above us, tinged red in the sunset. This castle could belong back in Brocéliande, but when I look up, the moon is already out. A full, *single* moon.

"Any idea where we are?" asks Raphael.

Ysolde stands, her face pale. "We can ask him."

A man wearing wellies and a tweed jacket steps out of the castle. He's carrying a large hunting rifle, and he aims it straight at us. "Not one step closer," he hollers in a Scottish accent. "This rifle is loaded with iron bullets, and I can hit all three of you before you say Jack Robinson."

I hold up my hands. "We aren't moving! We're staying right where we are."

"My English isn't so good," Ysolde whispers. "What is this Jack Robinson?"

"It's just an old human saying." Stupidly, tears spring to my eyes at hearing English again. "We're somewhere in Scotland. I was right. The portal key was intended to take Talan to Scotland."

"We're not Fey, we're demi-Fey!" Raphael calls back to the man in English. "We mean you no harm."

"Yeah? Not being funny, lad, but when I see pointy ears, I'm not exactly brimming with confidence."

"I'm undercover," I call out. "I grew up in Los Angeles. I'm not really Fey." I try to think of the most human things I can. "As a kid, I ate McDonald's Happy Meals with plastic toys. I drink Dunkin' Donuts coffee with vanilla flavor shots. My favorite food as a kid was corn dogs."

I turn to see Raphael staring at me, horrified.

The man keeps the rifle aimed at me. "Christ, lass, now I'm tempted to shoot you to put you out of your misery," he says, slowly lowering the gun. "Americans, here now, as well as the Fey. Not sure which is worse.

No offense, but you look proper Fey to me. You've got the pointy Fey ears, not the half-breed sort."

"It's glamour," I say. "We're agents working with the allied armies. My name is Nia."

He takes another step closer. "I'm Cameron. So, what are you doing all the way here? The war is mainly to the south, as far as I know."

"This is just where the portal dropped us. Do you have a phone? We need to get in contact with our superior officers."

"Phones are knackered. Stopped working completely all through Scotland a few weeks ago," he says.

"A telegram?" I ask desperately. "*Any* way to get in touch?"

He shakes his head. "We're back to the Middle Ages. Homing pigeons and messengers, that's all we have. My eejit cousin thought we could deliver messages by smoke signals, and he nearly burned his house down."

"Where are we, exactly?" I ask.

"We're at Castle Menzies. We have a bunch of war refugees staying here now, escaping the Fey soldiers. I'm the bloody welcoming committee."

"Castle Menzies." I frown. "Where is that?"

"Near Aberfeldy."

I recall the weeks spent poring over Scotland's map with Avalon Tower knights, trying to figure out the best lines of defense against the Fey army. I turn to Raphael. "I know Aberfeldy. We're way too far north. The majority of our army is about a hundred and fifty kilometers south of here, near Glasgow. More than that, really, because there are no direct roads. We'll need transportation."

Going by the brief glimpses of Talan's mind, the portal he plans to use for this attack is about ten miles north of something called "Green Hollow." I'm almost certain that's Glasgow. Auberon will be opening a portal there.

Raphael glances at Cameron. "Can you tell us the fastest way to get to Glasgow?"

"You won't get there driving. The roads are in shambles. You won't get more than five kilometers with a car."

"Horses?" I ask desperately.

"I suppose you could get horses in town," Cameron says thoughtfully. He walks closer to us, scratching his cheek.

"We can't ride a hundred and fifty kilometers on horses in one day," Ysolde points out. "Especially not in our state."

"What if we get to a northern military post?" Raphael says. "Cameron says people are using homing pigeons. They might have those, or some similar way of delivering a message."

"There's one north of Perth," I say slowly. "That's closer. We could maybe get there in time."

Cameron shakes his head. "The ways to Perth are crawling with Fey patrols. There's no way you'll get through on horseback. You'll be captured in no time."

"We have to try," Raphael says. "Ysolde, you can stay here. Nia, you, too. I'll grab a horse and try to—"

"No way," Ysolde says.

I close my eyes. "Let me think. Cameron, there's a river nearby, right?"

"Aye, that's right. River Tay."

"Right!" My eyes snap open again, my excitement rising. "And the river flows right through Perth, doesn't it?"

"Aye," Cameron says. "It goes east, then south to Perth."

"We could take a boat to Perth," I say.

"We can get you a boat," Cameron says. "But it's a wild river, especially in the past weeks. I think the Fey magic makes it even rougher. Their presence has a certain wild effect on nature."

"That's all right," I say, grinning. "Ysolde here can handle a wild river. Right, Ysolde?"

"Is true," Ysolde tells the man in broken English. "I am what humans call a Mo-zets."

"Eh?" Cameron squints.

"She's an expert in whitewater rafting," I quickly say, hoping to avoid going down that particular rabbit hole. "Can you get us a boat? We need to get moving as soon as possible."

THE BOAT BELONGS to a local fisherman, who seems brokenhearted to sell it to us. "Used to fish in it with my dad down in the loch," he tells me, his voice cracking, "but he died two years ago, and with those Fey monsters everywhere, I cannae risk using it."

"I'm sorry about your father," I say, handing him two diamond rings that Talan gave me. "I understand."

"My family needs to eat, and we're running out of food. Shops are empty, markets are empty. A Fey patrol went into our town last week. They killed my mate and his wife for no reason at all." He stares at the rings in his hand. "Maybe with this, we'll be able to get on one of the outlaw boats to Ireland. Leave our home behind for now."

"You might be able to return soon," I say. "If we win this battle."

He raises a shaggy eyebrow at that. "Do you know what's going on, lass? The humans are getting massacred. This place will be overridden by Fey within days. I can only hope that Ireland's not next."

He turns, shaking his head as he walks away, shoulders slumped.

Ysolde sits in the back of the wooden boat, one with two benches and oars. We push our boat into the water, and I take the back bench.

At the start, the river doesn't seem rough, but within minutes, the water churns around us, the current sweeping us faster and faster. As we move, silky magic washes over my skin. I glance at Ysolde and see that her eyes are nearly shut, and her body is tense with concentration. She's pushing the current, giving us speed, and the water pulls us along much faster than I thought possible. Snow-dusted trees and rolling hills flash by, and droplets of water splash on my face as we accelerate. The water churns, nearly ripping one of the oars from my hands. I pull them into the boat, and Raphael does the same.

Ysolde doesn't need our help. As she takes control over the river, I curl into the damp bottom of the rocking boat and drift into the land of sleep.

* * *

"Nia!"

My eyes snap open, panic enveloping me as I struggle to understand where I am and what the fuck I'm doing. The world is rocking violently around me, and I'm shivering with cold, drenched with wintry river water.

Oh, right.

Blinking, I sit up, the boat wobbling.

The water around us is white, frothing with fury against jagged rocks. I look ahead, and we're hurtling toward an evil-looking boulder with alarming speed. I let out a yell as we veer to the left, missing the huge rock by a fraction of an inch.

Raphael is frantically rowing. I glance at Ysolde. Her eyes are rolling in their sockets, her lips moving without a sound, an aura of static magical power emanating from her.

"I've been calling you over and over!" Raphael shouts over the churn of the water. "Grab your oars."

Crawling back onto the bench, I snatch my oars from the bottom of the boat, the cobwebs of sleep still clouding my mind.

"Push us away from incoming rocks!" Raphael shouts. "Be on the lookout for more."

Up ahead, jagged rocks rise from the water like enormous broken teeth. I sink my oar in the water, turning us to the right. The current shifts and aligns itself with my oar, helping us along. The boat dodges, but not fast enough. We won't be able to escape both of the rocks.

"Aim for that large gap between them!" I shout back.

I paddle like a madwoman. The water rises sharply around us as Ysolde's magic transforms the river into long, straight waves by our sides, a magical funnel that helps to steer us. Working together, we manage to push the boat at the gap, but I quickly realize we won't fit through.

"Fuck!" I shout, as a terrible scraping sound fills my ears.

The boat shudders, then shoots through the rocks, splintered on the right side where it hit the rock. I frantically check the bottom of the boat for holes, but it looks fine. The hole, at least, is high enough that it won't sink us.

"We're fine, we're fine, we're fine," I mutter to myself.

When I look up, I see more rocks, and the river whorls around us. The air above the river spray shimmers with magic.

"Is that Ysolde's magic?" I ask.

"The land is reacting to the Fey army," Raphael shouts. "Ancient magic is now stirring, magic that has been dormant for centuries."

The river grows wilder.

* * *

My heart is still in my throat, my breathing ragged from effort. We've been struggling with the rocks for nearly an hour while all around us, the rapids roar. I grip the oars tight as I try to help steer. Battered by the current, we struggle to keep control.

Arrows pierce the water around us, and my heart skips a beat.

I look up to see Fey riders on horseback. They're gaining on us, galloping along the bank, their horses kicking up mud by the riverside.

"Archers!" I scream.

They loose more arrows at us.

These archers are fucking *fast*, and they're gaining on us.

An arrow thunks into our boat, the tip deeply embedded in the stern.

As I duck, another arrow whistles just above my

head. Three more fly behind me, one of them cluttering into the wood.

"They're aiming at Ysolde!" Raphael shouts.

My blood roars. They must've realized that Ysolde is using magic to steer us in the wild river. If she dies, we all die. While she's managing the magical energy of the water in a trance state, Ysolde can't duck for protection like I can.

Another arrow misses Ysolde by a hair. Raphael scrambles to his feet, the boat rocking dangerously.

"What are you doing? You'll tip us over!" I shout.

He grabs his bench and pulls, gritting his teeth. With a sickening wooden crack, the bench snaps free in his hand. He crawls over to Ysolde with the plank and holds it in front of her, shielding her from the arrows.

Two more fly at Ysolde and Raphael. One hits the shield, the other sinks into his shoulder. Blood pours down his arm. A third arrow flies at me, whistling over my head.

I glare at the archers. We've gone too far to die now. I pick up my bow and grab an arrow from the quiver, then take aim and fire. As we rock in the rapids, it should be impossible to properly shoot an arrow. When it finds its mark, I let out a gasp of surprise. One of the riders topples from his horse, an arrow in his side. His mount veers off course—right in front of one of the other horses.

Here, surrounded by water humming with magic, power vibrates within me. But it's not just my own. The ancient, dormant power of the Lady of the Lake has risen to the surface.

An arrow zings toward me. I stare at it. Time slows, and the arrow seems to be crawling through the air. I shift aside, and it whistles harmlessly by me. With a dark smile, I shoot another arrow, and it hits its mark.

Three soldiers down. Four to go.

"Nia! Look ahead!" Raphael shouts.

I twist around and let out a curse. Directly ahead of us, an enormous rapid roars. I drop the bow, grab my oar, and start paddling, though I'm not even sure where to. The boat tips into the rapid and dives, churning water filling it. As we're slamming against a rock, the boat turns sideways and becomes trapped in the frothing rapid, unable to break free. I try to push us away with the oar, and it snaps from my hand. The river devours it like a hungry beast.

Two more arrows thunk into the side of the boat. The four soldiers have halted their horses, and they're taking careful aim. We're no longer moving, and this time, they won't miss.

I grab my bow, my movement lightning fast. I fire another arrow, and one of them topples from his horse, an arrow in his neck. Dead before he has time to scream. The three others let their arrows loose. Two fly at Ysolde and Raphael, both hitting Raphael's shield. The third arrow flies at me. Again, time slows, and I lower my head as the arrow speeds by.

Another well-aimed arrow flies directly at Ysolde.

Raphael moves his makeshift shield just in time, and the arrow hits the plank.

The boat is quickly filling with water, and we're still trapped, slamming against a rock. At this point, we have mere seconds before we sink.

I scramble on the boat's floor and grab an oar. Roaring with fury, I sink it into the water. I feel the unyielding power of the turbulence that traps us and push against it with all my strength. The oar bends in my hands, creaking, and I snarl at it, willing it not to snap. And then, with a joint push from my oar and Ysolde's magic, we break free, hurtling down the river, arrows flying in our wake.

I look back as the riders are left behind, unable to catch up with us.

But the river is hungry now, and it demands payment. The water rages, and we hold on for dear life as the side as the boat tips and rises, then plunges down, down, down beneath the cold surface.

I hold my breath as the icy river swallows me. I don't know up from down. Under the water, my head slams against something hard, and the world floats away.

CHAPTER 41

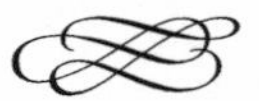

"Oh, for fuck's sake." The words, spoken in a Scottish accent, float into my mind, and my eyes flutter open.

I'm alive, my teeth chattering wildly. This, in itself, is a miracle. I'm soaked in freezing water, but I'm breathing.

Someone must have pulled me back into the boat because I'm lying on its cold, wet bottom. Somehow, the boat has stayed mostly intact.

I sit up to see Raphael and Ysolde still on the boat as well. They're trying to catch their breath, and they're drenched and shivering. Raphael's sleeve is crimson with blood, though he pulled the arrows out. Ysolde is deathly pale, with an almost blue tinge to her skin. I suspect she's the only reason we survived the last leg of our boat ride.

Raphael glances at me. "You're back. I had to drag

you out of the river, Nia. The water wanted to keep you, and can you blame it?" A little smile. "We're safe now."

We're pulled onto the bank by a burly guy in military overalls. A group of men in similar garb stand nearby, shouting contradictory instructions in different languages, some with accents that are clearly French, others that sound English.

A bunch of men bossing one another around in makeshift Esperanto? This has to be the allied military. I nearly weep with relief. We've made it.

As we're pulled ashore, one man offers me a chivalrous hand, which I'm grateful to accept. I carefully step out of the boat, and it takes all of my strength to remain on my feet.

They stare warily at my pointed ears. "Those are proper Fey ears, aren't they?"

"I'm demi-Fey in disguise," I say tiredly, "and so are they. I grew up in LA. Go Lakers. Look, we don't have much time. I'm with MI-13. I need to talk to whoever is in command. I have urgent intel."

"We have an MI-13 agent in our base with us," a man with a thin mustache says. "Will she vouch for you?"

"Probably," I mumble, glancing at the boat, where two men are helping a half-conscious Ysolde up. "What's her name?"

"Don't remember," he says. "She's blond and scary as fuck."

"One of the guys tried to grab her arse, and she broke his wrist in two places," another one says.

"Then yes, she'll vouch for me," I say, my voice cracking. "Viviane knows me quite well."

* * *

I'M SITTING on a military cot, waiting for someone to lead me to the base's commander. They took Raphael and Ysolde to the infirmary, while a soldier led me here to wait. They gave me fresh, dry clothes, warm woolen blankets, and hot tea.

A guard is stationed outside my tent to make sure I don't roam around.

No one is listening to me when I say I need to speak to the commander *right now*.

As I sip my tea, Viviane enters the tent, glaring at me, her blond hair pulled back severely. She folds her arms. "What the fuck are you doing here? What happened to Raphael? Who's the woman he's with?"

She fires questions at me without stopping to let me answer. I'm not sure she's *interested* in my answers.

"Why did you leave your position?" she goes on. "You had clear directives! Without you there, we won't be able to strike at Auberon and murder him and his fucking son. Did you talk to Nivene about this? How did you get to Scotland?"

My fingers tighten into fists. "Viviane…"

"You show up here in a fucking fishing boat. How the hell did you survive the River Tay in a fishing boat?"

"Viviane."

"I don't know what Raphael was thinking. Or what *you* were thinking. I don't know what anyone is thinking right now—"

"*Viviane*!" I scream at the top of my voice.

She winces, snaps her mouth shut, then raises her eyebrows. "What?"

"I'll tell you everything, okay? I'll give you a full, thorough briefing. I'll even write it down for you, if you want. But right now, I have incredibly urgent intel for the base's commander."

"What sort of intel?" asks a male voice.

I look behind Viviane to see a new person stepping into the tent: a man, forty or fifty, by my guess, his head shaved to stubble. Sharp green eyes. Strong jutting chin. I'm not very knowledgeable about military insignia, but he looks well-decorated. A large gun hangs at his side, a combat knife in his belt.

"Commander Pearson," Viviane says, her voice steadying as she turns to address him. "This is Nia Melisande. Dame Nia. She's with MI-13. An Avalon Steel knight. She's glamoured to look like a full-blooded Fey, but she's not."

"I see." His eyes are scrutinizing, digging deep. "And I understand you have some information for me?"

Finally. "The Fey are planning a trap for the human military. It will happen tonight. Prince Talan plans to lure your people in and slaughter them."

He shakes his head. "You're mistaken, Dame Nia. The Fey army is in disarray. Our scouts recently discovered that they're on the move to attack an abandoned base, exposing their flank. The joint human military is launching a full-scale attack this evening. They'll never expect it."

Frustration simmers. "That's the trap! They're not just expecting it, they're planning for you to attack tonight, in exactly that way. They plan to retreat, pulling our forces deeper. Then a second, smaller, elite trained force will assault from the north, backed by a dragon. Our army will be caught in the middle and will get cut down on all sides. It will be a massacre."

He frowns at me. "Our scouts detected no such elite trained force. Even if it's a small force, it would have to be at least a few hundred Fey soldiers—"

"Two thousand."

"We would have seen them."

"No, they're not here. They've been amassing for weeks in Brocéliande. They're coming through a portal."

Silence settles in the tent, and the commander scrubs a hand over his jaw.

"How certain are you of this?" Viviane asks, her blue eyes piercing me.

I take a deep breath. "Fairly certain. My intel is from two days ago. I took one of his portal keys, but he doesn't need it. Auberon can open portals. I don't know what the limits are on his magic—I only know that he can do it, and that he plans to do it tonight. You have to warn everyone."

Viviane and Pearson exchange looks.

"That's impossible," Pearson says. "We don't *have* a way to warn them. The Fey magic has completely disrupted our communications. We work with messengers and homing pigeons, and a pigeon will take about three hours to get there. Our assault will begin to mobilize in less than two hours."

"Send the pigeon now," I say. "They might have enough time to turn back."

Pearson shakes his head. "They won't. And we're losing the war, Dame Nia. Even if your intel is true, we have no other option."

"He's right, Nia," Viviane says softly. "We can't turn this around now."

I want to shout at them, but I see the hopelessness in their eyes.

Then, a tiny kernel of an idea starts to blossom in my mind.

"How long would it take you to send a small force to Glasgow?" I ask.

Pearson considers that. "The roads between here and Glasgow are more or less intact, and we have two old trucks that still work. I estimate that we can do it in two hours. Maybe two and a half."

"But we don't have more than twenty or thirty people we can send there," Viviane says.

"That's enough." I shakily stand. "Send me with them."

"What for?" Viviane asks. "You can't change the outcome of the battle with just thirty people, Nia."

"*If* I manage to shut the portal, I can stop the elite Fey force from coming through. The portal is just a short distance north of Glasgow." It might be the only way to ruin Talan's plans.

"You can shut the portal down?" Pearson asks.

My Sentinel powers haven't worked on a portal—yet. But my powers have been growing for weeks in Brocéliande. In theory, it could work.

"I can't promise it. But it's possible. And frankly, none of us have a better idea, do we?"

CHAPTER 42

I sit on a bench in the truck's open-air cargo area with a few other soldiers and Viviane. Another truck follows behind us, and a light dusting of snow falls, stinging my cheeks.

Viviane sighs. She looks exhausted. "When this is over, Nia, I want a chance to get back to Brocéliande. I miss the red moon. And the korriberry tarts the way my mum used to make them."

"When did you leave?"

"It was just after the famine started. My mum knew things were going to get bad for a demi-Fey like me, so we moved to England. But I miss Brocéliande. It's my home. We had a little cottage in the Melian Forest, and my specialty was picking mushrooms to cook with. I could identify all of them. When I lived in London, I used to dream every night that I was back there in the rich forest with red moonlight."

I smile at her. "We'll find a way to get you back."

She frowns, surveying the landscape. "We should be near the portal now, if your prediction is right."

"Let me focus." I take a deep breath, trying to tune in for the feel of the portal magic. The noise and vibrations of the engine aren't making it easy to focus, but the soldiers are keeping quiet.

I glance around at the rugged, wild landscape—rolling snow-dusted hills, the frosted heather and grasses that sparkle under the winter sun. From this point, we can see all the way to Glasgow, though it's partially shrouded in mist. I inhale the scent of pines, moss, and damp earth, trying to clear my thoughts.

But I feel my powers fizzling within me. Without sleep, I can't seem to summon the power I need to even find the portal, let alone close it.

As the minutes tick by, I can feel Viviane's nerves fraying. Finally, she says, "Are you *sure* it's somewhere here?"

"I'm pretty sure," I say.

Which is close enough to the truth. I think there's about a fifty percent chance that it's around here.

But the longer this goes on, the more I start to doubt myself. What if I got it all wrong? What if I only saw part of the plan—or what if in the past two days, the plan changed?

Then something twinges between my ribs.

"Wait!" I whisper, touching my chest. Then, louder. "Wait! Stop the truck!"

Viviane bangs her fist on the tiny, smudged window between us and the cab. "Stop the truck!"

Pearson is sitting in the front with the driver. I see him tell the driver something, and the truck slows and stops. I shut my eyes so I don't see the looks of the people around me. So I don't feel them watching me. When the truck is silent, I can concentrate.

Yes. I can sense it, that familiar, vibrating tug—just like the portal we went through yesterday. It twines around my ribs, beckoning me closer. I point with my finger, my eyes still shut. "The portal is that way."

"How far?" Viviane asks.

"I don't know. About two hundred meters. Maybe three hundred."

She nods. "That's good enough. Let's triangulate to be sure."

I nod. If I can point to the direction from a different position, we'll be able to pinpoint the *exact* location of the portal.

Viviane checks a compass, then her map. She opens the window between us and the cab and tells Pearson and the driver to take us a few hundred meters down the road. As soon as the truck starts, I lose my sense of the portal. I wait anxiously as we drive, praying that I haven't been imagining things.

The truck stops again, the engine going silent. I take a deep breath and close my eyes, and to my relief, I feel it again, sliding between my ribs, luring me closer. "That way."

I open my eyes and point in the direction I feel the portal's energy coming from.

Viviane checks her compass again. Then she looks out over the landscape, verifying our location on the map. She purses her lips as she triangulates the two vectors, then circles a point on the map. "Here."

I frown at it. The location tells me nothing. Is it really the place I saw in Talan's dark, twisted mind?

Viviane shoves the map in Pearson's face and points to the location I identified.

My skull is rattling with something like panic as they argue about how best to get there, and my fingers curl into fists. The pressure of the oncoming invasion is bearing down on me, making it hard to breathe. We veer off the road, nearly crashing into a pine tree. The truck shudders through a snowy field, and the second truck follows.

A few minutes, the truck stalls. The engine revs, the wheels screeching. We're mired in the muddy snow.

"Close enough," Viviane says. "Let's go."

I follow her off the truck, and the rest of the soldiers join us. The second truck rolls up, and more soldiers hop off onto the hillside. There are nearly thirty of us, I think, most of them armed with the guns the military use against Fey—old-fashioned rifles that shoot iron bullets. Like me, Viviane is armed with a crossbow, but she also wears her sword slung around her waist.

Magic tingles over my body. "This way."

The power of the portal pulls at me, luring me closer. Now I'm certain we're on the right track.

We march down into a misty valley, then up another hill. With breath puffing from our mouths like clouds, we climb the next hill, trying not to slip on the tall, snowy grass or trip on the craggy rocks that jut from the hillside. I'm out of breath, wheezing. I take a few puffs from my inhaler to open up my lungs, to stop the coughing.

"It should...be...right...beyond the top...of the...hill."

Viviane and Pearson suddenly drop to the ground, lying hidden in the tall grass. Pearson hurriedly motions for the rest of us to do the same. I flatten and crawl closer to Viviane.

"You were right, Nia," Viviane says grimly, peering over the top of the hill. "The portal is definitely here."

From the top of the rocky hill, I look down, my stomach sinking.

A portal has opened—a rip in the landscape. And a legion of Fey soldiers has already begun to step through, their weapons gleaming.

CHAPTER 43

The hill overlooks a large valley with a small stream running through it. Talan must have chosen this location to keep the soldiers hidden as they step through the portal into Scotland.

My heart thunders. There are already dozens of them, a hundred at least. They pour into the grassy valley below us, clustering in groups. Most are heavily armored, carrying enormous swords. They've brought horses with them, too. They're inspecting their gear, preparing for battle. A few men wear command insignia on their armor, and they're barking orders. As I look, five more Fey materialize from thin air.

The journey through the portal looks as rough for them as it was for us. They land hard on their hands and knees, and one of them vomits where he lands.

"We have to strike now," Viviane whispers.

"Are you insane?" Pearson hisses. "They outnumber us eight to one."

"And soon it will be twelve to one, then fifteen to one, then fifty to one," Viviane says. "And that's *before* the dragon shows up. Right now, many of them don't look too healthy. The longer we wait, the worse our chances are."

"The passage through the portal is disorienting," I explain. "It takes time to adjust."

"Close the portal right now!" Pearson says. "Before more show up."

"It'll take me some time," I say. "And they'll probably notice my magic when I do it."

"Then we'll supply you with cover fire," Viviane says grimly. "Most of our group will stay with you. We'll send others to attack the Fey as they're coming through the portal. They'll be at their weakest right after they appear."

The five new Fey arrivals are ushered away by a sergeant.

A few seconds later, five more show up, the portal humming as they arrive. It's much larger than the ley portal from the Avalon dolmens. This one is *immense,* a vast tear in the fabric of space—a black hole with ragged edges, as though it were violently ripped from the world. It's big enough to allow hundreds of soldiers through. Big enough to let a dragon through.

The blood drains from my face.

Pearson starts commanding his men, positioning them hidden atop the hill, rifles ready. In the tall grass, fifteen human soldiers take their positions around me, protecting me. The others quickly beeline to a higher point, where the craggy hill rises up to the north. From there, they'll have the best angle to fire at the Fey as they arrive.

As the Fey march through the portal, one group at a time, Talan's plan takes shape.

I clench my jaw in frustration, cursing myself for not getting us here sooner.

"Okay," Viviane says. "Start, Nia. We'll provide you with cover and take out as many as we can while you try to close it."

I nod and dig my fingers into the snowy earth. Through the soil, I feel the buzz of powerful magic, and I try to understand its structure.

As I focus, a volley of explosions thunders through the air. Near the portal, a few Fey soldiers fall to the ground, some screaming. Two of them are lying still, bleeding from their heads. Now, like an anthill that's been kicked, the soldiers beneath us scurry for protection, readying their swords and bows. Commanders call out instructions, and one of them is instantly gunned down. Pearson must have told his men to target the officers first.

I try to block the chaos from my mind and focus on the portal. Wrapping my powers around it, I push at it, threading my own crimson magic into the gaps, but the magic of the portal doesn't react to my attempts.

Below, the Fey are scrambling, regrouping. One of the commanders manages to get a cluster of soldiers in formation, protected by a line of shields. Behind the shields, Fey archers aim high and let their arrows loose. I hear a scream as an arrow finds its mark.

From the gaping portal, ten new soldiers materialize. The Fey army is moving faster now. Someone must have given the order to rush. Though they seem dazed by the passage, their weapons are drawn, and they're ready to fight as they come through. A volley of iron bullets takes three of them down, but the others quickly run to the cover of nearby boulders.

I exhale, tugging at my energy reserves. I channel the tendrils of red, summoning my power into a great ball, and *fling* it at the portal.

The portal swallows it, a black hole devouring red ribbons of my magic.

And now, it's caught the Fey's attention. The Fey are more attuned to magic than humans are. At the feel of my magic rushing down the hill, many of them turn their heads toward me. Someone shouts a command.

And with a blood-curdling battle cry, dozens rush toward my position. My breath goes still, my body shaking with primal fear.

The Fey raise their metal shields against incoming bullets and charge. Archers cover them as they storm up the hill. Many of them fall to our fire, but arrows land around us, some hitting our own men.

Agonized screams echo through the valley, and my blood roars. Clenching my fingers, I unleash another magical torrent. Red streaks through the air, soaring for the portal.

This time, I feel something different, a glimpse of a crack in the portal as the Fey soldiers come through.

The portal magic grows vulnerable, weaker, as the Fey travel through it, I realize.

Before I can make use of this discovery, three Fey warriors bear down on me, yards away, their teeth bared in grimaces. A bullet takes out one of them, and he twists and topples backward down the hill, but the other two keep coming, and they're not ten feet away. I look at them, petrified. I reach for an arrow, knowing that it's already too late—

A blade swings, sending one soldier's head flying, and the rest of his body collapses onto the hillside. Viviane stands over him, her sword dripping blood. She pivots to the other and breaks his nose with the pommel of her sword, then kicks him brutally in the chest. He tumbles down the slope.

"Nia, get that fucking thing closed!" she shouts.

I turn my attention back to the portal, blocking out the screams and volleys of bullets around me, sending a tendril of magic at the portal, probing it carefully.

It flickers, and I see two worlds.

It's as if Brocéliande and Scotland suddenly exist in

the same place and time. I can still see a Scottish valley, the stream churning through it, our soldiers fighting the much larger force of Fey. But I can also glimpse the snowy landscape of Brocéliande spreading out and a military camp with white tents surrounded by high snow-capped mountains. The Fey soldiers stand in large formations—legions of them. A vast army waiting to charge through.

My heart skips a beat.

It's one thing to know that the advancing army numbers two thousand. It's a different thing to *see* them. Rows and rows of armored cavalry, archers, magicians, and knights. And behind them, a midnight-blue dragon raises his head, opening his maw to roar. The sound rumbles through my gut, making me want to run. Dread dances up my nape.

Now, mounted cavalry charge through the portal, and I can glimpse them *shifting* from one reality to the other, materializing in the battlefield here.

My double-world vision fades. I blink, my head pounding. The Fey horses are spooked and run in different directions. One collapses, crushing its rider. But the other riders take control of their mounts and manage to turn them to the hill.

They're charging right for us.

A volley of fire hits them. Some go down. Some don't. Through my fear, I force myself to focus.

When it opened, I saw the two worlds shift together. *That's* when I have to strike. But it's easier said than done. My mind isn't built to see two realities intertwined. I'm nauseated, and my head spins. Most of my magic is already depleted from my earlier attempts. I summon what I can of it, gathering the red flares, and send my power out to the portal. Now, the battle sounds seem muted in my ears. An arrow thunks into the ground a few inches away from me, but I don't lose my focus.

The portal shifts again.

The worlds coalesce.

More Fey are gathering to charge through, a group of archers and another group of heavily armored warriors. A man, taller than the rest, shouts commands at them, and his dark cloak billows around him. He turns to face me.

My heart sinks as I behold the shockingly beautiful face of the Fey prince.

His black hair catches in the wind as he roars orders at the men, urging them to move. Fear cuts me down to the marrow. He's going to come through the portal. He'll find me here—Brocéliande's worst traitor. The mistress who turned on her prince.

I dig my fingers deeper into the cold soil and focus my senses on the portal. I now have a sense of the complex energy that weaves it into the world. It's a masterful work of magic—an art form, like a tapestry. And yet, I can see its weaknesses. I can unravel it, thread by thread, if I just have enough time. I concentrate on one weak link and channel my power at it. The portal's magic vibrates under the onslaught of my power, thinning, about to shatter—

The archers charge through the portal, and a flash of raw energy runs through it as they do. The power jolts through my bones, and I grunt in agony, my concentration shattered.

The portal flickers again. Brocéliande disappears, and Talan is no longer in view.

In the valley before us, the archers all kneel, the warriors standing in front of them, protecting them with their shields. A hail of arrows flies through the air, more precise than before. Talan has now brought the best of his archers forward to eliminate our forces. He wants to end the threat from us as quickly as he can.

Pearson shouts, but his command is cut short as an arrow tears through his throat. Around me, I feel death closing in. The scent of gunpowder and blood fills the air.

The earth thunders as the cavalry gallop up the hill, hooves pounding. Fear keens in my skull.

Blood runs down Viviane's face, dripping into her eyes. "We're running out of time. It's now or never. Can you do it?"

This time, I'm certain. "I can do it."

"I believe in you, Nia. Stop those fuckers. Save us all."

She turns to face the incoming riders. "For Camelot!" she roars, and rushes at them.

I've never seen a warrior move so quickly. She leaps at the first, lopping his sword arm off. Pivoting, she's already throwing a knife at another. She blocks a sword swing, the metal blades scraping together, and manages to pull a rider off his horse. More men are upon her, and an arrow sinks into her side, but she doesn't stop. She's a whirlwind of thrusts and slashes.

Once, she told me that you beat your opponent by using everything you've got. And this is everything she has.

My heart pounds, a war drum in my chest.

Our few remaining soldiers join her, firing at the incoming Fey.

One by one, they fall, their blood mingling with snow. The world grows colder, darker. I can taste the blood in the air. I blink the tears from my eyes and focus once more on the portal.

It flickers and shifts, Brocéliande reappearing in the gap.

Terror sinks its claws into my heart.

The dragon is only fifty feet away from the portal. The monster opens his mouth to unleash a gout of fire.

Talan rides on his back, his dark cloak whipping in the air behind him.

For just a heartbeat, he looks my way, his dark eyes locked on me. I know he can't see me, but a shiver of fear runs through me. *He knows.*

Beating its wings, the dragon rises into the air.

I focus on the portal, searching frantically for the weak link. *There!* I channel all my fear, my desperation, my anguish at that one thin spot, and slam my crimson magic at it. It vibrates with the force and starts to crack.

The dragon runs for the portal, wings spread, flying for the opening. Talan grips it tightly, his mouth open in a war cry.

The dragon roars and belches fire.

My magic spreads, cracking red over the portal like a spiderweb of broken glass. And as the dragon flies for the gap, the cracks widen, shattering. The portal disappears, and the dragon's roar goes silent.

The Fey feel the portal die, and they stumble, disoriented, the world shifting around them. A few humans are still aiming at them. Bullets fly, hitting the Fey warriors, taking them down, one by one. Swallowing hard, I ready my bow and nock an arrow. My first bolt takes down a Fey archer, and my next kills a charging knight.

They don't know that we're outnumbered. They only know they're stranded in a hostile world, cut off from their forces, and that they're being shot with iron bullets. Someone shouts an order to retreat, and they turn and run.

With shaking legs, I manage to stand. On the slopes below me, bodies stain the earth with gore. The dead lie among the injured, and moans fill the air. As I catch my breath, I turn to see what's left of our forces. My throat tightens. Only four men are still standing.

Tears blur my vision, and I stumble over to Viviane, sorrow pulling me apart.

Her body is a mess, cut in countless places. Her pale blue eyes stare vacantly at the sky. Blood streaks her face, and I close her mouth, her eyes.

I choke out a sob.

I hated her when I met her. She hated me.

Then, somehow, she grew to be one of the people I trusted and admired the most.

And now, after giving Camelot everything she had, she's gone for good.

CHAPTER 44

I stand in a large tent in the main camp of the human allies, looking at a detailed map of the UK. It's a fresh map, clean, the paper sheet crisp. Little round markers signify the army positions. They seem so innocuous, but every X marks the place where thousands were killed and tens of thousands injured.

You can't smell the blood on the map. You can't hear the screams. You don't see the vacant eyes of the dead staring up at the sky, their jaws hanging open. Nothing on the map shows you the mangled limbs, the broken bones, the empty chair at dinner, the ashes scattered in a garden. There's no symbol for the man I saw on the way here, weeping by the side of the road, his entire body shaking. No marker for the moms rifling through old photos of the sons and daughters they'll never see alive again.

Sir Kay clears his throat, and I look up, blinking tears away. Raphael and Nivene stand by my side.

I feel Viviane's absence like a hole in my chest.

"Thanks to your intervention," Sir Kay says, "the Fey ambush failed. Without the reinforcements they tried to send, we've crippled their army." He points at a cluster of green pieces representing the Fey.

Even before the invasion of Britain, Sir Kay was growing quite old, but the war has taken its toll. He's pale and gaunt and walks with a noticeable limp. Before, he always wore his armor, but now he's dressed in simple clothes. He probably can't carry the armor's weight. Dark circles under his eyes make it clear that he's hardly been sleeping.

"Three dragons attacked the logistical base," Nivene says, pointing at another section of the map. "Because of Nia's intel, we were prepared with an enormous battery of Anti-Dragon Guns. Even with those, they were nearly successful in demolishing our base. But we wounded one dragon, killed another."

Her arm is bandaged. When I asked about it, she waved it away as a superficial burn. But I can see how she winces every time she shifts her arm.

"First time we managed to kill a dragon in this invasion," Sir Kay points out. "Ever since Auberon made them resistant to iron."

"Still," Nivene says, "if the Fey decide to attack us with all of their dragons, there's nothing we can do to stop them."

"Hopefully, the loss of one dragon and the crippling of another will make them hesitant," Raphael says. "And hopefully, they don't know how limited our capabilities are."

Raphael looks pale, haunted. After the battle, his healing powers were in high demand, draining him completely. And he's still injured, since the one person he can't heal is himself.

"For now, this failed assault of theirs bought us valuable time," Sir Kay says. "We're evacuating Edinburgh and Glasgow, as well as the surrounding towns. And we're amassing more allies. Denmark and Italy are sending reinforcements."

"But it won't be enough," Nivene says grimly.

"No." Sir Kay sighs. "This is what we're here to discuss."

A soldier hurries into the tent and hands Sir Kay a missive, then quickly slips out. He unfolds it and reads it carefully, his brow creasing.

"What is it?" Nivene asks.

"An update from our Seneschal," Sir Kay responds shortly. When he raises his eyes from the message, his face is even grayer than before.

"Is Avalon Tower all right?" I ask.

"It's fine. Things there are strained but...under control. For now."

Nivene and I exchange glances. We both know how much things are "under control."

"But this," Sir Kay continues, raising the missive with

his hand, "is just another reminder that we need to move quickly. If the war doesn't end soon, Avalon Tower will find itself in its own civil war. Tearing itself apart. And without us, the human allies don't stand a chance."

"So, what's the plan?" Raphael asks.

"I go back to Brocéliande," I say. "Get closer to Prince Talan. Cooperate with a team of assassins to take out the prince and the king. The loss of both of them at once will sow complete chaos."

"What?" Raphael snaps. "You told me you thought that he might have sensed you on the battlefield. You said he knows there's a spy in the fortress. He'll execute you as soon as you step back in Brocéliande."

"I think he sensed my magic. I don't think he knew it was *me*. He thinks I'm a harmless farm girl. What he sensed was the Avalon Tower agent he'd encountered before. He hasn't connected us."

Raphael's fists tighten. "And how long until he puts one and one together? Sir Kay, we can't allow this to continue. Nia isn't properly trained for this kind of undercover mission. There hasn't been time."

"I'd argue that she's already demonstrated quite the opposite," Sir Kay says softly. "Dame Nia has met our expectations and even exceeded them. She is truly worthy of her Avalon Steel rank. But yes, it's risky. Nia, are you sure you can pull this off?"

"Is there any alternative?" Nivene asks impatiently.

His eyebrows knit together, and Sir Kay glances at the missive in his hand. Then he folds it and pockets it away. "No. Nothing that I am willing to consider right now."

"I can do this." I glance at Raphael. "You're right. Talan will put one and one together, but only if I don't go back. If I'm there, I can convince him otherwise. I have a connection with him. I'll deepen the bond, make him trust me."

"The man is a killer. He doesn't trust anyone," Raphael says.

I ignore him. "Get the assassination plan ready. Nivene and I can go back through the portal we used before."

"This is insane." Raphael's voice is pure ice, and his silver eyes bore into me.

I shake my head. "Not insane. Desperate. We have no other options."

* * *

BACK IN BROCÉLIANDE, Nivene and I have been riding for days in the cold, our journey slowed by storms. As we draw closer to Corbinelle, lightning sears the sky, illuminating Perillos rising in the distance.

Corbinelle's city walls stretch out before us, carved with gargoyles. Torches line the walls, little orange specks from here.

Thunder rumbles over the dark landscape. Strange how they have lightning storms through the winter in Corbinelle.

At least we're already past the hailstorm that hit us yesterday, which rained enormous chunks of ice down on us. Or the blinding blizzard that lasted for hours and set our journey back a full day.

I've heard so many rumors at this point about Talan controlling the weather that I have to wonder if it's true. Is this his doing? The prince is probably furious. His plan has failed. Is nature raging on his behalf?

As we get closer to the city gates leading into Corbinelle, I feel it—a caress in my thoughts. The dark, silken murmur. The Dream Stalker is looking for me, and I'm back in his city. He's focusing hard, trying to find his mistress. I have to concentrate to keep the veil raised in my mind, making it thicker and stronger. He's working harder than ever to get into my thoughts.

Is he looking for me because he wants to kill me? Was Raphael right—and am I riding directly toward my own death?

Nivene pulls her horse to a halt before the open city gates, and I turn to look at her. "I'll leave you here," she says. "I'm heading off to find Meriadec."

"He might be at the farm, still."

"I'll find him. Then I'll meet you back at Perillos as soon as I can, yeah?"

I turn, riding through the city, past crowded timber-frame houses and taverns that beam with warm lights, the raucous sounds of laughter piercing the glass. My horse's hooves clop over the cobblestones. These little homes with their warm lights and jutting oriel windows look so cozy right now, but I'm heading for the terrifying castle that pierces the clouds.

I take the winding road up the gently sloped hill to Perillos and head for the main gate.

As I reach the gate, I nod at the soldiers.

One of them shouts up to me. "My lady, the prince has been looking for you."

I smile at him. "Well, I'm back."

They exchange looks that make me wonder exactly what sort of mood the prince might be in, but I ride on with feigned indifference, my heart thrumming in my chest.

As I bring my horse to the stables, this starts to feel like a terrible mistake. Coldness creeps over my skin.

Surely Talan has figured out the truth by now.

As I walk inside the fortress, I half expect armed guards to accost me, to chain me and drag me to the dungeon.

But no one does. Is Talan just biding his time?

I climb the stairs to my room, dread climbing up my throat.

There's no turning back now, though, is there? The soldiers have seen me.

I open the door and stagger into my room, out of breath.

Talan steps out of the bathroom, a towel around his waist. Water slides down his tan, muscled body.

It's hard to believe that just days ago, I saw him riding a dragon's back, ready to light a city on fire.

"Where have you been?" A knife's edge slides under his velvety tone.

"In hiding," I say in what I hope is a breezy tone. "I left a note behind. Arwenna wants me dead, and you were incapacitated. There was no one to protect me from another attempt on my life."

"I could have protected you if you'd stayed close to me, even at death's door." Ferocity laces his voice. He prowls closer, and darkness slides through the copper rings in his eyes. There's something in his expression I haven't seen before, something that I can't interpret. "Why did you not tell me where you were going? I searched everywhere for you. Your father said you visited the farm but left again. Even he didn't know where you went."

I swallow. "I'm here now."

"We have only hours left, you know. The moment my spies received word that you were returning through Corbinelle, I sent for Jasper. " He stares down at me, and the fresh scent of jasmine soap coils off him.

"A few hours left until what?"

"If you'd been here, Nia, I could have filled you in. You missed Arwenna's sham trial. She's already been found innocent of an assassination attempt."

My jaw drops. "She shot the crown prince with an iron-tipped arrow. Why would they find her innocent?"

He shrugs. "We had no proof, and Auberon needs her money. You were our only witness, and you were gone. Her family is wealthier than mine at this point. My father is demanding that I marry her tomorrow. He's hungry for the considerable dowry she'd bring, since he ran out of money to pay his soldiers long ago. He needs funding desperately. But I'm not letting it happen. We cannot let her get that close to the throne. And you shouldn't want it to happen, either. If she gets that much power, she will tear you to pieces like a child pulling off a moth's wings. And that's why you need to get moving, my beautiful mistress. Jasper will be here any minute to get you ready."

I blink. "For what?"

"He'll be designing your wedding dress. I can't marry Arwenna if I'm already married." He's searching my face, but I'm not sure what he's looking for. "I'm afraid we only have a few hours until we wed. Nia, this is the only way."

THANK you so much for reading Vale of Dreams!

If you haven't yet read it, there is a bonus chapter of Talan's perspective.

Lady of the Lake will be the third and final book starring Nia (but not necessarily the end for this world).

Please read on for an excerpt from another series that Alex Rivers and C.N. Crawford have written together.

SAMPLE OF AGENT OF ENCHANTMENT

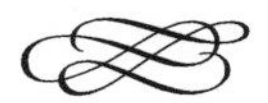

The following is an excerpt from Agent of Enchantment, another fae romance and adventure series from Alex Rivers and C.N. Crawford

* * *

THE FAE LAY on the ancient flagstones, candlelight dancing over his handsome features.

I had power over him now, and it intoxicated me. I was beyond taking things slow, beyond being careful. I was a fugitive, at the end of the line. I had very little to lose.

Standing below the towering stone arches of the ancient London church, I stared at him. Candlelight wavered around the nave, and high above me, thick shadows danced over the peaked vaults like malicious spirits. I took a deep breath, the battle over.

At least, I thought it was over.

As I drew closer, he seemed to rally, his lips curling into a grimace. With a roar, he leapt to his feet, charging me in a blur of movement. He moved impossibly fast, and yet to my eyes time seemed to slow down. His powerful arms swung like heavy pendulums, as if he were moving through a sea of honey.

Reflexes took over as I slid aside and let his fist pass me. Then, with both hands, I grabbed his wrist. Dipping my hips, I used his momentum to send him flying into a stone pillar. The crunch of his bones echoed off the vaulted ceiling, and dusty stone rained down on us.

The asshole had wanted to keep me in a cage, to torture me for fun. He wasn't going to see my merciful side.

With a dark smile curling my lips, I stalked toward him. A trickle of blood ran down his forehead, and he glared at me with his good eye. He snarled, a bestial sound—a predator, unused to being prey. As I came within reach, he tried to punch me in the stomach.

I slapped his hand away, then backhanded him across the face. His head snapped right, and he fell to the floor. I picked him up by the collar and hurled him at a row of pews. When he crashed into them, his body splintered the wood.

And yet he kept going, dragging himself up again, breath rasping.

This time I charged fast, intent on beating seven shades of shit out of him, but he was reaching for his boot. A knife? No. I recognized the familiar shape of a Glock 17, rising to point at my chest. My heart thundered. *Shit shit shit.* I dove, but not in time.

A gunshot echoed off the stone. Pain ripped through my side. Gasping, I fell back, clutching at my waist, my hands covered in blood.

He stood slowly, training the gun on me as I stumbled back, pain splintering my gut. The custom iron bullet seared me from within, and I fell to my knees.

Already the poison was spreading through my body, dizzying me. Quenching my magic. I gritted my teeth, mentally whispering my mantra. *Be prepared to kill everyone you meet.* Right about now, that wasn't working out so well for me.

His pale eyes flashing with fury, he pulled the trigger again, but it only clicked dully. The gun was empty. A small mercy.

"Well." He smiled wryly, walking toward me. "I guess I could always kill you the old-fashioned way."

I crawled away from him, gripping my gut, trying to block out the searing agony. "I should have known it was you. A fascination with power. Obsession with fear. You worship chaos…" Shivers wracked my body as the blood seeped through my fingers. "I profiled you all along."

"Mmm. Yet look where you are now, mongrel," he growled, eyes gleaming.

"Yeah, well…" I looked down at my blood-stained fingers. "I like to know that I got things right."

He kicked me in the stomach, right where he'd shot me. I gasped with pain, collapsing to my back, staring at the arched stone ceiling. Shadows writhed along the pillars, as if this place were cursed. And maybe it was—Smithfield, the vortex of slaughter. Moaning, I gritted my teeth.

The fae smiled, apparently enjoying my grimace of pain.

At the sight of his shit-eating grin, rage flared in me. *Fight, Cassandra. Always fight.* If only there were some way I could use my remaining magic… I grasped around me for metal, glass, anything.

"No one to save you anymore." He knelt over me, running a fingertip down my chest. "No more tricks. No more magic. Just me and you. Do you know what I think I'd like to do? Break your ribs, one by one. I want to see the fear in your eyes. What do you think, profiler? Will I enjoy it?"

A line of blood trickled from my mouth. "I think you need a more pro-social hobby."

He leaned over me, his pupils black as coal, completely devoid of feeling. "Ready to die, mongrel?" he asked, pressing his knee on the gunshot wound.

I screamed.

"I'll take that as a yes." His fingers wrapped around my throat.

As if in a dream, I stared into his eyes. So soulless, so empty, that I could see nothing in them but my own reflection.

* * *

FIVE DAYS EARLIER

Despite my Special Agent training, I nearly got myself killed three seconds after leaving Heathrow airport. I could handle snipers, knife attacks, poison, bombs—just not cars driving on the left side of the road.

But hey, in my defense, I was a bit preoccupied with the serial killer case I'd been called in to profile.

Anyway, three steps into the road, and it was all screeching brakes, honking, and the words "stupid twat" and "fuckwit" piercing the air.

And I'd been thinking everyone in England would be polite.

As the red-faced man continued his tirade ("Watch where you're going, fucking dozy mare!"), I jumped back to the sidewalk, cheeks burning. I took a deep breath, forcing myself to focus. I was in England now. The land of Shakespeare, Chaucer, and—as I was quickly learning—inventive swearing. They drove on the *left* here, something I should really keep in mind.

Having oriented myself, I decided that maybe navigating my way to a bus in a foreign city in the middle of the night was beyond my capabilities right now.

I mentally scanned through everything I'd digested in my tourist guide on the plane: trains, the Underground, black cabs. Perhaps best to just get one of those.

Supposedly, the black cab drivers were required to memorize the entire city, street by street.

I turned, catching a glimpse of the yellow *Taxi* sign by a long line of cabs. Pulling my suitcase behind me, I hurried across the crosswalk, back toward the terminal. As I hustled past the airport's gleaming windows, I caught a glimpse of myself: pale skin, rumpled blond hair, wrinkled skirt, and coffee stains on my white sweater.

Apart from the gloriousness of my favorite black boots, I looked like shit.

I reached the line of black cabs, and a bearded man rolled down the window, leaning over. "Taxi?"

"Yes, thank you," I said, relieved. "I need to get to the Bishopsgate police station."

"No problem." He smiled. "Hop in. I'll get your bags."

I let him put my carry-on in the trunk while I slid into the back seat. *At least some of them are polite.*

The driver got in, switched on the engine, and rolled into traffic. I relaxed into the soft leather seat.

I stared out the window at the dark West London streets. I was pretty sure we had a long drive ahead of us to the other side of London—the part called "the City." It was the old section of London, the part the Romans had encircled with a wall nearly two thousand years ago. The wall had fallen, but the ancient Square Mile still had its own governing bodies, separate from the rest of London. The Square Mile even had its own City police force.

My phone buzzed in my pocket, and I pulled it out. My stomach churned as I watched the contact name slowly scroll across the screen: *Under No Circumstances Should You Answer A Call From This Ballsack,* it read.

That would be my ex-boyfriend.

See? Brits aren't the only ones who can swear creatively.

I'm not normally the angry sort, but when I'd come home to find that my boyfriend had left open a dating site on my computer (username: *VirginiaStallion),* the swears had just rolled off the tongue.

According to a quick Google search, the Virginia Stallion had also been quite busy swapping dating tips on bodybuilding forums. Apparently, wearing a nicely tailored suit attracts the ladies, and Valentine's Day can be a nightmare when you're "banging three chicks on the regular." All things I'd learned in the past two weeks.

You'd think I'd be more careful about the kind of men I let into my life. Lesson learned for the future.

Scowling, I shoved my phone back in my pocket.

The driver glanced back at me. "Did you come from America or Canada?"

"The US. It's my first time here." I bit my lip. "Have you ever encountered the phrase 'dozy mare?'"

"Did someone call you that, miss?"

"Based on the context, I'm assuming it wasn't a compliment."

"I wouldn't pay it any mind, love." He turned onto a highway. "You working with the police at Bishopsgate? I don't imagine you came all the way from America to report a crime."

"Just doing a bit of consulting," I said. "Insider trading cases in the City. White-collar stuff."

A lie, and one boring enough that he wouldn't ask any follow-up questions. I'd become quite used to lying after a few years with the Bureau, though I still lacked the skill of the Virginia Stallion.

"Right," he said. "The financial district. You ask me, half those people should be in jail. Mucking about with the stock market and all that. Screws it up for everyone."

"Couldn't agree more."

My lies bored even me, but I wasn't about to expose the fact that I was here to profile London's most famous serial killer since Jack the Ripper. Plus, it creeped people out when I said I was an FBI special agent. And it *particularly* spooked them if they learned I worked for the Behavioral Analysis Unit, as a psychologist who profiled criminals. All of a sudden, people got jittery, as if I were going to unearth their darkest secrets just by looking into their eyes.

We lapsed into silence as the cab sped along the M4. As we drove further into the city, I began to feel a change tingle over my body, as though my senses were becoming heightened. Here, in the center of the City, the streetlights seemed to burn brighter, washing the streets in white light. On a road called Chancery Lane, we drove past squat Tudor-looking buildings, the colored lights from the shops on their lower floors dazzling off puddles on the pavement. No one lingered on the dark streets at this hour, but for just a moment, I thought I heard the buzz of a crowd of people; then it faded into the distance again.

A shiver rippled over my body. I'd never been to London, and yet I had a strange sense of déjà vu here. *Get a grip, Cassandra.*

The driver turned to me. "You hear about the new Ripper murders in the City?" he asked.

"I did hear about them. It freaked me out. Nearly canceled my trip," I lied. "You don't normally get many murders around here, do you?"

"Not like you do. We don't have guns. But these murders... I wouldn't advise walking around at night if I was you. From what I hear, they didn't even put the worst of it in the papers. The girls they found, they was..." He cleared his throat. "Well, I don't want to scare you."

"I'll certainly be careful."

I didn't need him to tell me the details—I'd been poring over them for the entire flight, and before that, in my BAU office back at Quantico. I practically knew the depth of each laceration by heart. Still, the cab driver's concern was cute, and I appreciated it. I was quickly reviving my "polite" theory of Brits.

A few days ago, the City of London police had persuaded me to fly to the UK. The London FBI overseas office was slammed with other work, the attachés delving into investigations of terrorism cases and election interference. None of them had time for a serial killer, but I'd made my career off these cases. I'd been researching serial killers for the Bureau for years. The strange details of this case had piqued my Unit Chief's interest—enough that he was willing to foot the bill. And the City Police wanted to meet me as soon as I arrived—a Detective Constable Stewart was waiting for me, even at this late hour.

I rummaged in my bag, searching for some makeup and my mirrored compact. I pulled out a rose lipstick and dotted some pink on to my pale cheeks in the reflection. As I did, something glimmered in my blue irises—a hint of rushing water, like a rolling river.

I snapped the compact shut. *I am losing my mind.* I obviously needed sleep, or water, or perhaps several Manhattans.

I rubbed my forehead. I was supposed to head straight to the station to quickly meet the detective, and the details of the case nagged at the back of my mind.

The driver looked over his shoulder at me. "Lots of papers to go through, I imagine. With your sort of work."

"Oh, you have no idea. I'd better go through some of the financials now, in fact." Diving back into my bag, I pulled out the case reports the police had sent earlier that week. I flipped through them, taking care to shield the gruesome photos from the driver.

Over the past month, three young women had been found dead in London. The killer had slashed their throats and abdomens open. And just like Jack the Ripper, he'd claimed macabre trophies: a uterus from one, a kidney and heart from another. From the third victim, he'd taken her liver.

So was this a Ripper copycat? The papers certainly thought so. The UK tabloids were already gleefully declaring "The Ripper Is Back!"

I wasn't so sure we were dealing with the same mentality. The killer was almost certainly inspired by the Ripper, but he was killing at a much faster pace.

Staring at one of the crime scene photos, I shook my head. I'd never understood why Jack the Ripper had gotten so much attention. He was hardly the worst, in numbers or methodology. Perhaps it was the name that had inspired endless horror stories. Or the fact that the lack of resolution provided fertile ground for wild conspiracies. Whatever the reason, no one could quite let it go.

My phone buzzed in my pocket, and I grumbled under my breath. But when I pulled it out to glance at the screen, it read *Unknown Number.*

Tentatively, I swiped the screen. "Hello?"

"Agent Liddell?" It was a British man with a deep voice. A faint London accent, I thought.

"Speaking."

"I'm Detective Constable Gabriel Stewart. I'm the detective in charge of the serial killer cases."

"Right. Hi. I'm on my way to meet you right now." Gabriel was supposed to be my contact.

He cleared his throat. "I think you should come directly to Mitre Square instead."

I glanced at the time. It was past midnight. "Why?"

"There's been another murder." He paused for a moment as a siren wailed in the background. "Mitre Square is the location of the crime scene."

* * *

IF I HAD any hope that the crime scene would be reasonably contained, it evaporated the moment I turned down the narrow covered alley leading to Mitre Square. Blocked by a line of police tape, a small crowd jammed one end of the passage, barring my way. One of the men seemed to be leaning against the wall, half asleep, and the entire passage smelled of piss and beer.

Pausing, I pulled out my phone to call Detective Stewart.

"Hello?" The detective answered almost immediately.

"Detective, it's Cassandra."

"Who?"

"Agent Cassandra Liddell."

"Oh, right! Are you close?"

"I'm standing just outside the crime scene perimeter in Mitre Passage," I said. "Do you want to let me inside?"

"Sure, just wait until Officer Holbrook comes over to you. Flash your badge, and he'll let you right through."

"Maybe I should be more discreet with all these spectators around?"

He went silent for a moment. "Good point," he finally said. "I'll come for you myself."

I hung up, gripping my suitcase a little tighter and scanning the crowd. For all I knew, the killer could be lingering around here to watch the action. It was one of those weird quirks of some serial killers, returning to the scene of the crime to relive it. I wasn't sure exactly what I was looking for, as his previous history suggested he wasn't overtly psychotic or disorganized. But it wouldn't hurt to memorize the faces for later. I looked at them hard for a long moment, imprinting the view in my mind. Satisfied, I relaxed and took a deep breath.

Despite the fact that half the people here were three sheets to the wind, I could sense an undercurrent of fear beneath their drunkenness. My guess was that whatever lay beyond in Mitre Square was sobering them up pretty fast.

In all honesty, it wasn't just that I could sense their fear. I could actually *feel* it, like a physical charge. And right now, it was building in my system.

As always, it started with my heart. It began pounding faster and faster, each beat thundering in my ears. My fingertips prickled with what felt like a delicate electrical current. Despite the chilly night breeze, my face flushed, heat waves rolling over my body.

The first time I had described this to my friends, they'd just stared at me. I'd assumed everyone felt this way occasionally. Sometimes you're hungry, sometimes you want to sneeze, and sometimes you feel like the emotional energy of the people around you powers your body like electricity. Right? *Right*?

Apparently not. This was not a sensation everyone experienced. This happened only to me. And after talking about it a few times, and getting very weird looks, I stopped mentioning it. Energy? What energy? Ha ha, the only energy I know is energy drinks. I'm totally like everyone else.

Whatever it was, it came from strong emotions. Going to a football game in my hometown was... intense. I'd walk out dazed, a grin on my face, and when someone asked me if I'd enjoyed the game that much, I would realize that I didn't even know what had happened on the field. I knew what had happened in the *crowd*. They were thrilled, or disappointed, or angry... and I felt it blazing through my body like a drug.

But no other emotion affected me like fear did. And right now, an undercurrent of fear flowed through me. It focused me, sharpening my senses. Any fatigue from the flight dissipated completely.

I began shoving my way through the small crowd, rolling my stupid suitcase behind me. As I did, I glimpsed a media van parked in the road. Damn it. Nothing hurt a serial killer investigation more than public fear.

I reached the police tape, staring at the horrific scene before me. Spotlights bathed it in white light. About seventy feet away, on the other side of the square, a group of people surrounded a woman's body. Even from here, I could see the crimson pool glistening on the cobbles beneath her.

Most of the investigators surrounding the body wore white overalls that covered their bodies completely, surgical masks on their faces. Shoes were covered with white sterile wrappers, and their hands were gloved in blue latex. Only their eyes were visible as they scanned the scene intently, documenting and marking evidence.

A tawny-skinned man approached, eyeing me. Unlike the crime scene crew, he wore a suit and a gray coat.

"Gabriel?" I asked when he got closer.

He nodded, and motioned me through. I raised the tape and stepped under it, then leaned my suitcase against a wall before turning to him.

He shook my hand, his grip firm. I found it difficult to pull my eyes from his face. Broad-shouldered and tall, he towered over me, and something about his hazel eyes drew me in. Plus, with his bronze skin and strong jawline, he kinda looked like a movie star.

His body seemed tense. "Agent Liddell," he said. "I'm glad you could make it."

"Call me Cassandra."

"Okay," he said, his tone cold. "Cassandra."

It didn't take a PhD in psychology to pick out the chilliness in his voice. I guess I had a few ideas why he might not be thrilled to have me there. For one thing, American law enforcement agents hadn't always done well with the British police. We tended to ignore their pesky legal systems and make our own rules. Plus, FBI consultants in general had a reputation of disregarding local expertise. And if all that weren't bad enough, he was probably terrified I was going to have a chirpy American attitude and say things like "good work, team," or force him to high-five at the end of the day.

"Come with me." He turned and walked away.

I followed him. As we drew closer, my mood darkened. I began to pick up the details—the red gash across her entire body, throat to belly, and the dark pool of blood beneath her. Lumps of flesh glistened under the lights. A woman stood above her, photographing the carnage.

"We can stop here," he said when we still stood twenty feet away. "It's intense, and I doubt you need to see it up close to profile the killer. We can provide you with photographs later on."

"Thanks for caring." I raised an eyebrow. "I think I can handle it."

I marched forward. When I reached the body, I crouched by a man who eyed me warily beyond a pair of glasses. I could have sworn I heard him mutter something about Americans under his mask, but I kept my focus on the victim.

Up close, bile began to rise in my throat. She was young, no more than twenty, her face full of pain and horror, mouth ajar in a voiceless cry, eyes staring emptily at the night sky. Her dark hair spread out on the pavement between her arms, giving the impression she was falling. The killer had torn her shirt, exposing the top of her ravaged body. A deep slice exposed her internal organs, or what was left of them. The glaring spotlights highlighted her white skin and bones, shockingly pale against her crimson blood. And as if that weren't bad enough, he'd mutilated her face, slashing perpendicular lines in her cheeks. Dread roiled in the back of my mind. Somehow, the marks looked eerily familiar, like something I'd seen in a nightmare, but I had no idea why.

I tried not to imagine what she would have felt in those final moments, but the images came anyway. The gash on her throat indicated that the killer was likely standing behind her, but her expression left no doubt—she had felt the hand that gripped her, the blade that cut her.

I could only hope that the shock of the attack had overwhelmed her, dulling the pain of the knife wounds somewhat—that her mind hadn't been able to process the horror of what was happening to her. I *hoped* most of the damage had been postmortem.

As my mind roamed over the horror of her final moments, I was almost sorry I hadn't listened to Gabriel. But this was important. This was the murderer's work, and I had to see it up close. This was his sadistic form of expression, how his mind worked. I pushed my visions of her death to the back of my skull, trying to focus.

A steady buzz drew my attention. Several flies

roamed the open, bloody cavity. When a body was hours or days old, flies were valuable allies of the forensic team. A skilled investigator could estimate the time of death using fly and larvae samples taken from the body. But this corpse was fresh, and the flies were nothing but parasites, using the poor woman to feed their young.

I waved my hand to shoo the flies away. The coppery smell of blood overpowered me, and I quickly stood up. The flies returned, haunting the woman's wounds again.

I struggled with the desire to close her eyes, to soothe the tortured stare from her face. Somehow, that was what hit me the hardest: her eyes. Wide open and in pain. Maybe I couldn't feel her emotions on a visceral level, but they were written plainly on her face.

Stepping away from the body, I gritted my teeth, trying to picture the monster who would rip apart four young women like this. How many more would he kill before someone stopped him? Would I be able to help?

I was pretty sure I would. This was what I did best. I helped find men like him and put an end to their murder binges.

From the perimeter around the police tape, I felt the crowd's horrified energy, and it began to build my resolution. I wouldn't return to the US until we'd put this monster in prison.

"Are you okay?" Gabriel asked, handing me a pair of latex gloves. I took them and put them on, the synthetic material somehow reassuring.

"I will be," I muttered. "Looks like the viciousness is increasing."

"That was our impression as well," Gabriel said. "This one is the worst so far."

I looked around the small city square. There were no shop fronts here, just the back entrances of buildings, a fenced-in parking lot, and a tiny road. Still, it seemed impossible that he'd slaughtered her in the center of the city without anyone noticing.

"Do we have any witnesses?" I asked.

Gabriel shook his head. "No. A passerby found her at twenty past eleven. He saw no one near the body."

"Do we have an estimated time of death?"

"Yeah. Between eleven and eleven twenty."

"So he found her only minutes after she had been killed."

"Yes."

I frowned. "This doesn't make sense. Someone killed her and disemboweled her completely. It would have taken some time. How did he manage to do that without anyone noticing? Surely people must cut through here to get to the bars and restaurants I saw on Bishopsgate?"

"There isn't much light here without the spotlights. And most people out at this time in the City are likely plastered."

I looked around. The body was reasonably hidden from the nearby street, but anyone looking a bit carefully would surely have noticed it. "He must have been silent. And calm. This is... extraordinary."

"I agree. I've never seen anything like it."

"Any organs missing from the scene?" I asked, thinking of the previous cases.

"The heart, at least, but I'm not sure what else. We'll have a preliminary autopsy report tomorrow."

"Did you do a door-to-door? Did anyone hear anything?"

"We've only just found her," he countered. "And no one lives around here. Unless you wander further east, it's all empty banks and businesses at this hour."

I stared at the woman. "Do we have an ID?"

"Her name is Catherine Taylor," Gabriel said. "Nineteen years old. There was a driver's license in her purse, discarded by the body. We don't know if it's a coincidence yet."

"Coincidence?" I asked.

A sigh slid from him. "Jack the Ripper killed a woman called Catherine Eddowes in Mitre Square."

My throat tightened. Shit. Was he starting to mimic the actual Ripper? "The other victims weren't killed in places where the Ripper struck."

"This is the first that overlaps."

"And the other names didn't match the original Ripper's victims, right?"

"No. I imagine he is adjusting his signature as he goes along. But then, I'm no profiler, so perhaps I'd best leave all the complicated stuff to you."

I narrowed my eyes. Some British people were under the impression that Americans didn't understand sarcasm, and perhaps it was best if I just played along. "Right. Best leave it to the experts."

He stared at me for just a moment before the medical examiner interrupted. "Detective. Can you have a look at this?"

Gabriel crossed to the body. As he quietly spoke to the man, my gaze wandered to Catherine's eyes again. What had gone through her mind in her final moments? Had she thought of anyone she loved, or had the pain overwhelmed her?

My fingers tightened into fists. I wasn't sure if it was my own past coming to the surface, the way it sometimes did at times like this, but I suddenly had an overwhelming desire to catch her killer and kick the living shit out of him *before* I put him behind bars.

Gabriel knelt close to Catherine's mouth, inspecting it.

I leaned over to get a better look. "What is it?"

"There's something here. It's shoved into her throat. Hang on..."

The man crouching by the body handed Gabriel a pair of medical forceps. Carefully, Gabriel inserted them into the victim's mouth, grimacing as the metal rattled against the teeth. He struggled with it for a second, before finally removing a small piece of paper, spattered in blood.

"What the hell?" he muttered.

Carefully, he unfolded it, and I peered over his shoulder.

It was a note, the cursive letters looping over the paper.

> The King of Hearts
> Tears minds apart,
> Deep below the water;
> From Bedlam's den,
> He lures them in,
> Like lambs led to the slaughter.

For just a moment I heard the sound of a rushing river, before the noise disappeared again.

I shook sensation from my mind.

Gabriel rose, frowning. "What's he playing at?" he asked, more to himself than anyone else.

Unnerved, I swallowed hard. "Jack the Ripper left notes, right?"

"Scribbles on a wall. Some tosh about Jews. But nothing like this."

"And this is the first time our current Ripper has left a note?"

He was still staring at the paper. "The first one."

"Well, if you want my input…" I stopped myself short. I needed to avoid coming off like a know-it-all, or I'd alienate him immediately. "Perhaps we can discuss this tomorrow morning. I'll gather a few ideas during the day, and I'd be interested to know your thoughts as well."

Gabriel nodded. "Right. I don't suppose you have an initial assessment?"

"I'd prefer to do a bit of research first. But the note and the gruesome display indicate that the killer seems to enjoy the attention of being the next Ripper. Maybe part of his fantasy revolves around the media and the police. The tabloid headlines might increase his obsession. And if so, maybe he'd want to see us working his cases up close."

I watched him carefully, interested if he'd get what I was implying. He stared at me for a long moment, before glancing over my shoulder, at the crowd beyond the tape. Then, he turned to the photographer—a middle-aged woman with a very expensive-looking camera.

"I want detailed pictures of the crowd," he said in a low voice. "Don't aim the camera straight at them. I don't want anyone to avoid the picture."

She nodded, pointing her camera at the blood spatter around the body. Slowly, she tilted the lens slightly higher, so that it would catch the people behind the tape. She took a few photographs, nudging the camera left and right. She knew what she was doing. And so did the detective.

I'd already committed most of their faces to memory—the two men with beer guts in cheap suits who probably had low-level positions in one of the nearby banks; the man in the white hat with track marks up his arm; the cluster of teens who'd convinced someone to serve them beer, at least one of them more interested in trying to get laid than anything else going on here. But photographs would make it easier for other cops to study the crowd after the fact.

From a far corner of the square, a man in a gray suit approached us, a serious expression on his face. "Detective Stewart." He nodded at Gabriel. I pegged him at about fifty, his hair silvery gray. He wasn't bad-looking, like a giant George Clooney. He was at least as tall as Gabriel, and powerfully built. Standing next to them, I felt roughly the size of a young child. Was everyone in Britain a giant?

"Chief." Gabriel nodded at him, then motioned at me. "This is Agent Liddell from the FBI. Agent, this is Detective Chief Inspector Steve Wood."

"Oh, yes." DCI Wood's voice was deep, pure gravel. "The *profiler*."

He didn't sound thrilled either. It was becoming clear to me that the high brass had gone over everyone's head when they'd contacted the FBI. Still, he offered me his hand, and I shook it.

"So what are our preliminary findings?" he asked.

For a second I thought he was talking to me, but Gabriel cut in, "This murder is slightly different from the rest. More aggressive. More… public. And he left a note shoved in the victim's throat."

"Are we sure it's the same killer?" DCI Wood asked. "With the different MO—"

"The MO is the same," I interrupted. "The signature is different."

Damn it. I was doing that American thing.

The chief glanced at me. "Is that so?"

"Well, um, perhaps..." I blustered. *Ah, fuck it.* "The MO is the method used to commit the crime. In this case, cutting a young woman's throat with a knife is the MO. It's how he's killed all his victims. The signature is what he did later to satisfy his emotional needs. Mutilating her body postmortem—that's his signature. But this time he left a note. His signature has been modified."

"I see." He nodded slowly. "And what does a different signature indicate?"

It was a sensible question, but his tone clearly implied he thought I was full of shit.

"Serial killers modify their signatures constantly," I said. "They evolve and change after each murder. A different signature isn't unusual, but it suggests that his emotional needs may have changed."

He looked at Gabriel. "What are your thoughts, Detective?"

Gabriel shrugged. "I agree with her assessment so far."

The crime scene technicians were wrapping the body's hands with paper bags, and someone had rolled over a stretcher.

How long would it take to clean all this up? Would

tomorrow's bankers stroll past the large stain on the cobblestones, not knowing why it was there?

As DCI Wood walked away, I nodded at the crowds. "How are Londoners handling the crimes?"

Gabriel frowned. "A mixture of fear and rage. They think it's a form of terrorism."

Irritation sparked. "It clearly isn't."

"For now, Wood is keeping the media in the dark, so they're creating their own narrative. Foreigners did it. That's the story."

I exhaled slowly. If Wood allowed this to continue, people could get hurt.

Gabriel stared at the body. Under his breath, I heard him say, *"The savage man is never quite eradicated."*

Surprised, I turned to him. "Thoreau. He's from my home town."

He seemed to study me for a minute, as if his curiosity had been piqued. "Where are you staying? I can walk you to the hotel."

"No need. I'm only five or ten minutes away—the hotel connected to Liverpool Street Station. And I don't imagine our killer will be striking again within the next fifteen minutes."

"Are you sure?"

"Gabriel," I assured him. "I'm an FBI agent. I can take care of myself."

* * *

As I walked through the City's winding streets, my phone buzzed, and I pulled it out of my pocket. I flicked open the screen, finding a text from Scarlett.

Things OK in Blighty?

She was into archaic slang. *Yeah, apart from all the serial killers,* I typed.

You need the serial killers, she wrote back. *Without them, you'd be out of a job.*

Weird slang and dark humor. That was my best friend's thing. *That's grim, Scarlett.*

After another minute, the green bubble popped up again. *Speaking of grim, please visit my favorite London spots: Anne Boleyn's execution spot, William Wallace's execution spot, the plague pits, and Kennsy's Fried Chicken, which is disturbingly addictive when you're drunk. XO.*

Scarlett consistently ruined my mental image of CIA agents. They weren't supposed to stumble around foreign cities drunk and eating fried chicken, but she seemed to get away with it. I wasn't going to argue that I was here for work, not a vacation, because she never seemed to get that concept.

I looked up from my phone at the city streets. Like I'd told Gabriel, I didn't get lost. I had an excellent sense of direction.

But I seemed to have misplaced myself a bit.

The streets in the "Old City" were contorted relics of a time before proper math or straight lines, when the whims of bakers and butchers overruled good sense. It seemed easy to end up off by a block or two.

A chilly night breeze nipped at my skin through my merino sweater. I listened to my suitcase scrape along the pavement, trying not to think of Catherine Taylor and the horrified look on her face.

Shivering, I slowed my gait when I noticed the road narrowing. Suddenly, the buildings seemed to loom over me. I frowned. I should be heading toward lights and traffic, not away from it. When I pulled out my phone, I could see I'd gone off course. Not by much, fortunately; I had taken a wrong turn one block back. I was one street away from where I should be. I could actually follow the alley all the way to the main street, but something didn't feel right here.

I checked the map again. The name—Catherine Wheel Alley—didn't inspire a lot of confidence. Wasn't that a sort of medieval torture device? And after what I'd just seen, the name "Catherine" alone conjured images I'd prefer to revisit in the warmth and safety of my hotel room.

From somewhere behind me, footfalls echoed off the walls. *Fuck, I do not want to meet the kind of people who are out at this hour.* I began hurrying forward. Maybe I *would* just keep going on the same way. But a man stepped from the shadows in front of me, blocking my way in the narrow alley. He wore jeans and a grey hoodie and his hands were tightened into fists, his body tensed as if ready to attack.

"All right, darling?" he asked.

Turning, I quickened my pace away from him,

heading back to Middlesex street. My footsteps echoed in the tight alley, the sound intermingling with the constant rumbling of my suitcase on the ground.

Another man appeared, sliding toward me like a wraith. This was the owner of the first set of footsteps I'd heard. My heart began to gallop in my chest.

"Where do you think you're going, beautiful?" he asked. I could just make out a pair of bright blue eyes and a mop of blond hair.

My hand flew to my holster—or where my holster would have been if I was back in the States. My beloved Glock did not get to join me on this trip.

The two men closed in on me. Blondie grinned, eying me up and down. "Don't you know there's a killer out in the City? Wouldn't want him ripping your pretty little body open, would we? That'd be a terrible waste."

"Why don't you let us take care of you," said the man behind me. "You just need to be nice to us first. You know how to be nice, don't you?"

A dark smile curled my lips. In training, I'd had to hold back from hurting men twice my size. And I didn't imagine these two men were particularly well-trained. I wouldn't hurt them if I didn't have to, but I would if I needed to. I rehearsed my mental motto in my mind. *Be courteous, and be prepared to kill everyone you meet.*

Blondie grabbed his crotch, his excitement nauseatingly apparent. "What do you have under your tight little sweater?"

Okay. Maybe the courtesy thing wouldn't last long.

My gaze flicked behind Blondie, to where the alley made a sharp turn. I could dip behind the corner. They'd rush forward, a predator's basic instinct. And then I'd leap out, catch them unawares.

"Excuse me," I simpered. *Always give your opponent a reason to underestimate you.*

I dropped my grip on the suitcase handle. I'd come back for it later if I had to.

"Excuse me," I said again, pushing past Blondie. If they let me out of this unscathed, we'd end it here.

But with Blondie pressing in on me in the narrow alley, I had to rub against his body to move past him. He let out an appreciative moan as I squeezed past, and grabbed my ass. I choked down my revulsion.

I broke into a run, giving the impression of a frightened woman—prey. I was breathing hard—not an act. When I reached the corner, I ducked behind it, listening to their oncoming footsteps. When Blondie rounded the corner, I lunged forward with a lowered shoulder, catching him in the gut. The leverage was perfect and he went down hard. But his body had been much heavier than I'd expected, like a brick wall.

Worse, he instantly bounded to his feet, in an unexpectedly catlike movement. His speed disturbed me. He was too fast for an untrained goon.

His friend rushed me and reflexes took hold as I rammed my fist into his nose. The sound of crunching bone echoed off the walls, and he stumbled back, hollering.

I whirled to face Blondie. I was now between them, with nowhere to run. The alley was narrow enough to allow anyone to block the way completely.

Blondie's face was a mask of rage. "I'm gonna have fun taking you for a ride, bitch," he snarled, his voice like sandpaper on a log. "And since you've got on my wick, I'm not gonna be gentle."

He lunged, grabbing for me, and I took a step back, kneeing him in the groin. He folded in half, sputtering something in a language I couldn't name. And yet, the sound of those strange syllables made the hair on my neck rise. He raised his face and my eyes met his. Blood red circles, shimmering in the darkness. I froze at the sight, and felt arms wrap around me. His friend, from behind.

His throaty whisper was damp in my ear. "Gotcha, darling."

He held me in a vice grip, thrusting his hips against me. Despite the broken nose, he seemed to be enjoying himself. And I was quickly starting to panic. I wasn't normally on the losing end of a fight. What was *with* these guys? Performance-enhancing drugs?

I tried to elbow his stomach, but I couldn't move my arm more than a few inches. I let out a whimper, heard him laugh as I dropped my head.

And then threw it back, hitting his face.

On its own, a broken nose is a terrible thing. But I don't care what your pain threshold is, if someone slams you in a nose that's already been broken, you're going down. And he did—screaming, clutching his face. Music to my ears.

Before I had the chance to feel too good about my victory, Blondie punched me hard in the stomach, knocking the wind out of me. I stumbled back, and he stepped forward. Moonlight glinted off a blade in his hand.

I scrambled back against the wall, sliding down to the pavement. Fear climbed up my throat. My diaphragm spasmed, my lungs still struggling against the pain.

Something hit my left ear hard, agony exploding in my skull. Broken-nose guy had kicked me in the head. Pain ripped my mind apart, and my vision blurred. I stumbled back, crashing to the ground.

The world was going dark. Through my haze of confusion, a long-buried memory began to ring in my skull. A woman screaming. *Horace, don't!*

My gut tightened. *Not now...* I forced myself to focus, grasping at my consciousness, and I was back in the alley, woozy, my head throbbing painfully.

The blond man stepped forward, his red eyes flickering, and his head darted in a weird, reptilian motion as he *spat* at me. Instinct took hold and I rolled aside, the spit missing me by inches. There was a strange sizzling sound, and I glanced at the pavement. The asphalt hissed and bubbled where the spit had hit it. *What the fuck?*

Fog pooled on the ground, a blanket of gray making the asphalt nearly invisible. The temperature seemed to have dropped ten degrees. Surely this was the effect of a concussion. On the one hand, my body burned with a strange energy. On the other hand, the blow to my head dizzied me.

The man with the knife smiled a toothy, menacing grin, taking another step toward me. But before he could do any damage, his body was suddenly flung aside like a rag doll.

My brain scrambled to comprehend what was going on.

A dark silhouette stood where my attacker had been. Now, a third person had entered the picture. He was so tall that, for a moment, I wondered if it was Gabriel. But no; this man was even bigger—six-five at least. Wide shoulders framed against the night sky, a moss-green coat billowing behind him. A copper clasp fastened the front of his coat, shaped like a stag's head. Through the fog, I could make out his rich gold hair. Emerald green eyes pierced the fog, and there was something predatory in his glinting stare. A shiver ran up my spine. *Inhuman...*

I was losing my mind. Obviously, that had been a serious blow to my skull.

Broken-nose guy snarled, charging for us, a knife appearing in his hand. The newcomer moved in a blur of green—so fast I couldn't track his movements. I just heard a snap. My attacker groaned, the knife tumbling from his hand.

Grasping the alley wall, I pulled myself up, my mind still muddled from the blow. The giant was grappling with the second attacker, his movements preternaturally fluid. The thug flew six feet, then crashed on the ground, smacking his head against the pavement. No fancy rolling this time.

Both attackers rose to their feet, trying to hurry away. I lunged after them, but the newcomer grabbed my arm, his grip tight as iron.

"Leave them," he growled.

His grip sent an entirely unexpected surge of electricity through my body. I'd wanted to connect my boot with the attackers' faces one more time, maybe get a chance to call the cops. But the feel of the stranger's hand stopped me. It was almost as if power rolled off his body, and an unnatural energy seemed to root me in place.

Slowly, I turned to look at him, and when my gaze met his, I froze.

His green eyes bored into me, his fingers still tight on my arm. I had the sense that he was restraining himself, and that he was far, far more dangerous than the two men he'd just chased away. He exuded pure menace, a tightly coiled lethality.

And yet, his oddly feral beauty mesmerized me, his perfect gaze stirring some long-dormant part of my brain—the part that whispered of forest trysts on beds of moss, fingers digging into dirt with wild abandon.

Despite his raw masculinity, his lips had a deeply sensual look. Black lashes framed his green eyes, which were locked on me—his fascination apparently as great as my own.

I stared at the chiseled planes of his face, then let my gaze roam over his body. Under his green coat, he wore a tight gray sweater. It looked expensive as hell, stretched over a powerfully muscled chest. My pulse began to race out of control.

He smelled of moss and sage. Some sort of power seemed to charge the air between us.

I found myself unable to move.

I wasn't sure if it was my fear, or the carnal way he stared at me. Surely no one had ever looked at me that way before. I felt my body responding to him, growing warmer.

With a low growl, his eyes slid down my body, taking in my ripped clothes, lingering over my curves, and I had the strange sensation that he could see right through my clothes to the little Latin phrase tattooed under my right breast. When he raised his gaze again, it lingered on my mouth. His dark brows drew together, entranced. I have no idea what possessed me to do it, but I licked my lips, and his body tensed.

He snarled—actually snarled—and moved his hand from my arm to the nape of my neck. As I looked into his eyes, I was torn by two competing desires: one, to keep staring at him, and the other, to lower my gaze submissively. I fought the urge to look down, instead staring right into his eyes.

I should have been running away.

And yet, for some reason, I really didn't want to.

I was used to feeling emotions from other people, their fear or excitement. Normally, it only came from a crowd buzzing on intense emotions, but at that moment, I could sense two emotions rolling off his powerful body, a war raging in his mind. One emotion was desire; the other, pure rage.

As I watched, his eyes turned from green to the pale amber of sunlight.

Yep, I should definitely run the other way.

He leaned in, his breath warming the side of my face. "Stop what you're doing."

"What *I'm* doing?" I managed. I wasn't doing anything, except imagining my naked body sliding against his.

He slipped his fingers into my hair, gripping it. Our bodies were so close now, my peaked breasts skimming against his chest. I could almost feel his heart beating against me.

He pulled my head back to expose my neck. "I know your game." He spoke as if in a trance, but his movements were precise and controlled. Gently, his knee pressed between my legs, urging them open.

"What are you talking about?" I breathed.

He leaned in, and his teeth grazed my throat. The touch of his warm mouth against my skin sent a rush of hot desire through my core. I heard myself moan lightly, and his other hand found its way to my hip, tightening possessively. His thumb lingered dangerously close to my waistband, slipping lower onto my bare skin, over the hollow of my hips. The feel of his skin against mine —even a tiny amount—lit my body on fire. I had no idea why, but I arched into him, wanting more.

"You don't even know what you are, do you?" he growled. "And yet, you can't help yourself." His accent wasn't quite English—not like the London accent of the other two. It had a different lilt to it—Scottish, maybe? I didn't really care right now. I just wanted to shove my hands under his clothes.

My pulse was racing out of control, and I had the strongest desire to kiss him. As I looked up at him, the moonlight flickered over his face.

And then my heart skipped a beat. To my horror, two golden horns shimmered just above his forehead. Was this a trick of the light, or my battered brain playing tricks on me?

I clamped my eyes shut, panic claiming my mind. I was losing it—but of course that was destined to happen to me at some point. "Get away from me," I snapped. "I don't want you to touch me."

Slowly, he released me, stepping away, and I opened my eyes again. The stranger's irises had returned to their green color; the strange horns had disappeared.

His lip curled, as if disgusted with himself. The air around us had cooled, the mist thickening. "You don't have to ask me twice."

"I don't know what just happened. I have a head injury."

He backed away, his eyes narrowed. "You don't know what you are, and yet I'd be willing to bet that you feed off fear," his voice was a low growl, dripping with disgust, and something about his tone sent terror rumbling through my gut. "A *terror leech*."

My mouth went dry. How could he possibly know how I felt about fear? "What are you talking about?"

He coiled his fingers into fists, as if he were holding himself back from touching me again. Or perhaps from strangling me to death.

My body began to cool again, but my heart still pounded. "Right. Well, thanks for your help. Perhaps you have another alley to haunt."

I could see his knuckles whitening, his jaw tense. He nodded back in the direction I'd come from. "You left your wheelbarrow back there."

"My what?"

"You've been injured." His tone dripped with hostility. "You look weak. I can help you with your wheelbarrow."

"My wheelbarrow?" I snapped. "You mean my suitcase?"

"Suit-case." The word sounded alien in his mouth, as if he was learning a new language. "You don't look as though you can manage it." His lip curled disdainfully.

I had absolutely no explanation for the overwhelming attraction I'd felt for him just moments ago, because he was obviously an asshole. And had I really seen horns? It must be a brief psychotic break brought about by the trauma of the attack, plus the head injury.

I mean sure, he looked like a god, but there was something not *right* about him. Something predatory and feral, like he was holding back from dragging me off as a conquest. Asking him to accompany me to the police station was out of the question. He would not step into a police station. With his muscles tightly coiled, his powerful body conveyed a threat of extreme violence. He was definitely not a man with a clean slate. The only reason I was talking to him at all was that he'd tried to help me.

"I'll be fine, thanks." As soon as the words were out of my mouth, dizziness overwhelmed me, and I faltered. His arm shot out, fast as lightning, gripping my wrist. Again, at the contact with him, an electrical charge surged through my body.

I yanked my hand away, glaring at him. "Like I said. I'm fine."

I turned, suddenly desperate to put myself as far as possible from this encounter. I walked a few paces, when it occurred to me that I'd at least need his name to file a police report. But when I turned, I found the alley completely empty again.

My chest tightened. Shit. I was definitely losing my mind. And given my family history, that was a very dangerous thing indeed.

* * *

I DROPPED down on the smooth hotel bed, my head throbbing from the beating I'd taken. I'd been on hold with the police for a good ten minutes. If I hadn't been psychotic before, the cheery elevator music droning through the phone threatened to put me over the edge.

The Metropolitan Police dispatcher had answered immediately, I had to give her that. She had very politely told me that since the actual crime occurred in the City of London, and not in Greater London, I'd need to be transferred. This, she had explained, was a matter for the City of London Police. I was promptly transferred. The dispatcher for the City of London was happy to hear that I was in no immediate danger, and transferred me to the constable in charge, who asked if this could wait until morning. When I said it couldn't, she put me on hold. Again.

The music droned on in my right ear. My left ear still throbbed from the kick, and I was not about to abuse it further with this ordeal.

At least the hotel room was luxurious—clean and modern: gray curtains, a sleek red armchair, and hanging ceiling lamps that cast buttery light over the room. From the enormous bed, I stared into a mirror, slightly horrified at my mud-spattered appearance and messy tangle of blonde hair. My blue eyes were wide open, still in shock. I looked like a crazy person. Which, incidentally, was now a distinct possibility.

Had that man with the red eyes spit acid at me? Had I really seen horns—and eyes turning gold? Not to mention that inhuman speed and grace. This was *not* a good situation. I could only pray the hallucination had been a result of my head injury and not the onset of a mental illness.

"Thank you for holding, Miss Liddell," the constable's voice returned.

"Sure. I just want to file the complaint. I was attacked by two men in Catherine Wheel Alley an hour ago."

"Do you need medical assistance?"

"No, I'm fine, I think." My fingers brushed against the bruise on my stomach, and I winced. My head still pounded. But the hell with it; I didn't feel like being prodded by a doctor right now. "I just want to report the attack."

"I understand, Miss Liddell. Why don't you come tomorrow to report it?"

I restrained myself from yelling at her. How would a Brit phrase this? "Don't you think tomorrow might be a bit late?"

"If you file a report tomorrow—"

"This is stupid. They'll be long gone by then." Okay. I was done with the pleasantries.

"I'm not sure what you want me to do about it. I'm sure they're long gone now."

I didn't even know how to approach the question. "Maybe… send a patrol there? It's ten minutes away. See if you spot the two assholes who tried to kill me?"

"There's not a lot we can do. I was mugged just last

month, myself. You really should be more careful in the future."

I blinked. Apparently the police operated differently here. "Are you serious?"

"There really is a limit to what the City of London can do about it, Miss Liddell. What would be best is if you come tomorrow morning, and file a report—"

"You know what? Forget it." I hung up, seething. I'd tell Gabriel about this the next day. He struck me as a serious police officer, at least.

Exhausted, I rubbed my eyes. It was nearly three in the morning here, but only ten p.m. on the East Coast. Scarlett would still be up.

I pulled out my phone, texting her. *I think I'm losing my mind. I saw some really weird shit tonight.*

A moment later, a green bubble popped up on my screen. *Welcome to my world. What did you see?*

I swallowed hard. *If I start losing my mind and send you texts full of jumbled word salad, promise me you'll make sure I get medicated.*

Sure, she typed. *But you're not losing your mind. Have a Manhattan and a good fry up in the morning.*

I dropped the phone on the bed. A fry up wasn't a bad idea.

I had to sleep, but first, I desperately wanted a shower. Alley dirt covered my body, I had a bootprint on the side of my cheek, and I was pretty sure the rancid smell of death from the crime scene clung to me.

I rose, crossing to the clean, white-tiled bathroom. I

turned on the water and adjusted the temperature until it was hot enough to make tea. Then, I pulled off my ripped sweater, tossing it in the trash. It was beyond repair. I unzipped my boots, and stepped out of the rest of my clothes.

I stepped into the shower, letting the sublime water rush over my skin. As the steam billowed around me, I couldn't help but think of that stranger—his fingers gripping my hips hard, his lips soft on my neck. I stroked my finger down my chest to my hipbone, where he'd grabbed me. My nipples began to harden. If I closed my eyes, I could almost smell his musky scent, and feel his muscled body against mine. I could almost feel his mouth sliding lower toward my navel...

My eyes snapped open again. I wasn't going to think about him again. I wasn't sure what had happened with him, but I needed to get a grip.

I grabbed the small shampoo bottle, pouring a dollop of vanilla-scented soap into my palm. I worked up a thick lather, forcing myself not to think of the heat that had raced through my body at the stranger's touch. I'd think of unsexy things: lampreys, taxes, British politicians having questionable relations with pigs...

For just a moment, I drifted asleep while still standing under the current.

Horace, don't! Her scream pierced the walls. Hiding under the table, I covered my ears with my hands. I tried to close my eyes and I couldn't, and I saw the blood trickle down her lips...

My eyes opened wide, my breath rapid and shuddering. Stupid. So stupid. I leaned against the shower wall to steady myself.

My brain was conjuring impossible visions—a long-forgotten trauma. An attack I'd heard, but hadn't seen. All those years ago, I hadn't actually been there to watch the blood on her lips.

My body tensed. I pretty much did everything in my power not to think about that.

Tears stung my eyes. It felt like my own mind was punishing me in the worst way possible.

Why had I gone into this disturbing field in the first place, especially given my own history? I could have become a school psychologist, or an addiction counselor. Someone who helped the *living,* who had a part in their growth. It sounded nice, but… that type of work just didn't light my world on fire.

According to a goateed man in my counseling psychology class at Tufts, forensic psychologists were all "trauma junkies." Goatee Man—a clinical psychologist—believed that profilers like me haunted the dead and the depraved because we were fundamentally flawed. Apparently, it was a way of sublimating our own sadistic impulses into something socially acceptable. Asshole.

That wasn't the only thing we argued about. According to him, personality, temperament, intelligence—it was all completely genetic (which raised the question, what was the point of psychologists in the first place?).

But that brought me to the real reason I needed to understand killers' minds. I *needed* evil to be environmentally-created, and I made it my life's mission to prove it. I wanted to understand how a psychopath's background shaped him into what he was—the violent parents, the brain damage, the sexual abuse—how it all fit together to create a monster. That was the real reason I haunted the dead and the depraved.

I shook off the old, stale arguments, and turned off the tap. I stepped out, feeling the warm water trickle down my body. The cold bathroom floor sent a shock through my feet. I grabbed a soft white towel and dried off, leaving wet footprints all over the bathroom floor.

Finally, the brutal day had ended. All that was left was to brush my teeth and go to sleep. As I crossed into the bathroom and passed the mirror, I spotted a strange movement from the corner of my eye. I whirled, my body tense. What the hell was that? I thought I'd seen something in the mirror, but it was just my mind playing tricks on me.

A sigh slid from me. Just the mirror, and my own terrified expression in my blue eyes. It had seemed... different a second ago. Almost like there was a stranger in the room with me.

Obviously, the night's events had screwed with my senses. It didn't mean I was losing my mind, though, right?

I hoisted my suitcase onto the bed and unzipped it, rummaging through until I found a pair of black underwear and a tank top. I slipped into them. When I pulled the cotton shirt on, it clung to my damp back. I'd been too tired to dry myself properly.

Grabbing my travel kit, I turned for the bathroom. But as I did, I froze, a shiver inching up my spine. I was almost certain I saw something moving in the mirror again… something that was no longer there.

I closed my eyes, breathing deeply through my nose. Okay. The next time that happened, I was booking an appointment with a therapist. If I was going to descend into insanity, I would do it in the most responsible way possible.

I couldn't risk turning out like my dad.

ACKNOWLEDGMENTS

Thanks to C.N. Crawford's coven, my fantastic readers' group on Facebook, and all our readers who have helped to support us over the years. We are so privileged to share our stories with you, and you have made our dreams come true!

Thanks to Linsey Hall for reading and giving feedback on the romance sections. Also, thanks to Evelyn, Cara, and Marissa for beta reading and giving us helpful feedback.

Three amazing editors helped to refine the text, to make the writing smooth and clear: Lauren Simpson, Lexi George, and Jena O'Connor.

Rachel from Nerd Fam helped to get the word out by organizing my marketing campaigns and consulting with us.

Our fabulous cover designers are Merrybookround, who did stunning work on the ebook, paperback and dust jackets, and Coverdungeonrabbit who did beautiful work on the naked hardcover.

Thanks to K.F. Breene, Laura Thalassa, Shannon Mayer, Linsey Hall, Eliza Raine and Leia Stone for emotional support.

ALSO BY ALEX RIVERS

A full list of C.N. Crawford books can be found here.

https://www.cncrawford.com/books

Find out more in C.N. Crawford's coven.

Made in the USA
Columbia, SC
06 January 2025